# The Alien Mate Index

## Book 4: Severed

## Evangeline Anderson

PUBLISHED BY:

Evangeline Anderson Books


The Alien Mate Index

Book 4: Severed

Copyright © October 2016 by Evangeline Anderson

# Dedication

With love to all my Kindred readers. If you like *Kindred*, I think you'll love *Alien Mate Index* as well. I write these books with all of you in mind. I feel very blessed to have such awesome people to pretend with me.

Hugs and Happy Reading to you all!

Evangeline

*To be the first to find out about new*

*releases join my newsletter at*

*www.EvangelineAnderson.com*

### ***Author's Note***

Severed can be read as a stand alone novel but if you want to go back and read Abducted, Protected, and Descended, the first three books in the Alien Mate Index series, you can find them in both print and ebook here:

EvangelineAnderson.com/connected/alien-mate-index

# Table of Contents

The Alien Mate Index

Book 4: Severed

Evangeline Anderson

# Chapter One

## Rylee

"You can have the apartment in South Beach and the BMW but *I* get Mr. Puppers." Daniel Forester-Jones, soon to be just Daniel Forester again, leaned back in the crappy plastic seat in my new office and crossed his arms over his chest.

"No. Absolutely *not.*" His soon to be ex-partner, Jacob Forester-Jones, frowned at him. "I brought Mr. Puppers into this relationship and I am *leaving* with him."

"God knows he's the *only* good thing you brought," Daniel sniffed. "Oh, no wait — *herpes.* You brought that too. Can't forget about *that.*"

"Daniel," I said, trying to interrupt the fight which was rapidly developing right in front of me. "Jacob. Come on now, what happened to an amicable divorce?"

I'm Rylee Hale and this is my life — helping people get separated and divorced from the ones they once loved the most. Needless to say, at times like this, it really sucks. But back to the argument playing out in my new office.

"Why, you little bitch!" Jacob glared at his partner, completely ignoring me and my conciliatory words. "I was very upfront with you about my status when we got married and we were *extremely* careful!"

"And yet you still managed to give it to me *anyway,*" Daniel flared. "And since you've given me such a *lovely* gift I'll never be able to get rid of, I think I should get to keep Mr. Puppers — it's only fair."

"You can't have Mr. Puppers — he's *mine!*" Jacob snarled.

"He likes me better than you!" Daniel snapped back. "It's glaringly *obvious.* I mean, who does he want to snuggle with at night? Who does he come running to with his little stumpy tail wagging when we walk in the door?"

"He goes to you because you've been sneaking him *treats!*" Jacob roared, his face turning an unattractive shade of puce. "The ones the vet says he shouldn't have. You're making him fat! *You're making my dog fat!*"

"*My dog! He's my dog!*" Daniel's face was bright pink. "*And I'll give him treats if I Goddamn want to!*"

"Gentlemen…gentlemen, *please!*" I raised my voice to be heard above their shouting. Still, they paid no attention.

"You mean the way you treat yourself?" Jacob shouted, jumping up. "All those carbs you scarf down are making you *fat!* You're addicted to gluten, you… you *fat gluten hog!*"

"I am not!" Daniel also stood, clearly in a rage. "You're just a Paleo *freak!* And for your information, *nobody* likes your famous seaweed and Sriracha Paleo rolls—they're *disgusting!* The last party you brought them to, everyone threw them away as soon as you went to the bathroom." He leaned forward. "Even *Hans.*"

Jacob paled. "You're lying. Hans *loves* my seaweed Sriracha rolls."

"No, honey, Hans only loves your *dick.* That's right—I know you're sleeping with him!" Daniel gave him a shove.

"So what if I am? He's a hell of a lot better than *you* are in bed!" Jacob shoved back.

It looked like they were going to come to blows—right there in my brand new crappy office—the one I'd only been in a week. The one I got at a reduced rent because I promised the landlord I was going to run a quiet, orderly office—so quiet, in fact, that he wouldn't even know I was there. In just a minute, *everybody* in the building was going to know I was there—especially if the punches started flying.

I had to do something, fast.

Jumping up, I pulled off one of my heels and pounded on my cheap plywood desk with it with a loud, *thwak, thwak, thwak!*

"Daniel! Jacob!" I shouted at the top of my lungs. "Both of you sit down *now!*"

That got their attention. Both of them were breathing hard and glaring at each other but finally they sat down in my cheap plastic Wal Mart chairs again.

"Now listen up," I said, narrowing my eyes at both of them. "I've had about enough of you two. I told you at the beginning of all this that I am *not* a divorce lawyer. I'm just a humble paralegal who hands out paperwork and helps you fill it out. I do *not* get paid enough to listen to all your crap. I don't *care* why you're getting a divorce. I don't care who's sleeping with who or who gave who herpes! And I most *especially* don't care who gets to keep *Mr. Goddamn Puppers!*"

"Well!" Daniel sucked in his breath and Jacob looked shocked.

"That's right," I said, crossing my arms over my chest. "I can cuss too...but I'd rather not." I took a deep, calming breath and settled lightly back behind my desk, slipping my shoe back on as I did. "Now why don't we all try to talk this out rationally? I know you want to end your marriage but there's no reason to end it *badly*. Have some dignity — some *self respect*."

"She's right," Jacob said stiffly. "I shouldn't have called you fat."

"You didn't just call me fat. You called me a *'fat gluten hog,'*" Daniel reminded him icily.

"*Daniel...*" I put a warning tone in my voice. I'm not a mom but I can do a fair imitation of one when I want to. That's what being raised by my Aunt Celia with my six rowdy cousins got me.

"Oh...all right." Daniel gave his partner a sulky look. "I'm sorry I said anything about the herpes. *And* your seaweed rolls."

"Good, this is good." I steepled my fingers and regarded both of them. "Now I can tell that both of you really love, uh, Mr. Puppers. So in the interest of getting these papers signed and your divorce underway, why don't we talk about a visitation schedule?"

So, we talked...

It took five hours to iron things out. *Five freaking hours*, otherwise known as my entire afternoon. Seriously, from noon to five I was busy making sure both my clients got enough quality time with their French Bulldog-labradoodle mix.

I'm not even a dog person.

If I had been a lawyer billing by the hour, I would have made *so much* money in the time it took to straighten things out. However, since I'm just a lowly paralegal, I was only making the fee I charged them to go over the paperwork in the first place.

I think it worked out to something like less than minimum wage—plus it gave me a pounding headache. When the two of them left, still glaring daggers at each other but with all papers signed and sealed, I collapsed and put my head on my desk, an Ikea special. The scent of plywood and cheap varnish assaulted my nose. I'd almost made enough during my hellish encounter to pay for it.

Almost.

I sat up and rubbed my temples. What a freaking mess—and to think I'd been so excited to have my first real clients! They had seemed like such a nice couple over the phone—Danny and Jakie they called themselves. I had been surprised they wanted a divorce at all, they seemed to get along so well.

So much for that.

I wished for the hundredth time that I could get some work that *didn't* involve divorce. I knew that sometimes dissolving a relationship was necessary—I'd had to dissolve my own to my no-good ex, Phillip, who was a real piece of work. But still, I would much rather be putting people together than tearing them apart.

"Should have been a wedding planner instead," I muttered to myself. But it would cost way more to get that business off the ground than just striking out on my own as a paralegal. So for now, at least, it looked like I was stuck doing quickie divorces for unhappy couples who wanted to murder each other right in my office.

With a sigh, I heaved myself to my feet. It wasn't a very auspicious beginning for my new paralegal firm—which had exactly one employee—*me*. But at least today was over. I could go back home to my tiny apartment which I now had all to myself since I'd kicked Phillip out two months ago, take an aspirin and a hot bath, and try to relax.

I trudged out the door and the long flight of stairs that led from the second floor to the first. I could have taken the elevator but it stuck between floors sometimes—a fact I'd found out the hard way my first day there. It was strictly stairs for me from then on.

I passed my neighbor in the hallway—a skinny twenty-something guy with fish-belly white skin and dirty blond hair twisted into long, scraggly dreadlocks. He had a Rastafarian air about him and always wore one of those multicolored Jamaican berets which looked like it desperately needed a trip through the washing machine.

"Hey, pretty lady." He nodded at me genially. "What it do?"

"Hi." I gave him a curt nod back. He was supposed to be a barber but none of the customers I ever saw going into his office — which was two doors past mine at the end of the hall—ever looked any different when they left. Well, their *hair* didn't anyway. Also, I often caught a waft of suspicious smelling smoke coming from the crack under his door. While I wasn't a *hundred* percent sure my neighbor was a drug dealer, I also wasn't surprised to see that his clientele usually had bloodshot eyes and dazed looks on their faces when they wandered out of his office.

There was nothing I could do about my suspicions, so I kept them to myself. Beggars couldn't be choosers and office space was expensive in Tampa. The small eight by ten cell of an office I was renting was pretty much the cheapest in the city. I knew because I'd shopped around a lot before settling on this place and giving my notice to my old law firm of Lauder, Lauder and Associates to strike out on my own.

*At least I'm out of **there**, anyway,* I thought, heading out into the parking lot where my beat up Honda Civic was parked. L.L. and A. had been an awful place to work, especially after my best work buddy, Zoe, ran off with a secret fiancé none of us knew about.

I frowned when I remembered the mysterious circumstances of her leaving. She'd vanished right out of the building—right out of the employees' bathroom, in fact. She hadn't given notice or anything and for a while, everyone thought she'd been kidnapped or abducted or something. Her two best friends, nice girls named Charlotte and Leah, had even insisted on opening a missing person's case on her and hiring a private detective to find her.

It still seemed strange to me that Zoe would leave in such an abrupt way without giving notice at work or telling the people she loved most what was happening to her. But she must have had her reasons. I had met her friend Leah again recently, when she was looking for help with her divorce, and she'd assured me that Zoe was fine. According to Leah, she had simply been whisked away to some south sea island where there was no phone signal, by her eager fiancé who kept her there for a romantic, extended honeymoon.

"Huh," I muttered to myself as I joggled the Civic's half-broken door to get it to open. "Wish somebody would whisk *me* away from all this crap!"

I had no idea that anyone was watching me at the time and even less idea that my half-formed wish would soon become a reality. If I had, I probably would have clamped my lips shut and gone home to hide under the bed, away from any shiny, reflective surfaces.

But I didn't have a clue. I started the car and drove away from my crappy little office for the last time, not having any idea what lay in store for me in the very near future.

# Chapter Two

## Lucian

"She's perfect," Drace growled, staring at the tall, (well, tall for an Earth girl anyway) female with creamy light brown skin and large black eyes on the AMI lightscreen.

I looked at my unintended bond-mate in some surprise. For once the big oaf was displaying some intelligence and taste. For the first time since Tanta Loro, the wise woman on our home planet of Denaris had told us we needed to find a Pure One to dissolve the accidental psy-bond between us, I agreed with him about something.

"She *is* perfect," I grudgingly agreed. "Did you see how well she handled the dissolution of the bonding between those two males?"

Drace snorted. "Fuck yeah, I saw it. She really put them in their places." He nodded approvingly. "I like a strong female."

"As do I," I admitted, surprised to find myself in agreement with him yet again. Through the psy-bond we unwillingly shared, I felt his surprise as well.

"Do you?" he asked bluntly. "I thought Fangers liked their females subservient."

"That's quite a large word," I said dryly. "I'm impressed. Though I'd be *more* impressed if you could refrain from using such derogatory terms for my people."

Drace scowled. "Just because I didn't go to the Queil University and spend four thousand credits an hour on my education doesn't make me stupid. I'm just not as high and mighty as you, you arrogant bastard. And what would you *prefer* I called you?"

"Just because I wasn't raised in the swamps of Yerbix and

actually had a proper education doesn't make me arrogant," I countered, my irritation rising. "And when you refer to me and my people, call us the Fang Clan—just as I have the common decency to call *your* people the Claw Clan. Although 'furry savages' might be more accurate."

"We're *not* savages. And I'd rather have fur over fangs any damn day." Drace glared at me and I felt his anger—always abundant and near the surface—bubbling up like molten metal in a pot. Gods, how had I gotten myself linked to such a crude savage? And one of the Claw Clan, no less, who were the sworn enemies of my own people.

"Gentlemen, if you please." The high piping voice that cut into our argument—one of the many we'd had since our accidental bonding—belonged to Char'noth. The diminutive blue being who looked rather like a three-foot long terga worm to me, swiveled his eye-stalks to look at both myself and Drace at the same time.

"Yes?" I asked coolly, holding my own temper in check with some difficulty. My bond-mate rubbed me the wrong way which was the exact opposite of the way psy-bonded males were supposed to react to each other. But then, what could you expect? Aside from coming from rival clans, we were *both* Alphas which went against the natural order of bonding in every way.

"I was simply coming to inquire if you and your, ah…life-mate, have chosen a female from our Index yet," Char'noth squeaked.

"He's not my fuckin' life-mate," Drace growled. "We're just temporarily psy-bonded, that's all."

"My *friend* here is correct," I said, frowning. "And as to a female, I believe we have settled on *that* one."

I pointed to the Earth female who was struggling to get into what appeared to be a very primitive vehicle. She really was surpassingly lovely—not that it was her appearance we were interested in. Drace and I had both seen the way she was able to separate the two males who came seeking her help. She sent them off in different directions with the clear implication that they were free of each other. Through her intervention, the link between them had been severed—which was exactly what my unintended bond-mate and I wanted.

"Ah—you have good taste—very good taste indeed, gentlemen," Charo'noth piped. "But also *expensive* tastes I am afraid. This female is the most costly subject we have in our current database." He named a price that made Drace suck in his breath.

"*That much?*" he demanded. "Why is that? Why should she cost more than any other Earth female? Well, aside from the fact that she's Goddess-damned gorgeous, that is."

He eyed our chosen female appreciatively and I couldn't say that I blamed him. Denari females generally have pale, pearly gray skin which is considered quite beautiful. But I had never seen such an exotic skin tone as this female's creamy light brown tint. Her large eyes were a liquid black fringed thickly with dark lashes and her hair was a profusion of black curls that framed her lovely face most attractively. As for her figure, it was exactly what I liked—full breasts with an ample ass and curving hips to match. She was, indeed, Goddess-damned gorgeous, as Drace had said.

*Well, at least we have the same taste in women,* I thought dryly. It was one of the qualities psy-bonded mates were supposed to have since they both had to be passionately in love with the female they chose to join in their partnership, completing the Triumvirate Bond.

Not that we wanted such a bond—the sooner I got free of my unintended bond-mate the better.

"This female is a *La-ti-zal*," Char'noth explained, breaking into my train of thought. "She is one of those blessed with special gifts from the Ancient Ones who sowed the seeds of life throughout the galaxy at the behest of the Goddess."

"How can you tell that?" Drace asked at the same time I said,

"How can you make such a claim?"

We both frowned at each other and I felt a surge of irritation going both ways through our link. It was aggravating in the extreme when we spoke the same thought at the same time and it happened more than I liked to admit.

"Do you see her aura?" Char'noth gestured with two of his many clawed hands at the warm amber glow around our chosen female. "That radiance denotes one with special gifts. This female glows more brightly than any other in the Alien Mate Index."

"She *does* appear to have a strong aura," I agreed grudgingly.

"But what is her gift?" Those rare females who are blessed to be *La-ti-zals* often have one specific gift given by the Goddess of Mercy.

"Right," Drace put in. "Is she a Healer? An Opener? A Knower? What?"

Char'noth's long, wormy body made a rippling gesture which I recognized as a shrug.

"That we do not know. We are working on a new device which will allow us to ascertain exactly what a particular *La-ti-zal's* talent is but it is not yet perfected."

"So we're supposed to pay through the nose just because she glows?" Drace grumbled. He looked down at Char'noth. "Look, we only need her for a minute. We just need a Pure One to touch both of us and dissolve our bond."

"My, ah, partner is correct," I said, looking at Char'noth. "After this Earth female performs the same un-bonding service for us which we witnessed her enacting on the other two males she was dealing with, we will let her go. You can return her to her planet with no ill effects. Then you can…" I cleared my throat. "Can sell her contract again to another male."

My own words made me uncomfortable for some reason I couldn't define. Maybe it was the idea of the little female being sold to some other Alien male. But then, that was the function of the AMI and it was the service Drace and I were buying from Char'noth and his fellow Commercians. Why should it bother me?

Apparently it bothered Drace too. I felt his unease through our link.

"I don't like it," he said abruptly. "I don't want her getting sold after we leave to just any male who might use her and abuse her."

"We don't even know her," I pointed out, through I secretly agreed with him.

"We know enough to know we're both attracted to her," he said. "Don't lie, Lucian—she makes your cock hard. I can feel it through our bond."

"Is that a good enough reason to pay full price?" I asked coldly.

"What—like you can't afford it?" He raised an eyebrow at me. "Thought you were some hot-shot litigator in your region."

"It's not a matter of credit," I said, frowning.

"Well then what *is it?*" he demanded. "Look, I might not be as rich as you, but I've got credit. I'll pay her entire price if I have to but I *don't* want her being sold to another male once we let her go."

Deep down, I agreed with him—which was probably why I was resisting. Still, I couldn't let him pay the female's entire price.

"We agreed to split the cost of this venture evenly," I said. "You don't need to take the whole expense on yourself."

"So you agree—we pay the whole amount and buy out her contract?" he asked.

I sighed. "Getting unbonded from you is turning out to be as expensive as a Triumvirate Ceremony to a female from the Feather Clan. But fine—we'll do it."

"Good." Drace turned back to Char'noth. "You heard him. We'll pay the full price but we want her sent back to Earth unharmed when we're finished."

"And no other male is to buy, bother, or in any way molest her," I put in. "Agreed?"

The Commercian nodded.

"Agreed. Though we do not usually allow humans to have knowledge of us, we have found that a single human who tries to report our existence is not believed by the rest. Therefore, I will affix it to the terms of your contract when we transport her up to the station."

"When will that be?" I was itching to get myself un-bonded from Drace and I could feel that he felt the same.

"Soon, Gentlemen. Let us wait and watch a little longer. I prefer to pick the right moment to bring the female through."

I didn't know what the "right moment" might be but now that the final dissolution of the accidental bond between myself and Drace was near, I found I could wait a little longer.

"Very well," I said. "As long as the process isn't interminable."

"As long as you don't take all night," Drace said, echoing my thought.

"Not much longer," Char'noth promised. She must be alone and in a private place. If too many Earthlings see her taken they will suspect our involvement in their lives and seek us out."

"That's sensible," I agreed.

"With any luck she is heading for her domicile now," the Commercian said, gesturing at the lightscreen where we could see our chosen female driving her strange little vehicle down a paved road filled with other such vehicles. "These Earthlings have many reflective surfaces in the places where they live — large, shiny, flat, glass panels which I believe they call 'mirrors'. Human females use them to check their appearance often — they are ideal for transportation."

"Like a 2D viewer?" I asked.

"Exactly." Char'noth nodded, his eyestalks bobbing. "We have only to wait until she gets to her domicile. Once she is there, I will lure her to one of the mirrors by playing discordant tones to get her attention. When she steps in front of the mirror, I will transport her directly to the station."

"How does your transportation device work?" Drace looked interested. "Does it use a trans-dimentional portal or —"

"I'm afraid that is proprietary information," Char'noth said stiffly in his high, squeaky voice. "We Commercians are extremely protective of our technology."

"Naturally you are." I frowned at Drace who shrugged.

"What? I like to know how things work."

"It doesn't matter *how* it works as long as it gets the female here to un-bond us," I pointed out.

"You're not saying anything I'm not already thinking." Drace glared at me. "Can't happen soon enough for me."

"Gentlemen, please," Char'noth waved several clawed hands for silence. "Look — she appears to be approaching her domicile. As soon as she is alone, I will lure the female to a mirror and transport her."

I closed my mouth on the angry words I'd been about to say. Soon the Earth female would be with us and the unbearable irritation of being bonded to an unsuitable mate would finally be ended.

We all watched avidly as the female entered a large,

rectangular building which appeared to house many smaller

# Chapter Three

## Rylee

I walked in to my apartment to find an unwelcome surprise.

My ex, Phillip, was lounging on my sofa with a beer in one hand and a belligerent look on his face.

Great, not this—not now. After the day I'd had, a confrontation with Phillip was the *last* thing I needed!

"What are you doing here?" I asked, deciding to take the bull by the horns as my Aunt Celia would say. "You know you're not supposed to be here. Did you forget something?"

"Yeah, babe—I forgot *you*." Standing, he put down the beer and swaggered over to me with a cocky grin on his face.

When I first met Phillip about three years before, he'd had a bad-boy air that I had found irresistibly attractive. With his thick brownish-blonde hair tied back in a pony tail and his big brown eyes he was also easy on the eyes—or he had been before he started drinking too much and spending most of his paycheck on drugs and other women. Now he had a beer gut and a scraggly, patchy beard which made him look like a bum.

I should have given him the heave-ho long before I actually did, but I hadn't known how deep his problems went. The drinking part was obvious because Phillip was a mean drunk. Not that he hit me—I wouldn't stand for that. No, he just got verbally abusive calling me a "bitch" and a "fat cunt" and screaming that I was ruining his life. Which was ridiculous because he was doing a damn fine job of ruining it himself—he didn't need any help from me. Afterwards he would cry and apologize and swear never to drink again—which usually lasted about a month before he 'went out with the guys' and got blackout drunk once more.

As for the drugs and the other women, I suspected both of them but I didn't have actual proof until the day I walked into my bedroom and found Phillip in bed with a skanky waitress from one of the grungy bars he frequented. They were trying to have sex but both of them were high as a kite so they weren't getting very far with it.

The waitress had a blissed-out expression on her face and she was laying flat on her back while Phillip crouched over her, fumbling with his crotch.

"Wow, babe, that's so good," she was moaning. "So good. *Soooo gooooood.*"

Phillip had his dick in his hand—as limp as a week-old stalk of celery—and was trying to aim for the hairy forest between her legs. Only he kept poking her belly-button instead.

"How can it be good?" he asked peevishly. "I'm not even in yet. Why is your pussy so shallow? It's like…only an inch deep."

"It's good—it's *really good!*" she insisted. "Just keep doing what you're doing, babe. It's *awesome.*"

It was a ridiculous scene and I would have laughed out loud if I hadn't felt so horribly betrayed. As it was I just stood there for a long moment, staring at them fumbling around in front of me before I swung into action.

I kicked them both out, threw their clothes after them and slammed the door in their faces. Later, after Phillip was finally gone, I dragged all his things out to the curb and left them there for whoever wanted them. I even got the locks changed.

As painful as the incident had been, I was glad it had happened. It had been a wakeup call for me—the boot in the ass I needed to get me moving. Up until I walked in on my ex and his hairy-waitress-whore, I'd been making excuses for him. But seeing them having sex in my bed—or *trying* to anyway—had snapped something inside me. The relationship which had started out sexy and daring and exciting had turned bad, I realized—had *been* bad for a while. That realization had enabled me to wake up, get out, and get on with my life.

Of course, Phillip had called me on the phone and ranted and raved and begged and pleaded. He called me plenty of nasty names—not the least of which was the "N" word which he hadn't previously dared to use, even when he was drunk—but I held my ground. I refused to talk to him, refused to see him, refused to even *think* about him if I could help it.

Which was why it was so disconcerting to walk into my apartment and find him lounging on the couch like he still lived there.

"What are you doing here?" I asked, frowning. "How did you even get in?"

He grinned, showing teeth which hadn't been brushed in a while.

"Called a locksmith and told him I locked myself out. He let me in—no problem."

"That's illegal," I said tightly. "They can't just let you in because you *claim* to live here."

"Hey, my name's still on the lease. This copy of it, anyway." He waved a piece of paper in my face. "Had a copy in my email. I don't know why I didn't think of it sooner."

"Maybe because you knew I never wanted to see your sorry ass again?" I said, crossing my arms over my chest. "Seriously, Phillip—after the day I've had, I don't need your shit right now."

"C'mon now, babe." His voice took on a wheedling tone I used to think was cute. "Don't be like that—I really *miss* you."

"Translation, you miss having a roof over your head. What happened, did that skanky waitress you were *trying* to screw kick you out?"

His face went dark and his eyes narrowed for a moment but then he made a visible effort to smile genially.

"She didn't mean nothin' to me—you know that. That was a mistake—I never woulda gone with her if I hadn't been drunk." He spread his hands. "But I've changed now—that's all over with."

"Let me guess—you're turning over a new leaf and you're never going to drink again and now you want me back because we belong together forever," I recited, giving him his old excuse almost word-for-word. I knew it by heart—I ought to, considering how many times I'd heard it.

"Well…yeah." Phillip stared at me earnestly. "I'm serious this time, babe—I even went to AA. Look, I got one of those chips they give you for attending the meetings."

He pulled a chip out of the pocket of his battered leather motorcycle jacket and held it out to me. I bent down and studied it briefly before looking back up at him.

"How stupid do you think I am, Phillip? This is a *poker* chip. Real AA chips have a triangle with 'Unity, Service, and Recovery' printed on them. I know—my uncle was an alcoholic."

Which was probably the reason I'd been drawn to one myself, since my Uncle Carl had been the only man in my life. Well, until Aunt Celia kicked him out for being a drunk, that was.

"They were out of that kind the night I went. That's why they gave me this one." Phillip scowled and shoved the poker chip back in his pocket.

"Yeah, right. You just can't stop lying, can you?" I shook my head. "Forget Alcoholics Anonymous—you need *Liars* Anonymous. Now get your lying, sorry ass *out* of my apartment before I call the police."

I held up my cell phone threateningly but Phillip darted forward and batted it out of my hand. It skittered into the corner of the living room and when I started to go after it, he blocked my path.

"I don't think so, *babe*," he snarled. "You and I belong together—you just need a little *encouragement* to see it."

He made a grab for me but I darted away.

"Get away from me!" I shouted, hoping the neighbors on either side of me would hear. "Leave me alone!"

"I'm not leaving." Phillip started advancing on me, arms outstretched to catch me. "We're back together, Rylee—you just need to accept it."

"You can't just *say* we're back together and have it be *true*," I argued, dismayed at the gleam in his bloodshot eyes. Was he on something? "I never want to see you again and that's *not* going to change no matter how many excuses you give or how many fake poker chips you wave in my face."

"We're back together," Phillip repeated doggedly, as though he could make it true by saying it enough. "Things are gonna be just like they were—even better, babe—you'll see."

"No! Now *get out!*" I shouted. If the neighbors *could* hear my shouting, nobody was doing anything about it. Was anyone hearing me at all?

Phillip continued to advance and I kept backing away, afraid to turn my back on him. I wanted to run out of the apartment but he had gotten between me and the door.

"We're gonna be together, Rylee," he snarled and reached in his pocket again. "One way or another we're gonna be together because I can't live without you."

"What are you talking about?" I demanded and was upset to hear how my voice was shaking. "What do you—"

"I can't live without you, babe," Phillip repeated. "And you sure as hell can't live without me."

Then he pulled something much bigger than a poker chip out of his pocket and pointed it at me.

A gun.

# Chapter Four

## Drace

"Get her out of there!" I bellowed at Char'noth. "Right fucking *now!*"

"Drace is right—that's some kind of weapon, you can tell by the way he's holding it." Lucian—the arrogant bastard—sounded like he was losing his cool for once. Not that I could enjoy his momentary meltdown—I was too busy having one of my own.

My temporary bond-mate and I had been watching with increasing unease as the female we had picked out was menaced by an Earth male who had apparently been waiting in her domicile for her to come home. From the gist of their conversation I gathered that she had ended their relationship but he didn't want it to stay ended. Though she repeatedly told him she wanted no part of his "sorry ass" as she put it, he wouldn't leave and now it looked like she was in real danger.

"Bring her through," I told Char'noth. "Or send us down there to defend her."

I felt a surge from Lucian through our link.

"Yes—send us!" he exclaimed, stepping forward. "We'll kill that bastard who dares to threaten our female!"

I nodded at him approvingly. For once we were in complete agreement. We might not see eye-to-eye on much else but at that moment we were ready to act as one to protect our chosen female—and pound the male who was menacing her into the ground.

But Char'noth was shaking his head.

"The equipment is set to receive a subject—not send. There is no time to recalibrate for the two of you. What is needed is a distraction. Watch."

He worked some of the glowing controls and we heard high, tinny notes echoing in our chosen female's domicile.

On the lightscreen, we saw the male who had been menacing our female with his weapon frown and cock his head to one side.

"What's that?" he demanded. "You got somebody in here?"

"What? No! I don't know." The female—whose name was either "Ry-lee" or "babe" (it was hard to tell since the male had called her both)—shook her head distractedly.

Char'noth played the notes again—he was trying to lure them to the large, flat surface he'd called a mirror which was located in another room of the domicile.

"There it is again—it's coming from the bathroom." The puny, scruffy-looking Earth male, who had skin which was an unhealthy dirty-tan color, several shades paler than our female's warm brown tones, glared at her. "You *do* have somebody in there. Is it another man?"

"What—you think I have a hidden lover who plays the trumpet on the toilet for the hell of it?" she demanded. "I don't know *what* that is."

"You're lying. Go." He motioned with his weapon for her to head towards the source of the noise. I clenched my hands into fists as I saw the muzzle of the primitive but effective-looking firearm sweep towards her face. If he hurt her…

An answering surge of rage and anxiety came from Lucian. Glancing briefly at my temporary partner, I saw the fear we both felt for our female on his face. It almost made me like him better. Almost.

Char'noth played the notes a third time and the two Earthlings finally entered the area the male had called "the bathroom." It looked like a fresher to me with an area to collect and dispose of waste and a booth with a nozzle mounted on the wall which might have been a personal cleansing unit. But none of that mattered— what caught my eyes was the large, flat glass mirror hanging on the wall. When the two humans stared into it, it was almost as though they were looking through a window right at us—although they couldn't see us.

Or could they? I saw both their eyes widen as they leaned

forward and the female breathed,

"What the *hell?* Blue…green…what?"

I figured she must be talking about our skin color. I have dark blue skin tones with green eyes like most of the males in my clan and Lucian has light green coloring with blue eyes which is usual for the Fang Clan. Neither of us would be remarkable on our home world of Denaris but to Earthlings who were only used tan and brown skin, it probably looked fucking strange.

I don't know why Char'noth decided to show us to our chosen female and her attacker—maybe as another distraction. But it only made the situation worse.

"I knew it!" the male shouted, waving his weapon wildly. "You've got other men in here. You're cheating on me!"

"I don't know *who* they are or what they're doing in my mirror!" the female protested.

"Yes, you do—you lying bitch!" The male leveled his weapon at her head. "If *I* can't have you, *they* sure as hell can't!"

"Bring her through!" Lucian shouted at the same time I growled,

"Now, Char'noth! *Now.*"

"Transporting," the high, ridiculous voice of the Commercian informed us.

There was a shimmer of light and both our chosen female and the male who was menacing her disappeared from the lightscreen…and reappeared at our feet.

# Chapter Five

## Rylee

For a moment I didn't know where I was. I felt dizzy and light-headed, as though I'd just been spun around really fast by one of those carnival rides that uses centrifugal force to pin you to the wall while the floor drops away under you.

I blinked to clear my vision, took a deep breath, and looked around.

I realized I *still* didn't know where I was.

All I knew was that I was sitting on a hard, cold metal floor with the two guys I'd seen staring at me through the mirror looking down at me.

They were both incredibly, ridiculously tall—like professional basketball player tall—but they weren't lean or skinny. Both of them had broad chests and plenty of muscles to spare bulging under their blue and green hides. At five foot nine I'm no delicate flower but next to them, I felt like I was surrounded by giants.

"Who...who are you?" I breathed, looking up at them. "And where am I?"

"You're aboard a station orbiting your planet," a high, thin voice answered me. It wasn't coming from either of the huge guys though. Looking around I saw a dark blue worm-looking thing about three feet high with googly eyes on stalks and multiple arms scuttling towards me.

"Ugh!" I gasped, scooting away from it. It looked like some kind of an insect with all those arms and legs and I do *not* do insects. I get enough of them living in Tampa, thank you very much. Especially roaches—I *hate* roaches—but I'm not really fond of any creature that skitters around and has more legs than I do. At second glance, I thought the thing looked more like a centipede than a worm.

My sudden motion put me right up against the legs of one of the two huge men—if they were men. When I looked up again, I saw it was the green one.

"What's wrong, little female?" His voice was deep and smooth and he leaned down to look at me anxiously. He was wearing black trousers and a gray jacket of some expensive, shimmery material with an elegant rounded collar that looked like it had been tailored to fit him. He looked like he belonged in a board room or a court room—someplace urbane and professional. If they admitted seven foot tall green people, that was.

"She's frightened—you're *frightening* her, Lucian."

The one with the blue skin glared at the green one and then bent over to look at me. He was also wearing black trousers but his were much tighter and he also had on a kind of leather vest that showed his muscular arms and chest. There was a leather band with some kind of sharp, jagged red things threaded onto it tied around his right bicep. In contrast to green guy, he looked like he belonged in a jungle or an Indiana Jones movie. Or maybe one of those extreme survival reality shows. He struck me as some kind of rugged explorer or someone who worked with his hands.

"It's all right, babe—you're safe here with us," he rumbled in a voice which was just as deep but considerably rougher than the green guy's.

"What?" I stared up at both of them, almost forgetting about the talking worm-insect thing. "*What* did you call me?"

"Babe." The blue guy frowned. "Isn't that your name?"

"No, Drace, her name is Ri-*lee*," the green one corrected him, pronouncing my name like it was a foreign word. "'Babe' is clearly a derogatory term."

"Actually, it's a term of affection—when it's used by the right person. It's a form of 'baby.'" I said and then thought, *did I really just say that? Am I really having a discussion on semantics with two huge blue and green guys in the middle of what looks like a space ship on a cheesy science fiction movie? Are they aliens? Have I been somehow abducted, right through my bathroom mirror?*

Apparently so.

"Oh God…oh, God, I'm sorry! I'm *sorry!* I swear I won't do nothing bad ever again—just let me go home!"

I looked over and saw Phillip was beside me on the metal floor, completely freaking out. His gun, I saw with some relief, was gone. But so were his clothes.

Come to think of it—so were mine.

Looking down at myself, I realized that I was completely nude—what my old friend Zoe would have called, "butt-nekked."

"Crap!" I wrapped my arms around my chest and squeezed my thighs together tightly. What the hell was going on here? Now that the first shock was wearing off I was beginning to panic. Where was I? Who were these people? What was going to happen to me?

"Please," Phillip moaned beside me. "Please, just let it be a dream! Let me wake up soon, *please!*"

His words gave me something to hang on to and I began to understand what was going on.

*A dream,* I told myself. *Of course – this is all just a weird, elaborate dream. I'm **dreaming**.*

I've always had extremely vivid dreams—I even kept a dream journal in college for a little while for a psych project—so this seemed completely plausible to me. Look at how quickly we had switched locations, from my bathroom to an alien spaceship or wherever this was, instantaneously. That was something that only happened in dreams, right? And how else could I understand the big aliens' language when they talked to me? Surely a dream was the only explanation for that.

And then there was the fact that Phillip, my slimy ex, was clearly contrasted with the two hot alien guys—both of them completely drool-worthy, though in different ways. Probably that was my subconscious telling me I needed to move on and start dating again. It was presenting me choices—would you rather be with an urbane professional with the world at his fingertips or a rough but sexy outdoorsman who works with his hands? That was a tough one—I really couldn't decide.

Now that I thought about it, it was all so clear—so obvious. The panic which had been threatening to overtake my mind dissipated and I could think again. But though I stopped panicking, I also couldn't stop shivering—the metal floor was *freezing* against my bare ass!

"Are you cold?" the green guy asked me. He had black hair and blue eyes, I saw. "May I offer you my *undla?*"

I had no idea what an "undla" was but when he started taking off his gray tailored jacket, I figured it must be the name for that article of clothing. He was every bit as muscular as the blue guy and his broad chest was mouthwatering, even if it was a light olive green like the rest of his skin. He draped the *undla* around my shoulders and I pushed my arms through the sleeves, which were much too long for me. The garment was warm from his body heat and carried a crisp, clean scent like expensive cologne and the smell of the ocean with a wilder tang underneath.

"Thank you," I said gratefully, pulling it closed around me. I would have buttoned it up but there were no buttons. It didn't seem to matter though, because the edges of the jacket stuck to each other almost as though they were magnetic and it closed neatly, hiding my breasts and sex.

As soon as I was covered, I had a moment of pure relief. Nobody likes to have that "naked in public" dream. Although my subconscious seemed to want to go one better and make me have a "naked in front of two huge muscular aliens on a spaceship" dream.

Thanks a whole freaking lot, subconscious.

"Allow me to help you up." The green guy had one hand under my elbow and was lifting me before I could answer him. The blue guy moved to help him, putting his hand under my other elbow. Between the two of them, they not only lifted me up—they lifted me right off the ground!

"Whoa!" I exclaimed as my feet rose two feet clear of the metal floor. "I'm good now, guys—you can put me down."

"Our apologies. My *friend* here can be a bit overeager at times." The green alien gave the blue one a withering look and they set me back on my feet.

"Asshole." The blue one glared back. "Ignore his high-and-mightiness," he said, switching his attention to me. "I'm Drace—Drace of the Claw Clan of the K'drin Jungle of the planet Denaris."

"And I am Lucian of the Fang Clan," the green guy said, smiling. He seemed to have extremely long, sharp teeth, which made me a little nervous. "Of the great desert city of Y'brith, also of Denaris."

Okay, as introductions went this was kind of freaky but I could deal with it.

*It's all right,* I told myself firmly. *Everything is all right – this is just a dream.*

"Nice to meet you both," I said, smoothing down the gray jacket. "And thanks for your, uh, assistance. I'm Rylee. Rylee Hale."

"Oh man, this is bad…this has to be a bad trip! I can't deal with this, man," Phillip wailed, breaking into our introductions.

Looking down, I saw my ex was curled into a shivering ball on the floor, scratching at his face and rubbing his eyes as though he thought he might see something different if he tried hard enough.

"Char'noth," the green alien named Lucian said with obvious irritation. "Can you put this Earthling away where he won't interfere with our conversation?"

"At once." It was the blue centipede thing again. Snapping its clawed fingers, it summoned ten or twelve other centipedes to come carry Phillip away.

"Oh my God!" I gasped, backing up again. (Hey, don't judge me for being girly—I'm very brave about lots of things but bugs aren't one of them. Especially three foot tall ones who speak talk.)

I felt something warm and hard against my back and a deep, harsh voice murmured, "Easy…it's all right, Rylee."

Looking up, I saw I had backed up into the blue guy—what was his name again? Oh right, Drace. He looked down at me and I saw he had dark brown hair and light green eyes which somehow went perfectly with his blue skin tones. This close I could catch a whiff of his fragrance, just as I had smelled Lucian's scent on his coat. Drace smelled wild and hot with a dark, animal spice that was as masculine as Lucian's cool ocean scent.

"Sorry," I said uneasily, taking a step away from him as the blue centipedes carried Phillip away, still moaning that he was having a "really bad trip, man." "I, uh, don't much care for bugs."

"The Commercians aren't bugs—just sentient beings who developed outside the Goddess of Mercy's sphere of influence," Lucian explained.

"Um, the Goddess of Mercy?" I asked, frowning.

"Sure—she who gave the seeds of life to the Ancient Ones and told them to spread them on every habitable world in our galaxy." Drace spoke as though this was common knowledge—something I ought to know.

I shook my head. "Uh, still drawing a blank, guys—sorry."

"She's from a closed planet," Lucian said, frowning at Drace. "They know nothing of the Goddess of Mercy or the Ancient Ones. She probably doesn't even know she's a *La-ti-zal.*"

I frowned at him. "What did you call me? A la-ti-*what?*"

"A *La-ti-zal,*" Lucian repeated patiently. "And a Pure One—a female from a closed planet whose people haven't mingled their DNA with any other race."

"Which is the reason we think you can help us," Drace said.

"Help you *what?*" I demanded. God, this dream just kept getting stranger and stranger! But since it didn't look like I was waking up any time soon, I figured I'd better play along with it.

Lucian sighed. "Our people—the Denarins, come of a race where two males bond together in order to procure a female as their mate."

"Wait," I said. "Two guys and one girl—that's how it goes in your world?"

"Exactly." Lucian nodded.

"Okay," I said. "I got it. Go on."

"Usually bond partners find each other as children, grow up together and call a mate together," Drace said, continuing their strange narrative. "But that wasn't the case with Lucian and me."

"We were accidentally and wrongfully bonded together during a Clan gathering when we both ate of a *ylla* roll that had a piece of the same bonding-bud in it," Lucian said.

"Bonding bud? Yulla roll?" I looked at them in incomprehension.

"The *ylla* is an aquatic plant which grows in the oceans of Denaris," Drace explained. "Kind of like your seaweed on Earth. It produces a flower that has binding properties. When two *usually* compatible males eat from the same flower or bud…" He frowned at Lucian. "It forms a psy-bond between them."

"A psy-bond?" I said.

Lucian made an impatient gesture. "It allows those who are bonded to feel each other's emotions and sense their location. It's very useful for life-mates who are *rightfully* bonded — they are more able to care for and protect the female the two of them share."

"But it's a fucking nuisance for those of us who don't *want* to be bonded together," Drace growled. "I've had this arrogant asshole's feelings in my head for two solar months now — it's driving me fucking insane!"

Lucian narrowed his eyes coldly. "Feeling your crude, uncontrolled emotions hasn't exactly been pleasurable for me either. I'll be only too glad to get you out of my head."

"Wait a minute, wait a minute," I said, holding out my hands. "Let me see if I understand this. You two come from a planet where everyone lives in threesomes, like, uh, constant ménage action all the time, right?"

Lucian and Drace nodded and I wondered what the women on their planet looked like. They must be some kind of huge Amazonian-type girls if they could take on two guys this size on a regular basis. The idea was enough to make me close my legs and wince in sympathy.

"Okay, and the *way* you get bonded is two compatible guys eat a roll made of the same seaweed flower?" For some reason I pictured both of them eating bright pink sushi.

Again they nodded.

"And you guys got bonded by accident and now you can feel each other's feelings but you don't want to," I finished.

"Yes," said Drace at the same time Lucian said,

"Correct."

I stared at them for a moment. Wow, this dream had to be the strangest I'd ever had. I was beginning to wonder if maybe the strange smelling smoke coming from my neighbor's office back at my work had anything to do with it. I had vivid dreams but my imagination usually wasn't quite *this* active. But there was nothing to do but play along until I woke up.

"Okay," I said. "Now that I have the facts straight, what do you think *I* can do about all this?"

"You're a Pure One, as we said before," Lucian said. "We were told by a wise woman back on our home planet that in order to get the bond between us severed we would need the touch of a Pure One."

"One that's not attached to another male," Drace put in. "You're not, are you?" he asked, nodding to the far corner of the space station where the blue centipedes had carried Phillip so he could cry and moan in peace.

"Am I still attached to Phillip?" I made a face. "*Definitely* not. He's a mistake from the past that came back to haunt me, that's all."

"Good," Lucian and Drace said at the same time. Then they glared at each other. Damn, these two *really* didn't want to be together. They reminded me a little of my clients from earlier that day. Only, presumably, there was no Mr. Puppers to fight over.

"So...you think *I* can separate you?" I asked.

"We *know* you can," Lucian said earnestly. "We saw you separate the two males who came to your place of business."

"You were watching me?" I asked in surprise.

"Of course. We wanted to be sure we found the perfect Pure One to set us free from each other," Drace said.

I sighed. So even in my dreams I was doing divorces—and this time it was an *alien* divorce. My subconscious was *really* trying to tell me something. I needed to get out of this business and find a way to do the wedding planner thing I'd been dreaming of before I went crazy.

"Okay," I muttered to myself. "I learned my lesson—can I please wake up now?"

Nothing happened. I was still standing in the middle of a spaceship with two huge, muscular aliens looking at me hopefully and my ex crying in the corner surrounded by blue centipedes.

Apparently my subconscious wasn't ready to let me wake up yet.

"Okay," I said a little louder, since my dream showed no signs of dissipating. "What you two saw was me helping two guys with their divorce papers because I'm a paralegal. *Just* a plain paralegal — not some magic 'Pure One' or la-ti-da or whatever. Also, those guys *didn't* have a psychic bond that was tying them together. All they had was a French bulldog-labradoodle mix named Mr. Puppers and a mutual case of herpes."

"But you helped them get free of each other," Drace insisted, a stubborn look on his chiseled features.

"Yes, but helping them 'get free of each other,' as you put it, *didn't* take any magic on my part. I don't know what kind of special powers you think I have but I assure you, I'm just an ordinary Earth girl trying to make a living." I shrugged. "So I really doubt I can help you."

"Will you not at least try?" Lucian asked quietly. "Please, *ma 'frela* — we are desperate. We swear to return you to your home as soon as you free us from each other."

I didn't know what *ma 'frela* meant but I could see the desperation in both their eyes. Somehow they were stuck together and they *really* didn't want to be.

*Well, it's just a dream — might as well try whatever they want,* whispered a little voice in my head. Then again, what if what they wanted was some kind of three-way sex ritual? The thought sent a shiver over me which made my nipples hard and the area between my legs feel hot and swollen for some reason. I pressed my thighs together tightly. Even in a dream, I didn't think I was up to taking on two huge guys at once.

"What do I have to do?" I asked, frowning up at both of them in turn.

"Just touch us," Drace said, sounding as desperate as Lucian. "The wise woman said that the touch of a Pure One would be enough to free us from our psy-bond to each other."

"Touch you *where*, exactly?" I said, wanting some clarification as my earlier worry came back full force. Surfing around on the Internet late one night I'd run across one of those "threesome" porn videos where a girl was jerking off two guys at once. It was called, *"The Wild Wankathon."* I had a sudden erotic image of me sitting between the two big aliens, holding their hard shafts in my hands and stroking slowly as they groaned at my touch. Then I pushed the weird fantasy away — I wasn't up for that mess.

"Anyplace there is bare skin," Lucian said.

"Okay." I nodded thoughtfully. That didn't necessarily have to be sexual. "Would a hand-shake do it?"

"A hand shake?" Drace frowned.

"Like this." I took a step towards him and held out my hand to him. Hesitantly, he held his out to me and I took it. His fingers were well made, very clean, and callused as though he worked a lot with his hands. His skin was warm and his touch was pleasant but I didn't feel any kind of magic or mystical power flowing between us.

"I don't feel anything," I said.

"Because you have to touch both of us at once," Lucian said, extending his own hand.

"All right." I reached somewhat awkwardly for his outstretched hand, crossing my arms to do it since my right hand was already enclosed in Drace's left.

The minute Lucian's big hand, (which looked manicured and was softer than Drace's though no less strong,) enclosed my own hand, something strange happened.

It started as just a tingle — almost a tickle — right in my solar plexus. The tickle turned to a warmth and then a tingling which began to spread through me in a slow wave that radiated out from my midsection to the rest of my body, almost like an electrical current running through me.

"What the...what's going on?" I tried to free my grip from theirs but Drace and Lucian both held my hands tight.

"Just wait, please, *ma 'frela*," Lucian said earnestly. "I can feel it."

"Me too — I think it's working!" Drace sounded excited. "Gods, *finally* we'll be free of each other!"

"Finally," Lucian echoed, his eyes gleaming.

I stopped trying to get free of them but the feeling growing inside me was making me *really* uncomfortable. The buzzing, tingling feeling was spreading warmth to every part of my body but especially to the more, *ahem,* sensitive parts, if you know what I mean.

To my discomfort, I felt the tingling growing especially intense in my nipples and the area between my legs. It felt almost as though someone was holding a vibrator—a really good one—to those places, teasing my tender nipples and torturing my suddenly swollen clit. I squeezed my thighs together as tightly as I could but it didn't do any good, the sensation continued to grow and with it came an unwilling pleasure I couldn't help feeling.

*What's happening to me?* I thought wildly. *This is going too far! Is this turning into some kind of a wet dream?*

The growing pleasure seemed to indicate that it was. I was beginning to feel closer and closer to coming but I fought the feeling grimly. It would be horribly embarrassing to lose control completely and have an orgasm in front of two complete strangers, even in a dream!

"Please!" I gasped. "Please, this is too...too much!" Fear made my palms sweaty and slippery.

With a final jerk, I was able to pull my hands free of their grip, just as a devastating orgasm hit me and I started coming harder than I ever had in my entire life.

# Chapter Six

## Rylee

"Ahh!" I gasped, sinking to the ground. I couldn't remember the last time I had come this hard. My whole body was affected—electrocuted by pleasure. I was panting, my nipples were hard and between my thighs I was slippery and wet and ready. My heart was pounding like it was trying to get out of my chest. And all this was all from holding hands with them for less than a minute.

I was beginning to feel scared—well, as scared as you can be when you're coming, anyway. What the hell was going on? I had never had such a vivid dream before—and shouldn't such an incredible orgasm have woken me up?

"Are you all right, baby?" Drace reached to catch me.

At the same time Lucian grabbed for me too. "Forgive us, *ma 'frela,* are you injured?"

I wound up cradled between them, both sets of muscular arms supporting me. Luckily, this time they weren't touching my bare skin—just the gray jacket-like thing Lucian had given me to wear, so there was no repeat of the strange, sexual tingling.

That didn't mean I wasn't *really* freaked out, though.

"Let me go!" I struggled to get away from them and they set me on my feet. I promptly sank back to my knees. Wow, that orgasm had been *strong!* My legs still felt like jelly. I didn't think I could get up if I tried.

"Are you all right?" Drace repeated, crouching down beside me.

Lucian did the same on the other side, looking at me with great concern.

"Did severing our bond wound you in some way?" he asked.

"I don't…think so." I took a deep, shuddering breath and tried to push the strange sexual pleasure away. God, that had been *weird.* "It was just really, uh, intense." I looked at them. "Did you guys feel anything, um, unusual or is it supposed to feel like that?"

Drace and Lucian exchanged a swift look and I wondered what they were thinking.

"What do you mean by 'unusual'?" Lucian asked at last.

"I felt…I mean…" I broke off helplessly, feeling my cheeks get hot. I wasn't about to tell them that holding their hands had given me the strongest orgasm of my life. That was *mortifying,* even in a dream. Although to be honest, I was beginning to wonder if this *was* a dream. Why was it so vivid? And why couldn't I wake up?

"I felt a sexual energy," Drace said at last, lifting his chin defiantly, as though he was daring Lucian or me to make fun of him. "It made my shaft fuckin' rock hard." He shifted uneasily. "I don't know what it meant—I've only ever heard of that kind of thing happening between partners in a really strong Triumvirate."

"Which we most certainly are *not,*" Lucian said, frowning. Then he added, reluctantly I thought, "I felt it too. But it can't be right—I've heard of touch-pleasure between Triumvirate partners but only when the bond is extraordinarily powerful. We weren't even doing anything sexual—just holding hands."

"Maybe it's because Rylee is a Pure One," Drace suggested.

The concern cleared from Lucian's sharp, handsome features.

"I'm sure you're right. The desire we all experienced was probably just the by-product of such a powerful severing. There is, after all, deep energy in a psy-bond—it stands to reason that breaking it would release some of that energy."

"Well, then…" I got up and brushed myself off, carefully avoiding their hands when they tried to help me up. "It sounds like my work here is done."

"I suppose so." Drace didn't sound very happy about it.

"Yes, you're right, of course, *ma 'frela.*" Lucian also didn't sound too pleased.

"Hey," I said sharply. "For two guys who were dying to be free of each other and go back to your own lives, you don't sound very excited. Come on—think about how great it will be to get back home to your own, uh, regions of your planet. The desert and the jungle..." I had already forgotten the weird geographic names they had told me but I did, at least, remember the climates.

"Of course." Lucian smiled at me, showing those sharp, white teeth again. I remembered that he said he was from the Fang Clan—did those teeth have anything to do with that? Or was it just a coincidence?

*Doesn't matter,* I told myself firmly. *And it's none of your business. Whether this is a dream or somehow real (which is completely impossible), it's about to be over. You're either going to wake up, or they'll send you back through the mirror to your apartment. Either way, you never have to think about any of this again.*

Not if I wanted to retain my sanity, at least.

Suddenly Drace said, "Shit!" in a low, angry voice.

"What's wrong?" I asked, turning to him in surprise. He was scowling, his face as dark as a thundercloud.

"What is it?" Lucian asked him.

"Just now, when Rylee said we should be happy to get back to our own homes..."

"Yes?" Lucian prompted impatiently.

"When she said that, I had this sudden urge—the feeling like I couldn't wait to get back to the city. To Y'brith." Drace ran a hand through his hair in a gesture of pure frustration. "I've never been to that fucking place in my life and I sure as hell don't want to go there! It's in the fucking desert, for the Goddess's sake! My home is the jungle—the trees and plants and—

"The rain," Lucian finished for him, frowning. "The drenching rains that flood everything, causing new life to grow." He shook his head. "I just had the deepest desire to go and see the jungle. But...I don't want to go there—I know I don't! It's too wet and humid—my people thrive on the dry heat of the desert."

"And when you said *that* I just had an urge to go walk through the fucking sand dunes!" Drace growled. "I've never even *seen* a sand dune—I sure as hell don't really want to go walking through one!"

"It didn't work." Lucian sank slowly to the ground and shook his head. "The severing of our psy-bond—it didn't work." He looked at me. "If anything, I think you might have bound us even more closely together."

"He's right—I could only feel Lucian's emotions before—but now I have his longings. His *cravings*." Drace shook his head, as though trying to clear it. "Why do I suddenly want *talabash* stew?"

"Because it's my favorite dish, probably," Lucian said dully. "And I'm guessing you enjoy *pilnar* cakes?"

"My mother used to make them," Drace admitted. "Gods, we are so *fucked*."

"I'm sorry," I said, feeling put on the defensive. "Sorry if I made your situation worse, somehow. But remember, I *told* you I don't have any kind of magic powers! And I only tried this because you begged me to."

"We aren't mad at you, baby." Drace looked surprised that I would think so.

"Drace is right—the fault is ours, *ma 'frela*," Lucian agreed. "We simply must have misunderstood what the wise woman said."

"We need to bring Rylee with us and go back to her!" Drace exclaimed. "Go back to see Tanta Loro. It's the only way—she needs to see all three of us at once."

"I think you're right." Lucian nodded and then both of them looked at me.

"Oh, no…" I started backing away, shaking my head. "I barely even know you guys—I'm not agreeing to go all the way across the universe with you. My aunt taught me not to get into a car with a strange man—let alone a spaceship!"

Lucian frowned and he and Drace exchanged a look.

"I'm afraid we are not asking you, *ma 'frela*—we are telling you."

"He's right," Drace growled. "You're coming with us."

"What? No—*no!*" I started backing away again but just then I heard a squeaky little voice behind me like a Disney character sucking helium.

"Is there a problem with your purchase?" it asked.

I whirled around to see the freaky three-foot tall talking centipede glaring at me with its round, bulging eyes on the end of their stalks.

"Crap!" I jumped back away from it—I just could *not* get used to that freaking thing—and found myself between Drace and Lucian again. Lucian had stood up so both of them towered over me.

"No problem," Lucian told the centipede coolly. "Just that we have decided to take our chosen female home with us to Denaris after all."

"And she does not wish to go?" The stalky, bulging eyes studied me dispassionately. "If there is a problem, we have several restraining devices which should work well. Would you care to tie her up? Perhaps to chain her and blindfold her? It is our experience here at the Alien Mate Index that these Earth females are much more compliant when they are bound."

"What?" I was beginning to get that sick feeling in the pit of my stomach again—that feeling that this wasn't a dream. "You do this on a regular basis? Kidnap girls from Earth and tie them up and sell them off?"

"But of course." The blue centipede made a kind of squiggly bow. "It makes us profit—which is all we Commercians truly care about. Why else would we go to the trouble and expense of setting up a transport station in your atmosphere and inundating your planet with translation viruses so that prospective Earth brides can understand the language of the Alien males who choose them?"

So *that* was how I could understand their language. This dream was getting less dream-like all the time.

I didn't like that one damn bit.

"We don't want to tie her up," Drace said. "Unless she won't come any other way." He looked at me. "But you *are* coming, baby—I'm sorry but we fuckin' need you."

"You...you two big jerks!" I shouted at them. "You promised you would send me back to my apartment if I tried to help you. You lied to me!"

"No, we promised to send you home once you had severed the bond between us," Lucian said, frowning. "But perhaps we can sweeten the situation a bit."

"Sweeten it how?" I demanded. "You're basically kidnapping me to drag me across the universe and do who knows what with me! I don't see how you can make me feel better about that!"

"Technically it's only to another quadrant of the galaxy," Drace said, as though that made it better. "And Lucian's ship has a fast hyperdrive—it's barely one solar day's trip from your planet to ours. We can have you back to Earth in just a few solar weeks."

"You're lying," I said, crossing my arms over my chest. "Nobody can travel hundreds of light years away and come back in only a few weeks. Not even at the speed of light."

"We don't travel at the speed of light," Lucian explained. "My ship makes a kind of bubble in spacetime which allows us to go faster than that."

"A bubble in—no," I interrupted myself, realizing I was actually entertaining the idea. "I don't care—I still don't want to go."

"You won't be the first of your kind to leave your planet," Lucian said. His deep, smooth voice sounded coaxing. "Drace and I met a female on our home planet who was also a Pure One and a *La-ti-zal*. She was traveling with a member of the Imperial Guards."

"Well goody for her," I said, frowning. "I'm still not okay with being taken away from my home planet to become your freaking sex-slave!"

"Who said anything about sex?" Drace growled, frowning. "You think we want to take you to our home planet so we can molest you?"

"Well, what am I supposed to think?" I flared. "After the way you guys made me feel when I touched both of you at once?" I could feel my cheeks getting hot but I made myself go on. "And that was only touching your hands! I can't imagine what would happen if you tried to…to…do *other* things at the same time. I mean, I—"

"*Ma' frela,* let me assure you here and now that Drace and I have no intention of harming or molesting you sexually or otherwise," Lucian said sternly, cutting off my fumbling protests. "We need your help to be free of each other as I told you before—

that's all."

"And we're willing to pay for your time," Drace added.

I frowned at him scornfully. "And how are you going to *pay* me? I really doubt we use the same currency and I don't know of anyplace on Earth that would do an exchange of Denarin money—whatever it is—for dollars."

"It's true our currency is different, but there are some substances which are popular as trading commodities on almost every planet," Lucian said. "Diamonds, for instance, or gold."

That got my interest. Maybe I could deal with this after all.

"Diamonds and gold, huh?" I said. "How much?"

Drace and Lucian looked at each other.

"How much do you have on you? Drace asked. "I only brought a couple of *prella*-sized bars in case we needed quick currency."

"I've got ten back at the ship and more on Denaris," Lucian said.

"Excuse me," I interrupted them. "What's *prella*-sized?"

"Show her," Lucian gestured at the other man.

Drace reached into the pocket of his tight black trousers which looked like they were made of some kind of leather and withdrew a long, flat bar of solid, gleaming gold. It was about the size of a king-sized Hershey chocolate bar but twice as thick.

"Oh my God," I murmured as he handed it over to me. It was extremely heavy and shiny and obviously real. I had never seen so much gold in one place at one time—it was kind of amazing.

"Well?" Drace asked, frowning. "What do you think?"

I narrowed my eyes at them. "How many of these did you say you'll give me?"

They exchanged another glance which they seemed to be doing more frequently. I wondered if my intervention really *had* bound them more closely together which made this non-verbal communication easier for them. I also wondered if they realized they seemed to be cooperating more.

"Say...fifteen bars?" Drace said and at the same time Lucian said, "Fifteen—not a bar more or less."

Fifteen solid gold bars. They might be a little hard to convert into money but my aunt had friends who knew people. Speaking of Aunt Celia, she would probably wonder where I had gotten myself off to. I hated to cause her pain and worry but we didn't speak that much anyway and if I was only going to be gone a few weeks...

*I could quit being a paralegal,* I thought, examining the gold bar in my hand. It gleamed mellowly in the lights of the spaceship. *I could open that wedding planner business after all – follow my dreams instead of always doing the practical, dull, sensible thing.*

It was a tempting offer—especially since Drace and Lucian had announced they were taking me with them, whether I wanted them to or not. At least maybe by agreeing to their payment I was making myself more of a partner and less of a hostage.

I hoped, anyway.

"All right," I said at last. "But I want to hash out the terms and sign a contract."

"This is no problem—we are set up for contracts between all kinds of species here," the blue centipede, who had been watching quietly, spoke up in his squeaky voice.

"Agreed," Lucian said and Drace nodded.

"I want to be gone from home no longer that one month—one *Earth* month. That's thirty days max," I said sternly. I figured that gave us plenty of time to get to their planet, see the old wise woman to sever their bond, and get me back home again.

Lucian frowned. "That may be cutting things a bit close, especially if she—"

"You said it would only take a few weeks," I interrupted him sternly.

"It shouldn't be a problem," Drace said. He looked at Lucian. "You've got a fast ship and Tanta Loro agreed to see us right away last time. I don't think she'd keep us waiting."

"All right." Lucian nodded. "Agreed."

"And I want the fifteen bars of gold even if you guys don't get separated," I went on. "I mean, I'll promise to do my very best for you and do whatever it takes to get you parted but I don't want to be blamed or stiffed if this doesn't work. You're paying for my time here, not just my supposed talent." Which I didn't have, even though they kept insisting I was "special" somehow.

Both of them frowned at this but finally Drace said, "I guess that's only fair."

"I suppose it is." Lucian sighed. "All right."

"And one more thing," I said, making sure to get all the terms of the contract down—I wasn't a paralegal for nothing. "*No sex.* Got it?"

Lucian looked offended. "You find us unappealing, *ma 'frela?* That's a great pity—we find you *ravishing.*"

Drace nodded. "It's one of the few things we agree on."

"It's not that," I said quickly. "I mean, you're both big and muscular and hot and...and I'm sure the girls on your planet would think you're a real catch." I took a deep breath. "But *look* at you— you're freaking *huge!* I mean, I'm considered tall for a girl on my planet but you guys make me feel practically petite."

"Ah—you're afraid we'd hurt you because of our size," Drace murmured. "Don't worry, baby—the females on our home planet aren't much bigger than you. We know how to be gentle."

I could feel my whole body getting warm at his low words and the way he and Lucian were looking at me. I wished desperately that I had on a bra and panties beneath the gray jacket I was wearing. I felt so *naked* without underwear!

"It's not just that," I said quickly. "I'm going with you in a professional capacity and I'm not some prostitute. I want it understood that this gold you're paying me does *not* buy an all-access pass to my body."

Lucian frowned. "Have we been disrespectful of you?"

"We can tell you're not a pleasure-girl, Rylee," Drace said, also frowning. "And we'd never treat you like one."

"All right, good." I crossed my arms over my chest. "And it's not that I don't find you two attractive but I'm not into casual sex— especially not with two guys at once."

"So you only have one male and one female when you make love on your planet?" Lucian asked.

"How does that even *work?*" Drace asked, shaking his head in apparent disbelief. "How can you be properly pleasured without one male to suck your nipples and another to taste and stroke your pussy?"

His words sent a hot rush through me and I had a sudden mental image of the two of them "pleasuring" me that way. I pushed it away quickly.

"We manage just fine, thank you," I said tightly. "The point is I want a no sex clause put in the contract—it's a deal breaker for me."

"As to that, you do not have to worry, *ma 'frela,*" Lucian said. "Only psy-bonded partners who *want* to be together wish to share a female between them and bring her pleasure." His face darkened. "And that is only when the bonded pair consists of an Alpha and a Beta. Drace and I are both Alphas."

I shook my head. "I don't understand—what does that have to do with it? And what does it mean—both of you are dominant?"

"It's one of the reasons we need to get our bond severed," Drace's face was as dark as Lucian's. "I'm sure as hell not going to act as the Beta."

"I feel the same." Lucian glowered at the other man. "I refuse to accept the subservient role—especially sexually."

Their explanation was still as clear as mud but if it kept them from wanting to make me into a sexual shish-ka-bob, I was okay with it.

"Fine," I said. "Then you won't mind putting a no sex clause in the contract."

"No, we don't object," Lucian said.

"Good. Then if we can just have it drawn up—" I began.

"Done!" The high, helium-sucking voice of the blue centipede thing interrupted me.

"What?" I exclaimed. "Where?"

"Here." It waved three of its clawed hands and a glowing screen that appeared to be made out of light was suddenly hanging in the air above our heads. On it, in perfect legalese, was a contract between myself, Lucian, and Drace detailing everything I had specified.

"Wow," I said, frankly impressed. Who knew he could whip a

contract up so fast? The little blue centipede was a better paralegal than I was!

*But I won't be a paralegal for much longer,* I told myself. *I'll sign this contract, get the gold, and come back home to open my own wedding planning business.*

If I didn't just wake up first and realize this was an incredibly vivid dream. But for now, I was going with it.

Already I could see myself, helping happy couples start their lives together. Doing cake tastings and floral arrangements and helping the bride pick the perfect venue and just the right dress...I've always loved weddings. It would be *so* much better and happier than helping angry couples end things. My heart felt as light as sunshine at the thought.

"We'll need some kind of written equivalent so we can sign it," Lucian said.

"Done!" Almost before I could blink, the centipede was holding out three copies of the contract on rich, creamy parchment which was thicker and heavier than any paper I'd ever felt before.

I checked my copy over just to be sure everything was there. Time limit—check...fifteen gold bars in payment—check...no sex clause (this one made me blush for some reason)—check. There were even lines by all three of our names, which I assumed was for our signatures, down at the bottom.

"Looks good," I said. "Does anybody have a pen?"

"Oh—you cannot sign this kind of contract with any writing implement." The centipede—who I was kind of getting used to— looked shocked. If a three foot tall blue alien centipede *can* look shocked, I mean.

"No?" I frowned at him. "Then how do you sign?"

"In blood," Lucian answered for him, as though it was no big deal.

"What?" I looked at him uneasily.

"He's right. Blood is binding." Drace nodded.

"But...I'm not going to slit my wrist just to sign a contract," I protested.

"You don't have to. Look." Lucian opened his mouth and I saw his teeth—the two where a human's canine teeth would be—grow suddenly long and sharp, almost like a snake's fangs. He pressed the pad of his right thumb casually to one needle-sharp point and I saw a small droplet of crimson blood well up on his green skin. Well, at least now I knew they bled the same color as me, despite their different skin colors.

As I watched, Lucian pressed the bloody pad of his thumb to the line on his copy of the contract beside his name. He then did the same for Drace's contract and also mine. He pulled a clean white piece of cloth which looked a little like a handkerchief out of his pocket and wrapped it around his thumb. Then he reached for my hand.

"Will you allow me? I can pierce your flesh quickly and efficiently."

"Um…" I held back, looking at those bright, white fangs uneasily. Even more than his immense height and his olive green skin, they made him seem scary and alien.

Lucian seemed to see the fear in my eyes.

"Come, *ma 'frela,*" he said gently. "I will not hurt you—you will feel barely a prick."

"Well…" I looked at him uncertainly and then eyed Drace. "Are you going to bite *him* too?" I asked, playing for time.

"No fucking way," Drace growled.

"Naturally not," Lucian said stiffly. "An Alpha of the Fang Clan bites only his bonded mates—his female and his Beta. Drace is neither of those to me."

"Oh, all right." I shrugged. "Well, then…how is Drace going to cut his finger?"

"Like this." The big blue alien suddenly produced the most enormous knife I'd ever seen. Seriously, I wondered how and where he'd been hiding it. The edge gleamed cruelly in the ship's light and I couldn't help gasping when he drew it over his finger, making a deep incision that began to drip crimson at once.

"Oh my God—look what you did to yourself!" I exclaimed. "That's really deep!"

"Just a scratch." Drace pressed his bloody fingertip to all three of our contracts as though it was no big deal. Then, instead of wrapping his finger in a handkerchief like Lucian had, he simply popped it in his mouth.

"What are you —" I began.

"Healing himself," Lucian said in a low voice. "Males of the Claw Clan are able to heal the wounds of themselves and their mates — it's one of their Goddess-given gifts."

Sure enough, when Drace took his finger out of his mouth, I saw that it was completely healed without even a scratch to show where the long, wicked blade had cut him.

"Oh my God," I said faintly. "That's…impossible."

Drace shrugged. "No it's not. I'll heal you too after Lucian pricks your finger." He cleared his throat. "If you want me to."

I looked at him and then at Lucian. Both of the big aliens were giving me strangely intense looks. I had the feeling they both wanted me to let them do this — to wound me and to heal me — although I couldn't imagine why. And I didn't exactly think they knew why either.

"Is this normal?" I asked, reluctantly extending my right pointer finger to Lucian. "I mean, with, uh, bonded mates on your planet?"

"It is normal for two males to take care of one female," Lucian admitted. He took my hand in his but instead of biting my finger, he pressed a gentle kiss to my fingertip instead.

For some reason the tender gesture made my heart bang against my ribs.

"But you don't usually see a Triumvirate including a male from the Fang Clan *and* a male from the Claw Clan," Drace said, frowning. "We're rivals — enemies."

Which was probably just another reason they wanted to be free of each other. I wondered if I could help them — I certainly hadn't been able to so far. But either way, I got paid — as soon as I signed the contract, anyway. Which meant I needed to get this over with.

I watched, unprotesting, as Lucian opened his mouth and pressed the pad of my index finger to the tip of his gleaming white fang.

I gave a little gasp but not because of the pain—I felt a bolt of pleasure go through me when he bit me as well. It wasn't as intense as the orgasm I'd had when I was holding hands with both of them at once but it most definitely made my nipples hard all over again and caused my pussy to tingle.

"Hey—you said no sex! It's right there in the freaking *contract*." I tried to jerk my hand away but Lucian held on to it for a moment.

"Carefully, *ma 'frela*. You don't want to injure yourself on my fangs." He let me go slowly, his big hand lingering on mine. "And I was not touching you sexually—it's just that the bite of a Fang Clan male can be quite…pleasurable to the right person."

"Is that why you won't bite Drace?" I said, beginning to understand. "Because it would be too intimate? Too, uh, sexual?"

Both of them frowned.

"Of course not," Lucian said quickly. "Drace is not my true mate or my Beta—he would get no pleasure from my bite—only excruciating pain."

"Not that I'd *want* pleasure from another male like that," Drace growled. "I'm no Beta."

Huh—there was something going on here. Something that made them want to be apart besides the fact that they had been bonded accidentally and were from rival clans. I considered it as I pressed my bleeding fingertip to all three contracts.

"Will you let me to heal you?" Drace asked, when I finished.

I cocked my head at him as I gave him my finger.

"Will you heal Lucian too? I think his thumb is still bleeding."

The big blue alien's face grew dark and he shook his head.

"I can't heal him for the same reason he can't bite me without giving me pain. We're not true mates."

"And *I* am no Beta either," Lucian put in, scowling.

Again with the "I'm not a Beta" thing. I was beginning to wonder about that but any questions I might have asked were wiped from my mind when Drace sucked my finger between his lips and began to lick it gently.

I won't lie—it felt exactly like he was licking me someplace else. Someplace south of the border, if you know what I mean. Not that I had much experience with that—Phillip certainly hadn't been interested in it. But it was still a strange sensation to feel the soft licking and sucking between my legs almost as much as I felt it in my wounded fingertip.

"Are...are you almost done?" My voice sounded high and breathy in my own ears. I wasn't surprised by the pleasure this time—I had halfway expected it after the feeling of Lucian's fangs sinking into me had given me such a jolt. But it was still uncomfortable to feel so incredibly aroused by the touch of someone who was still mostly a stranger.

Or was he? After everything we'd been through since we met each other, I was actually beginning to feel like I knew these guys, even if they were seven foot tall aliens.

At last, Drace let my finger slip slowly from between his lips.

"Finished," he murmured and there was a hunger in his half-lidded eyes that made something low in my belly clench with an answering heat.

*Stop it!* I told myself. *You just signed a contract saying no sex! And that's exactly the way you want it!*

"Well," I said, trying to make my voice sound light and unconcerned. "I guess that's that. We're all set to go."

"Oh man—this is so bad man! Please!" moaned Phillip from the corner.

I sighed. "Except for one thing."

# Chapter Seven

## Lucian

We had a long debate about what to do with the male who had menaced Rylee. Drace, predictably, wanted to kill him outright or at least flush him out the airlock and let him die in space. It was a crude solution at best, but I found myself agreeing with him—though I had no right to feel protective and possessive of Rylee, I did. Any male who harmed her or even *tried* to harm her deserved to die.

But to both our surprise, Rylee vetoed this idea. I could make no sense of this—the male had tried to kill her. Shouldn't she want to be rid of him forever? But despite the harm he'd done to her, she still didn't want him killed.

Char'noth offered to send the groveling, crying male back to where he had gotten him in the first place but Rylee didn't like that idea either. She understandably didn't want him invading her domicile while she was gone with Drace and me.

"What about a memory wipe?" I finally suggested. "We could clear his mind of you completely if you like," I told Rylee. "That should simplify your life when you return to Earth."

"You can do that?" She looked at me in awe.

I shrugged. "I can if Drace will help. It's a talent of the Fang Clan but we need a partner to make it effective."

Drace frowned and I could feel him considering through our newly strengthened link. What I was suggesting was something only rightfully bonded mates would normally do together and it took a level of mental and psy-connection which we hadn't previously had. However, since our first failed attempt at severing the bond between us had actually strengthened it instead, I thought we might be able to pull it off.

It also required a large measure of trust. I watched Drace as he considered my proposal.

"I guess we can try," he said finally. "If you really want to merge minds that way."

"It doesn't bother me if it doesn't bother you," I said. "And it's for Rylee."

I could feel his reluctance melting at that. Somehow, though we had just met the little Earth female, she had already worked her way under both our skins.

"If you could make him forget me that would be great," Rylee said eagerly. "Also, do you think you could make him forget he wants to drink and do drugs?" She made a face. "And *cheat?* He'd have a much better life if he wasn't so weighed down by his addictions...and his attraction to skanky women."

"Present company excluded, I'm sure" I murmured. "But actually, I'm afraid I can't erase your past paramour's proclivities and tastes—I can only make him forget *you*. If, for instance, he saw you on the street he might not remember you but he *would* still be attracted to you."

"Any male would," Drace pointed out. "She's fucking gorgeous."

The little female's cheeks grew rosy under her creamy light brown skin tones.

"Thanks anyway. Just making him forget me will be fine and I'll be sure he doesn't see me on the street or anywhere else. I never want to have anything to do with him again."

"Very well." I nodded at Drace and we attempted to get the whining, mewling human male between us. It was easier said than done—he kept falling on his face and moaning that he didn't want to die. His cowardly display was in direct contrast to Rylee's calm acceptance of the subject. It turned my stomach. Not even a Beta would whine and beg so shamelessly.

Finally Char'noth produced a set of manacles for the human's wrists and we hung him from a hook affixed to the ceiling. Why the Commercians had such extreme methods of restraint, I didn't know and didn't *want* to know. Probably to display Earth females to their prospective buyers. I didn't like that idea at all but there wasn't much I could say about it when I was using the restraints myself.

"All right," Drace said when we were standing on either side of the sniveling male. "Now what?"

"You put a hand on the human's right temple and I'll put mine on his left," I told him. "When we form a connection using him as a conduit, we should be able to enter his mind."

I had never actually tried this before but I knew instinctively I could do it—just as I knew the other gifts of my Clan would be available to me as soon as I found the right psy-partner. Drace wasn't that male but he would have to do, for now.

We positioned ourselves and I closed my eyes to concentrate. I could feel Drace concentrating too and then I was swooping forward, falling into a dark space I knew was the place behind our captive's eyes.

There was an unfocused blob of color which quickly resolved itself into shapes. It was the male—Phillip, Rylee had called him— pulling the projectile weapon from his pocket.

"Son of a bitch!" Drace said in a low tone and I knew he was seeing the memories as well.

"What? What is it?" I heard Rylee ask.

"We're watching the moment he pulled a weapon on you," I told her, not opening my eyes. "It's...unsettling."

"Unsettling? I want to pound this asshole into the ground," Drace growled. "I still don't see why we can't flush him out the airlock."

"How far do we need to go back?" I asked, Rylee, ignoring my temporary bond mate's outrage. "To get rid of his memories of you completely?"

"At least two years." She didn't sound very happy about it. "I stayed in the relationship way longer than I should. But I didn't want to give up—I'm not a quitter."

"You're not a coward, either," I said, examining more of Phillip's memories—some which featured Rylee and some which didn't. In the memories without her I saw him skulking around, often carrying and using his firearm as well as taking many illegal substances which made him even more unstable. He was a much more dangerous male than she seemed to realize.

"She's too brave for her own good," Drace growled in a low voice, obviously seeing the same things I was. "And this guy is a Goddess-damned asshole who didn't deserve her."

I was pretty sure I knew what he was talking about and it wasn't just the way Phillip had often gotten drunk and shouted at her. As we scrolled backwards through his past, looking for a time before he knew Rylee, we also saw the two of them in the sleeping platform together.

The sight caused a possessive growl to rise in my throat even though it was ridiculous—this had happened long before Drace and I met Rylee. Still, I didn't like the sight of her with another male.

Not that Phillip was doing much to please her.

As Drace and I watched, we saw how the human male seemed to only care about his own pleasure. He used Rylee's body selfishly, never considering what she might like or enjoy.

It made me angry to see how inconsiderate he was. Rylee was a rare beauty—a treasure. Any male privileged to attend such a female should feel grateful and do his utmost to worship her body properly with his own. Not just get on top of her and thrust a few times, grunting garbled endearments until he came.

Phillip hadn't even had the decency to make sure she was satisfied afterwards—he simply crawled off her and dozed, leaving Rylee to help herself.

Those parts—the parts after Phillip was already half asleep on one side of their sleeping platform and Rylee was bringing herself to pleasure—I tried not to watch too closely. It felt wrong to spy on her. Yet I couldn't help noticing how her slim brown fingers flew over the slippery, swollen interior of her pussy...couldn't help hearing her soft moans as she brought herself the pleasure her partner had denied her.

I felt Drace's arousal growing through our connection and knew he was watching as well.

"Gods," I heard him mutter but I didn't reply.

It made me uneasy to feel another male's sexual desire—it wouldn't have been so clear, so insistent, if he had been a Beta male. But bound to another Alpha as I was, I couldn't help feeling his strong emotions clearly, just as he felt mine.

To my relief, we finally found a point in Phillip's memories where there was no Rylee anywhere in sight.

"Here," I murmured to Drace.

"All right—what do we do?" he asked.

"Concentrate on removing Rylee. Wipe her from his mind completely as though you were rubbing out a drawing in the sand," I said and proceeded to follow my own instructions.

The action was unfamiliar to Drace at first but I felt him helping me and in less time than it seemed possible, all memory of Rylee had faded from Phillip's mind. It left some holes in his past but I managed to put in the suggestion that these were due to the substances he'd become addicted to. Maybe it would give him the incentive to quit them, as Rylee had wanted him to.

When we were finished, I was very glad to withdraw from his mind and I felt Drace's relief as well. Being inside the memories of a male who had been abusive and neglectful of our chosen female wasn't comfortable—mostly because I had to work almost every moment to control my temper and keep from breaking his unworthy neck.

"It's done," I said, opening my eyes. "We can send him back, just not to Rylee's domicile."

"There are plenty of reflective surfaces I can send him through," Char'noth assured me. "I will be certain to set him far from where your chosen female resides."

"Good," Drace said, frowning. "As far away as possible."

"Hang on," Rylee protested. "You can't set him down naked in the middle of India or Spain or somewhere. I mean—unless you're going to put some clothes on him?"

"Impossible," Char'noth told her. "Only living, organic tissue can be transported without considerable difficulty and expense."

"We've paid enough as it is," Drace growled. "I'm not spending one fucking credit more on this bastard."

"I agree," I said. "Send him down nude." Rylee started to protest but I shook my head at her. "No, *ma 'frela*—this male was cruel and inconsiderate to you. He deserves much worse than to be sent safely back to his home planet minus only his clothing and some parts of his memory. Or is it that you still have feelings for him?"

"What? No!" she exclaimed, frowning. "I just…feel bad for him. He wasn't *all* bad — not in the beginning, anyway."

"You're too kind hearted," Drace told her. "But you need to forget about this idiot now. If we're going to meet the terms you laid down in the contract, we need to get moving."

"Fine." She sighed and cast one last look at Phillip, who had a dazed, uncomprehending look on his face. "Just don't send him to France or Japan or anywhere like that. I mean, at least put him someplace where he speaks the language, okay?"

"It shall be as you say," Char'noth assured her.

"Thank you." Rylee nodded at the Commercian and though I saw a swift grimace of distaste pass over her face, she didn't gasp or try to run from him as she had at first.

Watching her overcome her fear of the many-armed alien gave me a new respect for her. She was brave and compassionate and beautiful and *ours* — mine and Drace's — for a solar month. I felt a surge of pleasure and possessiveness coming from my temporary psy-mate and knew he felt the same.

Without thinking about it, I went to stand to one side of Rylee. Silently, Drace took his position on her other side so that we were flanking her.

*Ours.* The thought echoed in my mind and in his as well, I was sure.

It didn't occur to me that I was thinking as though Drace and I were rightly bonded and had chosen Rylee the way any other psy-bonded males might choose a female mate to complete their bond. It just felt right to me and for the first time since I had experienced the other male's emotions within my own mind, I didn't feel exasperated or irritated or desperate to get rid of him. With Rylee between us, it didn't seem so wrong to know what Drace was feeling.

*Don't get too comfortable with it,* I warned myself. *This partnership can't last and you know it. We're both Alphas and that isn't going to change, no matter how beautiful and brave and desirable the female we've chosen is. This has to end and Rylee is the only one who can help us end it.*

I hoped.

# Drace

With Rylee's bastard of an ex-mate taken care of, we were finally free to leave the Commercian's station and re-board Lucian's ship. I saw the little female hesitate for just an instant before stepping through the airlock connecting us to the station. There was an expression of fear and indecision on her lovely face. Then she looked down at her copy of our contract, which she clutched tightly in one hand, lifted her chin, and took the step.

Lucian and I exchanged glances and I knew he had seen it too. Rylee had plenty of courage to go along with her beauty. It made me glad that we had chosen her from the AMI, even though we wouldn't have her for long.

I helped Lucian with uncoupling his ship from the Commercians' station and then he went to set a course for our home planet while I showed Rylee around.

"Wow…" She trailed her fingertips lightly along the polished copper of the walls as we walked down the main corridor. There was framed art at tasteful intervals lit by soft, indirect glows. "This is *amazing*. It's not at all like I thought a spaceship would be. I thought it would look more like the centipedes' station but this is different—it's like some kind of space yacht."

Even I had to admit the ship was a beauty—a sleek, Travian 6000 edition with spacetime bubble displacement tech and a hyperdrive second to none in its class. And it was built to the most luxurious specifications possible.

Personally, I still liked my own little star-jumper better. It wasn't nearly as fancy but it was cozier and it handled like a dream. But it wasn't as fast as Lucian's luxury behemoth and his ship was a lot roomier too—which was a good thing. On the trip to Earth we'd given each other a lot of space—mostly so we wouldn't kill each other.

"This is what five million credits will get you," I said to Rylee as she admired the brushed copper fixtures and large *zirgian* marble bathing tub in one of the freshers. "But Lucian can afford it—he's a high priced litigator. Negotiates a lot of trade agreements between

Clans. In fact, that's what he was doing when we were accidentally bonded at the Clan gathering."

"Really? If you two are from rival clans, why were you even near each other?" Rylee asked.

"Not on purpose, that's for fucking sure," I growled. "I was just there to deliver some work I'd promised to a client from another Clan."

"So these gatherings are like conventions—just for business connections and things like that?" she asked, with evident interest.

"Well, no..." I shifted uneasily. "They're mostly for males who haven't found a psy-bond mate yet. That usually happens in childhood so the psy-bond between the males has time to grow and mature with them until they're ready to find a female to complete their bond. I wasn't looking for a mate, though—I was fine being single. And so was Lucian, as far as I know."

It was a lie but I didn't see the need to tell her the truth—that I had watched the psy-bonded males all around me at the Clan Gathering with envy and despair. All my life I'd felt like a freak— an outsider because somehow I couldn't seem to find the right partner—couldn't find a Beta who could bind his life to mine so that we could call a female as our mate.

My parents—all three of them—had told me over and over not to give up, that someday I would find the right Beta and then the two of us would find the right female. But as I got older and struck out on my own, those reassurances dried up. Both my brothers found their mates and then found females to start families with. Then my sister was called to complete the Triumvirate of two males from the Beak Clan.

At last, only I remained.

I moved far from my hometown of Renth and buried myself in my work—making wood carvings for the holy temples of the various Clans and sometimes special pieces for private collectors. I only came out and socialized when I had to. It was easier to bear my unmated status in solitude than it was in a crowd where I felt like a single drop of water unable to flow with the rest of the stream.

I hated going to the Clan gatherings, even though my business demanded it...but I felt drawn to them too. I couldn't help thinking—even years after I should already have been mated—that I would somehow find the right Beta to psy-bond to. Couldn't help wishing that I would be able to trade my solitary existence for one filled with a family and a house full of children and two loving spouses to share it with.

And now here I was—bonded all right—but to another Alpha, which would never fucking work. I could still remember the sharp surge of elation I'd felt after eating the *ylla* roll when I suddenly had emotions that weren't my own inside me...and the crash of disbelieving anger and despair when I realized those emotions belonged to another Alpha and not a compatible Beta as I had hoped. Not just any Alpha either, but one from the Fang Clan, who were mortal enemies to my own Claw Clan.

It was *such* a fucking mess I wondered if we'd ever get it fixed.

Although now that I thought about it, my link to Lucian wasn't bothering me *quite* as much as it had been. Adding Rylee to the mix, even though we weren't really bonded to her, seemed to have sanded away some of the rough edges of our link, which had been irritating me since we'd first been accidentally joined. Of course, I still wanted to be free of the other male but the feeling of his emotions in my head no longer made me want to wring his neck—I wondered why...

"What's this room?" Rylee asked, breaking into my speculation. "Some kind of kitchen?" She was looking into a sleek, modern area with secure cabinets and a cold storage unit as well as a table with just enough room for three. There was also a huge, copper colored pot which was full of nutrient slime which could be simmed into any imaginable food.

"That's the food prep area. Lucian has the best in food-sim tech in here. You want me to make you something?" I offered.

"Thanks but..." Rylee yawned. "Actually, right now I'm just really tired. It's been a long, crazy day. Is there anyplace I can lay down? And, uh..." She looked down at herself. "Do you have anything else I can sleep in? I guess I should have thought about it before we left but I don't really have any clothes."

"I'll see what I can find," I promised. "But first, let's get you a room for the night."

"The night," Rylee mused as we left the food prep area with its large pot of nutri-slime and went down the long, curving corridor that led to the guest quarters. "But isn't it always night in space?"

"Technically, yes," I said. "But we hold with the standard twenty-seven hour solar day, just like we have on Denaris."

"Huh—our days are only twenty-four hours on Earth," Rylee remarked and yawned again. "I'm sorry—I don't know why I'm so tired."

"Like you said, you had a long day, baby," I told her gently.

She looked up at me, her black eyes flashing.

"Why do you keep calling me that?"

I shrugged. "You said it was a term of affection. I guess I was feeling...affectionate. I think Lucian feels the same way."

"Is that why he keeps calling me "*ma 'frela?* What does that mean?"

"I'm not the one to ask about Fang Clan dialect," I said. "But I'm pretty sure it means 'beautiful one' or 'lovely little one.' Something like that." I cocked an eyebrow at her. "Would you rather we only called you Rylee?"

"Well..." She frowned, considering. "We don't really know each other well enough for nicknames."

"Don't we?" I asked her quietly. I was thinking of the intense surge of sexual pleasure that we'd all experienced when Lucian and I held hands with her. From the rosy tint of Rylee's cheeks, she must have been remembering the same thing.

"I...uh..." she stammered. Then I opened the door to one of the guest rooms—the one beside my own—and her eyes lit up. "Oh—it's gorgeous in here!"

I had to admit she was right. The copper walls were lit from above and below with colored glows that switched slowly from pale blue to light purple to forest green, one tint shading into another so gradually it was hard to catch them doing it. For art, there was a shimmering display of *vanites* framed in a large plasti-glass aquarium which took up most of one wall. They also changed color, forming ceaseless patterns as they enacted their endless mating dance over and over, no two patterns ever the same.

"Oh," Rylee breathed, walking over to take a closer look. "They're like fireflies—multicolored fireflies!"

"Fireflies?" I asked, frowning.

"They're like a kind of bug back on Earth. They light up but usually only in yellow. These are like a living rainbow!"

"I thought you didn't like bugs?" I said, raising an eyebrow at her.

"I don't mind them as long as they're not *huge*." Rylee frowned. "And as long as they're not all over the place. These, uh, can't get out, can they?"

"Completely contained," I assured her. "They're only there for your amusement. Some people think they bring good dreams if you watch them before going to sleep."

Rylee yawned again. "I'm down with the sleep part. Is that the bed?"

She pointed to the large, flat sleeping platform which was hovering above the floor at about waist height to me—which was more like chest-height to Rylee. It was made of deep blue padded sensu-foam which cradled the body comfortably in any position. Neatly spread across it was a shiny silver tempra-quilt which would adjust to whatever body temperature would be most conductive to sleep for whoever used it.

Of course, the sleeping platform was huge because it had been made for Triumvirate use. Rylee was probably going to look like a doll in it.

"Yes, that's the sleeping platform," I said. "You need a boost up?"

"I *think* I can manage. Just don't look," she directed me. "In case this jacket thing rides up."

Gripping the sides of the sleeping platform, she hoisted herself up—or tried to, anyway. She nearly fell—would have fallen if I hadn't caught her.

"Hey—I told you not to look," she complained as I grabbed her by her waist and deposited her neatly on the platform.

"I caught the motion of you going over from the corner of my eye," I said blandly. "What was I supposed to do—let you fall?" I didn't add that I'd also caught the sight of her full, rounded ass which made me wish I could join her on the platform.

But of course, it wouldn't feel right if it was just the two of us—we needed another male—someone to lie on the other side of Rylee to help me pleasure her. For a moment I pictured Lucian there—the three of us wrapped in each others' arms, giving and receiving pleasure as we acted out our own mating dance, every bit as intricate and endless as the dance of the *vanites.*

I pushed the idea away—it was Goddess-damned ridiculous. We'd have no one to perform the Beta's duties and *I* knew I sure as hell wasn't going to perform them. I doubted Lucian would be interested either.

"You said you were going to find me something to wear?" Rylee said and yawned again. She really did look tired, poor little female. It made me want to tuck her in.

"Yeah—I think Lucian has a clothing-simulator somewhere on the ship. Just let me see what I can do and I'll be right back," I promised her. "Lights, dim," I added and the multicolored glows dimmed until they were barely visible. Only the shifting pattern of lights from the *vanites* allowed me to see Rylee's face.

"Okay, thanks." She had already snuggled down under the silver tempra-quilt and her eyelids were heavy. I wondered if she would even be awake when I came back.

"Sweet dreams," I murmured, brushing a strand of hair out of her face.

"Thanks. But I think I'm already dreaming." She sighed contentedly and closed her eyes.

Before I could ask what she meant, Rylee was already asleep.

I tucked the tempra-quilt more firmly around her shoulders.

"Sleep well, baby," I murmured. I couldn't resist the urge to touch her again—didn't even try. Gently, I stroked the curve of her cheek with one finger. Her skin was satiny soft and warm to my touch. She sighed and snuggled deeper under the quilt. Gods, she was beautiful!

I wished we could keep her.

But there was no point torturing myself with hopeless dreams.

Instead, I went to find Lucian.

He was in the control area of the ship, entering the final coordinates for our home planet. A vast array of perfectly designed controls surrounded him, calibrated down to the nth degree. Lights blinked and a 3-D holo display-map showing the stars and wormholes in our local quadrant floated in front of his face. When I walked in, he looked up.

"How is she?"

"Asleep." I nodded at the co-pilot's chair. "You mind?"

Lucian considered for a moment, then shrugged.

"All right. Why not?"

I sat, a little stiffly. We'd been trying to avoid each other as much as possible almost from the moment we'd been bonded. This was the first time I'd ever willingly sought my temporary bond-mate out for any kind of discussion but I felt like we needed to talk.

"She's really something, isn't she?" I said. "Brave…gorgeous… *Special*."

"She's a *La-ti-zal*," Lucian pointed out. "She *ought* to be special, especially at the price we paid."

"Any price is worth it to sever the bond. To be free of each other," I pointed out. "Don't you agree?"

"Yes, of course," he said quickly, scowling.

I shrugged. "Just asking. You seem sorry we paid."

"No." He was clearly on the defensive. "I never said that. But you must admit it's a lot to pay when we can't even keep her."

"Keep her and do *what* with her?" I demanded, even though I'd been thinking the exact same thing not five minutes earlier. "It's not like we can offer her a solid bonding and a proper fucking Triumvirate."

"I know." He glared at the controls. "The sooner we get her back to Tanta Loro so she can dissolve our bond, the better. I just…I wish I could have met her under different circumstances."

"Meaning with a bonded Beta psy-mate." I played aimlessly with the lighting controls, causing the overhead glows to brighten, then dim. "Yeah, I get it. Me too."

Lucian sighed. "It doesn't matter. I don't have room in my life for mates or a family."

"I guess they'd only mess up your work schedule, wouldn't they?" I said sarcastically. "Because who wants to come home to a female and a Beta and a domicile full of kids when they can work twenty-seven solar hours a day instead?"

His face went dark. "As a matter of fact, that's right."

"Don't bullshit me, Lucian," I growled. "I know you were lonely when we got bonded—as lonely as I was. It was one of the main emotions I got from you right from the start."

"You can learn to live with loneliness," he said stiffly. "It's much easier to deal with than having a whole set of unwanted emotions in your head."

"Well, I don't fucking want *yours* in my head *either*," I snarled. Standing, I headed for the door.

"Where are you going?" Lucian asked, his eyes narrowed with irritation I could feel clearly through our link.

"To find your clothing simulator. I promised Rylee I'd make her something else to wear."

"Fine," he snapped. "Don't bother me again while I'm piloting."

"Wouldn't fucking dream of it," I growled.

And just like that, the uneasy truce we'd had for a moment was ended.

# Chapter Eight

## Rylee

I woke up in the middle of the night in a strange bed with my heart pounding.

*Where am I?*

I knew it wasn't my apartment in Seminole Heights, the old central part of Tampa. For one thing, I didn't hear the constant rush of traffic from nearby 275 which ran just outside my bedroom window. Instead, there was a quiet hush of air circulating through some unknown filtration system.

I also missed the reflected headlights rushing across my bedroom ceiling. When I first moved into my little apartment, it used to bother me—the light glaring in the windows. Then I put up a pair of thick drapes so the white brilliance was muted, only able to slip through the crack between the top of the drapes and the ceiling. I found the lines of light from passing cars racing across my ceiling strangely soothing but I didn't see them now.

Instead, there was a window with a strangely shifting pattern of muted rainbow luminescence right across from the bed I was in. And speaking of beds, this one most *definitely* wasn't mine. I had a standard full bed—the largest size that would fit in my tiny bedroom. The bed I was currently lying in was *huge*—a vast, bewildering expanse of mattress that stretched out on either side of me and felt like the most luxurious memory foam I'd ever experienced. It was much bigger and nicer than the mattress I had at home.

I didn't like it.

*Where…? Why…?* I still couldn't figure out where I was or how I had gotten there. I had the feeling I should know but my brain was still fuzzy from sleep—I couldn't get it to answer my questions.

Suddenly something moved on the wall—a slithering, sliding motion like a shadow detaching itself from the blackness.

*Oh my God!* I sat up in the bed, clutching the strange, rustling blanket to my chest. It seemed to be made out of some kind of shiny metallic fabric which reflected the muted rainbow light from the window. It was the perfect weight—neither too thick or too thin but it *wasn't* the ratty old throw I'd had since I was a kid. That threadbare blanket was the only thing besides pictures that I'd salvaged when my mom died and I had to go live with my aunt. Phillip used to make fun of me for having an actual security blanket but I didn't care—I always slept with it—*always.* But it wasn't here.

*Where am I?* I thought again, beginning to panic. *And what – ?*

The shadow moved again, slithering over the glass window with its multicolored patterns this time, seeming to suck in the light like a moving black hole.

It was getting closer.

A breathless scream left my lips. Coming for me—it was *coming for me!*

Suddenly the door to my strange new bedroom slid open and I saw a huge, broad-shouldered shape silhouetted against the light spilling in from the doorway. The shape was at least seven feet tall—it looked like it belonged to a giant.

Black shadow monsters sliding around the walls, a giant coming into my room…I felt like a girl trapped in a fairytale—one I couldn't get out of.

"Please," I whispered, my mouth numb with fear. "Please don't hurt me!"

"Rylee?" a smooth, deep voice rumbled.

"Who are you?" I shrank even further back in the bed, pulling the strange silvery blanket all the way up to my chin.

"It's just me, *ma 'frela.* Are you unwell?"

*Ma 'frela—it means beautiful one.* Or *lovely little one,* a voice whispered in my head. Who had said that to me? I clutched desperately at the memory but when I finally brought it into focus, it didn't make me feel any better.

*Drace—he said that to me. And that's Lucian, standing in the doorway. I'm on a spaceship with them, headed for a whole different solar system, light years from Earth.*

"Oh my God," I whispered unsteadily. "It wasn't a dream. It really *wasn't a dream!*"

"What wasn't a dream, *ma 'frela?*" Lucian came into the room, his sharp, handsome features faintly illuminated by the glow from the window—no, not a window. It was a tank of some kind that held the rainbow-colored firefly bugs. More and more details were rushing back to me but they only scared me more.

*I'm here – I'm really here on a spaceship! With two strange men who aren't even men – they're aliens! I might never get home again! Trapped – I'm **trapped!***

My heart started pounding and suddenly it seemed like I couldn't get a deep enough breath. I could hear a frightened panting-gasping sound and realized it was me but somehow I couldn't stop.

"Rylee! What is it? What's wrong?" Lucian ran to my side and reached for me but I shied away from him.

"I can't," I whispered in a shaky, tearful voice. "I can't actually *be* here. I thought it was a dream! This is supposed to be a *dream.*"

"No dream, *ma 'frela.*" He sat down on the bed beside me and put a large, warm hand on my back, right between my shoulder blades. The pressure of his palm made me aware of the strange fabric I was wearing. *The jacket-thing he gave me when they first brought me to the centipedes' space station. I must have fallen asleep in it.*

I winced away from the touch, feeling more panicked than ever. Not only was my dream of being abducted and taken light years from home in a strange spaceship not a dream, the aliens that went with it were also frighteningly, impossibly *real*. Nothing was right—nothing was familiar.

Nothing was safe.

Suddenly another huge shape appeared in the doorway.

"What's wrong?" a deep, rough voice asked—Drace.

"She's having some kind of an attack." Lucian sounded grim and worried. "Maybe some kind of delayed reaction to being taken from her home world. I can't get her to calm down."

"Do you have sedatives in your med-aid kit?" Drace asked. "I'll go get her something to help."

"No, wait." Lucian put out a hand and the other man halted.

"What?"

"She doesn't need sedatives." It sounded like the words were being dragged from Lucian but he spoke them anyway. "I can't...can't calm her alone. Come here. Please."

"Why?" Drace held his ground. "You don't need me. You told me not to fucking bother you."

"Please," Lucian repeated steadily. "It takes two males to do this correctly and you know it. I'm not asking for myself. Do it for Rylee."

Drace hesitated for a moment more. Then he growled, "All right, Gods damn you." With a swift, angry stride, he came around to sit on the vast bed on the other side of me.

I was still nearly hyperventilating, my mind trying to come to terms with the fact that the freaky dream I'd thought I was having wasn't a dream at all. If you think about it, it's a lot to take in. I mean, it's one thing to believe there is intelligent life somewhere in the universe and quite another to actually be *kidnapped* by that life and taken to a galaxy far, far away.

I wasn't dealing with it very well.

"Get close to her—she needs both of us now," I heard Lucian saying. "We need to hold her between us."

I wanted to protest at this—mostly because I still had a vivid memory of our three-way handshake and the way my body had reacted so sexually to their touch. But my mouth was too dry to speak and I wasn't able to do much of anything as the two large, hard male bodies flanked my own and pressed against me. They weren't touching bare skin but their very presence in the bed on either side of me made me feel incredibly small and vulnerable.

I should have felt crowded and frightened and squished...and for a moment I did. Then I took a deep, gasping breath and a scent entered my nose. It was two scents, actually—one cool and sharp and the other warm and spicy. Both were somehow completely masculine. They mixed together and, like some strange aroma therapy, seemed to ease the horrible tension that had filled me to the brim like poisoned water.

I took another deep breath…and then another and another, breathing it in. My heart, which had been pounding so hard I could hear it in my ears, started to slow its frantic rhythm. The big male bodies on either side of me felt good—warm…safe.

I felt myself relaxing.

"Better, *ma 'frela?*" Lucian's deep, smooth voice murmured in the dimness.

"I…I think so." I put a hand to my forehead, which was wet with sweat. "I guess…I thought this was all a dream. I think I expected to wake up in my own bed. Instead…here I am."

"Is that what scared you? Waking up in a strange room?" Drace asked. He sounded as concerned as Lucian.

"Partly," I said. "But there was something else. It was—" Something dark caught my eye—the black, snaky shadow flitting over the tank again. I screamed breathlessly and held out a shaking finger. "There! It's there!"

"Where?" Lucian demanded at the same time Drace said,

"Lights on!" in a loud voice.

The walls began to glow brightly, making me wince and blink as my eyes struggled to adjust. I caught a brief glimpse of an inky shadow flitting away into the far corner of the ceiling, apparently frightened by the light.

"There!" I shouted, pointing.

Lucian jumped up and ran to look in the corner. He made a disgusted noise and tried to catch whatever it was, but it was too quick for him. He turned back to the floating bed, empty handed.

"What was that?" I asked in a shaking voice.

"*Skizix.*" Lucian still sounded disgusted.

"A *what?*" I put a hand to my heart which was pounding all over again.

"Parasites that hang around spaceports looking to hitch a ride on an outgoing ship," Drace explained.

He still had one muscular arm around me and I found I was huddling against his side like a scared little girl looking for comfort from her daddy. I made myself sit up a little straighter and took a deep breath.

"They're like semi-sentient shadows," Lucian said, coming back to sit on the other side of the bed. "They feed on dreams."

"What? Like they suck them out of your head when you're asleep like some kind of vampire?" I could hardly have been more horrified than if he'd told me they fed on blood like vampire bats.

"Not exactly." He sighed. "It's more like they feed on the emotions your dreams evoke."

"Which is why they like to slip into sleeping chambers and wait for you to go to sleep," Drace said, looking at me. "I should have checked for them before I left you alone in here. I'm sorry, baby."

"It's all right," I said automatically, although it really wasn't. I was *completely* freaked out. "So...is that thing, that *skizix,* likely to come back?"

"It's possible," Lucian admitted. He frowned. "They're very difficult to catch by hand. I'll have to get the ship fumigated when we get back to Denaris."

"Okay, well, I guess that's it for me." I sat up straighter and started to get out of bed.

"Wait—where are you going?" Drace asked.

"To find some coffee or whatever the hell it is you guys drink to stay awake," I said. "Because I am *definitely* not going back to sleep knowing that thing is prowling around."

"Wait." Lucian put a big hand on my shoulder to stop me. "*Skizix* don't actually do any harm—they mostly stay in the corners and feed from a distance. It won't actually *touch* you."

"I *know* it won't because I'm not giving it a *chance,*" I said stubbornly. "Come on—you guys must have some kind of stimulant around here. Where do you keep it?"

"You don't need a stimulant," Drace said unexpectedly. "You just need company."

"What? What do you mean?"

"Skizix only feed from unprotected sleepers," Drace said. "If you let us stay here with you, we can form a dream-shield around you."

"A *what?*" I shook my head. "What's that?"

"A protective mental shield those of the Claw Clan are able to form around themselves and others to keep away nightmares or anxious thoughts, I believe." Lucian sounded thoughtful. "Males in a Triumvirate often do it for their female mates." He looked at Drace. "Do you think it's possible? We of the Fang Clan don't have that gift."

Drace shrugged, his big, bare shoulders rolling. He and Lucian were both bare chested and wearing long, sleeping trousers in some kind of silky blue material.

"The Claw Clan aren't able to do a memory-wipe but I was able to help you do *that.* You should be able to help me form a dream-shield."

"I'm willing to try it for Rylee's sake," Lucian said, a bit stiffly. I had the feeling he was getting out of his comfort zone the same way Drace had felt uncomfortable when they fiddled with Phillip's memories. This was bringing them together — mentally? Emotionally? Anyway, in a way they weren't exactly comfortable with, but they were both willing to do it for my sake.

I was touched…but still a little uncertain.

"So in order to do this — to form this dream-shield — you'll both have to stay in here with me the rest of the night? I mean…we'd all have to, uh, sleep together?" My cheeks got hot as I said the words and I realized I really could have worded it better. *Great going, Rylee, you sound like a pervert.*

"Sleeping is *all* we would be doing," Lucian said blandly, obviously seeing my discomfort. "I'm sure we all remember the no sex clause in our contract."

"And you can trust Lucian and me to honor that," Drace said. "Whatever we may think of each other, we're both honorable males. There will be no actual sex between us."

"Well…all right," I said hesitantly. "As long as I get to keep my clothes on. Such as they are." I shrugged around in the oversized jacket.

"Oh — I simmed you some other things." Drace got off the bed. "You were already asleep by the time they were finished. I'll get them."

He came back with several strange-looking outfits which he hung in a kind of foldout closet that appeared in the wall of the bedroom when he tapped it. Then he handed me a long white gown with spaghetti straps. It seemed to be a thinner version of the silky material his and Lucian's sleeping trousers were made of.

"Oh... thank you." I ran the ultra-soft fabric through my hands. It whispered across my fingers like the finest, most delicate silk. "This feels *amazing*."

"It's sleeping cloth. Most of our night clothes are made from it on Denaris," Drace explained. "It's never too hot or too cold—much like the tempra-quilt you're under."

I looked down at the shiny silver duvet which had seemed such a poor substitute for my old security blanket. Maybe it wasn't so bad after all.

"I'll be right back." I hopped—and I do mean hopped because it was a long way down—carefully off the bed and went into the bathroom—what they called the fresher.

I had to pee by then. Earlier, Drace had briefly explained the way to use the strange alien toilet, which seemed to be kind of a cross between a bidet and an airplane toilet. I managed it without too much of a problem, even though the suction part of it was stronger than expected, and then decided to change.

After scanning the walls carefully for any stray dream-stealing *skizix*, I slipped off Lucian's gray tailored jacket and slithered into the slinky white night gown.

I looked down at myself and bit my lip. The fabric felt amazing against my bare skin but it left very little to the imagination. You could clearly see the outlines of my berry-dark nipples under the thin white material, which was stretched tightly over my full breasts. It clung to my hips and ass too, emphasizing how hippy I am, which is something I usually try to camouflage.

I frowned indecisively. Should I really wear this in front of Drace and Lucian? More to the point, should I sleep between them with it on? It was so *thin* it was barely there at all. Also, though it fell to my ankles, the top was cut low and the nightdress was sleeveless, ensuring that we were sure to have skin-to-skin contact of some kind since both the guys were shirtless.

When they'd put me between them before, I'd had the bulky jacket which formed a barrier between my skin and theirs. What would happen when that barrier was removed? Would I have another intense, unlooked for and unwanted orgasm if I rolled over in the middle of the night and wound up brushing their bare skin?

"Rylee? Are you well?" Lucian's deep, smooth voice from the other side of the fresher door interrupted my worried internal monologue.

"I'm okay. I'm just...not sure if I ought to wear this," I confessed.

"Don't you like it?" Drace asked and I could picture him and Lucian standing there together, both of them frowning. "Did I make it too big or too small? I had to guess your size and making female clothing isn't exactly my area of expertise."

"It's beautiful and it fits like a glove," I assured him—which was part of the problem. "It's just, uh, kind of revealing."

"Revealing?" Lucian deep voice sounded intrigued. "How do you mean?"

"How do you think?" I snapped. "I'm just...not used to dressing like this, especially around guys I barely know." Then again I was about to go sleep in a bed between the two of them— maybe I should revise that to "guys I'm getting to know." Probably better than I should. Oh dear.

"Don't be shy, baby," Drace said, his gravelly voice coaxing. "It can't hurt to let Lucian and I see you—we're only going to be together the one solar month before we go our separate ways. Less if Tanta Loro can get us separated sooner."

"Well..." I could feel myself weakening. Maybe it wouldn't hurt. What else was I going to do—change back into the bulky jacket? The night gown was much more comfortable. "All right," I said at last, opening the door and stepping out with my arms crossed securely over my breasts to hide my nipples. "But you can't say anything about my hips and thighs—I'm working on them but no matter how much I diet, I can't seem to do much about them."

"Are you suggesting we would complain about your curves?" Lucian sounded surprised as his deep blue eyes took me in. Drace's pale green eyes were likewise roaming over my body, barely hidden by the thin white dress. For a moment, I thought how strange it was that each man had eyes that matched the other one's skin coloring.

"Well, I mean…my hips *are* pretty big," I said, thinking of all the times Phillip had called me "fat ass" and "hippo" and "thunder thighs." God, why had I put up with that for so long? Mostly because he only did it when he was drunk, I supposed. He always apologized for it with tears in his eyes the minute he sobered up but that didn't matter — the damage had already been done.

In retrospect I was angry at myself for letting him make me feel so bad about my body. So what if I was hippy and had a big ass and thick thighs? This was *me* and no amount of diet and exercise was going to do much towards changing it. I knew because I had been trying for most of my life.

Of course, tell that to my ego, which was feeling pretty fragile as both sets of male eyes took me in, wearing the slinky, clinging nightgown. I waited, biting my lip as they looked me over.

"Well," I said at last when they didn't seem inclined to say anything. "Are we going to get back to sleep or not?"

"In a moment." Lucian was looking at me hungrily — eating me up with his eyes, my Aunt Celia would have said. "Give us just a moment more to drink in your beauty."

"Stop," I said, feeling my cheeks get hot. "You don't have to say that just to make me feel good."

"He's not — your curves are beautiful, baby," Drace assured me in a thick voice. "*You're* beautiful. I knew white would look amazing with that gorgeous skin of yours."

I looked at them both and knew they were being sincere. There was no way to fake the desire I saw in both the green eyes and the blue ones. An electric tingle ran through me. The idea that two huge, muscular alien men found me exciting and sexy made me feel simultaneously nervous and hot at the same time.

Have you ever been lucky enough to have that feeling — you know, the one you get when you *know* you're the prettiest girl in the room and all the guys are looking at you and wanting you? Well, me either but right at that moment, I *did* have that feeling and it was nice — *more* than nice.

Every girl should get to have that feeling at least once in her life.

"Well...thank you," I said at last in a voice that squeaked just a little. "I'm, uh, glad you guys like it. The gown, I mean. But I'm not just worried about the way it looks."

"What other concerns do you have, *ma 'frela?*" Lucian murmured, his eyes still half-lidded with lust as he looked me over. "And what can we do to assuage them?"

"I'm not sure you can," I said. "I'm worried about, um, skin-to-skin contact. I mean—the top of this dress is pretty skimpy and neither one of you guys is wearing a shirt."

"Why should that bother you?" Drace frowned. "Do the males of your planet only sleep fully covered?"

"No and it's not that," I said quickly. "It's the way we all, uh, *reacted* last time we had direct skin-to-skin contract. You know—when we were all holding hands?" I gave them a meaningful look, raising my eyebrows.

"Ah...I understand your concern." Lucian nodded thoughtfully. "But I think the reason that happened was that we were all concentrating on breaking the bond between Drace and myself. Any time a bond is weakened or strengthened it causes a release of energy. That was what contributed to our, um, *arousal* is, I suppose, the polite way to put it."

"Arousal, nothing. I nearly fucking came in my flight leathers," Drace growled. "I can see why Rylee would be worried about that. We can't be worrying about getting mentally jerked off every time we brush against each other. And we're going to have to be doing more than brushing against her to form the dream-shield—we'll both have to have a hand on her bare skin. Not in a sexual way," he added quickly, seeing my uncertain look. "Just to hold the shield in place."

"I really don't think it's going to be a problem," Lucian said. "Since we're not attempting to sever the bond this time. But the only way to be sure is to try."

"Well..." I couldn't really see any way around it. It was either give this a try or try to stay wide awake by myself and hope that damn shadow thing—the *skizix*—didn't come back. I knew that

Lucian had told me they only stayed on the walls to feed but I couldn't shake the idea that it would come right up to me...maybe even cover my face—ugh! Just thinking of its inky form slithering over my pillow, getting closer and closer made me shiver.

"Okay," I said at last. "But if things start getting too, uh, *intense,* I want to stop right away. All right?"

"Agreed," Lucian said and Drace nodded.

"Fine." I took a deep breath. "Then let's go to bed."

# Chapter Nine

## Rylee

Settling down under the silver quilt between their large, warm bodies made me feel like a kid again.

Way back when I was really little, before my parents died in a hit and run and I went to live with my Aunt Celia, I used to sleep between my mom and dad when there were thunderstorms. I can still remember the wonderful sense of security—the feeling that nothing could hurt me—I used to get when I was snuggled up in between them. I got that feeling again now as I made myself comfortable between Drace and Lucian.

But the feeling of complete comfort faded the minute both of the huge alien males turned to face me.

I was lying on my back, scanning the ceiling for any freaky *skizix* and I couldn't help feeling uncomfortable when they both turned on their sides, each propped up on an elbow to look down at me.

"Hey," I said, shifting around some. "Uh, do you guys really have to *stare* at me to do this?"

"If you're worried that we're staring at your luscious body, don't be," Lucian assured me.

"Speak for yourself," Drace murmured. "I'm definitely fucking staring—I can't help it." His green eyes were still scanning my body, making me feel more nervous than ever, especially since I had my arms down at my sides and my breasts were really visible through the thin white fabric of the gown.

"Hey," I said. "My eyes are up here."

"I know—they're beautiful too," Drace rumbled. He looked briefly at Lucian. "Wouldn't you agree, bond-mate?"

"Bond-mate?" Lucian raised an eyebrow. "That's the first time you've called me *that*."

"Well, it's true." I thought Drace sounded a little defensive. "I mean, for this situation, anyway. And we both know our bonded status is only temporary."

"True." Lucian nodded. "All right—what do we need to do to form this shield?"

"We need to touch Rylee's skin," Drace said. "Maybe if we both put a hand on each of her arms…"

"All right." Lucian put one large hand on my right shoulder and Drace put his hand on my left shoulder. I looked down, interested in the contrast between their skin tones and my own. Aunt Celia had never liked me dating Phillip—she warned I'd be sorry for dating a "white boy." I wondered what she would say now if she could see me with a blue boy and a green boy…at the same time.

*Okay, don't think about that,* I told myself sternly. *Remember, none of this is supposed to be sexual.*

Only it didn't feel that way—nonsexual, I mean. Though I didn't get the intense, orgasmic experience I'd had when we all held hands and tried to break their bond, I *did* feel a subtle but strong current of desire running through me…through all three of us, I thought. It was just enough to turn my nipples into tight little peaks and make my pussy feel swollen and hot between my thighs.

I should have felt uncomfortable—and I did, at least on one level. But on another level—a more primal level—I *liked* it. Then I felt guilty for liking it. Aunt Celia raised me pretty strict and she'd been plenty disapproving when I moved in with Phillip without being married to him. But at least I'd been dating him with the intent to stay together—I didn't even know Drace and Lucian and there were *two* of them.

*Stop it,* I told myself again. *Just stop!*

I squirmed around some, unable to decide how I should feel, unable to stop the current of desire that was tingling through me, making me feel hot and guilty and restless.

"Lay still, baby," Drace murmured. "This takes concentration."

"I'm trying," I said. "I just feel…" I trailed off, too embarrassed to tell exactly what I felt.

The two big aliens seemed to understand, though.

"We feel it too," Lucian murmured. "It isn't as strong—as overwhelming—as it was when we tried to break the bond but…"

"It's definitely there," Drace finished for him. "But it's okay—actually, it's a good thing."

"A good thing? What do you mean?" I asked, frowning.

"Well, like Lucian told you, building a dream-shield around your female is about blocking out frightening or anxious or negative images and thoughts. But in order to do that, you have to replace them with something else—something positive. Like this…"

Suddenly I had a mental image—a picture right behind my eyes I could tell wasn't mine. It was the three of us in bed together, just as we were now, only this time no one had on any clothes. Big hands were roving over my body, olive green and deep blue contrasting with my own creamy brown, plucking at my nipples…cupping my pussy…touching me everywhere while I moaned and arched my back, kissing first Drace and then Lucian…and then back to Drace again.

"Drace!" I exclaimed breathlessly. "You promised nothing sexual!"

"I said we wouldn't have to *touch* you in a sexual way," he said. "And we aren't—we just have to replace any bad images with good ones. These are pretty fucking good if you ask me."

I privately thought they were pretty good too —or extremely arousing, however you wanted to put it—but I wasn't about to admit it.

"We signed a no-sex contract," I pointed out, wishing my voice didn't sound so breathless.

"Are either of us penetrating you?" Lucian asked in a reasonable tone. "Are we touching you with anything less than respect?"

"Well…no," I admitted. "But you can send me positive images that don't involve the three of us, you know…"

"We can *try.*" Drace sounded doubtful. "Though the way our bodies react to each other might make it hard." He shifted in the bed and I felt something hot and stiff brush against my hip. Hard indeed.

"Allow me," Lucian volunteered. "I believe I have the idea of how it's done now."

"Be my guest." Drace nodded at him.

"All right. Let us all close our eyes," Lucian murmured.

Dutifully, I closed my eyes and found myself standing in the middle of a meadow filled with star flowers.

I don't mean that the flowers were shaped like a child's drawing of a star or that they had five points or anything like that — I mean they were actual tiny stars. White and blue and yellow and red burning balls of energy growing from pure black stalks. I had the feeling if I picked them I would singe my fingers but that was all right — I didn't want to pick them. I just wanted to stand there and admire their beauty.

"Oh," I whispered. "This is wonderful!" The star-flowers weren't the only attraction. The sky overhead looked like a Van Gogh painting — pure cerulean blue with whirling pinwheels of gold and silver.

"A beautiful scene for a beautiful female," Lucian said softly.

"You're good at this," Drace murmured, sounding impressed.

"Thank you — just as you were good at the memory-wipe. It seems we're surprisingly good at mastering the talents of each other's Clans."

"You're both amazing," I said dreamily. "How do you have these incredible mental abilities? I mean, is it just you, or do all extraterrestrials have them?"

"Each Clan on Denaris is blessed with different talents," Lucian said. "But no, not all males of the Twelve Peoples have them."

"I'm certain our abilities will be nothing to your *La-ti-zal* powers when they come out," Drace said. "Though I've heard it can take a while for that to happen."

I still thought they were wrong about that — about me being special and having special gifts, I mean — so I wanted to change the subject.

"So this is normal for your people?" I said, the words spilling out before I thought about them. "Two guys and one girl? I mean, don't you ever get jealous? That would be a *big* problem for us on Earth."

"There is no jealousy between proper bond-mates," Lucian said. "They both have one goal in mind—to pleasure their shared female."

Suddenly I was no longer alone in the amazing field—Lucian came to stand beside me, on my right.

"In other words, it's not about them—it's about her," Drace rumbled. And then he was on my left.

"But why?" I asked, looking back and forth. Their faces were incredibly clear in this vision—if I didn't know we were sharing a dream-fantasy, I would have thought we were really there in that magical star field together. "Why do you always *have* to have two males to one female? Is it just for preference or custom or is there some biological reason?"

"It has to do with the predators on Denaris," Lucian replied. "Back at the dawn of our time, our entire race was nearly wiped out by a carnivorous creature called a *kr'awn.*"

"A what?" I asked frowning. "What did it look like?"

"Extremely large with black fur," Drace said. "It had no eyes—it hunted entirely by scent. And it had fangs longer than Lucian's."

"Very funny," Lucian said dryly. "But it was no laughing matter. Now the *kr'awn* are extinct but back then, in our early pre-history, they were plentiful and very hungry."

"They fed only on our females," Drace continued the story. "Somehow they were able to find them and tell the difference between male and female by scent. So many females were taken our clans began to die out. We didn't have enough females to repopulate."

"That's awful! What happened?" I asked, interested.

"Two warriors of one of the early clans banded together, swearing to care for a single female and pleasure her equally with no jealousy between them," Lucian said. "She agreed to be with them both and they swore to protect her with their lives."

"The *kr'awn* never bothered males, you see," Drace said. "The warriors found that by shielding their female with their bodies when a *kr'awn* was near they could cover her scent and keep her safe. When other clans saw this was working, they adopted the pattern too. An Alpha and a Beta join together and then find a female to complete their Triune bond."

"Over time we evolved to make it a necessity in more than one way," Lucian went on. "We no longer have to protect our females from the *kr'awn* – as I said, they are extinct. But no male of Denaris is able to father a child by himself. It takes the DNA of two males to start a child in their bonded female's belly."

"But how do you *do* that? I mean do you take turns or…or what?" I could feel my cheeks getting hot and I kept my eyes tightly shut as I spoke. Better to stay in the dream world Drace and Lucian were projecting the three of us into than to open my eyes and see both of them leaning over me with that hungry light in their faces.

"Are you asking how we make love?" Lucian's voice was soft and sensual in my ear. In the vision we were sharing, he turned my face towards his and brushed his knuckles lightly over my burning cheek.

"Well, I mean…yes, I…I guess so," I stammered, filled with a mixture of shame and intrigue.

"First of all, we don't rush it." Drace was suddenly behind me, one big hand cupping the curve of my waist. "We bring our female pleasure and make her come over and over before we even think of penetrating her." As he spoke, he brushed my hair away from the side of my neck and bent down to place a hot, open-mouthed kiss on the tender flesh there.

"Oh!" I gasped, but I didn't make any move to get away from him. "And how…how do you do that?"

"Firstly with our hands." Lucian was facing me, standing in front of me as Drace stood behind. He cupped my breasts through the thin white nightgown (we were wearing the same thing in this vision as we were in real life) and thumbed my nipples lightly.

"Ah!" I gasped. Though I knew it was just a vision, I swore I could feel his hands on me – and Drace's too as they slid up and down my sides, stroking my curves while he kissed my neck.

*It's just a vision – it's just a dream,* I told myself. To reassure myself, I opened one eye and peeked down at myself. Sure enough, we were all three still just lying in bed and the guys were touching my shoulders—nothing else. Nothing sexual.

That made me feel a little better. This was all a dream…a fantasy. I could do what I wanted to with no consequences.

I shut my eyes again and breathed, "Tell me…tell me more."

"We also pleasure our females with our mouths," Drace growled softly from behind me. His tongue slid down the side of my neck until he was standing once more on my left.

Without being asked, Lucian relinquished my left breast and concentrated instead on the right. Somehow, in that quick, unthinkable way of dreams, they were both kneeling before me. They were so tall their faces were right on the level of my chest—I could feel their hot breath against my tender nipples through the silky nightgown.

"Wait," I gasped as Drace began to peel down the top of my gown. "Don't…not…I don't want to be, uh, bare."

"You don't want us to touch your bare skin, baby?" he growled, looking up at me. "You do realize this is all in our heads?"

"And we're simply trying to show you how things work with our people—to answer your question," Lucian pointed out in that deep, smooth voice of his.

"I…I know. I just…I don't want…to go too far," I whispered.

Lucian shrugged, his broad, bare shoulders rolling. "Very well—this material is thin enough to work through. As I was saying, we use our mouths to pleasure our females, too."

Before I could protest any further, he sucked the ripe point of my right nipple into his mouth.

I moaned breathlessly. Despite the thin fabric of the nightgown between my breast and his mouth, I could still feel the heat and wetness as he sucked on me, could still feel his tongue tracing my aching peak. I even thought I felt the faint prick of his fangs, bracketing the tender point.

"And we always pleasure our female at the same time," Drace rumbled. He was watching Lucian suck my nipple with a kind of drugged desire in his eyes. I had the strange feeling that he got almost as much enjoyment from watching the other male lap and taste me as he would get from pleasuring me himself.

Before I could ask him about it, he had already taken my left nipple between his lips and was sucking hard and long through the thin fabric of the nightgown.

"*Oh!*" I moaned helplessly.

It was *amazing* how realistic this shared fantasy was—I could swear it was really happening! I could *feel* their hot mouths on me, teasing me through the silky material of my gown. Lucian was using his tongue to trace around and around my aching right nipple and Drace was using his teeth, tugging very, very gently at my left peak in a way that sent sparks of desire straight from my breasts down to my swollen pussy.

The current of desire which had started flowing through me the moment they both put their hands on me was growing stronger now. The trickle had turned into a river which was rapidly becoming a flood.

A flood—that was how I felt—flooded with desire and only a third of it was mine. It swirled around me, that tide of pleasure, teasing my nipples and making my pussy ache and throb. My clit was like a second heartbeat between my legs and I could feel myself getting closer and closer to the edge. It was scary and amazing and intense and I knew if it didn't stop soon I was going to come.

*Come – I'm going to come so hard if they don't stop!* That thought— the thought of losing control in front of them yet again—snapped me back to reality. At least the last time touching them had made me come, we'd all been dressed (more or less) and standing in a public place which wasn't conducive to doing anything else. This time we all had on fewer (and thinner) clothes and we were in bed together. If I let them bring me to orgasm again—even in this strange dream-state we were all in—who knew where it might end?

"Wait!" I gasped, opening my eyes completely so that the scene in the star-meadow with the Van Gogh sky vanished. "Please, don't! I...I *can't.*"

"Forgive us." Lucian was once more leaning over me, touching only my shoulder. "You're so beautiful, *ma 'frela,* I fear we went too far."

"Still, she *did* ask," Drace pointed out. "How we make love."

"I asked you to tell me—not *show* me," I pointed out breathlessly. I couldn't help looking down at my chest as I spoke. I was half expecting to see two wet spots on my white nightgown, right over my aching nipples. But though my ripe peaks still tingled and throbbed, there was nothing to see—the white fabric was dry and undisturbed.

Too bad I couldn't say the same for myself.

"You see?" Lucian murmured, also looking down at the berry-brown points of my nipples which were extremely visible through the thin nightgown. "We haven't actually touched you at all, Rylee."

"Well, it *felt* like you did," I whispered. "I'm sorry I freaked out. I, uh, I've never done that. Not with two guys at once, anyway." My cheeks were hot and I wondered why I had said such a thing.

To my surprise, Drace shook his head.

"I haven't either. Haven't shared a female with another male."

"Nor have I," Lucian murmured.

"What?" I frowned at both of them. "But I thought that was how you guys worked—what you did. You just finished telling me the whole reason you have to have two guys to one girl."

"Yes, but only when you find the right Beta and then the right female to complete your bond," Lucian said. "Neither Drace or I have found a male we wish to share a female with."

"He's right." Drace nodded.

"You seemed to be, uh, sharing pretty well there in our, uh, dream-fantasy thingy," I pointed out, still flushed with embarrassment.

"We did, didn't we?" Drace looked at Lucian speculatively but Lucian only shrugged dismissively.

"We were simply answering your question—showing you the ways of our people."

"I think I've seen enough," I said, though my whole body was still throbbing with desire.

"But you still don't know how we make love," Lucian pointed

out. "I believe your question was do we take turns..."

"Or do we penetrate our female at the same time," Drace finished for him, a soft growl in his voice.

They were both leaning over me, still looking at me. It was a little frightening to be the center of their complete attention — they were both so *big* and their eyes were trained on my face as though they wanted very much to know what I was thinking.

"Um..." I bit my lip, not certain if I wanted them to continue.

"We can tell you without showing you," Lucian murmured.

"He's right — the dream-shield is in place," Drace agreed. "There is no need to return to our shared image."

"All right," I whispered, my curiosity getting the best of me at last. "Tell me then — how do you manage? And don't show — just tell." Which is, of course, the exact opposite of what they tell you in just about any creative writing class. But I wasn't looking to write about this, I just wanted to understand my guys.

It didn't occur to me then that I was thinking of them as "mine." The thought didn't even enter my head — it just seemed so natural, so right somehow. The innate possessiveness came and went without making an impression on me — then, anyway.

"Well, as I said earlier, we begin by pleasuring our female and getting her ready to receive us," Lucian murmured. "There are, of course, many ways to do this. Often both males will suck her breasts, as we showed you."

"Or one may tend to her breasts while the other spreads her legs and laps her sweet pussy," Drace growled softly.

"They...they do?" I whispered breathlessly. As I said before, Phillip was never much interested in this particular act. In fact, I'd never dated any guy who was.

"Mm-hmm. The idea is to make her come and help her open up for what is going to happen," Lucian told me.

"What *does* happen?" I asked, a touch impatiently. "Do you guys take turns, uh, making love to her?"

"Sometimes," Drace answered my question. "There are plenty of ways for three people to enjoy each other. But for bonding and breeding purposes, we have to enter her at the same time."

"What?" I bit my lip and some of the tingling pleasure that had been pouring through me died down a little. "Both of you at once? In the, uh, same hole?"

Lucian nodded. "There is no other way. In order to forge a bond or start a child, both males must thrust to the end of their female's channel and fill her to the brim with their seed."

"Again, at the *same time,*" Drace emphasized.

I winced and pressed my thighs together.

"But...but how is that even possible? I thought you said the females on your planet weren't much bigger than me?"

"They're not," Drace assured me. "But we have chemicals in our semen and saliva which help a female to open for us." He frowned. "Of course, they have to be applied in a very specific way..."

"Which is generally the duty of the Beta," Lucian went on. "But when done properly, it's more than possible for a female of a compatible species to open herself enough to take both our shafts deep in her pussy."

"I'll take your word for it," I said and shivered again. I couldn't imagine having to have two huge shafts inside me at the same time. Especially since I was betting both Lucian and Drace were on the extra-large side of the scale.

"You'll have to," Drace said, his voice harsh. "Since neither of us is a Beta."

"So...you have to have an Alpha and a Beta or it won't work? The, uh, bonding and breeding, I mean?" I said, still feeling hot and flushed all over.

"Technically any two males could bind a female to them," Drace said. "But no self-respecting Alpha would perform the duties of a Beta beforehand."

"It doesn't matter—Rylee isn't here to bond with us. She's going to help us *break* our bond," Lucian reminded him.

"Yes, I know." For a moment I thought Drace sounded almost wistful—as wistful as he could sound, anyway, with that deep, gravelly voice of his.

"Um..." I shifted a little, still feeling warm and flushed. I was beginning to think I had more information than I needed and it was time to stop talking about this extremely charged subject.

"Yes, *ma 'frela?*" Lucian asked, looking down at me. "Are you unwell?"

"Just tired," I said, though I had never felt less sleepy in my life. "Maybe...maybe we should try to get some actual sleep now?"

"And excellent idea," Lucian remarked. "We need all the rest we can get before we go see Tanta Loro tomorrow."

"If she'll see us again so soon," Drace muttered.

"She will." But from his tone, Lucian wasn't as sure as he would have liked to be.

"We should get some sleep then."

"True enough. Lights Dim," Lucian said. The lighted walls dimmed until the room was as dark as it had been when I first woke up and found myself alone in a strange bed.

But this time I wasn't afraid—this time I wasn't alone.

*It'll be all right,* I told myself as I closed my eyes and tried to get to sleep. *Everything is going to be just fine. I'll get them split up and be back on my way to Earth in no time.*

Only for some reason the thought bothered me. I couldn't understand why but while I was trying, I finally got sleepy. Tomorrow I would walk on an alien world hundreds of light years from Earth and face who knew what challenges but for tonight, at least, I was warm and safe and completely protected between the two big, male bodies.

With a contented sigh, I finally drifted off to sleep with my guys on either side of me.

# Chapter Ten

## Lucian

I woke up with a soft weight pressed against the side of my chest. A warm, feminine scent drifted to my nose and my eyelids fluttered lazily open just a crack. The room was dim and I was lying on a comfortable surface, broad enough to stretch out on.

There was another scent in the room as well—the scent of another male.

*Another male and a female – our female.* The thought drifted lazily through my brain. For once I wasn't waking up alone. I was in the sleeping platform with my bond-mate and our female—all was as it should be. She was beautiful and perfect and my bond-mate and I were there to protect her, to keep her safe and love her. We were a unit the three of us—together we were whole.

I thought with pleasure of the way we had shared her between us the night before. Both of us sucking her sweet, ripe nipples…making her moan as she surrendered to our touch. Gods it felt good to *share* a female! To finally have a partner to help me please her—after so many long years—to have things as they should be.

There were places a lone male could go to get his needs met, of course but they were few and far between on Denaris. And it always felt *wrong* to take a female by myself. No matter how much pleasure I gave her, I always knew she deserved more—that there was something lacking. *Someone* lacking.

*Not lacking anymore,* whispered a little voice in my head. *You're finally complete.* I sighed in contentment and stretched, careful not to wake the others.

I wasn't the only one stirring. Someone else shifted and the scent of the other male—my bond-mate—grew stronger.

My nose wrinkled. He didn't just smell like another male—he had the unmistakable dark, commanding scent of an Alpha.

That was wrong.

*Not my bond-mate...not my female. I don't have either. I am alone. I've always been alone, I'll **always be** alone. That is my life.*

The thoughts drifted up to me like acrid smoke, spoiling my perfect mood.

I frowned and grew more alert, my eyes opening wide as the last of the pleasant dream was cleared from my head like cobwebs. Where was I and why were there two other people sleeping with me?

After a moment, my eyes adjusted to the dim wall glows and I saw that Rylee was lying asleep across my chest, her long, curly black hair half obscuring her face. Lying on the other side of her with one long arm thrown over the curve of her hip was Drace.

The night before came back to me in slow sections...hearing Rylee cry out in fear, coming to comfort her and then asking Drace to stay and help me ease her fear.

Why had I done that? Why had I asked another Alpha to help me soothe her?

*There was no choice,* I told myself, uneasily. *Everyone knows a female needs two males to look after her, to tend and comfort and cherish her.*

*A female from **Denaris** needs that,* whispered an accusing little voice in my head. *But Rylee comes from a planet where they join in twos, not threes. Admit it, Lucian—it wasn't Rylee who needed another male near to feel complete, it was **you**.*

That, of course, was ridiculous. I had been on my own for years and from an early age I had accepted that I probably wouldn't be able to form a bond. I had tried of course, but I simply didn't fit with any of the Betas from the "good families" my parents brought me into contact with.

When all of the "suitable options" had been exhausted, my parents had, in effect, given up on finding me a psy-bond mate. My fathers were the Chief and Under-Chief of the Fang Clan respectively and my mother was extremely prominent socially. The idea of inviting a male who wasn't from one of the best blood lines on the planet to join with the only son of their Triumvirate was unthinkable.

Over the years I had looked myself—I had even found several Betas while attending school who would have been happy to bond with me. But none of them fit the standard my parents held—none were of the right social class and clan to be added to our family tree. None of them were good enough.

Eventually I gave up too. Better to be cold than hurt…better to be distant than lonely.

So I grew up knowing I would always be alone—that I would never have a partner to share a female with or any children to raise. I didn't mind, I told myself—truly I didn't. I buried myself in my work, went to the schools my parents deemed acceptable, and made friends with the people I would work with later in life as a highly paid professional. I did everything that was expected of me.

Until I got myself accidentally bonded to another Alpha. And not just any Alpha—an Alpha of the Claw Clan.

My parents still didn't know the situation I now found myself in—nor did I intend for them to find out. I was bonded to a male they would doubtless consider a mortal enemy—a male they would hate on sight. I could just see their faces—my Alpha Father scowling, my Beta Father disapproving and my mother—worst of all—conveying her disgust and displeasure with a delicate lift of her perfectly formed brows.

They had called me several times lately, wanting to set a date for a family meal but each time I put them off. Until I could extricate myself from the accidental bond to Drace, I needed to steer clear of my family.

*Be fair,* whispered a thought in my brain. *He isn't as crude as you feared at first and he's actually quite intelligent—he picked up on the memory-wipe technique incredibly quickly. And he was willing to stay and help comfort Rylee, even after your rude words to him.*

It was true but none of that changed what he was—what *I* was. I could never get away from my bloodlines or my family clan and legacy. But even if I could have, the fact still remained that both of us were Alphas.

I could imagine what would happen if Drace and I walked into a party thrown by my mother or one of her crowd. Even if I dressed him in the finest clothing, his scent would give him away. I could almost see the polite smiles and laughter as we were introduced…and the hostile and disgusted looks we would get after we had moved on. Polite society among the Fang Clan was exactly that—polite, but *only* to your face. The moment you turned your back, your reputation would be ripped to shreds if you committed even the smallest social blunder. And bonding myself to another Alpha was more than a small blunder.

It wasn't that I cared what people said, but it would ruin not only my reputation but that of my parents as well. Also, my business relationships would suffer. They would wonder which of us—Drace or I—played the Beta during our more…intimate moments. And if the consensus was that *I* took on that role, other males of good families would wonder if I was strong enough to litigate and negotiate for them.

It would be a social disaster.

*None of that is going to happen,* I told myself uneasily. *We'll be in orbit around Denaris in another solar hour and Tanta Loro will tell Rylee how to sever our bond. In fact, I should probably go check and make sure the ship is still on course.*

I extricated myself from the tangle of limbs on the sleeping platform, being careful not to wake anyone.

Rylee kept sleeping but as I got off the sleeping platform, the beatific smile on her face suddenly twitched to a frown.

"No," she muttered in her sleep, one hand sliding over the spot where I'd been lying. "No…*wrong.*"

"It's all right." On impulse, I bent down to smooth her hair away from her face and kiss her cheek.

She moaned and snuggled closer to Drace—but only while I touched her. The minute I straightened up, she shifted away from him and frowned again.

I didn't have time to analyze her strange sleep behavior. Instead, I headed to the control area to be certain we were on course. With any luck we'd get this taken care of—maybe even today.

But for a moment before I left the sleeping chamber—just a

moment—I looked back at Drace and Rylee still tangled in the tempra-quilt and my empty spot on the sleeping platform. I stood there and remembered the feeling I'd had when I first woke up—the feeling that I was where I belonged with the people I belonged to—people who belonged to me.

Then I pushed the ridiculous thought out of my mind and left.

* * * * *

# Drace

"So…what is this?" Rylee looked down at her plate uncertainly. "It looks like, uh, fluffy mounds of turquoise toothpaste sprinkled with small, purple balls."

"I don't know what 'toothpaste' is but those are *Tegral* eggs with *binta* jelly," I told her. "One of my mother's specialties."

I dug into my own portion as we sat around the table in the food prep area. I had done the cooking—often thought of as a Beta or female task—because Lucian had been busy piloting the ship. He was sitting with us at the table, now, though, with a plate in front of him. It wasn't lost on me that this was the first meal we'd shared. Despite having been bonded for some time, we'd avoided eating together and making conversation during meal times—until now.

"I've never had *tegral* eggs," he remarked, taking a bite. A look of surprise came over his face. "Delicious!"

"Thanks," I muttered. Lifting my chin, I looked at him. "Your turn to cook next time."

He stared at me for a long moment then nodded shortly. "Agreed."

"I'll take a turn too," Rylee offered. "If you'll teach me how to use that big copper pot. The food-sim, I mean."

She'd watched with interest as I used the food-sim to bring my favorite first meal recipe into existence. It wasn't hard—you simply placed the thought capture pad against one temple, pictured the food you wanted, and the sim would create it from the nutrient slime it used as raw material.

Rylee had thought the slime itself was disgusting but when I explained that the food the sim created didn't have the taste or texture of the green substance, she'd shrugged her shoulders and said, "All right—I'll try it. I won't make any promises about finishing it but I'll try."

I liked that about her—our Earth girl—the fact that she was adventurous and willing to experiment. I thought of the way we'd pleasured her the night before. Though it had only been in a controlled dream-fantasy, Rylee had allowed Lucian and me to taste her ripe nipples. The memory of her writhing between us still made me hard.

I wondered if it was the first time Lucian had ever shared a female with another male—I knew it was for me. And even though it hadn't been technically *real,* it had still been damn sexy.

I'd had females on my own of course—a male has needs and there are places that cater to lone males. But it wasn't the same as sharing. I had liked the feeling of having another male helping me pleasure the female I cared for—that we *both* cared for. Liked it a hell of a lot. Probably too much.

*This is temporary—this time with Rylee and Lucian,* I reminded myself. *Don't get used to it.*

"I'll teach you to use the food-sim on the return journey," Lucian said to Rylee, spearing another bite of eggs. "Maybe you can make us some Earth cuisine."

"That sounds nice. I make a mean marinara sauce." Rylee took a bite of her *tegral* eggs and chewed slowly. "Which is actually *kind* of what this tastes like. Like spaghetti with…" She popped one of the *binta* jelly balls into her mouth. "With malted milk balls," she finished, making a face and swallowing quickly. "*Squishy* malted milk balls. Eww."

"You don't like it?" I frowned. "Sorry about that, baby."

"It's not that I don't *like* it," she said quickly, and I could tell she was afraid she'd hurt my feelings. "I like both things separately very much. They just…don't seem like they would go together."

"It's an acquired taste," Lucian said, eating some more.

"Well *you* certainly seem to have acquired it." Rylee raised an eyebrow at him. "Look at you go—you've almost finished your plate already."

Lucian shrugged. "I think it's because my bond with Drace was accidentally strengthened — I crave what he craves."

"I know the feeling, bond-mate," I murmured. "I crave what you crave as well."

We exchanged a glance and then both looked at Rylee. I couldn't forget the sweet way she'd panted and moaned as we sucked and tasted her tender nipples and I bet that was what Lucian was thinking about too.

Today our chosen female was wearing another one of the outfits I'd made for her using the clothing-sim — a short red sand-dress such as a Denarin female would wear to the beach — which fell only to her mid thighs. It was cut low in the front and even lower in the back and the tight, silky material outlined her full breasts beautifully.

Rylee had complained about not having some items of clothing called a "bra" and "panties." I had managed to make her the panties — tiny, skimpy undergarments to cover her sex — but the bra eluded me though I tried several times. According to Rylee I kept getting the straps and cups reversed but the garment she described was complicated and hard to imagine, let alone create. In the end she had sighed and said that if I didn't know what a bra was, the women on Denaris probably weren't wearing it so she would go without too.

Looking at her now, I was glad she'd decided not to try and cover her breasts with anything but the sand-dress. Through the thin fabric, I could see the points of her tight peaks — they made my mouth water. I wished that Lucian and I could take her back to the sleeping platform and taste those peaks again — for real this time. Taste them and suck them and then spread her thighs to lap her hot little pussy until she begged for both of us inside her…

Through the link between us, I could feel a lust that matched my own. Lucian was feeling desire too — I would have bet the commission on my next ten projects he was thinking exactly what I was thinking…wanting the little Earth female the same way I did.

"You two stop looking at me like that," Rylee said, breaking the silence that had somehow fallen around the table.

"Like what, *ma 'frela?*" Lucian murmured, his blue eyes half-lidded with need I felt echoed in my groin.

"Like *I'm* what's on the menu instead of these, uh, eggs." She poked her *chanook* – a two-pronged eating utensil with a round bowl at the other end for liquids, into the mound of eggs still on her plate. "Like you're a couple of big, bad wolves and you want to eat me up."

"We'd love to eat you, baby," I murmured, running my gaze over her luscious, curvy body. "Love to taste how sweet and ripe and juicy you are."

"For once I have to agree with Drace," Lucian shot me a brief, one-sided smile that showed his fangs. "Nothing would bring us greater pleasure than to take turns licking between your thighs."

"Lucian! Drace!" Her face was flushed, her light brown skin rosy, but I didn't think she was really angry with us. Maybe more angry with herself for feeling the same desire we were feeling – because she *was*, I could tell. Her scent was sweet and ripe – aroused like it had been last night. Gods, she was fucking gorgeous! I wished for a moment that the three of us were really together – that Lucian and I were her mates, teasing her over the first meal table. Teasing in a way that might lead to more…

Of course that was impossible. Even if my family would accept a Fang Clan male as my mate, (which I doubted) we were both Alphas. I might be willing to take on some of the cooking or other Beta duties if we were truly bonded, but there were some things I was *not* fucking prepared to do. Some things I –

A high, shrill beeping sound interrupted my thoughts. Lucian lifted his head and frowned.

"That's the proximity alarm – we've reached Denaris. We're home."

"Good," Rylee exclaimed. "I can't wait to see your planet! So where are we going – where does this mysterious Tanta Loro live?"

Lucian and I exchanged glances and I said, "The beach. We're going to the beach."

# Chapter Eleven

## Rylee

"Wow, this is some beach." I looked down at the pure silver-white sand that was seeping into my shoes, which were kind of like wedge heels without tops They were bright red to match my dress. How did they stay on my feet without straps to hold them on? Well, they were made entirely out of some kind of foam that molded itself instantly to my foot. When I put them on, my feet sank in to them almost an entire inch, like I was stepping into really firm bubble-gum and then they just stuck to me.

I had been concerned at first but Drace had assured me they would come off when I wanted them to. In the mean time, they were surprisingly good for walking through the fine, powdery silver sand on the Denarian beach.

The silver-white sand wasn't the only beautiful thing about the alien beach, though. The water was a clear azure blue that sparkled like a gem. There was no sign of seaweed or any kind of trash littering the shore either—apparently the Denarins were sticklers about littering. Here and there little piles of pink and purple seashells lay scattered in the sand like heaps of polished jewels.

Tall, palm tree-like plants swayed in the soft, salty air, their bluish-purple fronds sharp against the pale blue-green sky. Roosting in their branches were tiny bright pink things. I couldn't make them out until one flew down to the beach to peck at something—then I saw they looked like tiny pterodactyls, no longer than my finger, with crests of green feathers growing from the tops of their heads.

It was all so gorgeous and exotic I hardly knew where to look first. And except for the strange coloring of everything (and the tiny pink pterodactyls) it was surprisingly Earth-like. Well, except for the people.

There were a few other couples—or I guessed I should say threesomes—visiting the beach. Some even had children with them. I noticed that the men seemed to come mostly in shades of blue and green—although I saw some red skin tones as well—and the women were a pearly gray. And just as Drace and Lucian had told me, the women were mostly my size or maybe even a little smaller. Watching one, who looked to be only around five foot three walk by, flanked by two massive seven-foot tall males, I wondered how the tiny woman managed to accommodate her huge husbands…and shivered.

*Good thing I don't have to worry about that!* I told myself. Then, remembering the dream-sequence I'd shared with Drace and Lucian the night before, I felt a stab of guilt. In the clear light of day I had to wonder why I had allowed them to do that to me, even in a dream. But still, the memory of having both of them touching and tasting me at once, the feeling of their big, hard bodies on either side of me, their hot mouths sucking my nipples at the same time, started a little fire in my belly. One I couldn't put out, no matter how much I scolded myself.

Trying to put the whole thing out of my mind, I looked around, wondering how the Denarins would react to the sight of an Earth girl.

A few of the natives looked askance at us, but not as many as I would have thought. Lucian had assured me that Denarin males often traveled outside their own planet to find the right female to bond with. Maybe that was why no one was very interested in the strange alien girl who had showed up on their beach.

Actually, my two guys seemed to get more strange looks than I did. People would look at the two of them, their noses would wrinkle, and a look of disbelief or confusion would come over their faces. Some of them shook their heads or muttered to each other. But though they had to be seeing the strange reaction too, Drace and Lucian kept their heads high and refused to acknowledge the way people were staring and talking.

I wanted to ask what was going on, but I decided to wait until we were someplace more private, like wherever this mysterious Tanta Loro they kept talking about stayed. I still didn't understand why they had brought me to the beach in the first place—did she have a house here? As far as I could see, the only structure built on the silvery sands was a little hut made of the wood of the bluish-purple trees.

As we got closer, I saw the beach hut was a kind of open-air shop with shelves filled with strange products whose uses I couldn't begin to guess. There was a bored looking young man sitting inside the hut, behind the counter. He was reading what might have been a girly magazine—that was, if a magazine had crystal clear pages you could see through and all the pictures moved,.

I noticed something else about the "magazine"—every single picture displayed a threesome. There were always two males with one female between them and some of the things they were doing made me blush. It was porn—pure and simple but the young Denarin guy, who had reddish skin and black hair, didn't seem the least embarrassed when we walked up to him.

"Hello." Lucian rapped on the counter for service and the guy put down his magazine—though he didn't bother trying to hide it.

"What do you need, good sirs?" he asked in a bored voice. "A filter-frond to block the light? Maybe a privacy shield so you can pleasure your female without prying eyes seeing?"

"That won't be fucking necessary," Drace growled, looking menacing. "And watch your mouth around our female—she's a lady."

"Oh!" The young Denarin sat up straighter and I saw his nose wrinkle as he looked between Lucian and Drace. "Forgive me—I, uh, made a mistake. I thought the three of you were a Triumvirate. But of course I see now that must be impossible."

"Why would it be impossible?" I demanded, putting a hand on my hip. "Because I'm from another planet?"

"No, of course not, beautiful lady!" The young man was looking more and more uncomfortable and embarrassed. Well, it was about time he got embarrassed about something since being caught ogling porn didn't apparently faze him.

"Why, then?" I persisted.

"Rylee…" Lucian said in a low tone but the young Denarin was already answering.

"Well…because both of these esteemed males are Alphas," he said. "So they cannot be bonded together even if…" He trailed off.

"Even if what?" I asked, frowning.

"Even if their, uh, scent says they are. Bonded, I mean." He looked truly miserable now and I was beginning to feel sorry for him, especially considering the way Drace was glaring at him and Lucian was frowning.

I finally began to understand what was going on—apparently what they'd told me about not wanting to be stuck together because they were both Alphas had some actual substance to it. Somehow everyone on their home planet could tell what they were and the fact that they were together—and none of them approved.

Now all the reactions of the other threesomes we'd seen on the beach made sense. We were getting the same kinds of looks that an interracial couple or a gay couple might get if they went to a less progressive part of Earth. Or anywhere people were bigoted assholes, really.

For the first time, I understood their desperation to be free of each other. It was one thing to be out and proud about it but neither Drace or Lucian *wanted* to be together. They were like two straight guys somehow stuck in a gay partnership—they were being stigmatized for something they weren't, which is never any fun.

"As a matter of fact, they *are* bonded," I told the shop keeper briskly. "But we're about to take care of that right now." I turned to Drace and Lucian. "All right, guys, why are we here?" I asked. "I mean, why did you take me to the beach? It's pretty and all but I thought we wanted to get down to business. Where is Tanta Loro?"

"Tanta Loro?" The young Denarin's red skin turned a dirty pink color and I realized he had suddenly gone pale. "You're going to visit the *sea witch?*"

That got my attention. "Sea witch? Nobody said anything about a sea witch—you guys said a 'wise woman.' I was picturing a little old lady with puffy white hair and a cat sitting on her lap while she served us herbal tea."

"What?" Drace frowned. "What is a cat? And why would a wise-woman have white hair?"

"A cat is a kind of animal on Earth," I said. "A pet. And on Earth, at least, when people get old and wise—well, old anyway—their hair often turns gray or white."

"Tanta Loro is very ancient and wise," Lucian said thoughtfully. "But I'm afraid she has no hair at all."

"What—she's bald?" I asked, surprised.

"No—she hasn't got hair because she's got tentacles," Drace growled.

"Tentacles?" I stared at him. "We're going to see a sea witch who has *tentacles?* What is this—the Denarin off, off, *off* Broadway production of the Little Mermaid?"

"What?" Lucian and Drace were both looking at me in obvious confusion.

"Never mind." I shook my head—this was getting bizarre. Well, at least I wouldn't have to worry about trading away my voice for legs since I already had them. But still…it was weird. "Listen," I said. "Just tell me—why are we going to see a witch?"

"Because she's the only one who can help us," Lucian said, frowning. "Don't worry, *ma 'frela,* you will be safe between us the entire time."

"Lucian's right—we won't let anything happen to you, baby," Drace assured me.

"So…you're really going to see her?" the shop attendant asked, wide-eyed.

"We are if you'll ever stop gawking and sell us some breath-weed," Drace growled.

"We need three doses to last at least two standard hours apiece. Do you have that?" Lucian asked him.

"Well…sure. I mean, of course I do." With trembling hands, the attendant reached beneath the counter where the porno mag was still displaying its moving three-way pictures and pulled out a small, shiny box that looked like it had been made out of a large clam shell. It was pinkish-red, curved on the top and bottom, and polished to a bright shine.

Opening the clam-box, the Denarin shop guy took out three tiny oblong objects about the size and shape of medicine capsules—

two blue and one red. Great—so we'd moved from *The Little Mermaid* to *The Matrix*.

He handed the pills to Drace who gave the red one to me. I looked at it, shining like a ruby in my palm, and wondered what I was supposed to do with it.

"Do you need vision drops? Or ballast?" the Denarin shop guy asked, putting away the clam shell box and motioning to the shelf behind him where, among the other strange objects, there were rows of shiny stones. They ranged in size from the size of a walnut to some that were bigger than my fist and reminded me of the polished geodes you can always find in the gift shop of the science museum. "I have different weights to fit all sizes," he said.

"Hmm…" Lucian nodded. "I believe I still have some drops left over from our last trip. But we do need ballast. We'll take six. Four large and two small."

"Right away." The shop keeper seemed to be in a hurry to get rid of us but he moved surprisingly slowly transporting the small geode-like stones. In fact, he only lifted one at a time, as though they were extremely heavy.

I went to pick up one of the larger ones and was surprised to find that it *was* heavy—too heavy for me to lift.

"*Oof*—what *are* these?" I asked, abandoning my efforts to pick up the fist-sized rock.

"Ballast rocks," Drace answered shortly, which didn't answer my question at all. He looked at Lucian. "I'll pay for these if you pay for the breath-weed. Deal?"

"That works." Lucian nodded.

"Very well then, uh, sirs." The shop guy brought out something that looked like a white pearl as big as my closed fist, round and smooth and gorgeous. He presented it to Drace first, who pressed his thumb to it as though he was going to let it take a fingerprint. But instead, a tiny, sharp needle shot out of the middle of the pearl and stabbed him. I saw it happen because he pulled back just a little at the last minute.

"Oh!" I gasped involuntarily. The milky white surface of the pearl took on swirls of red for a moment, then it cleared. Drace stuck his thumb in his mouth, clearly healing himself as he had after we signed the contracts the night before.

"Payment by DNA," Lucian explained, seeing my horrified look. "Each person's account is hooked to a sample of their DNA — it only requires a single drop of blood to verify and draw the credit from the account."

"Remind me not to open a credit card here then," I said faintly. I couldn't help thinking that if people had to be stabbed in the finger every time they paid for something back on Earth there would be a lot fewer impulse buys and way less credit card debt.

"Here you are, good sir." The shop guy presented the pearl to Lucian and he repeated Drace's performance, stoically allowing himself to be stabbed with the miniature needle. He didn't pull back as Drace had, however and I saw his mouth tighten — ouch, the needle must have gone in *deep*. I winced in sympathy.

"Paid in full," the shop guy chirped when the pearl took on swirls of red and then turned back to white again. "Thank you for your business, uh, sirs…madam." He gave a little nod to me.

Lucian just grunted and started to lift the extremely heavy geode stones off the front counter. But his bloody thumb slipped on the slick surface of one and he dropped it.

"Damn it!" he swore, grabbing for the falling stone.

Drace caught it right before it hit the sand and put it back on the counter. Then, to my surprise, he took the other man's wounded hand in his.

"Here." Lifting Lucian's hand to his mouth, he swiped the pad of the other man's thumb — which really was bleeding a lot — with his tongue.

"What — ?" Lucian looked almost as startled as the shop keeper, who was openly staring.

"Bond-mates take care of each other." Drace's deep voice was slightly defensive as he let Lucian's hand fall. "Even temporary bond-mates."

"I…" Lucian looked down at his thumb, which was completely healed now. Clearly he was at a complete loss for words.

"I thought you said you couldn't heal him?" I murmured to Drace. "Since you're both Alphas."

He shrugged. "Thought I'd try anyway. Looks like I can. Come on." Scooping up the incredibly heavy geode stones, he turned towards the beach. With a slightly stunned look in his eyes, Lucian followed.

Of course neither of them looked as freaked out as the shop keeper. The last time I looked back at him, he was still staring as though he'd seen something completely indecent happen right in front of him. Wow—for people who spent their lives having kinky three-way sex, the Denarins were a really uptight society!

I turned to follow my guys. Surely the wise woman slash sea witch was around here somewhere—but where?

\* \* \* \* \*

# Drace

"The bottom of the ocean? Seriously? We're going to the *bottom of the freaking ocean?"*

Rylee stared at me and Lucian with obvious disbelief.

"Yes, of course," Lucian said, frowning as he squirted some of the vision drops from the tiny plasti-seal bulb into his eyes and passed it to me. "Tanta Loro is one of the Half-Folk. They always make their homes below the waves."

"It's okay, baby," I said, trying to put her at ease as I squirted some of the drops in my own eyes. "We have the breath-weed to help us breathe and the ballast stones will allow us to walk normally on the sea-bed. And these drops will allow you to focus underwater just fine. Here." I handed her the bulb.

"But what about the water pressure?" she protested, even as she squirted some of the drops in her eyes. "Won't we be crushed?"

"Actually, we're not going that far down," Lucian said, taking the bulb back from her and tucking it into his trouser pocket. "Tanta Loro's fortress is on a submerged costal shelf not too far from our edge of the shore. Come—we'll show you." He took one of the blue breath-weed caplets and placed it under his tongue. Then he held out a hand to me. "Drace...the ballast?"

I pulled the ballast-stones out of the pockets of my worn flight leathers and handed him two of the large ones. Naturally the breath-weed didn't protect our clothing so we were going to get drenched—which was why I was wearing trousers I didn't care about. I arranged the other two large stones in my own pockets and helped Rylee put her own, small stones, into the side pockets of her sand-dress.

"Um...thank you." Lucian's voice sounded strange. When Rylee and I looked up at him, he was still just staring down at the stones in his hand. I saw that one of them had a smear of red on it— his blood. Lucian was looking at it as though he'd never seen anything like it before.

"Lucian?" Rylee asked softly. "Are you all right?"

"Fine." He tucked the stones in his pockets and looked up at me. "Thank you," he said again and this time I knew he wasn't just thanking me for the stones.

"Welcome." My voice came out rougher than it should have. I still didn't know why I had healed his wound. I doubted he would have done the same for me. Maybe I just wanted to show him I was as committed to this venture as he was—that I wouldn't leave him hanging even if things got rough under the waves, as they almost had last time.

The attendant at the shop had been right to get that worried look on his face when he'd heard where we were going—many of the Half-Folk were friendly with those of us who lived on land instead of under the sea.

Tanta Loro wasn't one of them.

In fact, she'd nearly had her guards skewer Lucian and me the last time we'd visited. It took balls to face her again but neither of us had even considered backing down—we needed to be parted too badly for that.

*But is it really so bad being joined to Lucian? He's an honorable male, even if he is a little stiff,* a little voice whispered in my head.

I frowned. I only had to remember the look on the shop attendant's face when I'd sealed Lucian's wound to answer that one. Even if I was sort of getting used to my temporary bond-mate, it wasn't like we could stay together. Our world wasn't kind to unsuitable bondings. We had to get this fixed.

"Come on," I said, tucking my own breath-weed capsule beneath my tongue and showing Rylee how to do the same with hers. "Let's go."

# Chapter Twelve

## Rylee

*I must be dreaming. This has to be a dream,* I thought as we walked slowly through the warm azure waves, getting deeper and deeper into the sparkling sea. But we kept walking and I wasn't waking up, despite the red pill I had tucked beneath my tongue. It had sort of stuck there and was staying in place without any effort on my part.

We kept walking. The heavy geode rocks in my dress pockets kept me grounded and the sand underfoot was surprisingly stable. Soon we were up to our necks—well, I was, anyway. Drace and Lucian were only up to a little over their elbows. As the water lapped against my chin, I began to feel panicky.

"Look, guys," I said, looking up at them. "I don't want to break our contract but I'm not sure if I can do this. I'm only an okay swimmer—I'm way better in a pool than in the ocean—and this is really kind of freaking me out."

"You won't have to swim, baby," Drace rumbled, taking my hand. "We'll just keep walking—the ballast keeps you grounded."

"Swimming or not isn't really the point," I said. "I just don't know how safe this is—are there sharks around here?"

"Sharks?" Lucian frowned.

"Huge man-eating fish with thousands of really sharp teeth," I explained.

"Oh, predators. No, the Half-Folk keep their area mostly clear of dangerous animals," Drace said. "Feel better now?"

"No," I said. "Because I don't like the idea of breathing water. I mean, I *really* don't like it. I know you said this little pill stuck under my tongue is supposed to make it possible but it just sounds weird and completely impossible."

"It *does* take some getting used to," Lucian admitted. "Would you like Drace and I to demonstrate how it's done first?"

"Yes, please." I crossed my arms over my chest. "Because I honestly don't see how it's possible."

"You're not actually going to be taking the water down into your lungs," Drace explained as he and Lucian scrunched down so they were also neck deep in the surprisingly calm sea on either side of me.

"The moment the water touches your face, the breath-weed will form a microscopically thin filter-membrane that covers the opening to your throat and nostrils," Lucian said. "You won't see it or feel it but it will be there."

"Water will enter your mouth but it won't be able to get down into your lungs," Drace went on, picking up the explanation. "The filter extracts the oxygen you need to breath and keeps the liquid out."

"It's an odd sensation at first, talking and breathing with a mouthful of water," Lucian said. "But you get used to it fairly quickly."

"All right," I said, crossing my arms over my chest—my pretty red dress was, of course, completely soaked and billowing around me in the waves. "Show me."

"Gladly." Lucian ducked his head underwater and looked up at us from under the blue waves. He said something but of course I couldn't hear him.

"What was that? What did he say?" I asked, looking anxiously at Lucian's black hair, floating like seaweed in the gentle current.

Drace grinned a little. "I think he said 'come on in, the water's fine.'"

"And...he's really able to breathe down there?" I asked, still watching him worriedly. With his pale olive green skin, he blended in with the light blue water surprisingly well—almost as well as Drace with his dark blue skin tones.

"You can see for yourself," Drace motioned to him and Lucian gave me a little wave. He was sitting cross-legged on the ocean floor now, reminding me of a game I used to play with my cousins when we went swimming. It was called "tea party" and the object was to hold your breath and sit on the bottom of the swimming pool long enough to pretend you were eating some cookies and drinking a cup of tea.

Lucian, however, wasn't holding his breath. Watching carefully, I could see his broad chest rising and falling—(he and Drace were both shirtless and completely mouthwatering, I think I forgot to mention that)—so it was easy to see.

"Okay," I said at last. "So you just…dunk your head under and start breathing?"

"That's right, baby." Drace smiled at me. "You want to try it? Or are you scared?"

I think it was meant as an honest question but I took it as a dare. Lifting my chin, I frowned at him.

"I'm not afraid," I said and ducked my head under the water.

At first I held my breath out of habit. I mean, who wouldn't? It's surprisingly hard to do something—such as trying to breathe underwater—that your brain insists will kill you. Finally, though, when my lungs felt like they were going to burst, I parted my lips and sucked in just the tiniest bit.

My mouth filled with briny water but it didn't taste like the ocean back home. It was less salty for one thing and it had an almost sweet aftertaste. It filled my mouth but didn't go down my throat, or up my nose for that matter.

I got brave and sucked in a little more. I felt my lungs expanding and realized I was doing it—I was breathing underwater! I could see too—thanks to the vision drops we'd all squirted into our eyes, everything was crystal clear.

It was bizarre and exhilarating like a waking dream. We continued our journey, but this time under the water. Of course, I felt a little like I was moving in slow motion and the salty taste of water in my mouth did take some getting used to, as Drace had said, but other than that I was perfectly fine. It was amazing.

When we talked, the sounds were strangely distorted until Drace pulled out some small, porous stones and put two in his ears like earplugs. He handed some to me and Lucian too.

"Sorry," he said as I pushed them carefully into my ear canals, making sure they weren't so far in they wouldn't come out again.

"Almost forgot about the sound-wave plugs. Good thing I had extras."

"They help," I said, once I had the small stones seated comfortably in my ears. "I can't believe I'm hearing and seeing and *breathing* underwater! I feel like I'm in a dream."

"No dream, *ma 'frela,*" Lucian said. He was on my right side and Drace was on my left. "This is the only way to visit the Half-Folk in their own world."

"Who are they?" I asked, looking around to see if I could spot any of them. To my disappointment, there was nothing but crystal clear water and silvery sand as far as my eyes could see. Well, except for a dark cloud over on our right. I wondered if it was a shoal of fish.

"They are one of the Twelve Peoples," Lucian said. "Those intelligent beings descended from the Ancient Ones who were given the seeds of life by the Goddess of Mercy."

"Um, okay," I said. "But what are they *like?*"

"Mostly peaceful," Drace said, sounding thoughtful. "There's never been much trouble between the land-living Denarins and the Half-Folk or Wave-Dwellers as they call themselves. We keep to the land and, for the most part, they keep to the sea. We share a lot of resources so we have to cooperate."

"That doesn't sound like how it would go on Earth," I said grimly, thinking of the way we'd polluted our oceans back home. Also, we were *so* not good at sharing resources. It was probably a good thing we didn't have to share our planet with a whole other sentient species.

We were getting closer to the big dark cloud and I could see now it wasn't a cloud at all—it was a kind of forest. A kelp forest with impossibly tall strands of dark kelp, purple on one side and deep green on the other, floating far over our heads.

"Do you have Half-Folk on your planet?" Lucian asked. "I thought humans were the only race on the planet—it's the reason you're Pure Ones."

"No, we're the only people there—that isn't what I meant," I said. "But look, you guys still haven't answered my question. What do these Half-Folk people *look* like?"

Suddenly, as if in answer to my question, two huge people came out of the kelp forest.

I say "people" but that was only half right. They were both men—or male, anyway—and from the waist up, they were as massive as Drace and Lucian with broad, muscular chests and shoulders and blond hair that floated around their faces. But from the waist down, well...

"They're lobsters," I whispered faintly, staring at the long, segmented bodies and chitinous, many jointed legs that ended in claw-like points instead of feet. "Oh my God, they're *lobster people.*"

"Hail, surface dwellers," one of the lobster guys said in a deep, sonorous voice. (Actually, he looked more like a lobster-centaur to me, only his bottom part was a lobster instead of a horse. Can you imagine a lobster the size of a horse? Don't—it'll give you nightmares.) "Why have you come to the domain of the Wave-dwellers?" he asked.

Lucian stepped forward. "We have come to consult with Tanta Loro," he said clearly. "Concerning some advice she gave us earlier. We need clarification."

"Once Tanta Loro advises, she does not speak on a matter again," said the other lobster-centaur guy. "Best you should be on your way." He yanked suddenly on a chain he was holding in one hand and a huge fish came swimming out of the kelp forest, apparently attached to the end of the chain like it was a leash.

I yelped when I saw the massive fish and jumped back—as well as I could jump underwater, anyway. I had been thinking horse-sized lobsters were bad but this was way, *way* worse. It was as big as one of those huge groupers who can swallow a whole car in one gulp, but it didn't have the stupid, complacent look of a grouper. Instead, its face was a nightmare, with huge, black staring eyes and teeth as long as my arm. They stuck out of its jaw every-which-way, a crazy game of razor-sharp pick-up sticks that looked utterly lethal. I couldn't see how this monstrosity could eat anything without chewing up its own face—not that I bet it let that stop it come feeding time.

"You said there were no sharks," I whispered to Drace accusingly. "So what's that thing?"

"A gnash-tooth," he muttered back. "Don't worry—Lucian and I won't let you get hurt, baby." Then he stepped up beside Lucian, making sure to keep me behind them.

"We have already paid the price for consultation and it was a high one," Lucian was saying. "But Tanta Loro's advice has not worked."

"We need to see her again," Drace added. "And we're not going until we do."

The two lobster-centaur guys raised their spears. (Did I mention they had long, silver spears with wicked-looking barbed points? Because they did, along with their freaking attack-fish.)

I was still hidden behind Drace and Lucian but I peaked out and felt my heart jump up into my throat when I saw their threatening stance. Then, for some reason they stopped and cocked their heads to one side, almost as though they were hearing something none of the rest of us could catch.

"Yes, Tanta Loro," one of them murmured. He looked at his partner and nodded.

"On your head be it, then," said the one with the huge gnash-tooth fish. "If Tanta Loro does not find your request reasonable, she will meet out punishment far worse than ours."

Worse than being stuck by eight foot long barbed spears or gobbled by the gnash-tooth? Wow, I was really hoping that this Tanta Loro wasn't upset with us for coming to see her!

"Come," the other lobster-centaur guard said. Turning, they both glided back into the kelp forest, taking their pet nightmare-fish with them.

Drace and Lucian looked at each other briefly and nodded. Taking a step back, they flanked me like some kind of honor guard. I understood they were putting themselves into position to protect me if there was any trouble. Gratefully, I grabbed their hands and squeezed.

Drace squeezed back and gave me a rueful grin.

"Come on, baby—we'd better follow them."

"You're sure we'll be all right?" I asked, my voice coming out squeaky, even underwater.

"It has to be," Lucian said grimly. "Don't worry, *ma 'frela.* Whatever else Tanta Loro may be, she is fair."

As we walked together into the shadows of the tall, waving kelp forest, I hoped he was right.

# Chapter Thirteen

## Rylee

"Why have you come to disssturb me again?" Tanta Loro had a deep, hissing voice that echoed in my ears like some kind of strange whale song. I wondered if maybe the echoes were caused by the walls of the structure around us.

I say "structure" because I'm not sure what else to call it—it certainly wasn't like any house or office building I had ever been in. It was shiny, pearlescent pink with a wide, round entrance that rose into a spiraling tower at least five stories above our heads. When we'd entered it, we'd walked up a curving, slippery ramp for what seemed like forever until we came to a large, central room where the walls were a much paler peach, but still with a pearlescent shine.

Really, I thought, what it resembled more than anything else was a giant seashell. *We're standing inside a giant seashell,* I told myself. *Standing in a giant seashell and talking to a —*

At that point, words failed me. Just like her house—if this *was* a house—Tanta Loro was hard to explain.

With all the talk about tentacles-for-hair, I'd been expecting her to be half octopus and break out into *Poor Unfortunate Souls* the minute we stepped in the room. But the reality was worse—much worse.

She had the top half of a woman—a *topless* woman, I might add. Her enormous breasts floated free with only two tiny purple seashells a la *The Little Mermaid* to cover her nipples. Other than that, her top half looked normal enough but her bottom half...well, that was another story.

Have you ever seen pictures of those huge, Japanese spider crabs? They're freaky because they really *do* look like spiders—giant ones with a sixteen-foot long leg span and bodies bigger than a man's head. That was what the bottom part of Tanta Loro looked like—a crab—a really big *scary* one.

Her hair was normal though—I didn't know what Drace and Lucian had been talking about there. It was slicked back into a sleek, black bun at the back of her neck where it showed really well since her skin was chalk-white.

"We followed your advice—your prophesy," Lucian said to her. "We found a Pure One to touch us both at the same time but it didn't sever our bond."

"It fucking strengthened it," Drace growled. "We're closer than we were before—that isn't what we paid for."

"You paid for a prophesssy," Tanta Loro hissed, swaying forward on her many long, spindly crab legs. "I cannot control how the prophesy playsss out."

"Be that as it may," Lucian said, frowning. "We still need help to be free of each other."

"Foolish sssurface dwellersss. You have what you need right in front of you, yet you do not sssee it. Iss this the one you brought to free you?" She swayed towards me and I had to fight not to run away.

I'm not afraid of much except bugs but her bottom half was *way* too bug-like for comfort. Also, she was *huge*—her top half was as big as the lobster-centaur guys. She towered over my head like some kind of strange, moving statue an artist with a sick mind had carved and left at the bottom of the sea.

"This is our chosen female, Rylee," Drace said, frowning at her. "She's under our protection," he added at the same time Lucian said,

"She is not to be harmed."

"I ssserve the Goddesss—I would not dream of harming a Pure One and a *La-ti-zal*. Come closser, child." She beckoned to me with two of her long, spindly crab legs.

My own legs were decidedly unsteady as I took a step closer and looked up at her. Tanta Loro leaned down towards me until her pale face was right in front of mine. She sniffed me, her nostrils wrinkling, and then she threw back her head and laughed.

"What the—" I stumbled backwards and almost fell. As she laughed, Tanta Loro's sleek black hair came down from its bun and floated all around her face.

Only it wasn't hair—long, thin tentacles waved around her chalk-white cheeks and forehead in a mesmerizing pattern.

*Tentacles,* I thought, my heart pounding. *Oh my God, they were right—she actually has **tentacles**!*

I don't know why the tentacle hair should have been more horrifying than the crab body but somehow it was. Maybe because it was so unexpected. At any rate, my horror didn't seem to affect Tanta Loro at all—except to make her more amused.

"Foolsss!" she cried, pointing at Lucian and Drace. "You sssurface dwelling *foolsss!* Do you know what kind of female you have chosssen?"

"She is a Pure One, just as you said." Drace put an arm around me protectively.

"And a *La-ti-zal,*" Lucian added, staying close to my other side.

"Yesss, ssshe is all thossse thingsss." Tanta Loro finally finished laughing and her "hair" settled down into a bun at the nape of her neck again. Then she looked at the three of us seriously. "She isss indeed a *La-ti-zal* but do you know what her power isss?"

"Well...no," Lucian admitted. "The Commercians couldn't tell us that—only that she had special powers."

"She doesss indeed have powersss," Tanta Loro hissed. She pointed one, bony finger at me. "She isss a *Binder.*"

"A what?" I stared at her blankly. "Look, I really don't think—"

"A Binder?" Drace growled, frowning. "That's impossible. We chose her because we saw her splitting two males apart."

"Drace is right—Rylee helps separate people," Lucian insisted. "She doesn't bind them together."

"She isss a *Binder,*" the crab-woman insisted. "Otherwissse the mere touch of her handsss to yoursss would have broken the bond between you. You have chosen the one female who can never help you sssever your bond—she can only bind you more tightly together."

"I...I don't believe it," Lucian whispered in a numb voice.

"This can't be right!" Drace insisted angrily.

My skin tightened and I felt a hot rush all over my body – the same feeling you get when you're being called out in front of a bunch of people and you know you did something really, *really* wrong. What if Tanta Loro was right? What if I was some kind of a Binder? The idea that I had some kind of untapped power sounded bizarre but was it really any stranger than the situation I currently found myself in, at the bottom of the ocean talking to a woman who was half-spider crab? Anyway, it would certainly explain how my intervention had strengthened the tie between them instead of weakening or breaking it.

"Guys…what if it's true?" I asked in a small voice. "What if I only made your situation worse?" I shook my head, twisting my fingers together. "I'm so, *so* sorry – I didn't know. Didn't know about *any* of this."

"Of course you didn't. It's not your fault, baby," Drace murmured roughly, turning to face me.

"Please don't think we blame you, *ma 'frela*," Lucian said earnestly, stroking my cheek. "We chose you ourselves because we felt drawn to you. The fault is ours."

"I guess…" I looked down at my hands. "I guess you'd better take me back to Earth and try…try to find some other girl to help you." For some reason the words wanted to stick in my throat. Which was silly – we'd made a deal, signed a contract – all predicated on the idea that I would be going back eventually. But now the idea of the guys – of *my guys* – finding some other girl to help them made me feel sick to my stomach.

Stupid, right?

"No!" The hissing, echoing voice of Tanta Loro drew us out of our little circle. "There musst be no one elsse!" she declared, pointing one long, many-jointed finger at Drace and Lucian. "Thisss female child isss bound to your fate – you will find no freedom without her."

"What are you saying?" Lucian demanded. "Is there still some way to sever the bond between Drace and myself if we keep Rylee with us?"

Tanta Loro threw back her head again but this time she didn't laugh. Instead her dark purple, jewel-like eyes rolled back in her head, revealing the milky whites. Her curving, ruby-red mouth pursed and her tentacle hair floated free and began to twist and braid itself around her pale face. Slowly, in a measured pace like someone reciting poetry, she began to speak.

"One chance has been given and that was enough
One chance, but you shall have two
To sever your bond, your kinship to slough
Listen well to what you must do

First find the key of Tanterine Gray
Lost and then found again soon
Gain it and go to the Temple of Ganth
By the light of the Quarreling moons

Within find the treasure—also a blight
The Claw that can sever your bond
But beware when you use it, you do what is right
Once severed, your love will be gone."

"God," I whispered softly when she appeared to be done. "What is all *that* supposed to mean?"

"It's a prophesy," Lucian murmured.

"Just what we need—another fucking prophesy," Drace growled.

Tanta Loro's eyes went back to their normal position and she let out a little gasp. Her long, spidery legs seemed to buckle under her and her tentacle hair went suddenly flat and limp.

"That isss all I have to give you," she whisper-hissed at us. "Go and do not return."

"But what does it mean?" I asked.

Tanta Loro suddenly drew herself up to her full height—I swear she towered up nine feet tall—and glared down at us.

*"GO!"*

Her voice echoed through the seashell house, nearly deafening me with its power. Clearly, we weren't getting anything else out of her.

"Guys," I said, dragging on both their arms. "Come on—let's *go!"*

Under the watchful glare of the two lobster-centaur guards, who had apparently come to see what all the shouting was about, we headed for the exit.

But as we were leaving, I threw one last glance over my shoulder and saw that the crab-woman was looking at me—just at me—her deep purple eyes blazing.

*"Binder!"* she hissed, swaying towards me. Her voice seemed to carry to my ears only because neither of the guys looked back at her. "Binder, beware the shadowsss and the thingsss that lurk in them! It is your death…your *death."*

I didn't know what she meant and I didn't *want* to know. I turned back around and ran.

# Chapter Fourteen

## Lucian

"First find the key of Tanterine Gray," Drace muttered, pacing up and down the length of the food-prep area. "What in the Frozen Hells does that *mean?*"

We were back aboard my ship—finally warm and dry though I still felt waterlogged. Visiting the Half-Folk who lived beneath the seas was always an undertaking. Drace and I were wearing our sleep trousers again and Rylee was dressed in her long white sleeping gown. We weren't actually planning to go straight to bed—I think we all just wanted to be comfortable.

And we *were* comfortable—physically, anyway. Mentally and emotionally, I was in a turmoil. The strange prophesy kept echoing in my head, making it hard to think past my misery.

Drace was too upset to sense my inner turmoil but Rylee seemed to pick up on it at once. She offered to take on the cooking duties, as long as Drace and I didn't complain about what she made. I had agreed absently and then sat myself down at the table with my head in my hands, trying to make up my mind what to do.

"The key of Tanterine Gray," Drace repeated again, still pacing. "For fuck's sake—what is she *talking* about?"

"Lucian knows, don't you, hon?" Rylee asked softly. She came to the table and sat a plate in front of me and then put another down in front Drace's place. "There—cheeseburgers. And remember, *no* complaining."

"He does? You do?" Ignoring the food, Drace came to the table and stared down at me, a frown on his strong features.

I sighed and ran a hand through my hair. Damn Rylee for guessing.

"Yes," I said heavily. "I know."

"Well, what is it then and how can we get it?" he demanded. "And why the fuck didn't you speak up earlier?"

"I didn't want to!" I shouted back. "Because—" I broke off, shaking my head.

"Because of what, Lucian? You can tell us." Rylee put a hand on my shoulder and her other hand on Drace's arm. I felt a current of calm run through me—was that coming from Rylee? Was she even now binding me closer to my temporary bond-mate—to the very male I was trying to get away from?

*A Binder – she's a Binder! You should pull away!*

And yet even if she was a Binder, as Tanta Loro had said, I couldn't make myself want to shake her hand off. Couldn't ask her to stop—her touch and through her, the touch of my bond-mate, felt too good. Which was damn scary.

"The key of Tanterine Gray refers to an artifact found at one of the sites of our earliest prehistory," I said in a low voice, not looking at either of them. "It's not really a key—it's a kind of triangular stone made of Tanterine—a rare mineral that's considered very valuable in some circles."

"And you know this *how* exactly?" Drace demanded, frowning.

"Because…" I scrubbed a hand over my face. "Because it was sold at auction in my home city of Y'brith not too long ago and bought for a large sum by a private buyer."

"That's great!" Rylee exclaimed. "Who bought it? Do you know?"

"I do," I said heavily. "It was bought by an off-worlder who makes his home in Y'brith—a Cantor male who goes by the name of Lord Mandrex. He's extremely wealthy and notoriously eccentric."

"That's the first piece of the puzzle solved then!" Rylee looked excited. "We can just go back to your home town and ask to meet with this Lord Mandrex and see if we can buy or borrow the key from him." She frowned at me. "Why do you still look so upset, Lucian?"

Drace answered for me. "Because going back to Y'brith caries a risk of someone seeing us and finding out we're bonded." His voice turned bitter. "Because Lucian here doesn't want to face his fucking upper-crust parents and admit to our bond. Do you?" he threw at me.

"Would *you* want to admit it to *your* family?" I snarled, glaring at him. "You don't know my parents—my fathers are the chiefs of our clan and my mother is the social leader of the city. If it gets out that I bonded with another Alpha—especially one from our clan's greatest rival—it will *ruin* them."

"Why does it have to get out?" Rylee asked, frowning at both of us. "Honestly, you two are such drama-queens. Why can't we just sneak quietly into the city and make a private appointment with this Lord Mandrex guy?"

"Actually, we *can*," I said slowly. "It would mean landing the ship outside the city limits and going through the desert but a stealthy approach *could* be made." I frowned. "It would be dangerous, though. The desert around Y'brith isn't called The Sands of Death for no reason."

"The Sands of Death?" Rylee sounded nervous. "That doesn't sound so good, Lucian."

"I think we should do it," Drace said, surprising me. "We can sim some protective clothing and go in at night. It'll be fine."

I looked at him gratefully. "Thank you—it's good of you to understand."

"'Course I fucking understand," he said roughly. "I didn't mean to ride you so hard about your parents—it's just...we come from different backgrounds."

"We do," I acknowledged heavily. "Very different."

"Well, I'm glad you two understand everything but *I* don't." Rylee was still frowning at both of us. "Look, I don't get why what your parents think should be such a huge deal. I mean, I know family is important but both of you are grown-ass *men*. You need to stand on your own two feet and tell momma and daddy to mind their own business."

"You don't get it, Rylee." Drace frowned. "It isn't just family—this is Clan protocol we're breaking, being bonded together. In some clans being bonded to a male of a rival clan can get you killed. And an Alpha being bonded to another Alpha is almost as bad."

"It won't get you killed in the Fang Clan," I said grimly. "Just shunned and socially ruined. That's all. Not to mention if my parents—my mother especially—found out I was bonded to another Alpha it would..." I blew out a breath.

"It would break her heart." Drace sounded a little more sympathetic now and I thought I felt less anger coming from his end of our bond.

"Yes," I said simply. "It would."

"I'm sorry. I guess I *didn't* really get it before now." Rylee gave me a hug, looping one arm around my neck and drawing me close for comfort. Then she motioned for Drace. "You too—come here."

Drace knelt on her other side and she put an arm around him too, drawing him close. We both put our arms around her and for a moment I allowed myself to press my face to the soft, yielding firmness of her right breast as Drace pressed against the left. She still smelled like the saltiness of the sea but underneath was her own slightly floral, deeply feminine scent which made my shaft ache despite my anxiety and doubt.

Once again a current of peace flowed between us—a current of caring and need and desire that made me want to take Rylee to bed and share her with my bond-mate all night long.

I sighed and pressed closer to her, breathing in her scent and Drace's too. The arm I had around her waist found Drace's and, without asking, I gripped his hand. I felt him hesitate and then he squeezed back. Immediately, the current intensified, bringing an almost euphoric warmth and pleasure.

*Three as One,* I thought. *One that is Three. The perfect number.*

Gods, it felt good to have her between us! To feel the comfort and understanding coming from my mates—*both* my mates. Because Rylee was embroiled in my bond with Drace too. By trying to break our psy-bond and somehow binding us more tightly, she had also become a temporary bond-mate. I understood that now as I hadn't before we'd gone to see Tanta Loro.

We were all in this together.

It was a good feeling, our three-way hug—so good I never wanted it to end. Just at that moment I felt that I didn't care about any of the consequences as long as we could just all be together.

A dangerous embrace.

*Don't forget why this has to end — why you can't be together,* whispered a warning voice in the back of my head.

I forced myself to sit upright, pulling away from my bond-partners.

"It's all right," I said and cleared my throat. "It will be all right — we'll simply have to be very, *very* careful to avoid my parents and anyone I know while we're in Y'brith."

"It's not your fault this happened to us," Drace offered. "I'd tell your parents so if you thought it would help. If they somehow found out, I mean."

For a moment I saw my bond-mate as my mother would see him — crude, loud, uneducated — or at least, not educated to her standards — the last male in the galaxy I ought to be bonded to. She wouldn't see Drace's bravery or generosity or the way he pleasured and protected our chosen female so selflessly. She would only see that he was the wrong class, the wrong clan, the wrong *one* for her only son. The ruin of her social status which she had worked so carefully to protect at all costs.

Come to think of it, she probably wouldn't much like Riley either. Males who mated off-worlder females were looked down on in the Fang Clan. It was supposed to be a last resort — something only a desperate male who had exhausted all other options would do.

But of course, I couldn't tell my bond-partners that. It would hurt them and though I once hadn't given a damn for Drace's feelings, I found I was unable to wound him now. My mind kept returning to the way he had healed my thumb — the way he had stood together with me to face Tanta Loro not once but twice. He was a good male, even if my mother and my fathers wouldn't think so. Even if being bonded to him and Rylee was a terrible shame on my family, I couldn't hurt or abandon them.

Not yet, anyway.

"It's all right," I said to Drace. "I thank you for your offer but I think it would be better if we kept the matter from my parents entirely. We *have* to get into the city without being seen."

"Agreed." He nodded. "That's exactly what we're going to do—but tomorrow, all right? It's late and going to visit the Wave Dwellers is fucking exhausting. I'm not up for a tramp through the desert on top of it."

"I'm all worn out too," Rylee admitted. "How about if we eat and go to bed?"

Her words seemed to resonate in the room and for some reason I found myself sharing a look with Drace.

"Do you want to sleep between us again, baby?" he asked softly. "Since Lucian hasn't had a chance to get the *skizix* problem taken care of yet?"

"Oh, um…" Rylee nibbled her lush lower lip—a distractingly erotic gesture although I don't think she knew it. "Will you…" She cleared her throat. "Will you need to…to build a, uh, dream-shield again?"

"If you want to keep the *skizix* out of the sleeping chamber, yes," Drace admitted. "Why—did it bother you the way we built it last night?"

"I…I'm not sure it bothered me *enough.*" Rylee sounded like she was slightly ashamed of herself for admitting it. "I mean, it was kind of, um, kinky. I know it seems normal to you guys but where I come from a girl with two guys at the same time is, well…" She trailed off, looking at both of us uncertainly.

"It's just a fantasy," I murmured, reassuring her. "Anything we do within our minds in order to build the dream-shield is just a phantom—an illusion. It's not as though it's really happening."

Although the Gods knew I wished it was. I wanted badly to share her with Drace, although I knew it was wrong.

"Well…" Rylee put her hands behind her back and entwined her fingers—a nervous gesture that pressed her full, creamy breasts out against the thin material of her night dress and put her tight berry-dark nipples on display. I had to bite back a groan as my shaft hardened.

Through the link I shared with Drace, I could feel my bond-mate's lust as well. But not just lust—he wanted to be careful with Rylee, to treat her gently and pleasure her well, just as I did. Our chosen female was a lady—we would treat her as such, if only she would let us.

"Baby..." he murmured caressingly, reaching out to stroke one large hand down her arm. "Come to bed with us. Just let Lucian and me hold you between us."

Rylee shivered and leaned into his touch, then she looked at me—an unspoken invitation. I put a hand on her arm as well, feeling her warm, silky skin under my palm, wanting her so badly I could barely breathe. Wanting to *share* her, the way it should be.

"All right," she whispered. "As long as we don't go too far and it all stays in our heads."

"Agreed," I said and Drace nodded.

Leaving the food forgotten on the table, the three of us headed for the sleeping chamber.

\* \* \* \* \*

# Rylee

I couldn't believe I'd agreed to this—agreed to let them do the whole dream-sex thing with me again.

*That's all it is—just a dream—a fantasy,* I told myself. *We won't really be doing anything but just lying in bed together. Hell, we won't even take off our clothes! Besides, we **have** to do this in order to form the dream-shield.*

But did we really? Weren't the guys just as able to form a shield with pretty mind images like the Van Gogh sky and the field of star-flowers as much as sexy images like the two of them sucking my nipples at the same time?

Just the thought of that—the memory of it—made me feel hot and cold all over. At that moment, I knew I wanted them—*both* of them—and that scared me.

*It'll be all right,* I tried to tell myself as Drace lifted me and put me down in the middle of the huge bed. He got in beside me, on the left side and Lucian got on my right in a pattern that was already beginning to feel extremely familiar.

They both rolled up on their elbows to face me and Lucian frowned.

"You're frightened, *ma 'frela* – I can smell the scent of fear on your skin."

"She's scared we'll go too far," Drace rumbled. Reaching out, he traced a gentle line down my cheek with one finger. "It's all right, baby – we'll be careful."

"And we will not touch you in reality – only in our minds," Lucian promised.

"Right," I said breathlessly. "Because touching in reality would, uh, violate our contract."

"Exactly. And we wouldn't want to do that," Drace murmured. "Come on, let's get comfortable."

"Lights dim," Lucian said and immediately the room went dark, lit only by the glow of the moving rainbow-lightning bugs in their glass tank across from the bed.

"Close your eyes – both of you," Drace ordered us, his deep voice slightly hoarse. "Lucian, help me. Let's set the shield in place."

I took a deep breath and we all closed our eyes.

This time there was no Starry Night or field of flowers – this time there was just the three of us in the bed.

Naked.

"Drace!" I gasped, looking down at myself. "Where did my gown go?"

And for that matter, where had their trousers gone?

The big blue alien gave me a lazy grin.

"Just thought we'd all be more comfortable this way. Don't worry – you're actually still dressed and so are we. Take a look and see for yourself."

I opened my eyes and saw that, sure enough, I was still wearing my long, white nightgown. Drace and Lucian also had on their sleep trousers. They were lying on either side of me, their big hands placed chastely on my bare shoulders. Absolutely nothing else was going on...in the real world.

But when I close my eyes and went back to the dream-world, things were different. Very different.

"Feeling better?" Drace asked, grinning at me. Naked, he and Lucian were every bit as muscular and mouthwatering as I had thought they would be. They were also *extremely* well endowed.

"Do you like what you see?" Lucian asked and I realized I'd been staring at their naked bodies for way too long.

"Is..." I bit my lip. "Is it real? I mean are you guys really this, uh, *big* in real life?"

"Hmm..." Lucian frowned and looked down at his dream-body. "Actually, I believe that Drace has shorted me a bit."

"Don't blame me," Drace growled. "I haven't exactly been paying attention to what you had between your legs, bond-mate — been too busy imagining what Rylee might have between hers."

"Ahh...you appear to have an excellent imagination," Lucian murmured. He cocked an eyebrow at me. "Well, Rylee? Does my bond-mate have you pictured correctly? And can we see for ourselves?"

I realized I was covering my breasts with my arms and keeping my thighs tightly closed to hide myself. Should I let them see me?

*Well, it is only a dream body,* I reminded myself. Sighing, I relaxed my stance, putting down my arm to show my nipples and opening my thighs. It felt naughty to show myself to my guys — especially both at once. But it was sexy too. And it was only a dream, so it must be okay. Anyway, that's what I told myself.

I heard a sharp intake of breath from Lucian and Drace gave a low growl of approval.

"Gods, you're beautiful, baby," he murmured.

"Stunning," Lucian agreed. "But tell us, has Drace done you justice? We have seen you naked once before, when we first chose you from the Alien Mate Index. But as I gave you my *undla* to wear, we didn't really get to, ah, *admire* you as we would have liked."

"Actually..." I looked down at myself and felt my cheeks getting hot. "It's pretty accurate," I admitted. "Except for the fact that I have a little birthmark that's lighter than the rest of my skin, right under here." I pointed to the underside of my left breast. "It's shaped a like a heart."

"I'd love to see that birthmark firsthand instead of just imagining," Drace growled.

"Now *that* would be going too far," I said lightly.

"Perhaps," Lucian said. "So other than the birthmark, Drace has drawn an accurate image of you?"

"Well…" I looked down at myself again and let out a little gasp.

"What is it?" Drace frowned. "Did I get something wrong?"

"Only if you really think I'm growing a freaking *forest* between my legs." I eyed the massive bushy growth Drace had imagined at the juncture of my thighs. To say it was big would be an understatement—it was seventies porn big—like a particularly fluffy cat had decided to curl up and take a nap between my legs big. It was huge.

"Hmm…" Lucian frowned. "That does seem to be…excessive."

"So it's too much?" Drace asked.

"It's *way* more, uh, hair than I have there," I said. "I usually keep up with the landscaping pretty well. Honestly, I—"

I stopped abruptly. The bush between my legs had disappeared completely, leaving my pussy mound bare and smooth. To my embarrassment, the button of my clit could be seen peeking from between my plump, naked pussy lips.

"Is this better?" Drace murmured.

"I…um…" Suddenly I realized I was lying there between them with my thighs spread wide and my naked pussy on display. Quickly I started to close my thighs, but Lucian stopped me with a hand on my knee.

"Please, *ma 'frela,*" he said softly. "Let us see you. Even if it is only a dream, you are beautiful."

"Well…" There it was again—the fact that this was only a dream. Reluctantly, I let him press my knee back against the sheets, opening me even more.

"So perfect," Lucian murmured. "So gorgeous."

"Such a pretty little pussy." Drace's voice was hoarse again. "Is that how you really look, baby? Did I get it right this time?"

"Yes," I admitted in a soft voice. "Only…only you made my, uh, clit a little too…visible. It's not usually that *prominent* unless I've been, um, touching it."

I could feel my cheeks heating as I spoke but I kept my legs open anyway. It made me feel hot to be on display for the two of them—hot and incredibly sexy. And still safe, since it was only a dream.

"Like this, you mean?" Lucian murmured. Reaching between my legs, he cupped my mound in one big, warm hand.

"Lucian…" I whispered in protest, but I didn't try to close my legs or stop him.

"It's all right, baby," Drace said softly in my ear. "Let him pet your pretty little pussy…stroke your clit a little so I can see what you're talking about. I want to get all the details right next time."

I knew I shouldn't, but somehow I couldn't seem to ask them to stop.

"All…all right," I whispered as Lucian spread my pussy lips open with his index and ring fingers. Then his long, middle finger slipped down into my inner folds and began to stroke and explore, sliding along the side of my tender clit in a way that made my breath catch in my throat.

The thing was, even though it was a dream, it felt so *real*. I swore I could really feel the big alien's hand on me, his fingers exploring me and stroking my swollen clit until I could barely breathe it felt so good.

"Gods, look how wet you're getting baby," Drace growled softly. "Am I getting that right? Would you get all wet and hot for us if Lucian was really touching you?"

"Yes," I admitted softly. "I…I don't think I could help it. *Ah*— that feels so *good!*"

"It could feel better," Lucian said. He looked at me, his eyes blazing. "Let us take your nipples in our mouths again, *ma 'frela*— this time with nothing in the way."

"Lucian's right—we can make it even better for you if you let us suck your sweet nipples," Drace growled.

I'm ashamed to say I didn't even think of saying no this time.

"Yes," I whispered. "Yes, do it."

"Our pleasure," Drace murmured. Leaning forward, he captured the tip of one thrusting breast between his lips and began to suck in long, hard pulls that made my nipple tingle and sent chills of desire straight down to my pussy.

Lucian did the same on the other side, taking my right nipple into his mouth and nipping very lightly before circling the sensitive tip with his tongue.

For a moment I looked down at myself, unable to believe this was happening, even in a dream. Here I was, lying naked on my back with a huge, muscular alien on either side of me. Both Lucian and Drace were sucking me, tasting and teasing my nipples with their hot mouths, while Lucian continued sliding one careful fingertip around and around my aching clit.

I was the picture of decadent, kinky sex—at least I fit the picture that came with that description in my own head. I could feel my pleasure building, the tingling sensations that shot between my nipples and pussy were soon going to be too much.

And then Lucian released my right nipple for a moment and looked at Drace.

"Fill her pussy with your fingers, bond-mate," he said, his deep, usually smooth voice ragged with lust. "Fill her and fuck her while I stroke her clit."

Drace stopped sucking for a moment too.

"With pleasure. If Rylee agrees?" He raised an eyebrow at me.

"Yes," I breathed, unable to stop myself. "*Do it.*"

"My pleasure, baby. " Drace reached under Lucian's hand, which was still stroking and teasing my clit, and guided two long, strong fingers deep into my hungry pussy.

I felt him filling me, pressing hard against the end of my channel and another jolt of sensation ran through me. I gasped and bucked my hips, unable to help my reaction as my pleasure jumped even higher. Oh God, I couldn't believe I was doing this but I couldn't seem to stop—couldn't even seem to *want* to stop. It felt too good, too *right* to be between them, their two big bodies bracketing mine.

"Gods, you're beautiful, baby," Drace growled. "Ride my fingers. Let us make you come."

"Yes," I whispered, completely shameless now. "Yes, but suck me again. *Please.*"

"Love to suck your sweet, ripe breasts, *ma 'frela,*" Lucian assured me.

He and Drace re-captured my nipples and started sucking again—hard—as they continued to stroke and pump my pussy in a rhythm that felt impossibly right. How they could be so in sync with each other when it came to making me feel good, I had no idea. I only knew they were doing it so, *so* right and I was about to come harder than I ever had in my life.

The heat between us built and built and built until suddenly it was too much and I felt myself coming...coming so hard I could barely breathe. My back arched, my toes curled, and my fists clenched at my sides.

*GodohGodohGod...so good! So good!*

"Drace...Lucian...*ahhh!*" I moaned breathlessly and threw back my head.

They stayed with me, riding out my orgasm, stroking and petting and sucking me as though I was the center of their entire universe and my pleasure was the only thing that mattered.

It made me feel like a goddess to be the center of so much attention. It was intoxicating...dizzying. I recognized, through the haze of delicious sensations, that it was a dangerously addictive feeling.

*Don't get used to it—it's just this once,* I told myself as the pleasure at last began to ebb.

At last, after what seemed like forever, the two of them withdrew and I lay there, panting in the bed, trying to get my breath. I was feeling sleepy and languorous but also kind of guilty. I definitely hadn't been raised to behave the way I just had.

"Um..." I looked back and forth between them, not sure what to do. "That was...really amazing," I offered at last, wondering if they would expect me to return the favor. "What now?"

"Now we get some sleep," Lucian said. "We can rest without fear."

"True. I would say the dream-shield is *definitely* set now," Drace said dryly.

"But..." I raised up on my elbows, frowning at them. "Aren't you guys feeling kind of, uh, unfulfilled? I mean you just gave me the best orgasm of my life but you didn't get to...you know, come yourselves."

Lucian frowned and Drace looked genuinely surprised.

"What happened between us was never about *our* pleasure, *ma 'frela,*" Lucian said.

"Lucian's right—just sharing you between us was the greatest pleasure." Drace leaned over and kissed my cheek. "Thank you, baby. You have no idea how much it means, being able to share a female with a bond-mate."

"Drace is correct—even in the dream realm, sharing you was exquisite," Lucian murmured.

I looked at them, still trying to wrap my head around it.

"Sharing is really *that* important to you? I mean, don't you guys *ever* have sex with just one guy and one girl?"

"It's possible." Lucian made a taste. "Just not...preferable."

"It feels wrong," Drace said bluntly. "Like something's missing."

"Like some*one* is missing," Lucian said and they shared a glance. "Here and now with the two of you is the first time I've ever felt...complete," he told us quietly.

"Me too," Drace offered. "And it feels fucking *amazing.*"

It was on the tip of my tongue to ask why they didn't just put their pride aside so they could stay together and find some nice girl to marry if it felt so amazing and wonderful to share a woman. But I didn't say it.

Two things stopped me—first, I had been able to observe first hand at the beach that day that there were more things than just their pride and very different personalities keeping them apart.

The second thing that made the words stick in my throat was the idea of them finding someone besides *me* to share. I knew it was ridiculous but I was beginning to get really attached to both of them. Our contract would be up and they would take me back to Earth soon enough—until then, I wanted to enjoy our time together.

Speaking of enjoying myself, I was feeing warm and contented and extremely sleepy just at the moment.

"I'm glad you guys had a good time," I told them and yawned. "Just as long as you know I would never, you know, do this kind of thing in real life." *Because I wouldn't,* I told myself. *I really wouldn't. That would be going too far – doing too much.*

"We understand, *ma 'frela.*" Lucian kissed me gently on the lips. "Thank you for allowing what you did."

Drace kissed me too, his mouth lingering sweetly on mine. "Go to sleep, baby," he murmured, when he pulled back. "You look tired."

I yawned again. "I am. Long day today."

"Another long one tomorrow," Lucian reminded us. "Hiking through The Sands of Death is apt to be somewhat unpleasant."

I wanted to laugh at his understatement but I yawned again instead. With a sigh, I turned on my side and snuggled down between my guys. I felt them draw closer and soon I was enveloped by the heat of their big warm bodies, one pressed against my front and the other against my back. Their mingled scent—sharp and clean and warm and spicy—swirled around me, making me feel safe and cherished and protected.

*It's all right,* I thought irreverently. *Everything is going to be all right.*

Then I closed my eyes in the dream world as well as the real world and slept.

# Chapter Fifteen

## Rylee

As it turned out, sneaking into the huge city of Y'brith by way of the deadly desert was more than a little "unpleasant."

It was getting near sunset by the time we parked Lucian's ship as close to the city gates as we dared and set out. Despite the late hour, the bluish-white Denarin sun was still way too hot and bright for my taste. And this is coming from a girl who lives in Florida — the freaking "Sunshine State" — so you know it was bad.

At least I was dressed for the desert — I'd traded in my flirty red sand-dress for a silver-tan, light-reflecting blouse and a billowy pair of lightweight trousers that gathered at the ankles and tucked into sturdy dune-shoes. The shoes were ludicrously wide in the toes, making it look like I had duck-feet, but they were uniquely suited for walking through the shifting sands. Also, they were *way* better than the ridiculous protective boots Lucian had tried to get me to wear.

The boots were made from thick, dirt-colored leather material with clumsy looking Frankenstein soles and they were thigh-highs. Not sexy, *Pretty Woman* thigh-highs, though — more like wading boots. They literally would have laced all the way up to my inner thighs if I'd put them on.

I had stared at the boots askance when Lucian held them out to me, fresh from the clothing sim. To my eyes, they looked unnecessarily hot and heavy — not to mention they were what my friend Zoe would have called "butt ugly."

I had taken one look at those boots and demanded to know if we were going to be wading through nests of rattlesnakes or pits of scorpions — I couldn't imagine any other reason to wear such ugly, heavy gear.

"Seriously, Lucian, is the sand we're walking through full of poisonous predators or something?"

"Well, no..." He frowned. "There are no dangerous creatures *above* the sand. Below it is a different matter."

"And are we going *below* the sand?" I asked.

He shook his head. "No, but—"

"Then I'm not wearing those." I shoved the long, ugly boots away. "I'd sweat to death in them trying to walk through the desert."

"They're for your protection, *ma 'frela*," he insisted.

I crossed my arms over my chest. "Then why aren't you and Drace wearing them?"

"I have a natural immunity to anything that creeps or crawls through The Sands of Death because I am of the Fang Clan," Lucian said patiently.

"Oh, I get it—and Drace gets your immunity because you two are bonded, right?" I asked.

Drace frowned. "Not really because our bond isn't sealed."

"Sealed?" I frowned. "This is the first I'm hearing of this—what does that mean?"

Lucian and Drace exchanged a look. "Members of our race form a psy-bond—usually early in life—that is binding in almost every way," Lucian said.

"But until they share a female, the bond isn't sealed," Drace finished for him. "That's why we thought breaking our bond would be possible—because we haven't shared a female."

"Um..." I couldn't help it—my cheeks were getting pink because I was thinking of the "sharing" we'd done the night before.

"I know what you're thinking, *ma 'frela*," Lucian said quickly. "But everything we three have done together has been in the dream realm."

"And even if it wasn't, there's no way Lucian and I could seal our bond—and bond you to us to form a Triumvirate—unless we both entered your sweet little pussy at the same time," Drace assured me.

"O-kaaaay." I lifted my chin and took a deep breath. It was time to stop talking like this—it made me picture what it would be like to be between them—for real this time. And I couldn't afford to start thinking like that. "So back to the butt-ugly boots," I said firmly. "Tell me again why Drace *doesn't* have to wear them, if he doesn't have your immunity, Lucian?"

He frowned. "Drace has on his leather trousers and the strength and abilities of the Claw Clan which are considerable. You have your *La-ti-zal* powers but…"

"But so far they haven't been very useful. Exactly the opposite, I know," I said quietly. "I really *am* sorry about that, you know."

"It is not your fault," Lucian said quietly. "Drace and I do not blame you for it."

"I know you don't and I appreciate that." I lifted my chin. "I'll still do anything I can to help you guys get this taken care of, you know. Tanta Loro seemed to think we needed to stick together, so we will. I'll stay with you until we get the job done—I swear."

"Your word means a lot to us, baby," Drace murmured, from where he was sitting, already dressed in his desert gear. "We know you'll see this through."

"I will," I said. "And not just because of our contract. This is a matter of honor now." It sounded kind of corny but it was true—I was determined to stick with them until I helped them get separated.

*Of course it seemed like you were doing your best to bring them together last night,* whispered a snarky little voice in my head.

*Shut up,* I told it, feeling guilty. *That was all in our heads—we didn't actually touch each other at all. That makes it all right.*

Didn't it?

"It is a matter of *our* honor to keep you safe," Lucian said, breaking my guilty train of thought and trying to give me the boots again.

I shook my head firmly.

"Nice try but I'm not wearing those ugly-ass boots," I told him. "You said we'd only be in the desert an hour tops, right? And we'll only be on the fringes of it—not in the deep desert where you told us it's really dangerous."

"It's true that the danger should be minimal but it *does* still exist." Lucian gave me a frustrated frown. "Even if there is only a one in a million chance you could be harmed, I don't want to take that chance with you, *ma 'frela.* You have…come to mean a lot to me. To both of us, I think." He looked over at Drace who nodded.

"He's right, baby," he murmured. "You're special. We don't want to risk you."

"If anybody is risking anything I'm risking myself," I insisted. "You said there's no danger on the surface of the sand which is where we'll be walking, so I'm going with the lighter and *slightly* less ugly shoe option."

Then I had put on the dune-shoes and that was that.

Now, as I hiked through the sand in the much lighter footwear, I congratulated myself again. Those long, ugly boots Lucian had wanted me to wear must have weighed fifty pounds. My thigh muscles would be *screaming* at me right now if I had worn them. It was hard enough getting through the dry, unstable sand in shoes specially made for it, let alone wearing what amounted to extremely ugly fetish-wear.

But even wearing the dune-shoes, walking through the hot sand under the hot sun was really no fun.

"This is crazy," I muttered as I slid and slipped my way through the sand dunes that led to the back entrance of the city. "First we're at the bottom of the ocean, then hiking through the freaking desert. What's next—mountain climbing?"

"More likely we'll be cutting brush through the jungle," Drace grunted, keeping his sand-visor low over his eyes to shield out the brilliant sunlight.

"Oh, yeah? I squinted and shielded my eyes as I looked into the distance. At least the city was getting closer—I could see the back gates rising like monoliths in the sand some distance away.

It was a shame we couldn't just fly Lucian's ship right in but then he would have had to identify himself and everyone would know he was back in town and come looking for him. (Everyone, presumably, being his super-snobby parents. Not that Lucian exactly *said* they were snobby—it was just a feeling I got and the way Drace rolled his eyes when he mentioned their social status.)

"Why do you say we'll be going through the jungle?" Lucian, who was leading our little expedition, looked back at Drace, who was heading up the rear. They were, as usual, keeping me between them.

"Been thinking about the prophesy," Drace growled, adjusting his visor again. "That line about the Temple of Ganth. I thought the name sounded familiar so I looked it up—it's an abandoned temple not far from Claw Clan grounds in the K'drin Jungle. So if we *are* able to locate this buyer and get the key from him, we're headed for my home territory next."

"Ah." Lucian nodded thoughtfully. "Another piece of the puzzle, as Rylee would say."

"Rylee would say she's sweating to death and needs a shower," I said. "So when are we going to get to—*ahhhh!*"

My last words ended in a scream because just at that moment my foot slipped into some kind of a hole in the treacherous sand. For a moment, I pinwheeled my arms, thinking I was about to trip and go flat on my face. Instead, my entire right leg slid down into the hole, as though I'd stepped into a pocket of pure nothing.

I cried out as I did an impromptu split. If I hadn't been doing Yin Yoga once a week for stress relief for the past two years, I probably would have torn a tendon or snapped a hamstring or something. As it was, the split hurt, but I was still okay. Well, as okay as I could be with my leg jammed to the hip in the sand.

"What in the Frozen Hells? You okay, baby?" Drace knelt beside me at once. He tried to pull me out, but I was stuck fast.

"Rylee!" Lucian came rushing back, more graceful by far than either Drace or me on the hilly sand dunes. "We have to get her out, *now!*" he told Drace, a trace of panic in his deep, smooth voice.

"I'm all for that," Drace growled. "Here—you take one arm and I'll take—"

That was when I felt something sting me. Or else bite me. I wasn't sure which it was—only that it felt like someone had heated two sixteen gage needles until they were red hot and then jabbed them into the tender flesh of my inner thigh.

"Ahhh!" I screamed again—this time in pain. "Oh my God—something bit me!"

Lucian swore, his dark blue eyes going wide with fear.

"We have to get her out—we *have to get her out!*" he shouted at Drace.

"Come on, then!" Drace snapped back.

The two of them each grabbed me under the armpits and heaved as hard as they could.

At first, it didn't seem like they could budge me—I was really stuck fast! Then, just as I thought my arms were going to come out of their sockets, I popped out of the ground like a cork coming out of a bottle.

Drace and Lucian staggered and we all fell over backwards in the sand. But the next minute we were up again and running for our lives, staggering and slipping over the shifting sands—because there was something coming out of the hole.

Out of the blackness boiled a huge cloud of flying creatures, each as long as my hand from the tip of my middle finger to the end of my palm. They hummed and buzzed angrily but they were so big the hum was more of a thrumming sound—something you felt rather than heard—vibrating the air all around you.

*"Moratas!"* Lucian shouted, urging us onward. "Death goddesses! Faster—run! We can't let the swarm catch us!"

I tried but the place where I'd been bitten or stung was aching and throbbing, making it hard to walk, let alone run.

My guys saw the difficulty I was having and they grabbed me under the arms again and dragged me along like a rag doll, the wide toes of my dune-shoes making wavy patterns in the sand as we raced through the desert.

"You didn't say anything about any fucking swarm of killing things," Drace roared at Lucian over my head.

"I've never seen them this close to the city—they're usually only in the deep desert," Lucian shouted back. "Come on—we have to get clear of them!"

"I thought you had immunity to anything out here," Drace demanded.

"I do, but that doesn't mean their bite doesn't hurt like fucking Hell!"

I could certainly attest to that. The feeling of being jabbed by red hot needles had never really ended. In fact, it was getting worse. Now it felt like someone was *twisting* the needles, trying to cause as much pain as possible. My entire leg was throbbing with every thudding step Drace and Lucian took across the sand.

Despite their best efforts, the humming, thrumming *moratas* – or "death goddesses" as Lucian had also called them, were getting closer. To my horror, one of them buzzed past my head and landed right on my billowing sleeve. I started to shake it off but I had to do a double take to be sure of what I was seeing first.

The *morata* had a body that looked like a cross between one of those huge grasshoppers you see in the spring sometimes, and a palmetto bug—which is, unfortunately, a huge, flying cockroach. But it wasn't the grotesque body or even the massive size of it that made me bite back a scream—it was the face.

The face—actually the entire head of the morata—was human. Small and chalk-white, it was the size of a Barbie doll head with short black hair, wide black eyes, and cruel red lips. I couldn't stop staring at it. It stared back at me and for an instant, I thought I saw pure hatred boiling in its ink-drop eyes. Then those curving red lips parted and two horrible long fangs shot out. It was going to bite me.

I shrieked breathlessly and shook my arm as well as I could while I was being dragged along with big hands under my armpits. It wasn't much but Lucian saw what was going on and batted the horrible insect-woman-thing off my sleeve before she could sink her yellow fangs into my arm.

"They're getting too close," he yelled at Drace. "Here—you take Rylee and run towards the city." He pointed to the huge, sand-colored walls with their black gates looming up out of the desert ahead of us. "They won't dare to follow you there."

He shoved me at Drace who caught me up in his arms, cradling me like a baby.

"What about you?" he shouted at Lucian.

"I'll draw them off." There was a grim expression on his face and I remembered what he'd said—just because he was immune to the bite of the *moratas* didn't mean it wouldn't hurt him to be bitten. He was sacrificing himself for us—preparing to bear what was surely going to be excruciating agony so Drace and I could get away.

Drace seemed to realize the same thing because he shook his head.

"You don't have to do this, bond-mate!"

"Yes, I do—get Rylee to safety! Now!" And before either Drace or I could protest, Lucian veered off towards a nearby sand dune. He gave a whistling-hissing-cry as he ran that seemed to draw the swarming *moratas* towards him. I saw the black cloud of buzzing, horror-headed insects aim right for him and I bit my lip in terror. Even with immunity, how many stings could he take before they killed him? Surely no one could survive many of those awful burning bites without dying!

I had only been bitten once and my leg felt like someone had dipped it in kerosene and set it on fire—I couldn't imagine having that sensation but ten or twenty or a hundred times worse all over my body.

For a moment Drace and I stood staring, then he said, "Come on," as though I had any choice, and began running with me still in his arms, aiming for the high walls that surrounded the city.

"No! *No!*" I beat against his broad chest, tears stinging my eyes. "No, we can't leave him back there—he'll die! He'll *die.*"

"You think I don't know that?" Drace's gravely voice was grim. "But he's right—we have to get you to safety first, baby. Once I do, I'm going back for him—I swear."

"I don't matter—I'm not important," I insisted. Despite the horrible pain in my leg and the disgusting humanoid insects, I had a strong—almost overwhelming—feeling that we shouldn't be parted. That the three of us needed to stay together, no matter what.

But Drace refused to slow down. "Hell yes, you're important—Lucian feels the same way I do. You're our female—we have to protect you," he insisted. "Anyway, look—we're almost there."

The city gates were looming closer. There was a wide road of some dirty-white stone extending out from them like a sidewalk to safety.

"Gonna leave you on the road where it's safe and go back for Lucian," Drace told me. Before I could answer he set me down as gently as he could, turned, and jogged back into the desert.

"Be careful!" I shouted after him and then felt like crying. What a stupid thing to say! How could he be careful when he was going back into that swarm of *things?* There was no way to stay safe in such circumstances.

*Both – I'm going to lose them both!* I felt tears welling in my eyes but a hot, dry desert wind whipped them away. The sun, which seemed like it had been setting for hours, suddenly dipped almost to the edge of the horizon. The city gates at my back cast long, ominous shadows over the shifting silver dunes—and over me. The wind picked up and seemed to hiss in my ears.

*"...beware the shadowsss and the thingsss that lurk in them! It is your death...your* **death."**

I shivered, suddenly cold despite the heat baking up from the stones under my feet. I wanted to get out of the shadows but when I tried to take a step, I nearly fell. My burning leg couldn't support my weight—not even a fraction of it. I was stuck standing on one leg, using just the toe of my other foot to balance.

"Drace!" I shouted, cupping my hands around my mouth to try and make my voice carry. "Lucian! Guys, where are you?"

The wind took my voice and whipped it away like a silk scarf, tossing it high before letting it die away to nothing in the empty, barren wasteland behind me.

I suppose at a time like this I should have been wondering how badly I was hurt and if I was poisoned or not. Or maybe I should have considered the fact that I was stranded alone on a strange planet light years from Earth with no chance of ever getting home.

Instead, all I could think of was my guys. Were Lucian and Drace okay? Or were they lost forever, buried under the weight of that horrible swarm of human-headed roaches, their bodies already being covered by the drifting sands of the desert?

At last the sun sank completely and not one but two moons rose in the Denarin night sky. One was vast and blue, much bigger than Earth's moon and the other was smaller with a pinkish cast. It seemed to flit around the bigger moon and I wondered hazily if it was orbiting the larger planetoid. Was it possible that Denaris's moon had a moon of its own? And why should I care since I was never going to see my guys again?

My throat was dry and sore from yelling and holding back tears but I shouted their names again anyway. Begging them to come back to me — to hurry up because I was scared.

"Lucian? Drace? *Please!* Please, come back to me — please!"

*It's too late. They're gone – gone,* whispered a nasty little voice in my head. *Gone and they're never coming ba –*

The sight of a large, male figure staggering out of the dunes to my right shut the nasty voice up in an abrupt and very satisfying way. Squinting into the moonlit darkness, I thought it was Drace — it was big enough to be him, anyway. But there was something strange about the figure. It was shaggy around the edges, almost…furry, which didn't make a lick of sense. But still, I couldn't shake the impression.

"Drace?" I whispered, my lips so dry they were almost cracking. "Drace, is that…is that *you?*"

The huge, shaggy figure seemed to shake itself and change somehow. When it came closer I saw that I had been mistaken — it wasn't furry after all. And it wasn't an it — it was Drace and he was staggering under the weight of Lucian, who was tossed over one of his broad shoulders like a sack of grain.

"Drace!" I could have cried I was so happy to see him.

I wanted to run to him but I didn't dare — my leg wouldn't let me move at all. I just had to stand there, planted in one spot as he made his way through the moonlit dunes until he got to me.

"Are you okay?" I asked anxiously when he finally reached me. "Is Lucian all right?"

"See for yourself." With a low groan, he deposited the other man on the ground at my feet and collapsed beside him, completely worn out.

I bent over Lucian as well as I could, feeling at his corded throat for a pulse. At first I couldn't find it but then, just as I was about to panic, I felt a strong steady beat against the tips of my first and middle fingers.

"He's alive!" I whispered and this time I couldn't help crying. *"Alive!"*

"…'course I'm…alive," a weak voice muttered.

"Lucian?" I reached for him and fell as my injured leg gave way.

He sat up, an obvious effort on his part, and caught me, cradling me in his arms. Drace was right beside him. He put a strong hand on my back steadying me. I felt surrounded by their warmth, by their big bodies.

*Safe,* I thought. *Now that we're all together again we're safe.*

"Lucian!" I whispered, pressing myself against his chest. "I thought…I was so afraid."

"I'm fine, *ma 'frela,*" he assured me. "I only passed out from the pain of so many bites—my body has already metabolized the poison." He frowned. "But you—you will not be fine if we do not get you some treatment quickly."

"What do you mean?" I asked. "My leg still hurts but actually it's feeling a lot better than it was. The burning sensation is almost all gone."

Lucian's face went pale. "It's feeling *better?* That's not a good sign, Rylee."

"What? How can less pain be a bad sign?" I demanded. "I mean—"

"We need to get to my apartment in the city as soon as possible," he interrupted me. "I have a dose of *morata* anti-venom there, in case a visiting business partner from another clan is bitten. We *must* get to it."

"Why?" I started to ask. "I mean—"

Just then, the world started to spin around my head, making me feel dizzy and sick.

"Frozen Hells, she's getting faint!" I heard Drace exclaim.

"The venom is working on her…one of the most potent in the world. We have to get her to the city—private transports by the gate," Lucian told him. "Can you help?"

"I dragged your sorry ass out of the desert, didn't I?" Drace growled.

"Yes, you did." I had a blurred impression of Drace nodding at the other man. "Thank you — you risked your life for me. You didn't need to do that."

"Bond-mates risk for each other," Drace growled. "That's all."

"But how did you keep from getting stung yourself? You didn't use your second nature, did you?"

"Had to. There was no choice," Drace said roughly.

"But—" Lucian began

"Come on," Drace interrupted. "Like you said, we need to get our female out of here."

I felt them lifting me again only this time it was Lucian carrying me. The shadows of the city gates fell over my face again, plunging me into darkness and I knew no more.

# Chapter Sixteen

## Rylee

My eyelids fluttered several times on the frantic trip to Lucian's apartment. I had a blurred impression of my guys hustling me into some kind of hovering vehicle and a male voice asking where they wanted to go. Lucian gave instructions and we rose up into the sky.

*Flying cars,* I remember thinking hazily. *Oh my God, they have flying cars, just like in the Jetsons.* Which was my favorite vintage cartoon when I was a kid.

I blacked out again and the next thing I knew, Drace was holding me in his arms while Lucian pressed his palm flat to the surface of a door made of rich, dark blue wood and trimmed in gold leaf. His handprint lit up and the door clicked open.

"In here," I heard him saying. "Put her on the couch—I'll get the anti-venom injection."

Drace settled on the couch across from the front door—a high-legged, plush affair with gold brocade fabric—still holding me. The pain was all gone from my leg now—in fact, I couldn't feel much of anything at all in my right thigh where I'd been bitten. I just felt spacey and cold—really, *really* cold, despite the big, warm, male body cradling me.

"Drace?" I mumbled, trying to focus on his face. "What...where...?"

"Don't worry, baby," he murmured, though his own face looked terribly anxious. "Everything's gonna be okay. Lucian has some medicine that will fix you right up."

"Here!" Lucian was suddenly beside me holding a weird looking thing in one hand. It looked sort of like a hypodermic but instead of one long needle, it had dozens of tiny short ones. The liquid it was filled with was a bright, vivid blue.

"What's that?" I asked groggily. "Looks like...you're about to inject me with...with Windex."

"Hold still," was all Lucian said before ripping open one of my billowing sleeves and jabbing the multi-needle hypodermic against the skin of my arm.

The minute the needles bit into my flesh, I felt a flaring heat through my body. Then the pain in my leg returned, only a hundred times worse.

"Ah!" I shrieked, jack-knifing in Drace's arms. "Lucian, that *hurts! It burns!*"

"That's a good sign—it's supposed to," he said grimly. "I'm sorry, *ma 'frela,* but I'd be much more worried if it *didn't* hurt."

As he spoke, the burning agony in my leg suddenly disappeared as quickly as it had come.

"Whew..." I breathed a sigh of relief as my muscles unknotted. I collapsed against Drace's broad chest.

"You okay, baby?" he asked anxiously.

"Yes. The pain is gone now." I wiped an arm over my forehead. "Glad that's over."

Drace looked relieved too but Lucian looked more worried than ever. What was it about this awful venom that made pain a *good* sign?

"It shouldn't be over this quickly," Lucian said. "The anti-venom gives pain for hours as it's neutralizing the poison infecting your system."

*"Hours?"* I stared at him in horror. I couldn't imagine experiencing that burning, stabbing agony for hours—I would go *crazy.*

"What does it mean that the pain faded so quickly?" Drace asked. "Come on, Lucian—what aren't you telling us?"

The big green alien shook his head. "That the anti-venom isn't working. Maybe because Rylee has different blood chemistry than a Denarin."

"Well, what can you do about it?" Drace demanded.

"First I need to see where she was bitten." Lucian looked at me questioningly.

"Here." I pointed to the loose trousers made of silvery-tan linen. "My right inner thigh."

Lucian didn't even try to get the trousers off me, he just grabbed the fabric and ripped a huge, gaping hole in it.

"Lucian!" I started to protest, then I saw the place where the *morata* had bitten me and the protest died on my lips.

There, on my inner thigh, were two tiny blood red dots. *Almost like a spider bite,* I thought sickly. But unlike a spider bite, there were crooked black lines running from the red dots—black veins of pure corruption tracing over the smooth brown of my skin.

"Oh my God," I whispered weakly. "That...doesn't look so good."

"It's *not* so good," Drace growled. "Look, Lucian, I know you want to keep a low profile but we need to get her to a house of healing *now.*"

"That won't do any good." Lucian snapped. He ran both hands through his hair in a gesture of pure agitation. "Don't you think I'd sacrifice my social status in a heartbeat to save our female? But what I just gave Rylee is the strongest anti-venom available. They won't be able to do anything for her in a healing house but make her comfortable."

"Make me comfortable?" I was feeling more and more unreal. "You mean make me comfortable so I can *die?*"

"They don't call the *moratas* 'death goddesses' for no reason," Lucian said grimly. "Unless it's treated quickly, their bite is invariably deadly to one who isn't of the Fang Clan or mated to one of the Fang Clan."

"Stop it, Lucian," Drace said harshly. "You're scaring Rylee."

"She is right to be scared—we all are." Lucian knelt in front of me, cupping my cheek. "*Ma 'frela,* this is on my head. I should have protected you better."

"You tried," I said numbly. "I was the one who didn't want to wear the ugly-ass boots. I'm sorry, Lucian—I should have listened to you."

"Stop it," Drace barked. "Both of you stop talking like Rylee is going to…to die." He coughed, as though the words choked him. "There must be something we can do — there *has to be a solution!*"

"But what can we do?" I asked. Lucian said the bite of the *moratas* is fatal to anyone who isn't Fang Clan or bonded to someone from the Fang Clan."

"That's it!" Lucian was suddenly on his feet again and pacing.

"What's it?" Drace demanded. "If you have a solution, now's the time to share bond-mate."

"You said it—'bond-mate'." Lucian pointed at him. "I was thinking last night when the three of us were together that you and I aren't the only temporary bond-mates in this equation — Rylee is too. She's part of us, Drace, even if only temporarily."

"Not enough to save her, apparently," Drace said angrily. "You only have to look at her fucking leg to see that, Lucian. If *I* didn't get any of your immunity, she *sure* as Hell didn't."

"It doesn't matter if either of you have my immunity — the question is can I give it to you now?" Lucian said.

"What?" Drace frowned. "What are you talking about?"

"Our tie to Rylee isn't strong because we haven't been physical with her — not really since every time we've touched her intimately we've been in the dream-realm." Lucian was still pacing, thinking this out as he spoke.

"Are you suggesting we bond her to us right now? That we seal our bond?" Drace asked. "Because that would be permanent, Lucian. I'll do it to save her life — I'll do anything. But that means you and I will never be free of each other."

"No," I said quickly. "I don't want you tying yourselves together permanently on my account." Besides, I knew the bonding process was sexual and right at the moment, with my right leg looking like a roadmap of Hell, I was *so* not feeling sexy. I didn't think I could handle the whole "two poles in one hole" thing even in the best of health, let alone when I was pumped full of deadly poison. "There has to be another way," I said.

"There's no time for further bonding now." Lucian waved the suggestion away impatiently. "I'm just saying that there might be enough of a connection between us for me to transfer my immunity to you, Rylee." He looked at Drace. "But you'll have to help too."

"Anything," Drace said hoarsely. "Anything to save our female—you know that."

"I know." Lucian gave him a grateful look and then turned to me. "I'm going to have to bite you, *ma 'frela,*" he said. "Bite you and inject you with my own essence which carries my personal antibodies against the *morata* venom."

"Um, okay," I said nervously, remembering how long and sharp his fangs could get. "Will it hurt?"

"As before, there will be a little pain at first when I penetrate your skin—then only pleasure," he promised.

"What can I do?" Drace asked.

"Since the anti-venom didn't work to neutralize it, you must suck the poison from her thigh," Lucian told him. "Whatever you do, do *not* ingest it. It's even more dangerous taken orally than injected into the flesh."

"Got it." Drace was already putting me down on the couch and crouching between my legs. He ripped at the desert trousers I was wearing, nearly tearing them all the way off me in his effort to get to the wound.

I got a funny, fluttery feeling in my stomach. The *morata* bite was very, *very* high on my thigh—so high that when Drace fastened his mouth over the two tiny wounds, his cheek was pressed against my panties. It made me feel nervous to have him down there—as I said, Phillip never had any interest in "going downtown" if you know what I mean.

But of course, there was nothing sexual about this situation. Drace was just trying to get the awful black venom out of my system. Right away, he started sucking and spitting like his life depended on it. Only it was *my* life that depended on it, I thought faintly. If this didn't work, if Lucian couldn't transfer his immunity to me...

*Don't think like that,* I ordered myself. *He'll be able to do it. He **has** to be able to do it. This is not how I die – killed by my own stupid fashion sense because I refused to wear the butt-ugly boots that could have protected me. I'll get another chance – won't I?*

I sure as hell hoped so. But before I could answer my own question, Lucian was standing behind me and leaning over the couch to whisper in my ear.

"Relax, *ma 'frela*," he murmured, tilting my head back and turning it to one side to bare my throat. "A moment of pain and then all is pleasure."

"All…all right," I whispered, suddenly more frightened than I wanted to admit. It was one thing to let him poke my thumb with those razor sharp fangs I saw growing from his mouth—it was something else entirely to let him sink them into my vulnerable throat. But what choice did I have?

"Now," Lucian whispered and then I felt the sharp double prick, like someone poking needles into my neck. Then his mouth latched onto me, just as Drace's mouth was latched on below, and something warm flooded my system.

Not just warm—hot. I don't know if you've ever had a CAT scan where they had to inject contrast into your veins but it was like that. A warm, flooding rush that swept over my entire body at once, making me gasp.

With the rush, came a pleasure like I had never known. It was as though a big, warm hand had somehow gotten beneath my skin and was stroking my entire body in all the right places, making me moan and arch my back because it felt so good.

"Lucian," I moaned, reaching up to tangle a hand in his thick, black hair. "Lucian, what's happening to me? I feel like…like I'm going to *come*."

He withdrew for just a moment. "Come then, *ma 'frela*," he murmured urgently. "The pleasure will help speed my essence through your body."

Drace looked up from my thigh. "I think I've gotten it all out now—what else can I do?"

"Feed the pleasure," Lucian urged him. "The more pleasure Rylee experiences, the more likely my immunity will take hold in her. Pleasure her, bond-mate—help her come."

"I don't—" I started to protest but Drace was already ripping my panties aside and pressing his mouth to my open pussy. At the same time, Lucian drove his fangs into my throat again, flooding me with more of his essence, more of the overwhelming pleasure.

I arched my back, thrusting my breasts up and Lucian tore at my blouse. Since we still hadn't figured out how to make a bra with the clothing simulator, ripping open my blouse put my bare breasts on full display. Lucian cupped them as he continued to inject me, twisting and tugging at my sensitive nipples while Drace bathed my pussy with long, hot strokes of his tongue.

I moaned, writhing helplessly between them as my orgasm hit me like a crushing wave.

"Lucian!" I wailed, one hand buried in his black hair and the other reaching down to fist tight in Drace's brown locks. "Drace! Oh my God, I'm coming! You're making me come *so hard!*"

And then the front door clicked open and a light, refined female voice said, "Lucian darling? What's all the fuss going on in here?"

# Chapter Seventeen

## Rylee

Have you ever been caught in the act of doing something either really wrong or really embarrassing or both? Like shoplifting or picking your nose or…I don't know, *having oral sex with two guys on a couch when one of their parents walks in?*

Well, anyway, I was having oral sex with *one* of them — Drace. Or he was having it with me, however you wanted to look at it. And the fact that I was having a screaming orgasm didn't help either.

The nice, refined-looking older lady with olive green skin a shade lighter than Lucian's and black hair just like his stood rooted to the spot right in front of the couch where our little three-way healing session had somehow turned into a three-way sex show.

"Oh my God," I gasped, when my brain registered that we were no longer alone in Lucian's apartment. "*Oh my God!*"

I struggled to get away but Lucian still had his head down with his fangs buried in my throat and Drace had his face pressed between my thighs and he did *not* want to stop licking. I don't even think either of them realized anyone else was in the room — they were *that* into healing and tasting me. It would have been amazingly hot if it wasn't so damn embarrassing.

The way they were focused on me and me alone presented a huge problem — as long as Lucian kept injecting me with his essence and Drace kept licking me like his favorite flavor of ice cream, *I couldn't stop coming.* And the woman — who I assumed must be Lucian's mom — just stood there, frozen to the spot, watching with a look of dawning horror spreading over her refined features.

"Lucian!" I gasped desperately as the waves of pleasure continued to roll over me. "Drace! Guys, stop — *stop!*"

"Don't wanna stop," Drace looked up, his mouth and chin all shiny with my juices. "Gods, you taste amazing, baby—I could eat your sweet pussy all night."

"Stop it—stop talking like that!" I begged him. "We…we have company."

"Company?" He frowned and looked around. "Where?"

"Behind you—in front of me," I panted. "I think…think it's Lucian's *mother!*"

"Mother?" Lucian must have finally heard me because he withdrew his fangs at once and stood up quickly. "*Mother?*" he said again, speaking to the woman who was still standing rooted to the spot with a look of horror on her face. "What are you doing here?"

"I might ask you the same thing!" Her voice trembled. "Lucian, your fathers and I have been missing you and you haven't been returning calls so I came to check on you and I find…find *this.*"

She gestured with one bejeweled hand—(Did I mention she had on enough rich and stylish jewelry to choke a horse?)—at Drace and me as though we were some disgusting, dirty garbage that had gotten into her son's tastefully appointed apartment by some dreadful accident.

"Mother—" Lucian began.

"I mean, who *are* these people? Did you go off planet to pick up some…" She pointed at me. "Some *trollop?*"

Drace growled and Lucian frowned.

"Don't speak that way about Rylee. She's a lady—you just happened to catch us in a, *ahem*, compromising position because you walked in without announcing yourself."

"Thanks," I muttered, sitting up and drawing the tattered remains of my desert clothing around me. It wasn't easy to cover myself since the guys had torn huge holes in both my trousers and blouse but I tried.

"And where and when did you find yourself a Beta?" Lucian's mother went on, as though he hadn't spoken. "I mean, we've discussed this ad nauseum, darling—there are simply *no* suitable Betas in our social class for you to bond with. So I thought we decided that you just simply *wouldn't bond.*"

"No, *you* decided that, Mother. You and my fathers." Lucian's voice was ice cold. "You decided that I should never have mates or a family of my own because none of my choices pleased you."

"And I'm not a Beta," Drace growled, standing up and turning around. "I'm an Alpha, the same as your son."

"You're a...a...what?" Lucian's mother got that shocked, horrified look on her face all over again. "Surely...surely not," she whispered, looking positively faint.

"Smell for yourself." Drace took a step towards her.

I saw her lady-like nostrils wrinkle and she made a face as though she'd just smelled dog-shit.

"You *are* an Alpha!" she exclaimed, fresh horror suffusing her face. "But why...how...?" Clearly she couldn't bring herself to finish the question. She just shook her head and looked at her son mutely for an explanation.

For a moment a look of pure misery passed over Lucian's sharp features. Then he took a deep breath and lifted his chin.

"Mother," he said calmly. "Meet my temporary bond-mates. This is Drace, an Alpha of the Claw Clan. We were accidentally bonded at a Clan gathering two months ago."

"The *Claw Clan?*" Lucian's mother looked like she might faint. "Lucian, are you trying to *kill* me?"

"And this is Rylee, the female who's helping us break our bond," Lucian went on flatly, ignoring her dramatic words. "She's a Pure One and a *La-ti-zal* so you might want to apologize for calling her a *trollop.*"

"A Pure One you say? From a closed planet?" She turned to me with renewed interest, though I noticed she *didn't* apologize for the name calling.

"From Earth," I said, standing up and holding out a hand to her while I clutched my torn clothing with the other hand.

Lucian's mother looked at my outstretched hand as though I'd offered her a dead fish and she didn't know what to do with it.

Suddenly I understood.

"Oh, sorry—on Earth when we meet someone for the first time we shake hands. But I'm sure you probably don't have the same customs we do."

"Actually, we do pat fingers." She showed how by raising both hands and lightly touching the tips of her long fingers together. "But I'm not sure where your hand has been lately, dear. So I'll just give you a verbal greeting if you don't mind."

"Oh...of course." I withdrew my hand, my cheeks getting so hot I was sure they were going to catch my hair on fire. "Er...sorry."

"That's quite all right, dear. Welcome to Denaris." She turned a laser-sharp look on Lucian. "Darling, might I have a word with you in the food-prep area?"

Lucian looked like he'd rather walk barefoot over a mile of hot coals but he only nodded. "Of course, Mother."

"Thank you, darling." And she led the way out of the richly appointed living room and around the corner.

"Whew..." I let out a breath. "Well *that* was awkward!"

"More than awkward—*wrong*." Drace was frowning like a thundercloud. "You know, I just couldn't find a Beta I clicked with and I thought it was the same with Lucian—but now I'm beginning to wonder. Did she and his fathers *really* decide he wouldn't be allowed to bond with anyone because they didn't approve of any of his choices? That's fucking cruel!"

"I don't know," I said thoughtfully. "If that's what they did to him, it *is* awful. But you've known him longer than I have."

"Yeah, but we didn't really start talking until you showed up, baby," he told me. "C'mon."

"Where are we going?" I asked as I followed him around the corner.

"To find out what's going on. Just keep out of sight and be quiet."

"Drace, no!" I put a hand on his arm. "We can't do that—it's eavesdropping!"

"The hell we can't! Lucian is our bond-mate—we need to know what the fuck is going on with him," he growled. "Are you coming with me or not?"

"All right," I hissed. "But we'd better not get caught!"

\* \* \* \* \*

# Lucian

"All right now, tell me how you got into this mess and how you intend to get out of it? How can you *possibly* break a psy-bond? It's never been done before!"

That's my mother—she's never been one to mince words.

Rapidly, I explained how Drace and I had ingested *ylla* rolls with pieces of the same bonding-bud in them and had become psy-bonded in the first place.

"But we haven't sealed the bond," I told her. "Which makes us think it will be possible to break it."

"You haven't sealed it *yet* you mean." She made a face, a delicate curl of her lip that indicated disgust. "But I saw what you were doing with those...those *people.*"

"Those people are my bond-mates, Mother," I said, frowning. "Even if their status is only temporary, I won't have you speaking ill of them."

"But, *darling,* just *look* at them," she nearly wailed. "Another Alpha—one of the *Claw Clan* no less? And that...that *girl.* If she's a *La-ti-zal* I'll eat my diamonds!"

"She *is* a *La-ti-zal,*" I snapped angrily. "I have witnessed her power first hand."

"Oh, and what's her power then? *Whoring?*" my mother demanded.

Of course then I wished I'd kept my mouth shut.

"She's...a Binder," I said reluctantly. "Rylee is a Binder."

"A *what?* But I thought you said you were trying to get *free* of them! Not bind them more closely to you!"

"We *are* trying to get free of each other." I couldn't keep the exasperation out of my voice. "But we were told by Tanta Loro—"

"What? You went to the Sea Witch?" My mother looked near fainting again—something she was prone to in her more dramatic moments. "This just gets worse and worse!"

"She was the only one who offered us any hope, Mother," I said grimly. "Even the Empress's own physician said we would be stuck together for life. Tanta Loro at least showed us a way out."

"And what way is that?" she demanded.

"There is a certain...artifact we need to get in order to sever our bond." I didn't want to tell her too much.

"What artifact? How can it possibly help you?"

"That's my business," I said shortly. All you need to know is that I'm working on it."

"Well you'd better work on it quickly," she snapped. "Do you know what would happen to your fathers and I if it were to become known that you were bonded to another Alpha—an Alpha of the *Claw Clan*? Who do you suppose they would think was playing the Beta's roll in all this?"

"I told you, Mother, we haven't sealed the bond so *neither* of us is playing the Beta's roll," I said through gritted teeth. "I know how bad this looks but don't worry—I'm taking steps to correct it. And I swear it won't impact you or my fathers."

"It had better *not.*" She crossed her arms over her chest and did her best to look down at me disapprovingly, just as she had when I was a small boy. The effect was somewhat mitigated by the fact that I was two feet taller than her now, but somehow she still managed. "If the ladies on the Fashion Council found out that my only child was bonded to an Alpha of the Claw Clan—"

"Don't worry, they *won't.*" I had to work to keep my voice calm and even.

"Just be certain you *don't* seal the bond or do anything else to strengthen your ties with those two either," she continued, as though I'd bonded myself to a couple of scruffy, disgusting indigents. No doubt to her, that was exactly what Rylee and Drace appeared to be. "Better no bond-mates at all than the wrong *kind* of bond-mates."

A sudden weariness overcame me—a sorrow so old it seemed it had been part of me forever.

"Yes, Mother," I said. "So you've been telling me my entire life."

Who could believe such a thing? That it was better to live a life of constant loneliness and emptiness rather than try to fill the void with someone of an "unacceptable" class or clan? That it was better to be alone than try to find someone to love outside the narrow strata of society my parents approved of?

I had.

I who had chosen to bury myself in my work and abstain from any kind of love because there were no "suitable" Betas to bond with. I who had sworn to myself that having a Triumvirate bond with another male and a female we both loved meant nothing to me.

I who had lied to myself for years.

"Now I'm not going to say anything to your fathers," my Mother said, interrupting my bleak thoughts. "Because I *know* you're going to get this fixed. And when you do, darling, I promise we'll try again to find you some suitable Beta to bond with and then the two of you can find a *nice* girl from the *right* class and clan to take as a mate. All right?"

It was on the tip of my tongue to say I didn't want anyone else besides Rylee and Drace...but then I stopped myself because it was ridiculous. We were on a quest to be free of each other. Why would I tell my mother I wanted to stay with them?

"Now, darling—" she began again but just then Rylee ran in to the food prep area, her torn clothes clutched in one hand and her eyes wild.

"Lucian, it's Drace!" she exclaimed. "Come quick—he just collapsed!"

# Chapter Eighteen

## Rylee

Lucian's mother trailed behind us as I led Lucian around the corner to where Drace was out cold.

We'd been standing there, eavesdropping for all we were worth and listening to Lucian's mother go on about social class and finding the right people to be bonded to when he'd suddenly put a hand to his head and then to his throat.

"What?" I asked, looking up at him. "What's wrong?"

"Not...sure." He shook his head as though to clear it. "Feel...strange. Dizzy. My throat burns."

"Burns?" I asked but just then his eyes rolled up in his head and he started to fall.

He was way bigger than me so even though I was right beside him I couldn't do much to stop his fall. I could only slow it down a bit. He was huge and *really* heavy—all muscle as I had observed on numerous occasions. So the most I could do was ease him down to the ground and turn him on his side, in case he threw up. Then I ran for Lucian.

I rapidly explained the details of Drace's collapse as he listened to his breathing and felt for a pulse.

"A burning in the throat, you say?" he said, frowning when I finished talking. "Damn it—he must have ingested some of the *morata* poison he sucked out of your thigh. I *told* him how dangerous it was!"

"What? But why wouldn't it affect him until now?" I demanded. "I mean, he was plenty frisky earlier. Uh, I mean..." I blushed and trailed off when I saw Lucian's Mom was listening in, a slightly disgusted look on her face.

"It's slow acting when orally ingested—slow acting but twice as deadly. Even anti-venom won't save him now—not that I have another dose of it. The only one I had I gave to you."

"Oh no!" I put a hand to my mouth. "Please, Lucian—can't you heal him the way you healed me? Can't you bite him and inject him with your essence and your immunity?"

He frowned and appeared to consider it.

"I *could* but Drace will not like it. He might even prefer it if I left him to die."

"What?" I nearly yelled. "What are you talking about? How could he prefer to die? You need to bite him, damn it! Bite him *now.*"

He sighed. "You don't understand, Rylee—in the Fang Clan, the Alpha bites for only two reasons—to heal and to pleasure his mates. The Beta, though he has rudimentary fangs, does *not* bite. So in biting Drace, I will be treating him like my inferior—my Beta— and stripping him of much of his dignity in the process."

"Look, I don't care about your crazy customs and who bites who," I exclaimed. "Drace needs help and you're the only one who can give it to him!"

"Lucian?" his mother said, interrupting our argument. "A moment, if you please?"

"I don't really have time right now, Mother," he said. "I'm trying to devise a way to save my bond-mate without emasculating him and making him hate me."

"But think about it, darling—why save him at all?"

"What?" Lucian and I said, looking up at her at the same time.

"What do you mean, don't save him?" I demanded.

"Think about it, darling—breaking a psy-bond, well—it's very tricky. In fact, it's never been done," Lucian's mother spoke only to him, ignoring me completely. "No matter what that Wave-Dweller witch told you, it's likely to be impossible. So the only way you'll ever be free of this...this *person* is if you just...let the bond die."

"You mean if I let *Drace* die," Lucian said flatly. "Don't you?"

"Well...yes. But just hear me out," she continued quickly. "You said yourself, treating him like a Beta is the ultimate insult. He'd probably *rather* die than have you do that. You should let him go with *dignity*, darling. Just let him slip peacefully away..."

"No!" I shouted, jumping to my feet. "What is *wrong* with you?" I glared at Lucian's mother. "How can you stand there and be so cold-blooded about letting someone *die*? Do you know that Drace just saved your son's life not an hour ago in the desert?"

"And I'm certainly very grateful for that, dear" she said coolly, looking down her nose at me. "But maybe you'd better stay out of matters you don't understand. As Lucian told you, treating another Alpha as though he was a Beta is the worse insult a male can give another male here on Denaris. It's better to just...let the bond *expire*."

I stared at her, disbelieving. She was talking about Drace like he was a carton of milk that was going bad anyway and should just be thrown out with the trash.

"Stop saying it like that!" I exclaimed. "Stop acting like it's only the bond that will die! Drace is a person—a fine, upstanding, honorable guy, er—male. And just because he's not of your social class or your clan doesn't make him any less worthy to live."

She put a beringed hand to her chest. "I never said—"

"Oh, yes you did!" I said. I turned to Lucian. "Tell me you're not going to listen to this! Tell me—"

But I broke off when I saw he was already kneeling over Drace's still form with his fangs extended.

"Lucian, no!" His mother's eyes widened. "Don't do this!"

He looked up briefly.

"I have to, Mother—Rylee is right. Even if Drace hates me for what I'm about to do, he deserves the right to live."

"Fine." Her lips thinned down to a white line. "Do what you want—throw your life away! Just *don't* let anyone else know what you're doing. The family status *must* be preserved at all costs."

Lucian didn't answer. Instead, he sank those long, gleaming fangs of his deep into Drace's throat. I saw his mother from the corner of my eye, her face all pinched and angry.

"I cannot watch this," she said stiffly, and left, picking her way across the floor as though the gorgeously woven carpet was land-mined with dog turds.

I watched her go, wondering how she could live with herself. Then I heard a shout and a scuffling sound.

Turning, I saw Drace with Lucian's fangs still buried in the side of his neck. He was fighting and fishtailing, his back arching and his heels in their thick desert boots drumming on the floor.

"Oh my God!" I gasped, rushing up to them. "Drace! Lucian—is he okay? What can I do?"

Lucian, of course, couldn't answer me—he was too busy injecting his essence into the other male. It must have been burning Drace because he was trying to get free and a deep growl was rising in his throat.

I frowned. It hadn't hurt or burned when Lucian had injected *me*. In fact, it had felt *amazing*. It…

My thoughts trailed off as my eyes came to rest on the crotch of Drace's black trousers. There was an unmistakable bulge there, straining against the tight leather.

Drace wasn't in pain—he was having intense pleasure. But from the look on his face, he wasn't enjoying it—not a bit. His eyes were open now and his teeth were bared in a grimace of pure rage.

At last, Lucian withdrew and sat back on his heels, looking down at Drace.

"There," he said dryly. "You won't die now, at least."

"You fucker," Drace said thickly. In one swift move he sat up and punched Lucian squarely in the jaw.

\* \* \* \* \*

## Drace

"Stop it! Stop, you two!" Rylee was suddenly all over me, keeping me from punching my bastard of a bond-mate again by putting herself between us.

"Get out of the way," I told her, trying to get around her to Lucian. "He deserves it and he knows it."

"Lucian just saved your life!" Rylee exclaimed. She grabbed my face in both her soft little hands and made me look her in the eyes. "Do you hear me? He saved you—the way you saved him by carrying him out of the desert!"

"Yeah, well I didn't treat Lucian like a fucking Beta to save him," I snarled.

"I had no choice." Lucian was sitting across from me, rubbing his jaw with one hand. "It was either bite you and inject you or watch you die."

"You should have let me die, then!" I shouted. Inside the tight confines of my leathers, I could feel my shaft throbbing shamefully. It was wrong to take pleasure from the touch of another Alpha and yet Lucian had forced it on me, the fucker.

I wanted to kill him.

"Stop it!" Rylee insisted again. "Listen to me—both of you. I don't understand why you're being like this and *I don't care!* The fact is, you both saved each other's lives because you *care* about each other. You need to accept that and move on!"

"I can't move on from this," I snarled. "He shamed me."

"How? Why?" She looked at me, an expression of exasperation on her lovely face. "Stop fighting and *explain* this to me, damn it! Why is it okay for Lucian to bite and heal *me* but not to heal *you* the same way?"

"It is because the bite of the Fang Clan gives sexual pleasure," Lucian said, answering for me. He sounded weary past the point of exhaustion and the look on his face was one of pure defeat. I could almost feel sorry for him—almost.

"So *what* if it gives sexual pleasure?" Rylee demanded. "I don't care if Lucian biting you made you come in your freaking pants—at least you're *still alive!*"

"A male without honor has no life," I growled.

"Oh, so he stole your honor by biting you and injecting feel-good juice into your neck?" She put a hand on her hip. "Get over it, Drace. You're acting like he bent you over the bed and...and did you up the ass!"

"I might as well have," Lucian said shortly. "I told you he would not appreciate being saved in such a way."

"Are you *serious?*" Rylee looked at both of us, her black eyes wide with dawning comprehension. "You really put biting on par with *screwing?*"

"It gives the same pleasure—it makes you come," I pointed out. Although I hadn't—it was a near thing, though. A few more minutes with my bond-mate's fangs buried in my throat and I would have gone off like a fucking rocket.

*Sick bastard,* I thought but I didn't know who I was thinking about—Lucian or me.

"And what's so wrong with that?" Rylee wanted to know.

"It's wrong because of the way our relationships work," Lucian explained wearily. "Drace would have had no problem with me penetrating and injecting him if he were a Beta. But since he is not, I have denigrated his honor and his status as an Alpha."

"So…you're homophobic but only towards other Alphas." Rylee shook her head. "I swear to God, this three-way stuff you guys have going on here is *crazy* confusing."

"It's hard to understand if you haven't been born into it," I admitted grudgingly.

"I'm *trying* to wrap my head around it." She stared at us. "So is this why everyone on the beach was giving us such nasty looks? Because they could smell that both of you were Alphas and they thought you were doing things together that only an Alpha and a Beta should do?"

"That and the fact that they were probably wondering which of us played the roll of Beta," Lucian said dryly.

"But why does *either* of you have to play that roll?" Rylee asked.

"We don't and we don't want anyone thinking we do," I growled. "Why do you think we need to be separated?"

"But—"

"Drace is right—we can't go on like this." Lucian sighed and ran a hand through his hair. "Tomorrow I'll contact Lord Mandrex and ask for a private meeting to see if he'll sell or loan me the key."

"Fuck tomorrow—call him tonight," I snapped. "The sooner we get free of each other the better."

"All right." Lucian's face went cold. "I'll place the call. But I'd ask that the two of you remain out of sight of the viewscreen."

"Why is that, *bond-mate*—are you ashamed of us? Afraid the rest of the city will find out your dirty *secret?*" It was a fucking low blow and I knew it but I was still so *angry* with him for treating me like a Beta the words came out before I could stop them. Hell—I didn't even try.

"No," Lucian said stiffly. "I am *not* ashamed. But Mandrex has a sharp business sense. If he gets even an inkling of our desperation to get the key from him the price will be more than any of us can afford."

"I think Lucian is right—we should let him do the talking." Rylee crossed her arms over her chest. "But first I want the two of you to make up."

"Make up?" I frowned at her. "What are you saying? You want me to forgive what he did?"

"In light of the fact that he saved your life? That's *exactly* what I want."

"You're wasting your time," Lucian said coldly. "Any Alpha—especially one from a primitive group like the Claw Clan—would hate another Alpha who penetrated and injected him."

"You think I'm primitive?" I snarled. "Why? Because I used my second nature to save your sorry ass? Or because your mother doesn't approve of me?"

"Pick one," Lucian snapped. "And leave my mother out of it. She just wants what's right for me."

"Like condemning you to a life of loneliness and desperation because none of the available Betas was good enough for your family?" I asked. "Yeah, Lucian, sounds like she really gives a huge fuck about you. Congratulations."

The minute the words left my mouth, I knew I had gone too far. Lucian's face went pale with rage and his lips thinned down to a narrow line.

"That," he said in a voice colder than a night on the dark side of the farthest moon, "Is none of your fucking business." He stepped up to me and poked one hard finger in my chest. "Don't talk about my mother or my family and stay *out of my life!*"

"*I'm trying!*" I roared, leaning in towards him to get right in his face. "Trying like hell to get out of your fucking life, you Fang Clan bastard!"

I think we would have come to blows if it wasn't for Rylee.

"Guys...*guys!*" She stepped between us again, putting a hand on each of our chests. Immediately, I felt a current of peace and love flowing from her. The feeling that I wanted to forgive Lucian—that I *had* to forgive him—suffused me like a drug.

*No—it's a trick—a trap! She's a Binder,* I reminded myself. *Lucian offered me the greatest insult one Alpha can give another—it can never be forgiven.*

I stepped away from her touch, breaking the current and all my rage returned. Across from me, Lucian stepped away too.

"Guys..." Rylee sounded near tears now. I hated to make her so upset—it tore me up inside. But I couldn't let go of my wounded pride.

Apparently, neither could Lucian.

"There are guest rooms along the central hallway," he said, still using that voice that could freeze boiling mercury. "Please feel free to make yourselves at home—both of you."

"So..." Rylee bit her lip, a look of uncertainty coming over her face. "So we're not all going to, uh, sleep together tonight?"

"I don't think that would be advisable," Lucian said. "After all, we want to be free of each other. Every time we have any kind of *intimacy* between us, it only binds us closer together."

"He's right," I made myself say, even though the thought of sleeping by myself instead of across from my bond-mate with our female between us gave me a bleak, empty feeling inside. "The closer we get, the more we bond. We need some distance," I said.

"Fine." Rylee swiped at her eyes which looked suspiciously bright. Her normally vibrant feminine scent was muted and sad.

"Fine," she said again. "I guess I'll go find myself a room and take a hot bath."

"There's a clothing sim in the utility room," Lucian told her. "Perhaps Drace can show you how to use it while I'm placing the call to Mandrex."

Then he turned away, leaving Rylee and me to stand alone, looking at each other. Only Rylee wouldn't look at me—she just turned her face away and swiped at her eyes.

"Come on," her voice was muffled. "Show me how to make something to sleep in. I need some rest."

I privately agreed with her and I noticed, even as we wandered down the long central hallway of the apartment that Lucian was already calling up the coordinates for Lord Mandrex.

*Soon,* I thought to myself. *We'll be free of each other soon.*

And wondered why the thought didn't bring me any joy.

* * * * *

# Lucian

"Ah, Mr. Nx'xis. Of the Fang Clan, isn't it?" Lord Mandrex asked when his personal attendant ushered him to the viewer and he appeared on my screen.

"It is." I struggled to keep my demeanor calm, despite what I'd just been through. I could still hear my bond-mate's voice ringing in my ears, *"I'm trying — trying like hell to get out of your life, you Fang Clan bastard!"*

Of course, what had I expected Drace to do? *Thank* me for treating him like a Beta? In the time we'd been together, despite our mutual distrust and dislike, neither of us had offered such a serious affront to the other.

Rylee, of course, didn't understand—she thought Drace ought to be grateful that I'd saved his life and not worry about anything else. But I had known what a grave insult I was offering my bond-mate, had known that he would hate me for penetrating and injecting him, and yet I had done it anyway. Even though, as my mother had so coldly pointed out, allowing him to die would have severed our bond and taken care of all my problems.

But I couldn't do that—couldn't let him die. It wasn't just my sense of honor that prevented me, either. There was…something else.

What? Why? Why had I saved Drace, even knowing he would hate me for it and that it would complicate my life even more? Why—

"…asked why you called me so late, Mr. Nx'xis. Is there a bad connection on your end?" Lord Mandrex's voice cut into my private misery and I jerked my head up to see he was watching me with a quizzical look on his face.

Like all Cantors he had sharp, aquiline features, bronze-sheened skin, and wide, jewel-like blue eyes that seemed to spin and shift. Some said they had hypnotic powers but I had never cared to stare long enough into a Cantor's eyes to find out for myself. *Unlike* most of the rest of his people, Mandrex had long black hair. Most Cantors had fine blond tresses like spun gold.

Mandrex *did* have the most important attribute of the Cantors though—a set of huge, feathery wings, vast enough to support a male and, some said, a female as well, the rumor being that Cantors mated in flight. The feathers of Lord Mandrex's wings were black instead of white or silver—another anomaly—and he kept them folded neatly at his back, wearing them rather like a black cape that rose above his shoulder and enfolded his body in darkness.

I wondered why he chose to live here, on Denaris, rather than on his home planet. Our planet's gravity was too heavy to allow a Cantor to take flight so he was stuck on the ground, unable to soar like the rest of his kind. Still, he seemed to like it fairly well—he'd even immersed himself in Denarin culture enough to become interested in buying artifacts from our past. I just hoped he'd be willing to sell them as well.

"My apologies," I said quickly. "There was a bit of static on my end for a moment. I'm sorry for calling you so late but I was hoping to catch you in time to set up a business meeting for tomorrow."

"A business meeting, is it?" He looked at me quizzically. "But what business can you and I have to conduct? You're a litigator—

you facilitate deals between the different clans, do you not? But as a Cantor, I am a neutral party—I have no need of litigation with any of my clients or business partners."

"That isn't exactly the kind of business I had in mind," I said, frowning. "You recently acquired an artifact—the Tanterine Key."

"Ah, yes..." He steepled his fingers and stared at me thoughtfully from those whirling, crystalline blue eyes. "The prize of my collection. And that's saying something—I've quite a number of antiquities from my adopted world's past."

"Yes, I know," I said evenly. "I wondered..." I took a deep breath. "Wondered if you would meet with me to discuss selling it. Selling the Key."

Mandrex frowned. "Out of the question."

"What about allowing me to *lease* it for a while, then?" I asked, trying not to sound desperate.

"You want to *lease* it? Lease it and do *what* with it?" A look of curiosity passed over Mandrex's dark face.

"I'm sorry, I can't tell you that," I said evenly. "But I could swear that the Key would be returned in the exact condition you leased it to me."

"You intrigue me, Mr. Nx'xis." He steepled his fingers under his chin again. "But I'm afraid I still won't meet with you."

"May I ask why not?" I said, keeping my voice calm though inside I was raging. "On what grounds do you deny me?"

"Oh, I'm not denying you," he said mildly. "Not at all."

"What? You just said you wouldn't meet with me!"

"I said I wouldn't meet with you as in you *alone*." He gave me a white smile which was somehow predatory. "I also want to meet your new bond-mate and the female the two of you have chosen together."

"What?" It felt as though all the blood had been drained from my body at once. *"What* did you say?"

"Your bond-mates," he said, crossing one leg casually over the other. "Bring them with you and I'll meet. Without them, my door is closed to you."

"But how...how did you know..." I couldn't even get the question out.

"Let's just say I have eyes and ears all over this city." Mandrex gave me his predatory grin again. "The hover-transport operator who drove you to your apartment is one of those in my employ. He thought two bonded Alphas and an obviously wounded off-world female staggering out of the desert might be of interest to me so he snapped a few images."

"Images?" I choked out, my blood turning to ice water in my veins. My mother's relentless harping on preserving the family status leapt immediately to my mind and wouldn't leave.

"Of course he had no idea who you were," Mandrex went on, oblivious to my reaction. "But imagine my surprise when I saw *your* face in those images, Mr. Nx'xis—you, a prominent business leader and a member of the most important family in all of Y'brith."

"Are you planning to blackmail me?" I asked stiffly, my stomach clenching like a fist. "Is that what you're leading up to?"

"Not as such." He looked thoughtful. "I think you can answer some questions for me...help assuage my curiosity on some matters of, shall we say, Denarin *intimate* relations."

"I don't—"

"Come tomorrow evening. My domicile, just an hour after sunset," he directed. "And bring your bond-mates with you. Both of them."

"But the images," I said urgently. "What about the images?"

"Ah yes, those." He smiled mockingly. "Don't worry, Mr. Nx'xis. I can keep your secret...for a time."

Then the viewscreen flickered and his image was gone.

# Chapter Nineteen

## Rylee

"What the fuck does he want with all three of us?" Drace growled as we stood in the wide marble entry hall of Lord Mandrex's private mansion and waited for him to make an appearance.

The marble was pure black shot through with streaks of copper and there were thick marble pillars that matched — a row of them on either side of us. Standing between the tall black columns stretching up to the vaulted ceiling above made me feel like a child lost in a strange, alien forest.

At least I was dressed for the occasion. I was wearing a low-cut red gown which brought out my creamy skin-tones and some heels to match which I'd made in the clothing simulator at Lucian's place. I had my hair just right and I was looking pretty damn hot, if I did say so myself. Lucian and Drace were also wearing dark, formal suits, much like the one Lucian had had on when they first got me from the Alien Mate Index — they were both looking extra spiffy tonight. But even though the three of us were dressed to the nines, I couldn't help feeling intimidated by the huge house we were in.

"It does seem strange that he wanted to see all of us," I said tentatively.

"I don't know what he wants," Lucian said stiffly.

He'd been cold and withdrawn all day as we waited for our audience with Lord Mandrex. And Drace has been angry and growly. Neither of them was speaking to the other. It was enough to make me want to shake them both — only I knew it wouldn't do any good.

Last night I had slept in a bed alone and had been surprised by how much I missed them. Not just the dream sex, even though it was nice—I missed having their two big, warm bodies on either side of me. Missed the feeling of closeness, of being cherished and protected. It made me sad to see them so angry with each other, especially since it seemed like they had no real reason to be. So what if Lucian had penetrated Drace with his fangs? The two of them were acting like homophobic idiots and there was no need for it.

"Maybe the reason Mandrex wants to see all of us has something to do with you, Rylee," Drace speculated. "Something to do with you being a Pure One? Your kind is incredibly rare—he might want to know where we got you."

"Well I hope you're not going to tell him! It's bad enough the Commercians are selling unsuspecting Earth girls without you two advertising for them," I said, frowning.

"It's doesn't matter what he wants—I don't like the fact that he knows about the three of us at all," Lucian snapped before Drace could reply.

"You said he got the information from the taxi driver...er, the transport driver, I mean?" I said. "And that he has lots of people like that reporting to him?"

"Apparently," Lucian said shortly.

I frowned. "But that's so weird. Why would he have a whole network of spies spread out over the city?"

"You never can tell about Cantors and Mandrex is shifty even for one of his kind," Drace growled. "There have been rumors about him...rumors about why he lives here instead of his home planet of Cantor...reasons his own people don't want him—"

"Ah, Mr. Nx'xis, Mr. Gr'nez, and Ms. Hale, I presume." A deep, melodious voice which filled the entire entryway with echoes and interrupted Drace's words.

We all looked up and saw Lord Mandrex standing at the top of a long flight of black marble steps. He was dressed in a dark, fitted suit with a black feathery cape to match. The cape rose higher than his head and rustled when he moved. I wondered what it was made of but then I remembered what Lucian had said about Cantors—they could fly. So it wasn't a cape at all—the black feathery mantle around his broad shoulders was a pair of wings.

As he walked down the long flight of steps to greet us, I wished he would spread them out so we could see them—they had to be huge if they could lift a man his size into the air. He was every bit as tall and muscular as Drace and Lucian but with coal black hair and blazing, electric-blue eyes that seemed to swirl hypnotically. His skin was coppery—and I don't mean just dark tan—it literally had a coppery, metallic sheen to it.

"Lord Mandrex," Lucian said, answering our host's greeting. "I've come and brought both of my *temporary* bond-mates with me, as you requested. Can we please discuss business now?"

"Certainly." Mandrex nodded genially. "But would you care to join me for dinner first? I always find I'm in a better mood for business after I eat rather than trying to deal on an empty stomach."

We all glanced at each other, although it was mainly Lucian and Drace glancing at me and me looking back. I found I missed the way they'd communicated silently with each other back before they started fighting. The rift between them still seemed silly to me— Lucian had saved Drace's life just as Drace had saved his in the desert. They ought to be thick as thieves. Instead, there was a cold wall of ice growing between them and nothing I did or said seemed to be able to thaw it.

"Of course we'd love to have dinner with you," I said, when neither of the guys answered. "I'm from Earth so I'm still getting used to Denarin food. It will be a pleasure to try Cantor cuisine as well."

"Oh, I'm afraid I eschew all things from my home world—even the food," Mandrex said, shifting so that his black wings rustled. "But my chef has prepared some delicious dishes from both the desert and the jungle regions of Denaris that you may not have tried yet."

*Food from both Drace's home region and Lucian's,* I thought. That couldn't be a coincidence. Was he trying to prove exactly how much he knew about us? And if so, why?

"Would you care to take my arm? The dining chamber is this way." Lord Mandrex held out a black-clad arm to me.

I took a step towards him and saw, for the first time, that he had a jagged white scar running down the left side of his face. It started at his temple, barely missed his eye, and ran all the way down to his jaw line. The scar was well camouflaged by his long black hair but when he moved his head it was clearly visible.

I looked at Lucian and Drace to see if they would object to me walking with a strange man. Lucian was frowning and Drace was glaring but since neither of them said anything, I put my arm through Mandrex's and allowed him to lead me past the staircase and down a long central walkway.

As we made our way to the dining room, I thought that Lord Mandrex must really be loaded. Lucian's apartment was gorgeously expensive and well appointed but the mansion we were walking through now—really more of a small castle—was filled with rich tapestries and works of art in glass cases, all placed at tasteful intervals. Everything looked like it had cost a fortune.

Many of the works of art appeared to be quite old—ancient pottery and tools from some bygone Stone Age era of Denarin pre-history. I wondered why a guy from a whole other planet would be so interested in the history of someplace else entirely. But then, maybe he was just really into exploring other cultures. Or maybe, as Drace had hinted, his own people didn't want him so he had decided to immerse himself in the art and language and culture of someplace else entirely.

At last we reached the dining room and I saw one last, massive glass case standing in front of the richly carved double doors. I say glass but I'm not sure what the material was that made up the case—only that it was a clear cube which seemed to hover in mid air at a fixed point—the same way the sleeping platform bed hovered on Lucian's ship.

Inside the hovering cube was a black velvet pillow. Lying on it was a triangular stone about as big as my clenched fist. It was a strange mottled color—bluish-gray mingled with specks and swirls of brilliant orange. There was a hole in the center of it but it wasn't completely round—there was a notch at one end that tapered up towards the highest, thinnest point of the triangle. I thought it looked like one of those weird, multicolored crayon rings you can find in craft shops sometimes only it was much larger than a ring—more like bracelet-sized.

"Behold," Lord Mandrex said to me, nodding at the case. "The Tanterine Key—the oldest relic of Denarin prehistory ever to be discovered. Dealers of antiquities estimate its worth in the hundreds of millions of credits. I, myself, paid a considerable sum to own it when it came to auction."

I bit my lip. Was he telling us the key wasn't for sale…or that we couldn't afford it? Because I was pretty sure we couldn't. Gold bars not withstanding, I had an idea that Lucian was rich but not *that* rich. Of course, his *family* might be that rich—they might be willing to pay millions of credits to find a way to sever his improper bond but I wasn't sure. As for Drace and myself, well, I got the feeling that Drace was a regular blue collar guy and I was just a starving paralegal. There was no way Mandrex would be getting much out of either of us.

"It's very lovely," I murmured, nodding at the Key.

"Not as lovely as you, my dear." But I had the idea he was paying me an empty compliment. There was something about those whirling, electric-blue eyes…they were cold, distant. As though he'd been hurt in the past and had absolutely no intention of risking his heart again.

Then again, I might have just been reading things into the situation.

"Thank you," I murmured.

Mandrex nodded and ushered us inside a two-story dining room that looked like it could double as a ballroom in a pinch—if they had that kind of thing here.

A single long, high table with a silver tablecloth dominated the room. It was set with thin, oval plates decorated with a swirling turquoise pattern and multiple alien-looking eating implements. On one side were three place settings right in a row. On the other, there was only one. Taking the hint, Drace and Lucian and I went to the side with three. We sat down with Lucian on my right and Drace on my left.

Lord Mandrex seated himself across from us and snapped his fingers twice. Immediately four uniformed servants ran forward, all carrying steaming dishes held out at arm's length. With a flourish, they set the plates down in front of all of us at exactly the same moment and vanished as quickly as they had appeared.

I looked down at the plate in front of me and had to fight not to wrinkle my nose.

It appeared to be a large serving of long, thin strips of…well, it *looked* like noodles covered in brown fur. But not like someone had stroked a cat and then dusted their hands over the noodles — more like the noodles themselves had somehow sprouted long, straight hairs right out of their pale, fleshy sides. Mixed in among the furry noodles were large, flat black disks, about the size of a silver dollar. The resulting dish was, shall we say, *less* than appetizing.

"Ah yes," Mandrex said grandly. "This is *ylla-reth*, a high holiday dish from the area around Y'brith."

I looked at Lucian who nodded and picked up a pair of golden tongs. He used them to stir his hairy noodles. That sounds really wrong, doesn't it? But believe me, it doesn't sound half as wrong as it looked. This was some seriously nasty-looking food.

Of course, I would never say that I thought the food looked nasty out loud. Instead, I copied Lucian's actions, but without much appetite. The hairy noodles and black disks were making my stomach churn. Still, I didn't want to be impolite so I used my tongs to bring one furry noodle to my lips. It was as tough and dry as carpet liner and had about as much flavor, plus the hairs got stuck in my teeth. It was *awful*.

"Do you like it?" Lord Mandrex inquired, smiling across the table at me.

"It's very, uh, chewy," I said, trying to smile. "A very unique dish. I love trying new things. What is it made of?"

"In the very center of the Sands of Death is a deep cavernous hole which leads many leagues down to the Sunless Sea," Mandrex informed me. "Growing from the walls of this ancient cavern is the *ylla* moss. It hangs in long curtains right down to the sandy ground around the sea. Intrepid epicureans shear off sheets of the moss and cut it into long, thin strands. It's boiled quickly in the clear juice of the *yazzen* fruit and served piping hot."

"So…moss? These are long strips of moss?" I lifted another hairy noodle with my tongs questioningly.

"Indeed it is but you're eating it wrong," he informed me. "You have to split open the blood mollusks first and mix their bile with the *ylla* moss to get the most flavor."

"Blood...mollusks?" I asked hesitantly. "*Bile?*"

"Observe." Mandrex picked up another piece of silverware which looked like a tiny golden hammer with a sharp point on one end. He held one of the flat black disks steady with his tongs and gave it a sharp tap with the pointed end of the hammer.

There was a brittle cracking sound and what looked like dark red blood started seeping out of the shattered black disk. It sizzled and sent up a sickly-sweetish cloud of pink steam when it hit the hairy noodles, which immediately went limp.

"And *now* you can eat it," Mandrex demonstrated by putting down his tongs and hammer and picking up a pair of golden chopstick looking implements. Without hesitation, he shoved a mouthful of the now-limp, bile-covered, hairy noodles into his mouth.

"Oh, um..." I looked down at my plate which was now even *less* appealing than before Mandrex had showed me how to prepare it.

"Would you like some help?" Lucian positioned one of my flat, black blood-mollusks with his tongs and cracked it sharply for me before I could answer. "Stir it quickly," he advised as the blood-like bile came hissing and sizzling out to mix with the noodles. "The bile needs to coat all of the *ylla* moss strips for the best flavor."

"Oh, of...of course." Swallowing hard, I picked up my own set of long, needle-thin golden chopsticks and began swirling them through the steaming mixture. I really, *really* didn't want to eat this but since everyone else—even Drace—was digging in, I felt I had no choice.

This time the hairy noodle I brought to my mouth tasted less like carpet liner and more like dirty, raw liver. Seriously, if you've ever gotten mud or dirt in your mouth by accident, that was what it tasted like.

Dirt and raw organ meat. Wow, who wants seconds?

I didn't gag or spit it out but it was a near thing. I've always hated liver—my Aunt Celia used to make it at least twice a month and I always tried to be at a friend's house for supper on liver nights.

Of course, I couldn't excuse myself from the table or say anything about how nasty the hairy noodles in bile sauce were. I just kept swirling my chopsticks through them and pretending to eat without actually putting anymore of the awful stuff in my mouth. I also drank lots of the fizzy pink drink in the long, elegant goblet by my plate. Its taste was pleasant if somewhat weird—it reminded me of a cross between champagne and cherry Kool-Aid.

At last Mandrex snapped his fingers again and the servants appeared and whisked the dishes away.

I was hoping dinner was over but no such luck. The next course was set before us almost immediately—large, golden bowls with silver lids on top. The servants removed the lids at exactly the same moment, like it was some kind of dance routine they'd practiced and I blinked at what was revealed. It looked like a bowl of pure black oatmeal with gray lumps in it. There was also half of a pink, plum-sized fruit with blue seeds on a small plate beside it.

"*Serri-serri* porridge with *jub-jub* juice," Lord Mandrex informed us, picking up a long handled golden spoon with a tiny, wedge-shaped bowl at the end of it. "From the K'drin Jungle."

"Your chefs must be pretty fucking adventurous," Drace remarked, picking up his own spoon. "We never eat this except during the festival of the Watchful Moons because it's so damn dangerous to make."

"How is it dangerous?" I asked, poking my own porridge with my wedge-shaped spoon. I wondered what the gray lumps were—they didn't look very appealing. "What could be dangerous about porridge?"

"It isn't the porridge itself which is dangerous, my dear," Mandrex told me. "It's the savory *challa* eyes mixed into it which are perilous to collect."

"*Challa* eyes?" I poked a gray lump again but it just sat there. Was it some kind of plant that looked sort of like an eye when it was fresh but just looked like an ugly lump once you cooked it? That seemed like the most logical explanation.

"You have to awaken them with the *jub-jub* juice." Mandrex picked up the pink fruit which had been sliced in half to show its blue seeds. "Go on." He nodded, urging me to do the same.

I picked up the fruit and held it over the bowl of black porridge just as Mandrex was. Lucian and Drace were doing the same.

"Now squeeze," Mandrex instructed.

I did—we all did—sending a spray of pinkish-purple juice down onto our bowls. Immediately all of the gray lumps quivered and popped open revealing...

"Ugh!" I gasped, dropping the messy *jub-jub* fruit and pushing back from the table. "Eyes! They're really *eyes!*"

Indeed, I now had a bowl of black oat-meal-looking sludge dotted with many tiny golden eyes with large, dark pupils. It looked like a Halloween joke dish—ha-ha, try these worms and dirt I made out of crushed Oreo cookies and gummy worms. Only this was for *real*.

"Of course they're eyes," Drace said, as though it was perfectly reasonable to eat bird's eyes for dinner. "From the *challa* bird. You can only catch them during nesting season when they're separated into individual territories."

"Is that so?" I asked faintly, still staring at my eye-oatmeal.

"Yeah." Drace scooped up a spoonful of his own porridge with a particularly large golden eye right in the middle. "They have razor sharp beaks and poison feathers. You mess with one, the whole flock comes after you to peck you to death if you're not careful."

"They sound awful," I said. "Why...why would you want to eat their *eyes?*"

"Pretty much the only part of them that isn't poison," Drace said and took a big bite of the awful oatmeal.

"Try some," Mandrex urged me. "It's an acquired taste, I'll admit but the eyes pop most delightfully between your teeth."

I scooted back to the table and looked at my eye-studded oatmeal once more. The golden orbs seemed to be staring up at me, daring me to take a bite. Daring me to put one of them in my mouth.

*I can't,* I thought. *I just can't!*

But if I didn't, would Lord Mandrex take offense? We were here to try and butter him up enough to get him to loan us the Tanterine Key. If I refused his food, he probably wasn't going to be feeling too friendly towards us.

*You swore you'd do everything you could to get Drace and Lucian separated,* I reminded myself. *This is part of that.*

Taking a deep breath, I scooped out the smallest eye I could find with a big bite of black oatmeal—hoping to hide the taste—and put the whole thing in my mouth.

The flavor of the porridge wasn't bad—bland and slightly sweet, not that different from plain oatmeal back home. Then I bit into the eye.

It was every bit as horrible as I had imagined it would be. It popped like a grape between my teeth and then my mouth filled with a salty, bitter slime that was like raw egg whites in consistency. The rest of the eye was chewy, like days-old bubble gum, and had a rancid-pepperoni flavor I found nauseating.

I fought not to gag and swallowed as quickly as I could. Picking up my fluted glass, I took a big chug of the pink, fizzy drink inside, draining it completely. A servant re-filled my glass unobtrusively and I drained it again.

Moss-strips with blood-clam sauce and black oatmeal with eyes—what a menu. What was for dessert—chilled monkey brains? Ugh!

"You might want to go easy on the *tambord,*" Mandrex said, nodding at my glass, which was being refilled for a third time. "It's mildly alcoholic and known for lowering inhibitions."

"Oh, it's just so tasty, I couldn't stop," I said weakly, trying to hide the fact that I'd been guzzling my drink to get the disgusting raw-eyeball taste out of my mouth. I knew I ought to eat some more of the porridge—maybe I could just eat around the eyeballs and only get the oatmeal. But I just couldn't make myself do it. Instead, I stirred the stuff with my spoon, trying to hide as many of the eyeballs as I could in the thick black sludge.

At last, Mandrex snapped his fingers again and announced, "Dessert!"

The awful black eye-ball oatmeal was mercifully whisked away and I felt my stomach clench with anxiety. What could possibly be next? After the first two courses, I couldn't imagine how awful dessert might be.

I couldn't have been more surprised when instead of some new disgusting culinary abomination, a pastry that looked like a pastel Rubix Cube was put in front of us.

"Wow..." I looked at the thing from all angles, turning my dainty golden plate to do so. It appeared to be a cube made up of many tiny pastel cubes, all about an inch square. There were lavender cubes, sky-blue cubes, blush pink cubes, and mint green cubes. All of them were individually iced, a little bit like petit fours, and appeared to be made to be detached from the rest of the square cake easily.

I felt the knots in my stomach begin to relax. The dessert was beautiful and by far the most appetizing thing I'd been served so far.

"This is the one dish I still serve which comes from my home planet," Lord Mandrex said, plucking a pale peach cube from his plate and putting it in his mouth. "Mmm... *Nandra* cake. I cannot bear to eschew it."

I thought about asking what it was made of but then decided I didn't want to know. Tentatively, I picked out a lavender cube and placed it on my tongue. The icing around it melted and a delicate, sweet, slightly floral flavor filled my mouth. To my surprise and relief, I liked it.

I tried a pink piece and got a different, but still tasty flavor. Then a blue piece, then a green piece. All of them were good, especially after the awful first and second courses. Eating the *Nandra* cake was kind of like eating extremely light and airy sponge cake flavored like flowers. I drank more of the fizzy *tambord* with it since it made me extremely thirsty and by the time we were finished with dessert, it's fair to say I was feeling a little bit tipsy and much more relaxed.

I think that was exactly what Mandrex wanted.

"Now," he said, when the last dishes were cleared and the servants had left us with several more bottles of *tambord* in case we were still thirsty. "You wanted to talk business?"

"Yes." Lucian cleared his throat and sat up straighter. "We wanted to know about leasing the Tanterine Key from you."

"For what purpose?" Mandrex raised one jet-black eyebrow at him.

"I'm afraid I can't disclose that," Lucian said.

"Oh. Well, then, I cannot lease you the Key." Mandrex made a mocking face of disappointment. "Still, it was good of you to come to supper. Thank you very much for your company and I hope the three of you have a lovely evening."

"Wait!" Drace barked as Mandrex was getting up from the table. "We'll tell you."

"He already knows enough about us," Lucian hissed.

"Well, he's about to know more." Drace's green eyes blazed. "Lucian and I—we were wrongly bonded," he told Mandrex. "And we're trying to sever our bond. We need the Tanterine Key to do that."

"Oh? Does it have some kind of severing properties I am not aware of?" Mandrex asked.

"We don't know," I said. "We only know it's part of the prophesy we were given by Tanta Loro. It's vital that we have it or these two…" I looked pointedly at Lucian and Drace. "Will be stuck together forever. Which they do *not* want."

"Most interesting." Mandrex stroked his chin, which had one of those adorable clefts in the center of it. With his whirling blue eyes and those big black wings, I thought he looked like a fallen angel— one who was more likely to lead you into temptation than deliver you from evil.

"I'm glad you find our plight amusing," Lucian said tightly. "Now that you know our reasons for needing the Key, could you find it in yourself to lease it to us for a short time?"

"I'll consider it. What are you willing to pay for the privilege of using the Key?" Mandrex asked.

"What do you want?" Lucian asked levelly. "I can pull upwards of a million credits personally. My family can get more if I ask."

"Ah, but asking would mean admitting to your fathers you're bonded to another Alpha—a great shame in your culture," Mandrex pointed out blandly.

"True," Lucian said stoically. "But we'll do anything that's necessary to get the Key."

Mandrex leaned forward, steepling his fingers under his handsomely cleft chin.

*"Anything?"*

"Well...yes." Lucian looked at him uncertainly. "Why—what did you have in mind?"

"Something you might find rather...unusual," Mandrex said.

"Unusual how?" Drace asked, scowling suspiciously.

Mandrex sighed and leaned back in his elegantly scrolled, high-backed chair.

"I am, as you know, attempting to adopt the Denarin culture as my own. I love the art and the music and the food—even the more unusual dishes."

*That* was certainly an understatement, but I didn't say anything about it out loud. I wondered what might be coming next—what in the world did Mandrex want from us in order to let us borrow the Key?

"I am, in fact, completely comfortable with all aspects of Denarin culture except one—the idea of two males sharing a female."

Drace snorted and Lucian looked at Mandrex in apparent disbelief.

"Forgive me, Lord Mandrex, but that is the very *essence* of our culture. No matter what clan we come from the idea of sharing a female, of protecting her with a partner you can trust to back you up in any situation, is at the core of our very identity."

"I know...I know...and I'm *trying* to embrace it." Mandrex made a curt gesture with one hand. "It's just foreign to me. Cantors are *fiercely* monogamous. The idea of sharing a female I care for—

that I love, if I could ever find such a female—makes me tremble with rage."

"I don't know how we can help you then," Drace remarked. "The idea of having a female to yourself with no other male to share her with seems as wrong to us as our sexual needs seem to you."

"But I *want* to understand it—I want to *embrace* it." Mandrex leaned forward again, eyes blazing like blue flames. "I want you to show me the beauty of it."

"Show you *how* exactly?" Lucian asked, frowning.

Mandrex looked at him levelly. "I want a private exhibition. I want to see the things the three of you do firsthand—I want to see the *beauty* in it."

"So...you're asking us to put on a *sex* show for you?" I stared at him in disbelief. I had been mostly quiet during the discussion because I was still feeling slightly tipsy from all the fizzy Kool-Aid-champagne I'd been drinking throughout dinner. But now it seemed time to speak up.

"Essentially, yes," Mandrex said mildly. "And in return I will loan you the Tanterine Key *and* keep the secret of your shameful Alpha-on-Alpha joining to myself."

"This is blackmail!" Lucian exclaimed. "What we do together in the privacy of the sleep chamber isn't for you to judge!"

"There will be no judging involved, I assure you—I only want to observe, *not* participate in any way."

"I don't get it," Drace said roughly. "You're fucking rich. Why ask us to perform for you? Why not hire some pleasure girl and a couple of pleasure boys to act it out for you?"

Mandrex raised one black eyebrow. "And have it bruited about that Lord Mandrex is a perverted foreigner who only came to Denaris because he has a fetish for watching three-way sex? No..." He shook his head firmly. "I value my reputation as much as you value yours, you know. Far better to ask the three of you, who have something to hide. This way, you will keep my secret and I will keep yours. Neither of us will betray the others because the stakes are too high. Besides..." He cocked his head to one side. "If I hired sex workers to act out the scene that is all I would get—acting. I want to see a Triumvirate with genuine affection between them."

"You'd best look elsewhere then," Lucian said bitterly. "Drace and I have no affection between us — why do you think we're working so hard to be free of each other?"

"He's right — we fuckin' hate each other," Drace rumbled.

"No, you don't!" I snapped, surprising myself. "Whether you admit it or not, the two of you *care* about each other. You *saved* each other's *lives*." I looked back and forth between them. "And it doesn't matter what you had to do in order to do that — it still counts. And you still *care*."

Neither Lucian or Drace answered me but Mandrex looked surprised and interested.

"A lovers' quarrel, it would seem. Would you then, gentlemen, at least both admit that you care about the female you share between you?"

"Of course we care about Rylee," Drace growled, moving closer to me. "We'd protect her with our lives."

"She is our lady — we are sworn to keep her safe at all costs," Lucian put an arm around me protectively.

"Fascinating." Mandrex nodded. "Given the feelings you both have for your female, it should be most interesting to watch you share her."

"Wait a minute!" I protested, some of my tipsiness wearing off. "We can't...we've never..."

"Our bond is not sealed — we're not a true Triumvirate, nor do we plan to become one," Lucian said sharply. "So we have no intention of performing bonding sex with our female in front of you, just for your viewing pleasure."

"You don't have to perform bonding sex," Mandrex said. "I just want to see the three of you together — to see your interaction." He shook his head. "I still can't understand how it's possible for the two of you to share a female and not feel any jealousy when you watch your bond-mate take her."

"Nobody's taking anybody anywhere," I said quickly. "At least..." I bit my lip. "Not until we talk about this some more." I looked at Mandrex. "Can we have some privacy?"

"Certainly. In fact, allow me to lead you to another, more *intimate* setting to discuss my offer."

He rose from the table and led the way out of the vast dining room, his feathers making whispering sounds as the tips of his wings dragged against the richly carpeted floor.

Without a word, the three of us followed him. I think we all wanted to talk—we were bursting with things to say. But none of us felt like we could really cut lose until we were in private. At least, I know that's how *I* felt.

*I can't believe you're even considering this,* whispered a little voice in my head as we followed Mandrex down a long hallway that led off from the main corridor. *What is **wrong** with you even **thinking** about agreeing to this?*

*It's in my contract,* I tried to tell myself. *That I'll do anything I can to help them get free of each other.*

Of course, there was also a no-sex clause in the contract—one I'd put in myself. If we went through with this, we would be breaking that part all to Hell. I told myself, a little uneasily, that it was all right if *I* broke it, since it had been my idea in the first place.

But there was another reason besides the contract and the promises I'd made to stick with Lucian and Drace until the end that I was considering Mandrex's proposal instead of rejecting it out of hand. I felt—felt *strongly*—that this was the only way to get the two of them back together. Which of course was silly—the whole idea was to break them apart. But I missed the way they'd been—their cooperation, the way they'd shared glances that communicated more than words could say. The way they worked together to pleasure and protect me and make me feel comfortable and cherished. I *missed* that and I wanted it back.

Even if the three of us were only together for another few days, I wanted them to be *good* days.

*I can make that happen,* I thought and felt a strange little tingle running through me. A power I hadn't known I had was awakening…growing.

*You're a La-ti-zal…* It was a ghost of a whisper, meant only for me. Did it come from inside me…or somewhere else? I didn't know and didn't really care. *You're a Binder. You alone can restore harmony between your males.*

*Yes,* I thought. *I can bring them back together this way...I know it.*

The question was, how far would we have to go in order to achieve my goal?

# Chapter Twenty

## Rylee

"I can't believe we're even fucking *considering* this," Drace growled, once we were installed in a large, richly decorated bedroom with the door shut firmly behind us and Mandrex on the other side.

"Oh? And you have a better idea for getting the Key?" Lucian snapped. "By all means, please *share* it."

"Stop it, you two," I said, before Drace could growl back. "This is the only way to get the Key and we all know it."

They both looked at me in surprise.

"And...you're willing to do this?" Lucian asked. "Despite our contract?"

"I swore I'd stick by both of you until the bitter end," I said grimly. "Until you're separated. But right now, the two of you need to get a little closer together."

"I'm not getting close to him," Drace snarled.

"I feel the same," Lucian said coldly.

"Well then it looks like the two of you are going to be stuck together forever. Because I'm not doing a damn thing to help you get that Key until the two of you make up and promise to play nice together."

I went over to the bed—a vast, round mattress as big as a small stage—and sat on the edge, my arms crossed over my chest. My low cut gown pulled down at the gesture, pushing my breasts up in two swells.

I could feel both sets of eyes—the green and the blue—on my breasts and my body under the tight, sexy gown. I could almost hear them weighing their options. On one hand, they *needed* the Key. On the other, they were still super pissed off at each other.

But there was a third factor at play here. They wanted me—wanted to *share* me—badly. I sat up a little straighter, letting the red gown pull lower until the dark circles of my areolas were just visible above the low-cut neckline. My heart was racing but I tried to keep my face calm.

"Come on, guys," I said, a little more gently. "Don't let your wounded pride keep you from getting what you need. That's foolish."

Lucian melted first. Turning to Drace he spoke in a low voice.

"Forgive me for treating you as I would a Beta," he said, looking the other man in the eye. "It wasn't my intention to denigrate you—I only wanted to save your life as you had saved mine and there was no other way."

For a moment Drace just stood there, scowling.

"Drace," I prompted gently. "Come on—accept his apology. This anger is just eating you up inside, honey. Let go of it."

"I…" Drace took a deep breath. "I forgive you," he said at last, the words halting and choked. "I know you were only trying to save me."

"I'll never do it again—treat you like a Beta, I mean," Lucian promised swiftly. "I…do not like to be at odds with you. I miss the harmony we found when Rylee joined us."

"I miss it too," Drace admitted in a rough voice. "A fucking *lot*."

"Good—this is good!" I exclaimed, sitting up straighter. There was still some resistance between them—I could feel it. But I thought I knew how to get rid of it. "Now hug each other."

"What?" Both of them looked at me in disbelief.

"Come on…" I got up and went to them. Putting a hand on each of their broad backs, I concentrated for the first time on using the mysterious power I felt tingling inside me. "Come together," I told them in a low, commanding voice. "Drace, take Lucian in your arms."

Slowly I could see some of their reluctance fading away. Drace reached for Lucian and wrapped his arms around the other man in a bear hug.

"Lucian," I murmured. "Hug him back. Show Drace you care."

I saw Lucian's arms go up and then, hesitantly, he folded them around his bond-partner. After a moment, he squeezed, returning the other male's affection.

"I'm sorry," Lucian said hoarsely, a more heartfelt apology than before. "I didn't mean to hurt you, bond-mate."

"You saved my life," Drace growled back. "I guess it doesn't matter how you did it."

"That's good." I felt a warm glow inside me, spreading outward like a tiny sun expanding and sharing its warmth. "So good. This is exactly what the two of you needed."

"What all *three* of us needed," Lucian amended. Without discussing it, he and Drace opened their arms, accepting me into the middle of their embrace.

"All three," Drace echoed.

I put my arms around both of them and squeezed as tight as I could. I can't even begin to explain the happiness that filled me at that moment. I felt a sense of rightness I couldn't deny—didn't want to deny. Was I willing to do this with my guys—to get sexual for the personal edification of Lord Mandrex? Well, if it meant more of this feeling then yes—yes, I was.

"So we're going to do this?" Drace asked, breaking the silence first and putting my thoughts into words. "We're really going to put on a show for Mandrex?"

"I think that has to be up to Rylee," Lucian murmured, pulling away a little to look at me. "She's the one who asked for the no sex clause in our contract in the first place."

"I also promised to do anything I could to get the job done," I said. "I'd say this falls under that promise, only..." I bit my lip. "I think we need to have some limits. Some boundaries."

"Agreed," Lucian murmured. "No sealing of our bond for one thing."

"Definitely not," I agreed. "That would defeat the purpose and…" I cleared my throat. "And it would be going, uh, too far."

"How far should we go then?" Drace asked. "Are we allowed to touch you? Taste you?" There was a gleam in his eyes and I couldn't help thinking of the way he hadn't wanted to stop licking my pussy. The thought made me feel like I was blushing all over and yet, I also felt heat starting between my legs as I remembered his hot tongue lapping me there.

"Yes," I whispered. "You…you can touch me and…and taste me."

"I can't wait." Lucian was giving me that hungry look now too. "Can't wait to slip my tongue deep in your sweet pussy and lap your juices, *ma 'frela.*"

"What about penetration?" Drace asked, looking at me. "Ejaculation?"

"Um…" I felt my heart begin to beat triple time in my chest. It was one thing to agree to let them do things they'd already done. But this…it might be going too far.

"Just say if you would rather we didn't penetrate you, Rylee," Lucian said softly. "We won't be upset."

I liked the way he was referring to himself and Drace as "we" again—liked it a lot.

"I'll say *maybe* on penetration," I said after a moment's thought. "But no to, uh, ejaculation. I mean not…" I was feeling like my face was on fire now but I made myself finish. "Not *in* me anyway. That wouldn't be, uh safe."

"Just to remind you, you cannot get pregnant with us unless both of us were buried to the hilt in your pussy, coming at the same time inside you," Lucian reminded me.

"Still…" I fidgeted, looking down at my hands. "I just…don't think it's a good idea."

"She's right," Drace growled. "When you come in a female, it's a sign of possession—of ownership. It's going to be hard enough letting Rylee go when the two of us are separated without marking her by filling her pussy with our seed."

"Agreed." Lucian nodded again. "All right—then I think we have an idea of what we will and won't do."

"Very good," a voice came from somewhere overhead, making us all jump—*Mandrex's* voice. "Then if you're ready to proceed, I am ready to watch."

"What? You fucking bastard—have you been listening to us all along?" Drace demanded, looking up at the ceiling.

"Of course. I wanted to see if you could reach a consensus. Since you have, I'll come back and join you."

There was a click, like a hidden microphone being switched off and then Mandrex came into the bedroom. He was wearing a black mask that covered the top part of his face, showing just his eyes. It was surprising how much anonymity that gave him. In fact, I found myself feeling much less self-conscious than I normally would have at the idea of someone watching me just because of that mask.

He sank down on a large, plush armchair opposite the round bed, which had a dark green spread on it, and crossed his legs. He had the air of a man settling down to watch an enjoyable entertainment.

"Now," he said, when he was settled comfortably. "As I am the possessor of the Key which you three want, I will be directing this little scene. And please don't worry," he added when Drace and Lucian both started to protest. "I heard your terms to each other—I know what you are and are *not* willing to do."

He smiled charmingly and I thought again how much like a dark angel he looked. The angel of temptation, urging us to do things we knew were wrong and yet wanted to do anyway.

At least *I* wanted to do them. Did that make me a bad person? I decided I didn't want to think about that now—it wasn't relevant. Right now all that mattered was getting the Key from Mandrex and this was the only way to do it.

"Hmm…" Mandrex hummed thoughtfully, looking at us from behind his black mask. "You know, despite my natural resistance to the Triumvirate relationship, I find I like the way the three of you look together. It is most…sensuous."

"We're glad you like what a pretty picture we make," Drace growled sarcastically. "But what do you want us to *do?*"

"To start with? Simply kiss. I want to see each of you kiss Rylee in turn while the other male watches," Mandrex directed.

Well, that was easy enough. I was still standing between them but I was more turned towards Lucian. I reached for him and he took me in his arms eagerly. My mouth found his and he gave me a sweet but urgent kiss, the tips of his fangs pressing lightly against my lips as he tasted my mouth.

"And now kiss your other paramour," Mandrex said.

Lucian let me go and I turned to Drace, reaching for him just as eagerly as I had Lucian. His kiss was rougher than Lucian's—more wild though no less sweet. I could feel the need growing inside him—inside both my men—and knew it would have to be satisfied soon.

"And now all three of you," Mandrex murmured. "I want to see the two of you kiss your lady at the same time."

Lucian and Drace didn't hesitate and I was glad all over again that I'd made them hug and make up. This situation would have been beyond awkward if they were still angry with each other. They leaned towards me, pressing their cheeks together so that I could kiss both their mouths at once. It was a sweet, three-way kiss that left me breathless and longing for more.

Mandrex was watching as we finally broke the kiss, a calculating look on his dark face.

"Interesting," he murmured, looking at us. "And it truly does not bother either of you to watch the other kiss your female?"

"No," Drace said and Lucian answered,

"Why should it?"

Mandrex only shook his head. "Fascinating. Very well, let us up the stakes. Lucian and Drace, the two of you sit on the bed and take out your shafts."

They exchanged looks that said, *What now?* But what else could they do? As Mandrex had said, he was the one calling the shots. Going to the bed, they sat down side by side and unfastened their trousers. Before I knew it, there were two hot, hard shafts poking out of the crotches of their formal suits.

"Now you, my dear," Mandrex said, nodding to me. "Go and kneel between them."

My heart pounding in my chest, I went and did as he ordered, kneeling by the side of the bed between my two guys. This close, I could see how hot and hard they both were. It made me think of the dream-state we'd shared when we had all been naked. They were every bit as thick and long as they had been in the dream-realm and if Lucian was a little longer and Drace was a little thicker, they were both bigger than anyone I'd ever been with in my life. It was frightening in a fascinating, sexy kind of way.

*It's all right,* I reminded myself, my pulse racing. *It's not like you're going to make love to them.* Which was a damn good thing because I didn't see how in the world even one of them would fit in me — let alone two. I knew that Lucian and Drace had said their bodies secreted hormones or chemicals that helped a woman open up and accommodate them but I didn't see how any chemical, no matter how strong, could help a girl take such huge shafts inside her comfortably without pain.

"Now touch them — both at once to start with," Mandrex directed.

I did as he said with only a little hesitation. Lucian hissed between his teeth when I took his long shaft in my right hand and Drace growled softly when I reached out and palmed his thick cock in my left. Their skin was hot and satiny smooth and I couldn't get my fingers wrapped all the way around either shaft though I *did* try.

"Pump them," Mandrex told me. "Stroke your lovers — give them pleasure, my dear."

What else could I do? Feeling a little like an actress in a porno but also extremely hot, I began a slow slide back and forth, stroking up and down with my fingers loosely curled around each long, thick shaft.

Drace growled again and Lucian murmured, "Gods, *ma 'frela,*" as I stroked them. Touching both of them like this, so intimately, I could feel a steady current of love and need and lust flowing between the three of us. It was almost magical — it made me never want to stop.

But soon Mandrex had other things in mind.

"Suck them," he ordered me, his deep voice thick with lust. "One at a time, please — to start with, anyway."

I turned my head to look at him. He was lounged in the armchair, legs spread wide and I could see a definite bulge in his black trousers. He could talk all he wanted about just wanting to *understand* the threesome aspect of Denarin culture but clearly watching us was also turning him on.

"Which one?" My voice came out high and squeaky and I had to try again. "Um, which one do you...uh, want me to suck first?" I asked, feeling completely unreal.

"Take Lucian's shaft in your mouth to begin with," Mandrex said. "And Drace, I want you to watch as she does so."

"No problem." The big blue alien watched with interest as I knelt between Lucian's thighs and brought his long shaft to my mouth. God, more than ever I felt like a porn star and yet, this didn't feel dirty — or not dirty in a *bad* way. It was more like I wanted to give my men pleasure. I loved the half-lidded look of anticipation on Lucian's sharp features as I lapped gently at the head of his cock. A small, clear droplet of precum formed on the tip and I licked it away, savoring his taste which was clean and briny, like the ocean.

"Enough licking — take him in your mouth," Mandrex ordered.

Heart beating, I complied, taking as much of the long shaft into my mouth as I could, sucking and swirling my tongue around it.

Lucian moaned and threw back his head, one hand coming up to stroke my hair.

"*Ma 'frela,*" he murmured. "Gods, your mouth is so sweet on my shaft."

"Drace," Mandrex asked. "How does it make you feel? To see another male fucking the mouth of the female you care for?"

"If it was just some other male, I'd be Goddess-damned furious," Drace growled. "I'd want to kill him. But Lucian's my bond-mate."

"So it *truly* doesn't bother you?" Mandrex sounded incredulous. "Look at the way she licks and sucks him — watch how he thrusts between her sweet lips. How does that make you feel?"

"It's fucking hot," Drace murmured and I could see, from the corner of my eye, that he was stroking his own shaft as he watched me pleasure his bond-mate. "I love watching Rylee sucking Lucian."

"Mmm…" Mandrex hummed thoughtfully. "Enough, my dear," he told me. "Now pleasure your other paramour with your mouth."

I gave Lucian one last sucking kiss and then moved over to Drace. God, I still couldn't believe I was doing this — going from one to the other with such ease. But it felt right somehow. And apparently my closet exhibitionist was coming out because I liked it — liked putting on this kinky little show for my guys. My pussy was wet and throbbing between my legs and I was willing to bet my panties were soaked with my juices.

Drace's shaft was thicker, as I said before, so it was harder to get him in my mouth. But I did my best, lapping and kissing up and down his pulsing shaft, enjoying the wild, spicy scent of him, before taking the broad head of his cock between my lips and sucking as well as I could.

"Gods, baby!" he groaned and I felt his big hand fist gently in my hair. "You're sucking me so good — don't stop!"

"Very nice," Mandrex murmured. "Lucian, do you feel the same as your bond-mate? You enjoy watching your shared female pleasure him?"

"It is…most erotic." Lucian wasn't actually stroking himself like Drace had been but from the corner of my eye, I could see his long shaft twitching with need against his flat belly. "My bond-mate's pleasure is my pleasure," he said, his deep, smooth voice filled with desire.

"And what if she pleasures you both at once? How will that be, I wonder?" Mandrex sounded almost as though he was talking to himself. "Scoot together," he ordered Lucian and Drace. "So that your shafts are touching. I want to watch Rylee lick you both at the same time."

I released Drace with a last kiss and moved back, watching to see what would happen. I wasn't sure if they would go for this or not and for a moment, I felt a tug of resistance between them. Then they shared a look—another one of those *what else can we do*—glances. With a shrug, Drace scooted closer and angled his body towards Lucian. After a long pause, Lucian did the same. Soon the two of them were sitting in such a way that the broad heads of their cocks rubbed gently together.

For a long breathless moment, I took the time to appreciate their male beauty. Their skin tones were darker here—Lucian's olive green deepened to a dusky forest hue at his cock and Drace's shaft was a deep indigo. They were both utterly masculine and completely gorgeous and I felt my pussy tingle in anticipation at tasting them both at the same time.

God, I was *really* getting into this! Was there something wrong with me? But how could I help wanting to bring them pleasure? They were my guys and I was their female—the one they had chosen to cherish and protect. As I reached for both of them and pressed the green shaft to the blue more firmly, I knew I wanted to give them the same pleasure they'd given me in the past.

"Very nice," Mandrex murmured as I lined up their shafts so that I could lick both broad heads at once. "And…it does not bother you? Having your shaft touching another male's so intimately?"

He was addressing the question to both of them but it was Drace who answered.

"It's not so much that Lucian is another male—it's that he's another *Alpha*."

"It does feel…somewhat wrong," Lucian admitted, looking down to where the head of his cock was rubbing against Drace's. "But again, my bond-mate's pleasure is my pleasure. Being with Rylee—sharing her touch and her kiss—makes it feel right again."

"We would have to be pressed together anyway if we were both taking her—bonding her to us," Drace added and I thought I heard a deep longing in his voice, as though it was something he wished he and Lucian could do even though we all knew it was impossible. "It's a fucking intimate connection—no pun intended—but it's still the ultimate pleasure to service our female at the same time."

Wanting to demonstrate the pleasure between the three of us, I leaned forward and lapped both of them at once, letting my tongue glide over both broad heads. Drace groaned and Lucian hissed—a sharp intake of breath between his teeth.

"Gods, *ma 'frela,* so erotic," he murmured. "I like to watch you taste us both at once."

"Me too—it's fucking hot," Drace growled, the lust thick in his gravelly voice.

I licked them again and then rubbed their heads together, mixing the clear beads of precum that was now flowing from both shafts. Both men groaned again and then I was lapping and tasting, swirling my pink tongue around their blue and green shafts, tasting the flavor of the two of them mixed together in my mouth and wishing I could feel them together someplace else…

*What are you saying?* whispered a shocked little voice in my head. *Just look at them – they're huge! You'd never be able to fit even one in you – let alone two of them!* But I couldn't help it—the need inside me seemed to grow with each passing minute. It was an emptiness, a longing to be filled I had never experienced before. God, I wanted them—both of them!

"While this is most tantalizing, I think it's time we switched things around a bit," Mandrex said from his armchair. "I think the lady has done enough pleasuring—it's time for her to also be pleasured."

I sat back, releasing my guys reluctantly. They had been pulsing in my hands and I liked the flavor and the feel of them mixed together. It was, as Drace said, "fucking hot."

"Rylee, my dear," Mandrex murmured. "Tell me—which of your lovers do you find most pleasurable to have in your pussy?"

"I…um…" I could feel myself blushing and biting my lip. "I…"

"Neither Drace nor myself has entered Rylee with our shafts," Lucian said, interrupting my stuttering. "In fact, only Drace has had the pleasure of even tasting her."

"Is that right?" Mandrex looked surprised.

"We're trying to get free of each other, remember?" Drace said sarcastically. "Every time we're intimate it draws us closer together."

"And now I have put you in the position of having to draw closer together in order to get apart," Mandrex mused. "Most interesting. I would apologize if I didn't find the three of you together to be such an erotic sight. Unfortunately, if you wish to earn the right to use the Key, I'm afraid you must go on."

"We would expect nothing less," Lucian said evenly. "What is your next command?"

"Oh, I prefer to think of it as a *request*." Mandrex gave him a "cat that got the cream" smile. "And, as I said before, since the two of you have had such pleasure, I think it's time for Rylee to enjoy herself as well. Why don't you both suck her nipples to start with — at the same time," he added. "I like that — I like watching the three of you together though I still cannot picture myself in such a situation."

"You better fucking keep trying if you really want to fit into Denarin society," Drace advised him. He and Lucian looked at me.

"All right, *ma' frela?*" Lucian asked softly and Drace asked,

"Are you okay with this, baby?"

Biting my lip, I nodded. I had known I would have to get naked eventually, that the long red dress I was wearing would have to come off. I just hadn't expected it to happen so soon.

"Slowly, then," Lucian murmured, sliding down the top of my dress to bare my breasts. My nipples tightened immediately in the slightly chilly air. I shivered with a mixture of anticipation and fear. Part of me still couldn't believe that we were doing this — and doing it for an audience too! It was strange and hot and beyond kinky and yet I found I still wanted to continue.

Lucian and Drace were still sitting on the bed together but now they switched places with me, sliding to the floor and putting me on the bed so they were kneeling at my feet. Both of them were so tall they were still easily able to reach my bare breasts. And, as Mandrex watched, they each took a nipple in their hot mouths, just as they had in the dream-realm.

I moaned softly as my guys sucked hard on my tender nipples — I couldn't help it. I could feel the gentle press of Lucian's fangs bracketing my right nipple and the hot suction of Drace on the left. He pulled hard, taking as much of my breast into his mouth as he could while Lucian swirled his tongue delicately around and around on the other side, making me feel like I was going to go crazy with all the sensations.

"Very nice—very nice indeed," Mandrex murmured approvingly. I saw that his whirling blue eyes were half-lidded behind his black mask and the bulge in his trousers had grown even bigger. "But it could be even nicer, I think," he added. "Lucian, I think you said that Drace had tasted your lady in the past but you hadn't gotten the chance to taste her yourself?"

Lucian released my right nipple, which was dark and tingling from his sucking, and looked up.

"That's correct," he murmured.

I expected Mandrex to direct him to get between my thighs and believe me—I was completely ready for that. Though it made me embarrassed to admit it, my pussy was wet and swollen with need. I wanted my guys to touch me—to taste me—even if they had to do it in front of an audience.

So I was surprised at Mandrex's next words.

"Drace," he said. "Take your place between your lady's legs while Lucian watches."

If he was trying to provoke jealousy between them, I don't think he succeeded. Though I knew that Lucian wanted to taste my pussy, he also derived pleasure from watching Drace go down on me. Myself, I didn't know what to think.

"You'd better disrobe now, don't you think my dear?" Mandrex said to me while my guys switched around so that Lucian was sitting on the bed behind me and Drace was still at my feet.

"I...I guess so."

Blushing and trembling, I stood up and Lucian helped me peel down the red dress. When it was gone, I had on nothing but a pair of lacy black panties that Drace had made for me with the clothing sim. He still hadn't mastered a bra but he was getting better and better at making sexy underpants.

These were small and the silky crotch clung to my pussy lips looking painted on because they were so wet with my juices. To my shame, I could even see the outline of my clit peaking out from between my pussy lips—the tender little bump begging for attention. Attention Drace would soon be giving me.

"Very nice," Mandrex murmured, his whirling blue eyes taking in the state of my pussy. "Pull them down slowly, please Drace," he directed when the big alien hooked his fingers in the lacy sides of my panties. "See how wet she is—how much she enjoys your mouths on her," he continued as Drace slid the panties slowly down my thighs. "Her pussy is swollen with need—you must help her, my friend."

"My pleasure," Drace growled. There was a hungry light in his eyes as he pushed me gently to the bed, right into Lucian's lap. "Hold her, bond-mate," he told Lucian. "Help our sweet Rylee spread her legs wide for my tongue."

"I'll be happy too." Lucian positioned me so that my back was supported by his broad chest and reached around to cup my breasts. "Spread your thighs, *ma 'frela*," he ordered in a low voice. "Let Drace get a good, deep taste of your sweet pussy. Let him give you pleasure."

I moaned breathlessly, and did as he said. I couldn't believe the situation I was in—completely nude and being cradled in one man's lap while another knelt between my legs and prepared to taste me. And all while a third man watched. God, how had I gotten into this? And why didn't I want to get out of it?

I couldn't answer either question but in a moment, it didn't seem to matter anymore because Drace was bending over me and I could feel his hot breath blowing against my bare pussy.

"So sweet," he growled. "Can't fucking wait to taste you again, baby. Can't wait to fuck you with my tongue…" Then he leaned forward, spread my pussy lips wide with his thumbs, and took a long, hot taste, dragging his tongue over my slippery inner folds. The deliciously intimate sensation of his hot tongue on my open pussy made me cry out and jerk in Lucian's arms.

"Ah! Oh, God!" I moaned. "*Please.*"

"That's right, bond-mate," Lucian growled softly, watching as Drace tasted me. "Give our female pleasure—lap her sweet pussy and make her wet and ready. Put your tongue deep inside her."

"Gladly." Drace lapped me again, circling my aching clit with just the tip of his tongue and then diving in for more. He pressed his hot, wet tongue deep into my channel until I gasped and bucked against his mouth. And all the time, Lucian was cupping my breasts and twisting my nipples with a slow, hot motion that sent sparks of pure pleasure from my aching peaks to the throbbing place between my thighs.

"Drace!" I moaned, unable to stop myself from writhing all over Lucian's lap. "Oh, God…that feels so *good!*"

I hadn't really had a chance to appreciate his technique before, mostly because that last time he'd tasted me, I was on the edge of death and he and Lucian had been trying so desperately to pull me back. But now, naked and helpless between them, I was free to appreciate exactly how good Drace was at going down and let me tell you, he was *good.*

"It doesn't make you jealous at all?" Mandrex asked Lucian as they held me between them. "To watch another man pleasure your female? To see him lick and suck her open pussy?"

"He is my bond-mate," Lucian said simply. "Though I long to taste Rylee's sweet juices myself, I still love watching Drace give her so much pleasure."

"And why shouldn't you taste her juices?" Mandrex mused. "Drace," he ordered. "Look up for a moment, if you please."

As before, Drace was extremely reluctant to leave his spot between my thighs. He kept lapping and sucking, teasing my clit with just the tip of his tongue until I cried out and jerked against his mouth. At last, though, he looked up, his full, sensuous lips and chin shiny with my juices.

"Ah—I can see how much you're enjoying tasting your female," Mandrex told him. "But you shouldn't keep all of her sweet honey to yourself, my friend."

"What do you mean? You want Lucian to have a turn between her thighs?" Drace's voice was hoarse with lust.

"Not yet." Mandrex gave them both a slow smile. "Kiss him— share your lady's essence with your bond-mate."

"Kiss him?" Drace frowned and I thought for sure he wouldn't go for it.

"Why yes." Mandrex smiled pleasantly. "Is that a problem?"

"He's not a Beta," Drace growled. "Hell yes, it's a problem."

Uh-oh—here we went with the whole Alpha/Beta thing again. I was still trying to piece together the rules. Could the Alpha kiss the Beta but not the other way around? I put my hands on both of them, making sure I was touching bare skin.

"Guys," I murmured, concentrating on sending a current of peace and caring to them both. "We have a common goal here. I know neither of you is into kissing other males but we need to come together over this, no matter what kind of taboo you have against it."

"To be clear about the 'taboo' as you put it," Lucian said, frowning at me. "Kissing between the two males in a Triumvirate isn't usually done. And for one male to kiss another means he is treating him in a subservient manner—as though he was a Beta." He cleared his throat. "But having said that...I will allow Drace to kiss me."

"You will?" I don't know who looked more surprised—Drace or me. But Lucian nodded firmly.

"I owe you one, bond-mate," he said to Drace in a low voice. "It's all right—for now, I'll play the Beta to your Alpha...just this once."

"All right." Kneeling up, Drace reached for the other man. Lucian leaned towards him, over my shoulder. I watched in awe as the two of them kissed.

Their lips met tentatively at first and then Lucian groaned softly and lapped at Drace's mouth—clearly he was enjoying my taste on his bond-mate's lips.

"Gods," Drace growled, breaking the kiss for a moment. "Open to me, bond-mate—let me share the flavor of our chosen female with my tongue."

Lucian hesitated for a moment, frowning.

"You said that you'd be my Beta," Drace reminded him in a hoarse growl.

"So I did." Leaning forward again, Lucian parted his lips and allowed the other male to thrust slowly into his mouth. They both groaned as Drace's tongue slid between Lucian's fangs and then their mouths clashed together in earnest.

I felt a fresh surge of heat between my thighs as I watched the rough, luscious kiss play out in front of me. God, the two of them were so sexy together! I loved the fact that they were sharing me—that they were enjoying sharing my juices so much and coming together at the same time.

At last they broke apart, panting.

Lucian looked at Mandrex, his eyes flashing.

"Are you satisfied now?"

"I will not be satisfied until your lady is, Lucian," Mandrex drawled, his own eyes glinting behind the black mask. "Tell me, since you say neither of you has entered her pussy, would you like to be the first?"

Lucian looked down at me. "That depends on what Rylee says," he murmured. "What do you think, *ma 'frela?* Will you allow me to enter your sweet pussy with my cock?"

I bit my lip, feeling my breath come short. God, we were really getting in *deep* here. Was I really willing to do this—to go this far?

*I have to,* I thought. *There's no other way to get the Key.*

"Yes," I whispered at last, looking up at him. "If...if you're gentle. And careful."

"Of course *ma 'frela.* I would never hurt you," he said softly, stroking my cheek.

"Do you want me to watch?" Drace asked, looking at Mandrex. "You think I'll get jealous when I see my bond-mate's shaft sliding into our female's pussy?"

"Will you?" Mandrex looked intrigued.

"Did Lucian get jealous when he watched me tasting and tongue-fucking Rylee's pussy?" Drace raised an eyebrow at him. "No—he told me to fuck her deeper."

"So he did," Mandrex murmured thoughtfully. "Which is why I want you to do more than watch—I want you to participate."

"Participate *how* exactly?" Drace looked at him warily.

"I want you to insert your bond-mate's shaft into your female's pussy," Mandrex purred. "Help him enter her, Drace."

A stubborn look came over Drace's granite-like features.

"Fuck you," he said shortly.

"Oh, have I said something wrong?" Mandrex looked more intrigued than offended. "Have I hit upon another one of your 'taboos'?"

"During bonding sex, it is the Beta who prepares the female to be entered by both of her males," Lucian said in a low voice. "He helps to insert his Alpha's shaft into her pussy and then licks her tender little clit and the areas they are joined as the Alpha pumps inside her. The chemicals in his saliva in combination with the precum of the Alpha are what allow her to open to both males at once for bonding and breeding purposes."

"So the Beta licks her while the Alpha fucks her," Mandrex mused. "Most interesting."

"Fuck *interesting*. No true Alpha would willingly put his mouth that close to another male's shaft," Drace growled. "Kissing Lucian was one thing but I'm only gonna go so far."

"All right then." Mandrex nodded, apparently not at all offended. "In that case, you can simply hold Rylee steady while Lucian enters her. Will that offend your Alpha sensibilities?"

Drace looked relieved. "No, that's fine. I'd fucking *love* that."

"Well then—up on your knees, my dear," Mandrex said to me. "Let's have a good view of your lover's shaft filling that sweet little pussy of yours."

Biting my lip, I got to my hands and knees on the bed. Lucian positioned me so that my left side was to Mandrex and knelt behind me on the mattress. Drace was in front of me, his muscular arms around me, comforting and holding me. I nuzzled close to him, breathing in his spicy scent to calm my nerves as I felt the broad head of Lucian's shaft nudging my inner thighs.

God, I couldn't believe we were really doing this! I had never felt so open or so vulnerable as I did at that moment, kneeling between my two lovers as one of them prepared to open me with his cock. I was shivering with some emotion that felt like a strange combination of fear and desire and yet I still didn't want to stop.

My guys seemed to understand my feelings because both of them were petting me. Four big, warm hands were sliding all over my body, caressing my hips and thighs and ass and shoulders and throat and back.

"It's all right, *ma 'frela*," Lucian was murmuring. "I'll be gentle with you, I swear I will."

"You'll be fine," Drace told me. "Everything is gonna be fine, baby."

"Enough of this — enter her now, Lucian" Mandrex ordered. "I want your bond-mate to watch as you slide your shaft deep inside Rylee's pussy."

"All right, but I am taking my time. I don't wish to hurt her," Lucian said. He sounded like he was frowning but of course I couldn't tell since he was behind me. "Spread your thighs a little wider, Rylee," he murmured in a low, commanding tone. "It's time for me to be inside you now."

Moaning a little, I did as he said, opening my thighs so that I felt my pussy lips part for him, offering myself to him. My clit throbbed like a second heartbeat and my nipples felt tender and exposed as my breasts hung down, almost brushing the round mattress.

"That's good," Lucian told me, caressing my hips again before he fit the head of his cock to the mouth of my sex. "Very good, *ma 'frela.* I'm going to enter you now — going to slide my shaft deep in your tight little pussy."

I moaned again as I felt his broad head breach my entrance. God, he was really going to do this — he was really going to slide his cock deep inside me and I was going to let him. More than that — I *wanted* to let him.

I bit my lip as I felt Lucian's thickness begin to stretch my inner passage. God, he was big! I couldn't imagine what it would be like to have both him *and* Drace inside me. I really hoped Lord Mandrex wouldn't ask that of us — this was hard enough.

Drace seemed to sense my uncertainty and fear about being stretched open by his bond-mate's cock because he comforted me gently, his big hands stroking my hair and shoulders.

"It's okay, baby," he murmured, his big hands warm and soothing against my skin. "Just relax and let Lucian into your sweet, wet pussy. Just let him get into you nice and deep."

"I...I'm trying," I whispered, looking down at my hands, fisted in the green bedspread. "Really, I am."

"No—look up, Rylee," Mandrex ordered. "I want you to be looking into Drace's eyes when Lucian bottoms out inside you."

"All...all right." I tried to look up but it wasn't good enough for Mandrex.

"Drace, tilt Rylee's chin back and look at her," he ordered. "I want you to see it in her eyes when your bond-mate finds the end of her channel. I want you to look at her when the head of his cock kisses the mouth of her womb."

Drace tilted my chin and our eyes met. He held my gaze steadily as the last few thick inches of Lucian's long shaft entered my pussy.

"Oh!" I moaned when I felt him touch bottom inside me. "Oh, *God.*"

"Is he all the way in you, baby?" Drace murmured, stroking my cheek. "Can you feel his cock filling you up?"

"Y-yes," I stuttered. "I do...I mean, he is."

"That's good, baby." Drace leaned down and kissed me gently, his deep voice filled with tender approval. "I know it's not easy but you're doing perfect. You're so brave and beautiful, taking Lucian's cock all the way inside your tight little pussy. And it's so damn hot to watch you take it."

"That's right, Rylee," Lord Mandrex purred, his deep voice thick with lust. "Open yourself—submit to your lover's cock and let him fuck you."

I bit back a gasp. Was Lucian really going to do that? Was he really going to *fuck* me? I had thought—hoped—that he might just enter me and thrust once or twice. But now I wasn't sure what Mandrex had in mind.

"What...how much do you want...want him to do?" I asked him, my question coming out in a high, uncertain voice. "I mean I thought…thought you just wanted Drace to see Lucian, uh, slide inside me. Not…not actually…"

"Fuck you?" Mandrex looked at me speculatively. "Yes, actually having Lucian fuck you would seem to indicate completion. As in, he would need to thrust deep inside you and leave a load of his cum in your pussy."

I bit back a little moan as his erotic words started a forbidden fire in me. *I don't want that,* I told myself sternly. *I really don't want that.* But as my inner pussy stretched to accommodate Lucian's thick shaft, my body wasn't so sure.

"You said you understood our limits," Drace reminded him harshly.

"Yes, but I never said I wouldn't push them," Mandrex said silkily. "And is that the *real* reason you don't want to let your bond-partner come in your female's pussy? Or is it because you'll feel left out if he comes inside her and you don't?"

"For the last time, you cannot make us jealous of each other." Lucian's deep voice was exasperated. "I know it's difficult for you to understand but my bond-mate's pleasure is my pleasure and vice versa. If you asked me to pull out of Rylee this moment and allow Drace to enter her and make love to her instead, I would do so without a moment's regret."

"Lucian's right. Sharing our female and making sure she has pleasure is what gives us pleasure," Drace said, frowning. "Not being the one and only one to take her. You can't seem to get it, Mandrex—how fucking lonely it would be having a female all to yourself with no one to share her with."

"It seems I can't." Mandrex shook his head and sighed. "Very well—I will stop trying to make you jealous if Rylee will agree to let at least one of you finish within her."

I bit my lip again. Penetration we'd agreed on, but *no* ejaculation. That had seemed really important at the time we'd been laying our ground rules. Now, however, I found it didn't seem like such a big deal. After all, I knew I couldn't get pregnant unless both of them were in me at once. We couldn't even get bonded this way. And…I found I wanted to do this. Wanted to feel the pleasure of my men peak inside me.

"Rylee doesn't have to—" Drace began angrily and at the same time Lucian said, "You cannot require her to—"

"It's all right," I said, raising my voice to be heard. "It's all right—I'll do it."

"Ah—very good." Mandrex nodded his head, smiling. "And which of your paramours do you wish to let come to completion inside your sweet body, my dear?"

I took a deep breath and squeezed my eyes shut for a moment.

"Both," I said, in as strong a voice as I could manage.

"Rylee!" Drace sounded shocked. "Baby, we can't."

"It would bind us too tightly together," Lucian agreed.

"I didn't mean I wanted both of you, uh, in me *here*." I wiggled my hips slightly, making Lucian moan with the delicious friction. "I just meant…this." I pushed at Drace's broad chest lightly. "Lay back," I told him. "It'll be easier to show you that way."

With a bemused look on his face, he lay on his back on the mattress in front of me, his hard shaft still sticking out of the black trousers he was wearing. Propping himself up on his elbows, he looked up at me.

"Now what, baby?" he murmured.

"Now, this," I said. Bending lower, I took his long, thick shaft in my hand and began licking and sucking the broad, plum-shaped head.

Drace groaned and stroked a hand through my hair.

"Gods, baby," he murmured. "Your mouth is so sweet."

I stopped what I was doing just for a moment and looked behind me to where Lucian was watching, mesmerized as I sucked his bond-mate's cock. Widening my stance, I opened myself to him even more and said in a voice that hardly trembled at all, "All right—now *fuck* me."

With a low groan, Lucian did as I asked. Pulling almost all the way out of me, he thrust in again, hard and deep all the way to the end of my channel. I moaned with pleasure as he touched bottom inside me and leaned down to take Drace's cock in my mouth again.

It was like an out-of-body experience—I felt like I could almost float up and look down on myself and wonder who that girl was between the two guys doing all kinds of naughty things. I think it was because I was acting in a way I never would have acted back home on Earth. Doing things I might have thought were morally wrong. But here, with Lucian and Drace, they seemed incredibly, inevitably right.

As the three of us moved together, I remembered once running across some three-way porn on the Internet. It was a woman being shared between two men, just as my guys were sharing me now. I had turned away in disgust, thinking that the woman was being used, that she had become nothing but a fuck-toy for two horny guys.

But I saw things differently now. What was happening to me was different because I knew that Lucian and Drace really cared about me. No matter how high their passions ran, they were both still very careful with me. Neither of them thrust too hard or hurt me in any way. And both of them were still stroking all over my body, whispering how hot I was, how much they cared about me, how beautiful and brave I was to take them both this way.

I didn't feel used. I felt cherished. Cherished and protected and *loved.*

*No, you don't really love them anymore than they really love you,* whispered a practical little voice in my head. *That's impossible because when this is all over, the three of you are going to go your separate ways. So don't even think that, Rylee!*

But I didn't have to think it—I *felt* it.

I don't know how long it went on for—the push and pull of being between them. Feeling Lucian's long shaft invade me over and over, thrusting to kiss the mouth of my womb with each stroke as I took as much of Drace's thick cock into my mouth as I could, sucking and swirling my tongue around his hot flesh. I only know I felt a current of love and caring flowing between the three of us that made me feel like I never wanted it to end.

At last, though, our three-way rhythm grew more intense and I felt my pleasure building, like a wire tightening in my belly. The thrust of Lucian's shaft inside me, the way Drace reached under me to fondle and caress my breasts and pinch my nipples, was getting to be too much. I needed to come and I wanted to feel my men coming with me.

As though by a mutual, unspoken decision, I felt both of them speed up. Lucian's long, slow thrusts became faster and faster and Drace, who was fucking carefully and shallowly into my mouth, became more erratic in his motions.

"Gods, baby," he moaned, stroking my hair as he watched me suck him. "Your mouth is so sweet. Gonna come soon—can't help it."

"I am too," Lucian groaned. "But I want Rylee to come with us." I felt one of his big hands slide from my hip down to where we were joined and then long, clever fingers were stroking over my swollen, aching clit. At the same moment, Drace twisted my nipples, pinching and tugging lightly to send lightning bolts of pleasure through my entire body.

I moaned around the thick shaft in my mouth and then I felt the wire that had been twisting tight in my belly snap and my pleasure was flooding me, washing over me in a warm wave that threatened to drown me with its intensity.

"Gods, *ma 'frela*—I can feel you coming. Coming all around me," Lucian gasped hoarsely. I felt him swell even bigger within my pussy and then a gush of heat spurted deep inside me bathing my inner channel and the mouth of my womb with his cum.

At the same time, Drace groaned and I felt his shaft swell between my lips. He would have pulled away but I hung on to him. I'd never been much for swallowing before but this time I *wanted* to. Drawing close to him I took as much of his cock in my mouth as I could and caught the first hot salty spurt of his seed on my tongue.

Drace gave an inarticulate cry and stopped trying to pull away. Instead he held steady and still allowing his cock to spurt in my mouth as Lucian's erupted deep in my pussy. And through it all my own orgasm seemed to go on and on, a shining river of pure pleasure that I thought would never end.

It did end at last, of course and the three of us collapsed on the bed together in a panting, sweaty, tangled heap. My head was pillowed on Drace's broad chest and Lucian's head was nestled in the curve of my waist, right above my hip. I couldn't remember ever feeling so perfectly good—so at peace. I felt a warm glow of love suffuse me and it seemed to spread to both the guys and then come back to me—a closed loop of adoration and affection that just kept growing and growing until I felt like I was floating on a cushion of pure contentment.

"Well, don't the three of you make a charming trio?" Looking up, I saw Mandrex standing over us. There was an unreadable look on his dark face and he had one hand in his pocket. "Are you certain," he said, speaking to all of us. "*Truly* certain that you will be able to bear to sever the bond between you? You look so satisfied...so right together."

There was a wistfulness in his deep voice that almost made me feel sorry for him. I wondered what had happened to him to make him choose the life of an exile so far from his home planet.

Drace, however, clearly didn't share my sympathy for the eccentric Cantor.

"You got what you wanted," he growled. "We did everything you asked—answering questions wasn't part of the bargain."

"My bond-mate is right," Lucian said, sitting up and tucking his shaft back into his trousers. "We have given in to your demands. I would ask that you honor your part of the bargain."

"Very well—if you still want to use the Key to be free of each other, it is yours to use."

Mandrex pulled his hand out of his pocket and held out the strange triangular stone with its orange and blue markings.

I reached for it but he pulled it back, shaking his head.

"Wait—I have only one stipulation. When your quest is completed I want the three of you—*all* three of you—to return it to me."

Lucian frowned. "Why do you specifically want all three of us? We'll be separated at the end of this."

"So you say but I want to see it for myself." Mandrex looked at us thoughtfully. "I want to see the end of this story."

Drace and Lucian exchanged a glance and then both of them looked at me.

I shrugged. "Why not?"

"Sure, I guess," Drace said.

"Very well—it's agreed." Lucian held out his hand. "The three of us will return to give you back the Key. And our thanks for the loan of it."

"Very well." But it was to me that the fallen angel handed the stone. "Use it well…if you really think you want to, little Pure One," he murmured. Then he turned away and left the room with a rustle of his tall, black wings.

I watched him go, safe between my two guys, and wondered what he had meant…and what he knew that I didn't.

# Chapter Twenty-one

## Drace

"All right—we have the Key. Now what?" I said, looking down at the fist-sized chunk of triangular rock in Rylee's palm.

We were back aboard Lucian's ship, lounging in the master sleeping chamber in our sleep clothes, thank the Goddess. One more night in that fucking Y'brith…one more crazy encounter with another rich asshole…or even just run in with my bond-mate's parents and I might have lost it.

"You're the one who said we needed to go to the jungle next—to K'drin," Lucian pointed out mildly.

I looked at him speculatively but there was no anger in his words. We were getting along a hell of a lot better since we'd "literally kissed and made up" as Rylee put it. I didn't know about that but I *did* know that sharing our female sexually had put paid to any bad feelings that had been between me and my bond-mate. Part of that was probably due to Rylee's *La-ti-zal* power of binding but part was just that I felt closer to Lucian now that I understood more of his background.

I still couldn't get over the fact that his parents had forbidden him to find a mate and a female because none of the Betas he'd found were good enough for them. It's one thing to try and guide your child's future but it's something else to forbid them to have one just because they might choose someone you disapprove of. That was fucking cold hearted as far as I was concerned.

Of course, it wasn't like *my* family would approve either, if they knew about Lucian and me. I felt a twinge of unease when I thought about that. We were going to be near my home village of Renth on the edge of K'drin Jungle—I would have to be damn careful not to run into anyone I knew.

I felt a little guilty about wanting to hide my bonding status from my family. But I told myself that Lucian had wanted to hide it from his family too—hell, any red blooded Alpha would. So he couldn't blame me.

"Drace?" Rylee said, snapping me out of my guilty thoughts. "Are you all right?"

"Fine...I'm fine." I cleared my throat. "And yes, we do need to head for K'drin. We'll need to get supplies and a reliable nav-tracker. You don't want to go into the jungle unprepared."

Rylee groaned and rolled over on her side. She was lying between Lucian and me in the center of the sleep platform.

"*Please* don't tell me this hidden temple we're searching for is in *another* place we have to walk instead of fly to. What good is advanced alien technology if you have to abandon it to tramp through the desert and the jungle?"

"Sorry, baby," I said. "But the jungle canopy is way too dense to admit a ship—even a small one. The only thing to do is to park the ship in the public port nearest the edge of the tree line and wade in on foot." I frowned. "We'll just have to keep a low profile."

"What about your place?" Lucian asked. "Can we stay there? Keep out of sight until we're ready to go?"

I shrugged. "I'd say yes but it's about a hundred leagues from where we need to be. The temple is actually closest to my home village of Renth—if it can be said to be close to anywhere, that is."

"Crap. Well, into the jungle we go, I guess." Rylee sighed. "Can you at least promise we won't run into any more of those awful goddess-insects?"

"The *moratas* dwell only in the Sands of Death," Lucian said dryly. "But there are many other perils in the jungle, I am afraid. Though at least there are no more *kr'awn* to worry about—the K'drin jungle used to be crawling with them, as I understand it."

"*Kr'awn?*" Rylee frowned. "Aren't those the big, black eyeless predators that nearly killed off your whole race?"

"That's them," I said, reaching for the tray at the end of the sleeping platform and popping an Earth fruit Rylee had called a "grape" into my mouth.

After coming back from Mandrex's mansion, she'd insisted on simming what she called "decent food that doesn't taste like carpet liner or stare at me while I eat it." I had thought the food at Mandrex's dinner party was pretty good but I was enjoying the Earth fruits and delicacies Rylee had made in the food-sim, too.

"Do not worry, *ma 'frela,*" Lucian told her, nibbling a slice of crispy, juicy fruit called an "apple." "They are all extinct now. Not a single one has been seen for over a hundred cycles."

"Well, that's *some* comfort I guess. So we know *where* we're going but what about *when?* 'By the light of the Quarreling moons,'" Rylee quoted. "What is *that* all about? Do we have to wait for a lunar eclipse or something?"

"The Quarreling moons is just part of the lunar cycle," I told her. "It's when our smaller moon, Frella, appears to be attacking the larger moon, Bantor."

"Attacking *how?*" Rylee wanted to know.

"Every few solar months, Frella circles just a little too close to Bantor," Lucian explained. "The overwhelming gravity of Bantor pulls rocks from the surface of Frella which makes it look like she is bombarding him with debris when in actuality, he is pulling it from her."

"Huh. Okay, makes sense." Rylee sighed and ate a grape herself. "Mmm...*so* much better than hairy noodles and eyeball-oatmeal!"

"I take it you didn't enjoy the repast at Lord Mandrex's home?" Lucian said blandly.

Rylee made a face. "Look, I don't want to disrespect your cultures, boys, but I have to be honest—that was some nasty-ass food."

"Don't worry about it," I said, eating a slice of apple and enjoying the crisp, tart-sweet flavor. "Most of the stuff Mandrex was serving us was high holiday cuisine—not normal, everyday food like you'd get if went to my mother's house for dinner."

Rylee arched an eyebrow at me. "Speaking of your mother, are we really going to be *that* close to your hometown down there by the jungle?"

I sighed. "I'm afraid so. Too damn close for comfort. We're going to need to be careful from the time we park the ship until we finally get into the jungle." I shrugged at Lucian. "Sorry."

"Don't be. We want to avoid a scene like we had with my mother at all costs," Lucian said, frowning. "The fewer people who know you and I are bonded, the better."

Rylee sighed and rolled over on her back to look up at the ceiling.

"You know, it's a shame everyone here is so narrow-minded about two Alphas being bonded. When you two aren't snapping each other's heads off, you actually make a really good pair."

"I agree," Lucian said in a low voice.

I looked at my bond-mate in surprise.

"You do?"

"Of course I do," he said, frowning. "We support each other. We save each other's lives…" He grimaced. "Even if it's not always in the manner we might wish."

"That's behind us now," I said roughly. "I don't hold it against you and I hope you don't hold it against me."

"You know I don't," he said quietly.

"Then why can't you two be together?" Rylee made it sound so easy. "I mean, you're not limited to this one planet. Why not just move someplace else the way Lord Mandrex moved from Cantor to Denaris?"

"You're overlooking a few little problems, baby," I said, frowning. "Lucian and I might work great together—well, better than we did anyway—but there's still the problem of sex."

"Oh right—because neither of you is willing to do the Beta thing." She arched an eyebrow. "You really won't bend on that? I mean, I know it's kind of kinky but you two kissed each other with no problem during our, uh, little encounter for Mandrex."

Her cheeks went dark as she said it but I noticed she wasn't shying away from what we'd done together—which was good. I wasn't ashamed of anything we'd done and I didn't want either of my bond-mates to be either.

"We kissed to share your juices, *ma 'frela"* Lucian pointed out to her. "And because Mandrex gave us no choice in the matter. In the normal course of a Denarin relationship, the males do *not* kiss each other. They concentrate on pleasuring their female."

"Besides, kissing is one thing," I growled. "Putting your face that near another male's shaft is another. There have to be limits."

"All right—I get it." Rylee sighed again. "I guess I just thought, I don't know…that maybe you could take turns. The way you do with the cooking."

I gave a bark of laughter. "There's a hell of a big difference between using the food-sim and preparing your female for bonding or breeding sex," I pointed out.

"And even if there wasn't," Lucian said. "Even if Drace and I *were* willing to put our differences aside and 'share' the load sexually the way we do with other household duties, it still wouldn't work for us to stay together."

"Why not?" Rylee asked. "I don't understand."

Lucian and I exchanged a look and I felt an instant of connection that all bonded mates get from time to time.

"Because, baby," I answered in a low voice. "The only way the two of us can work is with *you* in the middle."

"That's not true," Rylee denied, her cheeks going dark pink under her smooth, creamy brown skin. "You guys don't need me— you'd find another girl. Someone—"

"There's no one like you, *ma 'frela,"* Lucian said quietly. "You're a *La-ti-zal* and a Binder. Do you honestly think it's a coincidence that Drace and I finally started getting along after we found you? Before you came into our lives, we couldn't stand each other."

"You didn't *know* each other," Rylee protested. "You never gave each other a chance."

"We didn't fucking *want* to know each other before you, baby," I said softly. "Lucian is right, without you, he and I would fall apart."

"I…I just don't believe that's true." She sat up on the sleeping platform and crossed her arms over her chest stubbornly. "I think there's more affection and understanding between the two of you than you even know. But you're too…too *male* to admit it."

Lucian and I exchanged another glance.

"What does our gender have to do with it?" I asked.

"Never mind." Rylee shook her head. "Look, forget I said anything, all right? We all know you guys need to get separated and then I have to go back to Earth and live my life." Her face lit up. "I'm going to start up a Wedding Planning business when I get back. Start putting people together instead of tearing them apart. I've always wanted to do that."

"I'm sure you have, *ma 'frela*. You have a way of drawing people together," Lucian said, smiling a little. "Even those that don't *want* to be drawn together in the first place."

"Enough about that." Rylee reached for another grape. "Let's just relax and take it easy our last night on the ship before we have to head into the big, scary jungle."

"I agree," I said. "The K'drin is no joke. We should conserve our energy."

"So…" Lucian cleared his throat delicately. "What are the sleeping arrangements for tonight?"

"Oh…um…" Rylee bit her lip and I felt a rush of uncertainty coming from her. It occurred to me that I was starting to pick up her emotions now as well as Lucian's but I didn't say anything about it. It didn't matter if our bond had gotten stronger since we were ultimately just going to break it.

Clearly Lucian felt our female's uncertainty too.

"Speak your mind, Rylee," he said. "Neither of us will be upset. Do you not wish to sleep between us?"

"Do you guys *want* me to?" she asked, looking at first him and then me. "I mean, I guess I thought you weren't going to…"

"Share a bed?" I finished for her. "We never did before you came into our lives. But now…" I let the sentence trail off but Lucian finished it for me.

"It feels wrong *not* to," he murmured.

"It feels wrong to me too," she said softly. "To not sleep with you guys on either side of me. I was..." She cleared her throat. "I was miserable last night."

"I think we all were," I said. Leaning across the sleeping platform, I took one of her small hands in mine. "Baby, will you sleep with us tonight? Sleep between us, I mean?"

"It doesn't have to be in any way sexual," Lucian hastened to tell her. "I had the *skizix* problem taken care of while the ship was docked in Y'brith so there is no need to raise a dream-shield around you tonight."

She gave that soft, throaty laugh of hers I swore I could feel all the way down to my balls.

"After the show we put on for Lord Mandrex you think I'm worried about the two of you getting handsy?"

"We just want you to know there's no expectation...no obligation," I said earnestly.

"But there will be warmth and safety and comfort." Lucian took her other hand and immediately I felt a tingling current of connection running between us. It was like he and I were power sources and Rylee was the conductor between us through which vast amounts of energy could flow.

Lucian felt it too—I knew because I felt him feeling it. We *all* felt it. It was fucking incredible.

"Yes," Rylee whispered, squeezing both our hands. "Yes, I want to sleep with both of you tonight. Let's get ready for bed."

# Chapter Twenty-two

## Rylee

"So this is Drace's hometown." I surveyed the bustling marketplace from under the cover of the multicolored shawl I was wearing on my head.

"So it would seem." Lucian had a broad brimmed hat on himself, woven of some thin, blue straw. It managed to hide his features fairly well, although his olive green coloring, out of place in an area where most of the males seemed to have blue skin tones, still stood out.

"It looks like a happy place," I said, looking around at all the stalls set up along the dusty main road. "I wonder why he moved so far away?"

Lucian shifted. "It can be…difficult to stay in a place where everyone else you know is finding partners when you yourself cannot," he said in a low voice. "It's one of the reasons I take so many business trips myself—to get away."

"Maybe that's it, then," I murmured. I could see no other reason Drace would want to get away, even though Drace's hometown of Renth was very different from Lucian's.

Though I hadn't gotten much of a chance to explore the desert city of Y'brith when we'd been there, it had obviously been a teaming metropolis filled with skyscrapers and all the hustle and bustle of a major urban hub. Renth, sitting just on the edge of the wild K'drin jungle, couldn't have been more different.

It was small and quaint and everyone seemed to know everybody else. At least, they all seemed to be calling each other by name. I bet myself it was one of those places where everybody knows everybody else's business and isn't shy about sharing it. No wonder Drace had left Lucian and me on the edge of town with instructions to keep a low profile.

It shouldn't be that hard to just stay out of the way while Drace bought supplies, I told myself. At least it hadn't been so far. As long as we stayed to the far edge of the market and kept our faces covered, no one bothered us. But Drace had been gone a long time now—much longer than we had thought he would be—and I was beginning to feel uncomfortable.

I didn't mind the heat or humidity of the jungle town, although Lucian had commented several times he felt like he was breathing underwater. I'm a Florida girl, after all—heat and humidity were nothing new to me. No, what was bothering me was the large amount of *jalla* berry juice I'd had with breakfast that morning before we locked up Lucian's ship and headed for town.

The juice was one of the Denarin foods I actually liked—a pale blue liquid about the consistency of orange juice but with a flavor like fresh nectarines and raspberries and some exotic spice I couldn't name. It tasted amazing and when Lucian, whose turn it was at kitchen duty, had realized I liked it so much, he had simmed me a whole lot more of it on the spot.

Back on Earth, I would have tried to check the nutritional information—the sugar in juice can rack up the calories fast. But here on Denaris, I was kind of playing fast and loose with my calorie count. So I drank every drop of the sweet and spicy blue juice, enjoying it immensely.

I hadn't regretted it a bit…until just now. Because now I was beginning to feel the very real and urgent need to pee.

"Lucian," I said, shifting from foot to foot on the dusty road. "How much longer do you think Drace is going to take?"

"I don't know." He frowned. "My understanding is that they don't use credit much in the jungle regions. They prefer a system of bartering—which can take some time."

"Great," I muttered, shifting again. "Just *great*."

"Is something wrong?" He frowned at me in concern. "I can feel your discomfort. What is it, Rylee?"

"I...um..." I sighed and pressed my thighs together. "That juice you made me was really good but I, uh, think I drank too much of it. I have to...I need to find a ladies room."

"A 'ladies' room?" He frowned, looking at me as though I was speaking a foreign language. "Why should you need to find a room exclusively for ladies?"

"It's just a nice way of saying I need a restroom. You know – a bathroom? A place to relieve myself?" I said impatiently when he still continued to look confused. "I'm trying to tell you I have to *pee*, Lucian – really *badly*."

"Oh!" He frowned. "Well, I'm not sure if the trees around here provide sufficient privacy."

"I don't want to pee behind a tree!" I exclaimed.

I wished we could just go back to the ship but the parking area was over a mile away – I would never make it in time. I would just have to find someplace in town to take care of the call of Nature. But where?

"What about that shop there?" I asked, pointing to a quaint little store across the bustling, dusty street. "Do you think they'd have a restroom I could use?"

Lucian frowned. "*Possibly* but I really don't think it's a good idea for us to interact with the natives here."

"Why, because you're a Fang Clan guy?" I asked.

"Exactly." He looked grim. "We aren't openly at war with the Claw Clan but we're enemies just the same. Our second natures do not get along well at all."

"Second nature?" I thought I remembered Drace saying something about that earlier. Something about how he'd had to use his second nature in order to get Lucian out of the desert without being bitten by the goddess-insects himself? I wasn't sure but something like that.

"Yes – the forms we are able to take for defense if need be. Although those of my clan believe it is low and improper to do so. Anyway, I'm sure the people of Renth wouldn't take it very kindly if they knew one of the Fang Clan was in their midst."

I wanted to know more about the whole "second nature" thing but I felt like my bladder was about to burst.

"Well they don't *have* to know you're here," I said tartly. "I'll just go over myself."

"What? Alone?" Lucian looked worried and I felt a burst of anxiety coming from him. Ever since the little sex show we'd put on for Lord Mandrex's benefit, I'd been catching little snatches of emotions from both of my guys. "Rylee, I don't think that would be safe," he objected.

"Why not?" I demanded. "I'm a grown-ass woman—I can look after myself. I'll slip in the shop, use the restroom, and be back before you know it. It'll be fine."

Lucian still didn't look very happy about it. "Are you certain you can't…er, hold it until Drace returns? He could probably tell us the safest place—"

"Sorry," I interrupted him. "But I'm literally about to burst here. Look, don't worry." I put a hand on his arm and squeezed. "I'll be *fine*."

Before he could protest any more, I hurried across the dusty street, headed for the little shop.

The store was made of some kind of pale green wood that looked like it had been weathered by years of rain and wind. There were three steps leading up and a little porch on the front where several locals were chatting and playing what looked like a complicated game of alien checkers—or whatever board game they played on Denaris. Honestly, I didn't take the time to look very hard—I had to go so bad by now my eyeballs were floating, as my friend Zoe would have said. I ignored their curious glances and stepped inside, sliding the pale green door open to enter.

Inside, the tiny shop looked more than a little like an old fashioned General Store you might see on a Western…until you looked a little closer at the merchandise they were selling here. Along the wall there were black barrels filled with various things— a kind of purple grain…some things that looked like orange rocks floating in green liquid…a yellowish substance that looked a little like yogurt although I was sure it wasn't. There were also rows and rows of wooden shelves filled with alien food products that would have fascinated me if I hadn't needed to pee so badly.

Lucian and Drace had explained that not everyone used a food-sim to make their meals—in fact, most people still cooked the old fashioned way. I could see the appeal of that and I promised myself I would come back and do a little browsing if Drace said it was safe. But right now I really needed to get to a bathroom.

There was a long, wooden counter made of the same pale green wood as the outside of the store that ran along the front. Behind it was a small woman with pale, silvery gray skin and a stern look on her face.

"Um...hello," I said, approaching her tentatively. "How are you?"

"Fine—just fine." She nodded tersely. "And how can I help you today, off-worlder?"

"Actually..." I pressed my thighs together tightly. "I was wondering...hoping...do you happen to have a restroom I could use?"

"A *rest*-room?" She said the words as though it was completely foreign.

"A bathroom?" I said hopefully.

She frowned. "If you want a bath, you'll have to take one at your own domicile. We're not a traveler's hostel you know."

I sighed and I cursed the limitations of the translation viruses the Commercians had been sending through the hole in Earth's ozone layer. They were pretty good for helping me understand and communicate straightforward concepts but for subtle things, not so much.

It was time to be blunt, just as I had been with Lucian.

"I have to pee," I told her. "Really badly. Do you have a room I could do that in?"

"Oh!" Her face cleared. "Why didn't you just say so? Of course—we have toilet facilities in the back." She frowned. "But they're *not* for the general public. Not unless you can pay."

"I don't have any money...er, credit," I said despairingly. I was beginning to think I might wind up peeing right on her nice clean store floor which would *not* be keeping a low profile like Drace had wanted me to.

"That headscarf you have on is nice," she remarked and I remembered what Lucian had said about the Claw Clan people using a bartering system.

"It's yours," I said, unwinding it from my head and holding it out to her. "Just let me use your bathroom—*please.*"

She took the multicolored, jewel-toned scarf—which matched the deep blue tunic and leggings Drace had made for me using the clothing-sim—and examined it for a moment. Finally, she nodded.

"All right—this way."

She led me around the counter and to the back of the store, which was filled with boxes and stacks of dry goods waiting to be stocked. I followed her through the maze, wondering where the bathroom was. At last we came to the far corner of the storeroom and there we stopped.

"All right—here you go, off-worlder." She nodded curtly at the corner.

My gaze followed hers and I stared at where she was indicating with a sinking heart. I'd been hoping for a private room to conduct my business in but there was only a low wooden partition which was very easy to see over. On the other side of it was a tiled area about three feet square.

There was no toilet—just a hole in the middle of one black tile that led down into the ground. There were two narrow footrests—or what I assumed were footrests—on either side of the hole that were raised about three feet above the floor. Apparently, I was supposed to put my feet on the rests and balance myself in a squatted position before I let fly.

Wow, *that* was going to be fun.

It looked like something you might find in a third world country and it was certainly a far-cry from the luxury suction toilet that cleaned and blow-dried you aboard Lucian's spaceship. But beggars can't be choosers, as my Aunt Celia was fond of pointing out. And at least it didn't stink. In fact, there was a strong scent of flowers in the air, though I couldn't tell where it was coming from.

Maybe it was the Denarin equivalent of air freshener? Whatever—I was just glad the primitive toilet didn't smell as bad as it looked.

"Thank you," I said to the woman with pale gray skin.

"You're welcome," she said curtly. She turned to leave but I tugged at her sleeve, stopping her.

"Um…it's not that I'm not grateful but…you seem to be out of toilet tissue."

"What?" She frowned.

"You know…" I tried to think how to explain it. "It's a thin kind of paper you can use to…to clean yourself? After you, uh…" I gestured vaguely at the toilet hole and she gave me a disbelieving look.

"You must come from a very strange world. Why would we use paper to clean ourselves when we have a cleansing spigot?"

"A what?" I asked humbly. "I'm sorry, I've just never, uh…been to this part of Denaris before."

"Look," she said impatiently. Leaning down, she tugged at a dull silver pipe sticking out of the wall. It pulled out and I saw that it was attached to a long red tube that looked kind of like a garden hose. Oh—okay, *now* I understood.

"Got it," I said, nodding to her. "Thank you."

"Welcome," she said again and left me to it.

By that time I really did feel like I was going to burst. As weird as the situation was, I was willing to do almost anything to relieve myself. I climbed up on the three-foot-tall footrests and yanked down the royal blue leggings I was wearing. Then I squatted, balancing precariously over the hole in the floor, held my leggings out of the way, and finally let go.

Despite the weird position I was in and the uneasiness I felt about doing my business with only a single, low, wooden partition between me and the rest of the storeroom, it was sheer bliss. I closed my eyes and let out a long, *"Ahhh."* I couldn't help it—it just felt so *good* to finally get some relief!

I peed for what felt like forever but finally I was done. I wished for some toilet tissue but since there wasn't any, it was time to check out what the "cleansing spigot" could do.

Still balancing on the three foot tall footrests, I leaned forward precariously and reached for the metal pipe. It pulled easily out of the wall but I didn't see any way to turn it on. There was no knob on the wall and no controls on the pipe itself that I could see, or the long red hose it was attached to.

I felt like a fool, crouched three feet in the air over the toilet hole with my bare ass hanging out, fiddling with the silver nozzle. My thighs were beginning to feel the strain of being in the odd position for so long and now that my need to pee was relieved, I felt increasingly exposed. Anyone who came in would have a clear view of me over the low wooden partition—I needed to finish up and get out of here!

I shook the nozzle in disgust and stared down into its round, silver bore. How the heck did this damn thing work?

I had just about decided to give up and just let myself air dry—although that certainly wasn't my preference—when I happened to twist the silver nozzle to the right while I was holding the red hose it was attached to. Immediately a spray of pink water came gushing out. Unfortunately, I was still staring into the bore of the spigot when it happened, so I got a face-full of the pink, flower-smelling stuff.

"Oh!" I sputtered, teetering precariously on the high footrests. I nearly fell off but somehow I managed to keep my balance. I jerked the nozzle away from me and twisted it quickly, trying to turn down the forceful spray but I only made it worse.

Have you ever seen one of those videos on YouTube where the firemen are fighting to hold onto the fire hose but they can barely manage because there's so much water pressure pumping through it? It was kind of like that. The pink flower water (at least now I knew why the bathroom area smelled like flowers) started gushing out at a tremendous rate. I tried to point it away from myself, down to the hole below me, but the red hose whipped in my hand like an angry snake and the more I twisted, trying to turn it off, the harder it sprayed.

"Shit!" I gasped, holding it with both hands now. "Damn it, you stupid thing! You can't—"

"Who are you and what in the Frozen Hells are you doing in the back of my shop playing with the fucking cleansing spigot?"

The deep voice scared the hell out of me. I looked up with a gasp to see a tall, blue-skinned Denarin glaring over the wooden partition right at me.

"Oh my God!" The shock was too much. I tumbled over backwards, off the footrests, the wildly gushing hose still clutched in both hands.

As I fell back, the nozzle I'd been struggling to point at the floor came up. I had a confused impression of the tall blue alien in front of me getting sprayed right in the face with the pink water and then I hit the ground with a jarring bump flat on my back.

I cracked my head on the black tiles and all the breath was knocked out of me. For a moment, I saw stars—bright twinkles of light flashing in front of my eyes as I gasped to get some air back in my lungs. I lost my grip on the hose completely and it whipped through the air, spraying pinkish water everywhere while the strange Denarin guy bellowed and cursed and tried to catch it.

"Fucking...Goddess-damn it!" he shouted, snatching at the red hose which was dancing around like a cobra about to strike, spraying a solid gush of water. Just as he finally got one big hand wrapped around it and started twisting, the gray-skinned woman who had let me use the bathroom in the first place came running in. Behind her was a red-skinned Denarin male who was about an inch shorter than the blue-skinned guy.

"Porgy!" the woman exclaimed, when she saw what was going on. "What's happening? What are you doing?"

"Came in from the back to get some *gorgem* powder and found this strange off-worlder playing twisty-listy with the Goddess-damned cleansing spigot!" he growled angrily, glaring down at me as he finally turned off the nozzle. "I don't know how she got in here but look at this fucking mess! Cleansing solution *everywhere*— I'm dripping with it!"

"She sprayed you in the *face?*" the woman exclaimed and glared at me as though I had betrayed her in some way.

"Herself too, by the look of it," the red-skinned guy behind her remarked, looking at me.

"I'm sorry," I said—or tried to say, anyway. I was still trying to breathe after the fall I'd taken. "I couldn't...I didn't mean to..."

"What I can't figure out is how she got in here," the blue-skinned guy called Porgy said.

"*I* let her in." The woman put her hands on her hips. "She *said* she had to relieve herself. Traded me a headscarf for the privilege." She looked at me disapprovingly, lips pursed.

My head cleared some and I became aware that I was still lying on my back, dripping wet, with my leggings down, flashing all of them. Weakly, I rolled on my side, reaching desperately for my pants. God, this was horrible! I *had* to cover up!

"Someone should help her," the red-skinned Denarin said, clearly seeing the trouble I was having.

"Let her be, Kess," the woman said. "We don't know *what* she might be capable of."

"She's hurt." Kess reached for me anyway.

"I'm okay," I said quickly, putting up a hand to stop him as I finally found the waistband of my leggings and yanked them up. "I'm so sorry, I just—"

"What's going on here? What are you doing to my female?"

Lucian suddenly appeared in my line of sight. When he saw me lying on the floor, wet and helpless with two other males bending over me, his face went rigid with anger.

"Get away from her!" he hissed. Moving almost faster than my eye could follow, he was suddenly in front of me, putting himself between me and the perceived threat. "Touch my female and you *die*," he snarled, facing off the very surprised looking Porgy and Kess. (Their names would have made me giggle if I wasn't so busy being wet and miserable and humiliated.)

"Look out—he's Fang Clan!" the woman shouted.

"That's right." Lucian tore off the blue straw hat he was wearing for camouflage and bared his fangs in a hiss. "Come a step closer and you'll find out the hard way. Now get *back* from my female!"

"How dare you come into my own store and threaten me?" Porgy demanded. "Who the *fuck* do you think you are, fanger?"

"Please!" I sat up, holding out a hand, wanting to explain. What a horrible mess—I'd only wanted to pee and instead it looked like I'd started World War Three in the bathroom! If things came to blows and Lucian got seriously hurt, I would *never* forgive myself. "Please," I begged again. "This is all just a big misunderstanding!"

"Listen to the off-worlder female," Kess urged, frowning at the other two. "I think she's telling the truth."

"She sprayed me full in the face with cleansing solution!" Porgy roared angrily. "That's no fucking mistake! That's an *insult!*"

"You always were quick to claim insult, older brother." The new, familiar voice made my head whip around.

Drace came into view, his broad shoulders stiff with tension. It was really getting crowded in the cramped storeroom. Then my mind finally registered what he'd said—*older brother?* Did that mean that Porgy—

"Drace?" The big blue Denarin stared at Drace in disbelief. "What are you doing here?"

I saw a myriad of different emotions cross Drace's strong features and felt them as they passed through our bond. Anger...dread...worry...and finally, resignation.

"I'm here because I felt that my bond-mate and our female were in trouble," he said simply.

"Bond-mate?" The gray-skinned woman looked at him incredulously. "You claim this *fanger* as a bond-mate?"

"I do." Drace came to stand beside Lucian, who was still standing in front of me protectively. "All right, bond-mate?" he asked Lucian in an undertone.

Lucian nodded briefly, his eyes never leaving the other two males. "You claim kinship with these two?"

"Yes." Drace sighed. "Afraid so."

"How can you call him bond-mate? He's Fang Clan!" Porgy's nose wrinkled and he inhaled briefly. "And an *Alpha!* What the *fuck*, little brother?"

"He *is* an Alpha!" The woman's nose wrinkled too and she looked at us in obvious disgust. "Drace, what will your mother and your fathers say? This is unacceptable!"

"You think everything is unacceptable, Twyla," Drace remarked. I could feel his shame through our link—the shame of being bonded to another Alpha and having his family find out about it—but he kept his chin high and his voice steady.

"It's only a temporary bond," I said, as I got shakily to my feet. "We're trying to separate them. That's why I'm here—to help."

"Oh really?" Twyla eyed me sourly. "And here I thought your sole purpose was to trick honest people into using their facilities and then spray everything they own with cleansing solution."

"I lost control of the hose," I said desperately. "You have to know I didn't mean to do it!"

"How should I know what you do for fun, off-worlder?" she snapped.

"Her name is Rylee," Drace said, frowning at his sister-in-law, (I assumed that was what she was to him, anyway.) "And I'm certain she didn't come in here looking to cause any harm or damage."

"Drace is right," I said quickly. "And I really am *so* sorry! I never would have done any of this on purpose!" I wanted to cry with embarrassment—what a way to meet Drace's people! Knowing he was related to them made the whole incident about a thousand times more humiliating.

"It's all right, baby," Drace murmured to me and I knew he and Lucian both could feel my misery through our link. "We'll get this straightened out."

"*Will* we?" Lucian was still staring at Porgy, who had assumed a menacing air, his eyes narrowed and his hands balled into fists.

"Of course we will." To my surprise, Kess, the red-skinned male stepped forward, smiling. "Hello, female of my mate's sibling," he said to me. "I'm Kess—it's a pleasure to make your acquaintance."

"Um...hi." I wasn't sure if I should offer to shake hands. In light of the fact that I still hadn't gotten to wash mine, I decided not to.

"Well met," Kess said before turning to Lucian. "Bond-mate of my bond-mate's sibling, well met."

"Well met," Lucian echoed, looking a little less stiff and ready for a fight.

"Thank you, Kess." Drace nodded to him gratefully. "Well met."

"Well met indeed, sibling of my bond-mate." Kess gave him an easy, open smile and I thought he was by far the nicest of the three. Was he the Beta to Porgy's Alpha? It seemed likely. "So how long have the three of you been together?" he asked Drace.

"Stop pretending like this isn't a big deal, Kess," Porgy snarled, before Drace had a chance to answer. "This is wrong and you know it—my little brother can *not* be mated to another Alpha—especially not a fanger!"

"You'll treat my mate with respect, Porgy." Drace spoke to his older brother in a low, menacing voice and I felt his anger sizzle through our link. "I wouldn't disrespect Kess or Twyla."

"You don't have any reason to because *we're* in a *normal* relationship," Twyla snapped. "Your brother didn't go off and get himself mated to another Alpha and an off-worlder freak who plays in the personal relief area for fun!"

"Wow." I shook my head. "That is just *beyond* rude." I wasn't going to explain again how the whole cleansing-spigot-getting-away-from-me thing had been an accident. I refused to dignify her mean-spirited insult with another word.

"How dare you speak to our female that way?" Lucian snarled. He turned to Drace. "I think it's time we were leaving."

"I think you're right." Drace nodded curtly. "Come on—I have the supplies all ready to go."

"Go, then!" Porgy threw at him. "We'll see what our *parents* have to say when I tell them what you've done! As if it wasn't bad enough to have a mateless loner in the family, you had to go one better and find yourself *these* two to get bonded with!"

Twyla shook her head. "It's going to break your mother's poor heart, Drace."

"Twyla is right." Porgy sneered. "Wait until I tell her you're playing Beta to a fanger and you found some weird off-worlder freak female to tie the two of you together! What do you think she's going to do?"

Drace had been in the act of taking a step but now he staggered, as though his brother had physically hit him. I could feel his pain and the worry about how his parents—especially his mother—would grieve when they found out about us. Yet, he refused to reply to his brother's remark.

I couldn't stay silent, though. Swallowing my pride, I turned to the three faces—two angry and disgusted (Porgy and Twyla) and one sad (Kess).

"Look," I said, spreading my hands in a gesture of peace. "I think we got off on the wrong foot here. Lucian and I are only Drace's *temporary* mates and we're working to get the situation resolved. So maybe you could hold off on giving your folks a heart-attack for a little while, huh?"

"Temporary?" Twyla spit out the word like it tasted bad. "How can a psy-bond be *temporary?*"

"It's a pretty fucking permanent bond," Porgy agreed.

"It is when it's sealed," Lucian spat. "But my bond with your brother is *not* sealed. Nor do we plan on sealing it."

A little of the ugly hate cleared from Twyla and Porgy's faces and Kess looked confused.

"Wait—you have both a bond-mate and a female but you haven't yet sealed your bond?" he asked.

"We've been trying all this time to sever it," Drace explained stiffly.

Twyla put her hands on her hips. "And just how do you expect to do that?"

"With this." Drace out pulled the triangular stone Key and showed it to them.

Porgy leaned forward, a look of awe on his face. "Is that *tanterine?* That stuff's fucking priceless!"

"Amazing," Twyla murmured. She had a look on her face like Drace was showing her the Hope Diamond or maybe the Black Princess Ruby which is mounted on the British crown jewels.

"It is an extremely ancient and powerful artifact," Lucian said tightly. "With its help, we are going to sever the bond between your brother and myself. We were bonded by accident at a clan gathering and have been working to be free of each other ever since."

"Lucian is right—we're about to go into the K'drin to visit the Temple of Ganth," Drace said. "We were given a prophesy by Tanta Loro, the Sea Witch, that we would find something to help us sever our bond there."

"Well..." Porgy gave Drace a look of grudging respect that I thought had more to do with the priceless artifact in his hand than any admiration he might have for his little brother's determination.

"So you see," I said smoothly. "This whole bond thing will be...will be over before you know it."

My throat felt tight as I said the words but I didn't know why. I had a sudden thought—what would I have done without the bond I had to my guys just now? Both of them had felt my distress and had come on the run to protect me. It was nice to have that kind of backup. And it would be sad to lose it.

Still, I only had to look at the expressions on Porgy and Twyla's faces and remember Lucian's mother's reaction to understand why it was necessary. Drace and Lucian would never be able to stay together in peace. There would always be someone hating on them—someone saying they needed to be apart. Staying together would make their lives immeasurably difficult. Plus, it wasn't like I could stay with them to personally keep the balance between them, which both of them seemed to think was so vital.

*"This wouldn't work without you,"* Drace had said. Or something to that effect. Which was silly, I was sure. But it wasn't like it mattered—it wasn't like the three of us could stay together or even *wanted* to stay together.

*We have to break apart and go our separate ways,* I told myself. And wondered why it made me feel like crying.

"I *suppose* I can hold off on telling mom and our dads," Porgy said grudgingly. "As long as you *promise* you're taking care of this."

Drace and Lucian exchanged a glance and I felt sadness, hurt, and grim determination flow between them. It was Lucian who answered.

"You have our word on it," he said evenly. "Please do not shame my bond-mate before his parents. I have already had that unfortunate experience with my own mother—she was as upset as you are about our situation."

"Well, it can be an upsetting situation if you don't understand it." Kess gave us a compassionate look. "Did you say you were going to the Temple of Ganth, Drace?"

"We are." Drace nodded shortly. "And I think we should be leaving now."

"Surely not yet!" Kess protested. "We haven't seen you in over two solar years and now you have mates—even if they are only temporary ones. Come and have last meal with us and stay in our domicile tonight."

"Umm…" Lucian and I exchanged a swift glance and I saw Porgy and Twyla doing the same thing.

"I thank you," Drace began. "But—"

"I really don't think—" Twyla started.

"I insist," Kess said firmly, overriding both of them. "It would be a great shame on our Triumvirate if we didn't follow the laws of hospitality and invite family into our domicile." He gave both Porgy and Twyla meaningful looks. "Wouldn't it?"

"Really, Kess? You're going to invoke the law of hospitality?" Porgy growled.

"I don't need to invoke it, bond-mate. It was invoked the moment your kin came within the borders of Renth," Kess said quietly. "The only question is, will we honor it or violate it?"

"Fine," Twyla sighed. "But they have to promise not to discuss their…situation with the children. I don't need to be answering a lot of complicated questions."

"I think we're all of the opinion that the fewer people who know about our situation the better," Drace said dryly. "We'll keep it quiet in front of the kids."

"Very good—the invitation has been tendered and accepted." Kess clapped his hands together. "The only thing to do now is to gather the ingredients for my famous garro bean stew."

I shot a slightly panicked look at Drace. A look that said—*are we really going to do this?* Talk about awkward—having dinner and staying the night at his bigoted brother's house sounded like a freaking *horrible* way to spend the evening. I would rather be sweating in the jungle risking poisonous plants and ravenous animals than sit across from these people and break bread.

But Drace and Lucian both seemed resigned to it. Did it have anything to do with the "law of hospitality" Kess had mentioned? Maybe it was some kind of rule that if your family was in town you *had* to offer them a bed and some food?

It had to be something like that. Neither Porgy or Twyla looked at all happy to be having us as house guests but they had the same look of reluctant acceptance I saw on Drace and Lucian.

*I guess this is happening,* I thought unhappily, looking around the room at all the resigned faces. *Look who's coming to dinner.*

# Chapter Twenty-three
## Lucian

"This is delicious stew, Kess." Rylee smiled politely at the mate of my bond-mate's sibling or as she called him, "Drace's brother-in-law." The Earth designation sounded strange but accurate and I wondered uneasily if by extension I was also related to these backwoods Claw Clan provincials. Of course, it wasn't so much their social class that bothered me as their hostile attitude.

*It's the same attitude my mother had toward Drace, though,* I couldn't help thinking. Just because she was more refined about it didn't mean she'd been any less hostile. The fact was, wherever Drace and Rylee and I went, we were going to face hostility, even from our own families. *Especially* from our own families.

"Thank you. I grew the garro beans myself," Kess said, smiling. He was Porgy's Beta and he was acting affable and accommodating as only a true Beta can be. He and Rylee were straining to make conversation because Porgy and Twyla, seated across the table from us, were stubbornly silent.

At either end of the long, oval table sat the children—two boys on one end and two girls on the other. Clearly Porgy and Twyla's Triumvirate had been blessed by the Goddess although I was damned if I could see why—they certainly weren't the kindest people. Kess tried hard to make up for them, though—I appreciated that.

"Father's brother's mate, Lucian?" piped up one of the children—a little girl from the end of the table farthest from me. "Are you from the Fang Clan?"

I cleared my throat, ignoring the glare that Twyla was giving me from across the table. "Yes, I am, little one."

"Cool!" one of the boys exclaimed. "Can I see your fangs?"

I shot a glance at Drace who shrugged. *Up to you, bond-mate,* the gesture said.

With a shrug of my own, I opened my mouth and let my fangs extend fully.

There was a collective gasp of awe and admiration from the children.

"Wow!"

"They look so sharp!"

"Can you bite through solid plasti-steel?"

"Do you have poison in them?"

"One question at a time, please." I had to smile despite myself at their unbridled enthusiasm. I have always liked children, although I never expected to be able to have any myself.

Rylee was grinning and Drace was smiling too—a reluctant curve of his lips that gladdened my heart. I knew how uncomfortable my bond-mate felt in the domicile of his brother. Though the laws of hospitality dictated that we must stay here at least for a night, none of us were comfortable with the situation. Still, last meal was progressing fairly well and no one had shouted at or threatened anyone else so far. I considered that progress.

"Well?" the boy who had first asked to see my fangs said. "Can you? Bite through plasti-steel?"

"No," I said. "Although yes, my fangs are very sharp. And yes I have a fluid in them called 'essence' but it's not any kind of poison."

"It's not?" The child looked disappointed. "What's it good for then?"

I cleared my throat, beginning to feel uncomfortable.

"It's good for healing his mates," Rylee answered for me. "And..." she trailed off, biting her lip. Clearly she had just remembered the other purpose of my essence—to pleasure my bond-mates. "And other things," she ended lamely.

"What other things?" one of the girls demanded.

"Well..." I started uncertainly.

"Did you ever bite father's brother Drace with them?" the boy demanded.

"Uh…" I shot a guilty glance at Drace across the table but his face was like granite. *Admit nothing.*

"Excuse me, female of my father's brother," one of the little girls said politely to Rylee. "But where do you come from? You don't look like anyone I've ever met before, *ever.*"

Rylee smiled at her. "Well, I come from a closed planet called Earth. And did you know on my planet nobody knows that there are other people in the galaxy? We think we're all alone out there in space so you can imagine how surprised I was when I, uh, ran into your uncles…er, Drace and Lucian."

That statement sent them off and running and Rylee, who clearly liked children too, answered a myriad of questions. I felt relieved that the children's appetite for information had turned in another direction. But then, suddenly one of the children piped up,

"Father's brother, Drace — aren't you an Alpha?"

"Yes," Drace answered simply.

"And isn't your bond-mate Lucian one too?" the boy continued.

"Yes," I said, feeling Twyla's small, angry eyes boring into me from across the table. "But you see — "

"If you're both Alphas, how can you be bonded?"

"All right, children, time for bed." Twyla was suddenly out of her seat and bustling the children out of theirs.

"What?"

"But I didn't finish my stew!"

"What about dessert?"

"I don't wanna go!"

Twyla looked exasperated by this chorus of protests.

"Porgy, can you lend a hand?" she demanded. "It's the children's bedtime."

"No — we want Papa Kess!" one of the children begged. "He tells the best bedtime stories."

"Papa Kess has to stay with our guests," Twyla said, shooting Kess a dark look. "He invited them in the first place so it's his job to keep them entertained."

"Agreed," Porgy rumbled, also getting up from the table. "To bed, kids or I'll tan your backsides for you!"

The four of them ran scrambling down a long narrow staircase which led to the basement floor of the long, low domicile with Porgy and Twyla behind them.

"Sorry about that," Drace said to Kess who had an unhappy but resigned look on his face. "We didn't mean to make the kids ask questions."

"It's all right." Kess sighed. "I wanted some time to talk to you privately anyway."

"Privately?" I said. "Should Rylee and I leave?"

"No, no—this is for all of you." Kess settled back down across the table from us and looked at us earnestly. "I just want you to know...Porgy and Twyla don't speak for the entire family."

"They might as well," Drace said roughly. "You know they're only saying the exact same thing my mother and fathers would say."

"Well, they don't speak for *me,* anyway," Kess said firmly. "Drace, did you know I was a Halfer before I psy-bonded with your brother?"

"A what?" Rylee looked confused.

"Most Denarin males are born very clearly Alpha or Beta," I explained to her in a low voice. "But every so often there is one born who could go in either direction—a Halfer. Half Alpha and half Beta. When it comes time to bond, they have to choose which way to go."

"I didn't know that." Drace looked as shocked as I felt. "I just always assumed. You just...seem so *Beta.*"

"I am—now. But I didn't have to be—I chose to be." Kess looked at me and Drace intently. "It's a decision I have never regretted. I fell in love with Twyla at the same time Porgy did and I knew I could never have her unless I allowed the Beta side of my nature to rule." He shrugged. "So that's what I did."

"Why are you telling us this?" Drace asked blankly. "Neither Lucian or I is a Halfer."

"We're Alphas and we cannot be otherwise," I agreed.

Kess sighed again and ran a hand through his hair.

"I guess what I'm trying to say is that if you have some Beta tendencies you want to act on, well, there's no shame in that. Not as far as I'm concerned."

"Beta tendencies?" Drace looked at him doubtfully. "I don't—"

Kess blew out a breath. "Goddess, I'm making a mess of this. I just…want you to know not everyone is horrified and ashamed of your choice. I know how lonely you've been, Drace—how much it hurt you when you couldn't find a Beta who fit with you—one you could bond with. So you found another Alpha instead. And that's fine—it's better to be with someone you care for and who cares for you, than to be alone and hurting."

"Kess…" Rylee reached out a hand and placed it on top of his. There were tears glistening in her lovely black eyes. "That's beautiful. Thank you."

Kess shrugged and tried to smile.

"Just want you three to know I support you. And I know, at least a little, about what you're going through. It's not easy to be Beta when you could have been Alpha instead. But sometimes it's worth it."

"Um…thank you," Drace said at last. "That's…kind of you to say, Kess."

"We appreciate your wisdom," I added stiffly. Indeed, he had given us a lot to think about. I couldn't help wondering if he was right—if playing the Beta every once in a while could really be so bad, so wrong.

I wondered if Drace was thinking the same.

# Chapter Twenty-four

## Rylee

"How did everybody sleep?" I asked after we had finally said our goodbyes the next morning and left the long, low house with the thatched roof where Twyla and Porgy and Kess lived. I had to ask because Twyla had insisted on putting all three of us in separate rooms for "decency's sake." Myself, I had passed a very restless, unhappy night rolling around in a bed that seemed way too big and lonely.

"Poorly." Lucian sighed and ran a hand over his face as we tramped along the dusty road through the still-sleeping town. "It took me forever to get to sleep."

"Me too." Drace grimaced. "Tossed and turned all night."

"I missed you guys," I said honestly. "I don't like it when we have to sleep apart—I guess that's because of the bond, huh?"

"That and the fact that we love having you between us, *ma 'frela*," Lucian murmured, brushing my cheek with the backs of his fingers.

"It's nice to know you like being there, too," Drace added, giving me a kiss on the other cheek. He made a face. "I'm sorry my family was so fucking awful and Twyla insisted on putting us in separate rooms."

"They were no worse than my own mother when she found out about us," Lucian said calmly.

"And Kess was actually really nice and supportive," I pointed out. "I like him."

"He's always been very kind to me," Drace murmured. "In a lot of ways he's a better brother to me than Porgy. The things he told us…" He shook his head. "I never would have guessed he was a Halfer."

"His words were very…thought provoking," Lucian murmured.

I looked at both of them in surprise. Could it be they were actually taking Kess's advice to heart? If they could get over the whole Alpha/Beta thing… *There might actually be some hope for them — for us!* whispered a little voice in my head. But that was crazy, wasn't it? It wasn't like I wanted to leave Earth permanently and spend the rest of my life on a whole other planet…did I? *What have you got to lose?* asked that persistent little voice. *What would you really be leaving behind?*

Well, there was Aunt Celia but though she'd raised me, we had never been particularly close. I loved my cousins who were like brothers and sisters to me but they all had their own lives. And it wasn't like I had a job I loved or any really close friends — not since Zoe had left so abruptly…

"All right — here we are. The edge of the K'drin." Drace's deep, rough voice cut into my strange musings. "Now listen, you two," he said to Lucian and me. "The jungle is full of poisonous plants and hungry predators so let's stay close. Anyone wanders off, they could get killed."

Looking around, I could see why he was warning us to be careful.

The K'drin jungle was, in its way, as intimidating as The Sands of Death desert had been. Huge trees, as big as the giant Redwoods back home on Earth, grew at intervals. Some were so big around you could have driven a car through them, and all of them stretched hundreds of feet in the air. They had a strange, bluish-gray bark and their leaves were an even deeper shade of dusky blue.

In contrast to the giant trees, there were also shorter ones which were a more normal height. These had bark in different shades of green and gray and grayish-green with silvery-green leaves. Of course, there were plenty of vines and creepers too and I could hear hooting and howls and growls and rustling in the underbrush. There was a wet scent in the air — like rain forever just about to happen—as well as the smell of growing things. It made me think of a line from one of my favorite books back home.

"The Jungle eats itself and lives forever," I whispered and shivered.

"Are you well, *ma' frela?*" Lucian asked, frowning.

"I'll be fine," I said, trying to convince myself as well as him. At least I was dressed for adventure this time. The red, lightweight tunic and leggings set I had on was treated to repel any kind of stinging insects and the boots I was wearing, while not as high and heavy as the ones Lucian had wanted me to wear in the desert, were still sturdy and protective. The outfit might have looked a little strange back on Earth but I had sworn to myself not to let my fashion sense interfere with self-preservation again. I didn't care what I looked like as long as we all got out of this alive.

"Do we know exactly where we're going?" I asked, looking around uneasily.

"Got the nav-tracker right here," Drace said. "I put in a course to the temple—if we start now we should get there by moonrise."

"What?" I said, surprised. "So you can just put it in the GPS-thingy and have it lead us straight there? I thought it was some hidden ruin that nobody knew the exact location of. All Indiana Jones-y."

Drace laughed. "The Temple of Ganth isn't a secret—it's just a pain in the ass to get to. And people usually don't bother because it's just a stone slab floor with a single monolith standing in the middle. Scientists who study antiquities and past ways of life have been all over it but there's literally nothing else to see."

"Then I wonder what Tanta Loro expects us to find there? Where is the 'claw' she spoke of that can sever our bond? If no one else has been able to find it, how can we?" Lucian asked.

Drace shrugged.

"Who knows? Let's go find out."

He pulled out a short metal stick. When he thumbed on the button a pale blue beam of light shot out of it about three feet in the air.

"Whoa!" I exclaimed. "Cool light saber!"

"What?" He frowned at me. "What the fuck is a light saber? This is a brush-cutter. We'd never get through the K'drin without one."

To demonstrate, he swung the cutter and the pale blue laser burned through a thick swath of branches and a tangle of vines, making a hole in the jungle through which we could enter.

"C'mon," Drace jerked his head and swung the cutter again, making a way into the jungle. I followed him and Lucian came after, bringing up the rear.

The jungle closed around us in a claustrophobic tangle of gray and green and blue and I felt a shiver of fear run down my spine. We were beginning the last part of our quest—which was how I had started thinking of it—and I felt a sense of foreboding I couldn't understand or deny. For a moment I wished we could stop—that we could call everything off and find a way to be together instead. But I knew that couldn't be—we had to push on, into the jungle and find the Temple of Ganth.

There was no going back.

## Drace

I don't know how long we cut our way through the K'drin— long enough for my arm to get fucking tired, that was for damn sure. After an hour or so, Lucian asked to take a turn and I let him, warning him what to look out for when I did. He'd never used a brush cutter before but you would never know by the way he took to it. I couldn't help feeling pride when I saw how quickly he picked up the right technique and rhythm, swing, cut, step...swing, cut, step...

The pride I felt in my bond-mate's accomplishments made me remember Kess's words of the night before. About how being a Beta wasn't so bad. Rylee had asked Lucian and I why we didn't just trade off on playing the part of the Beta—much the way we had begun taking turns at other tasks like cooking cleaning, or now, cutting brush. Her suggestion had seemed crazy to me when she first made it but now I was beginning to wonder...would it really be so bad?

I had been furious with Lucian for treating me like a Beta after our ill-fated adventure in the desert. So angry that he'd slighted my

Alpha pride I didn't even stop to thank him for saving my life. I'd reacted the way I'd been taught to react—the way my big brother, Porgy, would act. But our recent visit with my brother and his bond-mate's words made me reconsider my actions and emotions. Why was it so awful to be treated as a Beta? Or to take a turn acting as one?

True, I had no attraction to other males, but I didn't find my bond-mate *unattractive* either. It was as I had told Lord Mandrex—his pleasure was mine and vice versa. And both of our pleasure came from making our female feel good. As long as Rylee was between us, did it really matter who was the Alpha and who was playing the Beta?

I frowned when the thought popped into my head. Was it possible that it wasn't so terrible to be bonded to another Alpha after all? Was I changing my mind about something I'd believed since I was old enough to understand the difference between male and female…Alpha and Beta?

*Doesn't matter if you are,* whispered a voice in my head. *Just because you changed your mind doesn't mean Denarin society has. Stay with Lucian and you'll never be accepted. You'll live your life as an outcast.*

And that was different from my life before I'd been bonded, *how* exactly? I'd been a loner—a recluse who only went out when I had to. So ashamed that I was unable to find a bond-mate I dreaded showing my face in public. People had cast pitying and mistrustful looks my way whenever I did dare to go out. I got the same looks now that I was with Lucian and Rylee but at least I wasn't alone when I got them…

It was a lot to think about and I had plenty of time to think. Lucian and I traded the brush cutter back and forth all day, keeping Rylee between us for safety. But though I heard plenty of predators prowling through the trees none of them bothered us. We stopped in a small clearing for lunch and to catch our breath and then pressed on, guided by my hand-held nav-tracker.

At last, just as the sunlight faded and Denaris's two moons rose, we came within sight of the Temple of Ganth.

# Rylee

"Wow…" I looked up at the moons, just visible through a break in the jungle canopy. There was a steady stream of rocks—they looked like pebbles but must be the size of boulders—flowing from the smaller pink moon to the larger blue one. It was a mesmerizing sight, especially surrounded as we were by the rustling jungle.

"'By the light of the quarreling moons,'" Lucian quoted.

"And there's the Temple of Ganth," Drace said. "Just as Tanta Loro said. This is one of the early places of our people. Some say this is where we first learned to live in threes instead of twos and developed the Triune psy-bond which keeps Triumvirates together."

I tore my gaze from the moons and looked to where he was pointing. A flat slab of stone glimmered silver-blue in the bright moonlight, looking almost like a lake.

Walking closer, I saw that the glimmering effect was caused by little glittery specs embedded in the blue-gray stone which made up the floor of what must have once been a huge temple. Around the edges, the stone was chipped and jagged and the jungle had thrown out creepers and vines as though to try and annex it. But somehow the middle of the temple floor had remained clear and surprisingly clean. In fact, it looked almost polished, reflecting the moons overhead like a mirror.

"It's beautiful," I said wonderingly. "Can we, uh, walk on it?"

"I don't think we have a choice," Drace said. "We have to find a way to use this." He pulled the triangular Key from his pocket and I was surprised to see that it glimmered in the moonlight too, just like the temple floor.

"Oh, is it the same stone?" I asked, taking it from him to get a closer look. "I thought *tanterine* was extremely rare and valuable."

"It is. The temple floor isn't the same rock but both substances have *lanzenite* specs," Lucian explained. "They glow and sparkle in the moonlight—especially when both moons are full as they are now."

We stepped up onto the sparkly stone floor and moved slowly towards the center.

Right in the middle of the temple floor was a huge monolith of shiny black. It had the same *lanzenite* specs as the floor and the Key, which made it glimmer in the moonlight like an accusing finger pointing straight at the sky. We walked up to it but I didn't quite dare to touch it. There was something about it…something that made me uneasy. Just under my usual range of hearing I seemed to be catching a deep, throbbing buzz which I thought came from the stone finger. I wondered what it was.

"The Finger of the Goddess," Drace said, indicating the monolith. "It's said it speaks with her voice when there is danger nearby."

"Is there?" I asked nervously. "Danger nearby I mean?"

Drace shook his head. "It's an old wives' tale. Don't worry, baby — Lucian and I will keep you safe."

"Thanks." I looked around. "Okay, we're here. Now what?"

"I don't kn—" Lucian began but a deep, rumbling growl interrupted him.

"Guys?" I looked around, feeling the uneasiness which had been building inside me morph into outright fear.

"Drace, you know the jungle better than we do. What was that?" Lucian asked.

"I'm not sure." His deep voice was grim. "It sounds like—"

The rumbling, purring growl erupted again. This time it sounded like it was coming from all around us—as though whatever was making it had surrounded us somehow.

"Whatever it is, it sounds hungry," Lucian said grimly. "Rylee, put your back to the monolith."

I was still reluctant to touch the black finger of stone, but I found myself backed up against it with Lucian and Drace standing in front of me protectively on either side. The growling was continuous now and behind me the humming of the stone finger had risen in pitch until it sounded almost like a woman singing a single, low, ominous note.

Suddenly a furry black form came slinking out of the jungle. It was hard to tell in the moonlight, but it looked kind of like a panther to me. Not just any old panther though—a huge one as big as a *horse*. I looked for the glitter of its eyes but I couldn't see any—the sleek, black, bullet-shaped head moved blindly in our direction, the wide nostrils flaring as it scented us.

"Is that a *kr'awn?*" Lucian sounded like he couldn't believe it.

"Shit!" Drace growled. "That's fucking impossible. But yes, that's what it looks like."

"A…a *kr'awn?*" My mouth was suddenly so dry I could barely speak. "Isn't that the predator you said nearly wiped out your race by…by eating all your women?"

"That's the one," Lucian said grimly.

"I…I thought you said they were extinct!" I whispered, my stomach clenching into a knot of fear. I was squeezing the *Tanterine* Key in my fist so hard I could feel it digging painfully into my palm but somehow I couldn't loosen my grip.

"They *are* extinct. Or, they're supposed to be," Drace growled. He pulled out the brush cutter and lit it up. I wondered how much good the miniature light-saber was going to be against a huge horse-sized panther. If Drace could get close enough he might be able to cut off its head. But would he be able to get that close without it ripping him in two?

"What are we going to do?" I asked softly, my voice wavering in fear.

"Protect you," Lucian answered grimly and Drace growled assent.

"Do you have your blaster, bond-mate? Between the two of us we ought to be able to take it down," he muttered.

Lucian patted himself down and cursed. "It must be back at the ship!"

"Take this then—I brought a spare." Drace drew another brush cutter from his pocket and handed it to Lucian who flipped it on. There was a buzzing hum and then both of them were holding the sleek light-weapons like swords.

"I'm ready." When Lucian turned his face to me I saw his eyes were glowing and his fangs were fully extended — I guessed he was going into fight mode. Drace was changing too — he didn't have fangs but his hair seemed to get shaggier and thicker, and it was sprouting along his shoulders and arms, almost as though he was growing a protective fur coat.

Was this the "second nature" they had spoken about earlier? I'd been imagining some kind of werewolf-like transformation but this was more like natural defenses coming into play. Like a cobra raising its hood or a lion shaking its mane.

"We can take it," Drace repeated, his voice even deeper and growlier than usual. "There's only one."

Then the undergrowth around us rustled and another huge black shape emerged. Then another…and another…and another. Soon there were five of the sleek predatory *kr'awn* ranged in a semi-circle with the three of us in the middle. I bit my lip to keep back the sounds of sheer terror that wanted to come out.

We were surrounded and there was no way out.

# Chapter Twenty-five

## Rylee

I could feel my heart pounding in every part of my body at once and my breath was coming in sharp, terrified pants. The growling got louder and louder as the pack of *kr'awn* advanced on us. They had huge, long fangs that glittered white in the moonlight. I could see them every time the huge animals snarled — which they did a freaking *lot.*

*Oh please,* I prayed, though I didn't know exactly who I was praying to. *Please, this is really bad! If we can just get out of here I swear I'll do the right thing. I'll turn my life around! I'll stop wasting time on things that don't matter and make my life count.*

"Get ready," I heard Lucian say in a low voice. "They're about to spring."

"They'll be aiming for Rylee," Drace said in a low voice. "We have to keep between her and the *kr'awn.*"

"Agreed." Lucian sounded tense and I felt a feeling of determination coming from him — from both my guys. I understood suddenly that they thought they were going to die here — that this was the end. But they wouldn't leave me, even though I was the one the huge predators wanted. They would stay and protect me, even if they died doing it.

The thought brought tears to my eyes and I swiped at them quickly with one arm. The other hand — the one still clutching the *Tanterine* Gray Key — I put behind my back, trying to steady myself against the Goddess's Finger.

The fist-sized, triangular rock in my hand scraped over the side of the black stone monolith and, to my surprise, a shower of sparks fell to the ground. They were long and bright and reminded me of the sparks that come from sparklers you light on the Fourth of July.

Then something shifted behind me and the note the Goddess's Finger was singing got suddenly higher until it was almost a scream. Before I knew it, I was falling backwards as the solid stone behind me gave way.

"Ahhh!" I screamed—I couldn't help it! I was falling *into* the monolith. A door had opened in its broad, sparkly black side right behind me. Only by grabbing the lip of stone around the door with my free hand did I stop myself from tumbling over backwards.

"What? What is it?" Drace demanded, his eyes never leaving the pack of *kr'awn* that had us surrounded. "Why are you screaming, Rylee? They haven't even pounced yet!"

"A door—guys, look!" I babbled. "There's a doorway and…and steps, I think."

"What are you talking about?" Lucian risked a glance over his shoulder and I saw his glowing eyes widen. "Goddess above—what is that?"

"A door in the Goddess's Finger. Come on—it's the only way!" I tugged on their shoulders, the Key still clutched in my hand. "Hurry—who knows how long it will stay open?"

"Could be a trap," Drace growled, also glancing behind him briefly.

"And it could be our salvation," Lucian said urgently. "Come on, bond-mate—the *kr'awn* are about to—"

Just then the biggest *kr'awn*—the one that had come out of the jungle first— hurled itself at us. Or should I say at *me* because I was clearly his target. His blunt black bullet of a head was pointed directly at me as he sprang and I watched as he came towards me— everything slowed down to a horrible slow motion by the terror that was rising inside me like a wave.

"Now!" Drace shouted and I saw the two blue beams of light swing wildly, carving into the huge, black body as the beast came for me.

There was a humming hiss and the *kr'awn* snarled angrily as the laser blades bit into its sides. It leaped away—somehow changing direction in midair—and landed lightly on the other side of the semi-circle of hungry *kr'awn* where it growled its defiance at us.

Clearly it hadn't been very badly hurt and just as clearly I would have been dead without my guys to protect me. But as brave as they were, they were no match for five hungry horse-sized predators.

"Guys," I said to them urgently. "Come on—hurry! In here before they try again!"

This time they followed me without protest and the three of us found ourselves on a narrow set of steps that led down into blackness.

I felt better when we were all inside but Drace and Lucian were still on high alert.

"The door," I heard Lucian mutter. "Do you think it's wide enough for the *kr'awn* to enter?"

"I don't kn—*shit!*"

I turned my head, afraid that Drace's curse meant the *kr'awn* had gotten inside. Instead, I saw that the door in the monolith was closing. As we watched, the two moons and the snarling animals outside slowly disappeared. And then there was nothing but silence and darkness.

"Well..." I took a deep, shaky breath. "I guess that answers *that* question."

"I have a lot of other questions, though," Drace muttered. "Such as how in the Frozen Hells do we get out of here?"

"We don't want to get out while that pack of *kr'awn* is still out there," Lucian pointed out. "Why don't we follow the stairs and at least wait until morning before we worry about exiting?"

"Sounds good." Drace sighed. "Rylee?"

"Sounds good to me too," I said. "But before we go any further, give me one of those light saber things so I can light the way. These steps are narrow and I don't want to trip and break my neck."

"Be careful," Lucian said, passing me his. "Maybe you should let one of us go first in case of danger."

"There isn't room to maneuver," I said, which was true. The staircase we found ourselves on was extremely narrow and tight— almost claustrophobically so. Both of the guys had to turn sideways to get down it because of their broad shoulders.

I took the laser tool and held it up like a flashlight as we went single file down the dark steps. It made me think of the Egyptian pyramids and how they were supposed to have secret passages that led into underground chambers. Some filled with gold…and some set with deadly booby traps. What would we find under the Goddess's Finger?

I didn't know but I hoped it didn't involve any more chances to get eaten alive by horse-panthers, at least.

The stairs curved down and down for what felt like forever but finally they ended in a large stone chamber. Our footsteps echoed on the dusty floor as we came to a halt, not certain where to go next. The vast, empty chamber stretched out before us into an unknowable void. Looking at it, I couldn't help thinking of all the stories I'd ever heard about miners getting trapped in cave ins or explorers losing their way in the subterranean depths and dying in some unexplored cave system when their light burned out. It was an awful thought and something I most definitely didn't want to happen to me.

The guys seemed to be feeling a little less threatened, though. At least, Lucian's fangs had shrunk back to normal and his eyes no longer glowed and Drace didn't look like he was wearing a protective fur coat anymore. I considered that a good sign.

"Look," Drace, who had the other light-saber said. "The walls—they have writing on them. At least—I *think* it's writing."

"Let me see." Lucian walked to the closest wall and examined it. "Looks like some ancient form of early Drusinian," he murmured.

"You read early Drusinian?" Drace raised an eyebrow at him.

"I wanted to be a scholar of antiquities once," Lucian said a bit stiffly. "My parents didn't approve—they wanted me to go into litigation." He shrugged unhappily. "So I did."

"We've both done things for our families we wouldn't have chosen, I guess." Drace sighed. "Can you translate this—see what it says?"

"I think so—with a little more light."

"Here." Carefully, I handed him my light-saber. (Yes, I knew they were mainly for cutting brush but I felt so much more bad-ass thinking of them as light sabers.)

"Thank you." Lucian took it and began to walk slowly, following the line of hieroglyphic-type symbols that ran in a wavering line along the wall.

*"Here is the tale of two and one that became three,"* he read, pointing to the writing. Sure enough, there were two male figures with broad shoulders and narrow hips standing together across from a very obviously female figure with breasts and curves. There were marks and lines around the pictures which must be some of the words. I was impressed he could read the words of the ancient language and hopeful too—maybe now we could figure out what we were supposed to be doing down here.

*"The evil and eyeless ones were devouring the females of the tribe for they found their scent delicious,"* Lucian read, as we walked along.

On the wall were pictures of three, sleek black *kr'awn,* surprisingly vivid despite the ancientness of the artwork. They were crouching, about to spring on the female figure who was cowering in fear.

*"The females were being taken and the people cried out in fear to the Goddess—save us! Save us or we shall surely all perish!"* Lucian went on, following the trail of writing along the wall.

Here there were pictures of many stick-figure people bowing and bending, their arms upraised to a being in the sky. The being was represented by a pair of eyes—obviously female by their long, curling lashes. They eyes were watching from a shining cloud with rays of light coming out of it.

*"The Goddess was sad and felt pity for the people,"* Lucian continued. *"She said to them—I have made you to be protective of your females and protect them you must. Two males must join with one female—lie with her and bond with her until the Three become One. Then the evil, eyeless ones will not be able to scent your females and you will be saved."*

As he read, we came to pictures that showed two male figures with a female between them. The ancient artist hadn't been shy here—both of the men had their shafts out and they were in the act of impaling the female between them at the same time. Just looking at it made me blush and squeeze my thighs together.

"Okay," I said softly as we finally came to the end of the writing—and the end of the wall because it ended in a corner. "I guess this is a kind of origin story of your people."

"It must be." Lucian was looking at the ancient symbols and writing with wonder on his face. "This is amazing. I wonder if the Chamber of Triune-bonding is down here?"

"That's a myth," Drace scoffed. "There's no such thing as the Chamber of Bonding."

"What kind of myth?" I asked.

"Supposedly it's an ancient chamber where the very first Triumvirate bonded." Lucian said. "Where their three-way union was blessed by the Goddess."

"Hmm. And I suppose a chamber like that would be private...like it would have a door to keep people out?" I stepped forward to the wall the one we had been following had dead-ended into. "Like this, maybe?"

The rough, brown stone wall where I was pointing was abruptly broken by a smooth panel of blue wood.

"Amazing!" Lucian's eyes flashed. "Look at this—it's *berra* wood. But this place is ancient—it should have rotted away years ago. Yet, it's solid." He made a fist and rapped on the door, which gave an echoing, hollow *boom*.

"Don't!" I exclaimed, feeling suddenly spooked by the loud noise in the empty, tomb-like space. "That's *creepy*. Just push on it and see if it'll open."

Drace put a shoulder against it and shoved. The door didn't budge an inch.

"Try pulling," Lucian suggested. Drace did. Still nothing.

Lucian tried and then Drace and then both of them together but no matter how they pushed and pulled the blue wooden door was completely steady and refused to move.

"Fucking thing..." Drace stood back from the door, frowning. "I guess it's not supposed to be opened."

"Not by brute force, anyway," Lucian said with a sigh. "But look…" His eyes lighted and he knelt on the dusty stone floor and pointed to the far corner of the door.

I leaned down to see what he was looking at and saw a little triangular knob of wood sticking out of the door. It was the same color as the rest of the door and easy to miss but once you noticed it, you couldn't unsee it.

"Wow," I murmured, looking at him. "Do you think…?"

"Think what?" Drace demanded.

"That this door opens only to the right key," Lucian murmured. "Go on, Rylee — try it."

I still had the *Tanterine* Key in my hand. Tentatively, I held it up against the triangular knob of wood. It slipped on perfectly and when I twisted it to the right there was a creaking sound and the blue door, which had seemed so solid and ungiving moments before, slowly swung open.

"Wow…" I breathed.

"Goddess above," Lucian murmured at the same time Drace muttered,

"Holy fuck!"

We had a right to be amazed — the chamber in front of us was dark at first but when the door slid all the way open, lights blazed inside it. We were blinded at first but when our eyes got used to the sudden brilliance, we saw something that couldn't possibly be.

In front of us was a large, circular bed, plenty big enough for three — even if two of them were as big as Drace and Lucian. The mattress was thick and piled with all kinds of furs and fur covered pillows. Seriously, it looked some kind of sexy-caveman porn setup. The fur-covered bed all ready for action and around it were placed ancient stone lamps that burned with soft golden flames, giving a romantic ambiance to the whole place.

But it wasn't just the fur-piled bed that amazed us — it wasn't even the first thing that drew our eyes. Standing on a pedestal, just inside the doorway, was a long, golden tool with four sharp points on one end. There was a kind of glow around it — like a force-field of some kind — that made it gleam and glimmer in a strangely hypnotic way. It was floating in midair with the sharp points poking towards the ceiling.

"What *is* that?" I whispered, feeling awed. It looked like a golden backscratcher, like the kind you can buy at the dollar store. Only a lot more golden and expensive and magical, than the dollar store variety, obviously. In fact, the way it was suspended in the middle of the glowing force field made me think of the dying rose in *Beauty and the Beast.*

"The Claw—it's the Claw Tanta Loro talked about!" Drace exclaimed. "'The claw which can sever your bond'—that's what she said!"

"She also called it a blight—a curse," Lucian cautioned him. "I think we should be carefu—"

But before he could finish his warning, Drace stepped forward and attempted to grab the golden claw. The moment his fingers touched the glowing field around it there was a *zapping* sound like a taser and the brilliant light glowed brighter for a moment, as though emitting a blast of energy.

Drace cursed in pain and yanked back his hand. "What the fuck?" he growled. "Why put it right there if you're not supposed to have it?"

"You're not supposed to have it *yet*," Lucian corrected him gently. "Look, there is more ancient Drusinian on the walls of the chamber. Let's see what it says."

We all stepped inside and Lucian pointed to the walls of the chamber, which were curved into a kind of oval. In fact, the whole room was kind of like being inside a giant, stone egg. There was something in the air—some magic or power I couldn't put my finger on that sent a tingling thrill down my spine. I wondered if whatever it was had preserved this room, keeping it safe and secure for centuries until it would be needed again by people like us.

*"Herein find the means to protect your female,"* Lucian read. *"The Chamber of Bonding admits all, bonds all, loves all.* So it *is* the Chamber of Triune-bonding!" He pointed excitedly at the wall where there were more pictures of two guys making love to one girl. *"If you have need to sever that which the Goddess has made between you, this chamber also holds the key,"* he continued.

"The Claw!" I exclaimed, pointing to where a picture of the golden claw had been drawn on the cave wall with little wavy lines of radiance coming out of it.

"So what do we have to do to get it?" Drace growled.

"Be patient, bond-mate." Lucian frowned at him and continued reading. *"But that which is not whole cannot be severed,"* he went on. *"A bond must be sealed before it is broken. Think well on what you do before you break what the Goddess has wrought and squander the love she has given."*

"Um...does that mean what I *think* it means?" I asked in the long silence that followed. "Are we going to have to..."

"Seal our bond before we can break it," Lucian finished for me. "No wonder Tanta Loro said Drace and I wouldn't be able to make it without you, *ma 'frela* – a psy-bond between two males can only be sealed when they bond a female to them."

"Makes sense." Drace frowned.

"Uh..." I shifted from foot to foot uncomfortably. "Do you guys actually...I mean, are we really thinking of...of doing that?"

"Of sharing you completely? Both of us making love to you at the same time, baby?" Drace's eyes were suddenly half-lidded as he looked at me.

"Gods, the feel of you between us...it would be so sweet." Lucian stepped forward, his eyes blazing with lust.

"Guys," I said desperately. "I'm not sure about this. I mean, we're all uh, dirty and grimy from trekking through the jungle all day."

"That must be why the ancients provided a cleansing pool— look." Lucian pointed to the other side of the round, fur covered bed and I bit back a little gasp of surprise.

Inset into a hollow place in the floor was a long, oval pool just a little bigger than the bed itself. It was so quiet and still I hadn't even noticed it but when I took a step closer, I saw little wisps of steam rising from it. There was even a little pile of round, hand-made looking soaps at one end of it. Yup, all ready for a bath. *A three-way bath,* my mind whispered.

Unbidden, an image rose before my mind's eye — the three of us naked and washing each other in the pool, rubbing all over each other's bodies with soapy hands. Then climbing out and making love on the fur-covered bed, touching and tasting…taking and opening…

"This…this is some kind of a sex cave!" I exclaimed, taking a step back from the pool and the bed. "The people who built this *wanted* everybody who came in to have all kinds of kinky, menage a trois sex in here!"

"It *is* the Cave of Triune-bonding," Lucian pointed out mildly. "But I fear my bond-mate and I are getting ahead of ourselves…and forgetting the 'no-sex' clause in our contract."

"Lucian's right," Drace said. "This is the exact thing you wanted to avoid, baby — hell, that we *all* wanted to avoid — from the very beginning. Sealing the bond." He looked at Lucian. "You're *sure* that's what the walls say?"

Lucian scanned the hieroglyphic writing again. "Unfortunately, yes. You cannot break an unsealed or partial bond."

I took a deep, trembling breath.

"Look — I promised I'd stick with you guys to the end and its not that I don't want to keep that promise. And it's *also* not that I don't want to be with you — I *do*. I care about you both. I…" It was on the tip of my tongue to say that I loved them but somehow I couldn't — couldn't let myself go that far. "I *want* you," I said instead. "It's just…you're both so *big*. I'm afraid you'd split me in two!"

"Is that all?" Lucian looked relieved and Drace chuckled a little.

"Is that *all?*" I demanded. "Isn't that *enough?* I mean, I know you guys are supposed to make some kind of hormones that make a girl, uh, stretch but I just don't see how you could possibly — "

"Prepare you to take us both?" Lucian murmured. "Ah, but *ma 'frela,* you haven't even given us a chance to try."

"He's right, baby — if you give us a chance, you'll see how gentle we can be…and how good it can feel to have both of us inside you at once," Drace promised softly.

I bit my lip indecisively. On the one hand the idea of taking two such huge shafts inside me at the same time was freaking scary. But on the other hand…

*On the other hand, look at their faces,* whispered a little voice in my head. *They want you…they care for you the way you care for them, Rylee. If they promise to be gentle, you know they will be. And besides, why don't you admit you want this to happen…that you've wanted it for days, ever since the show you put on for Lord Mandrex?*

I had to confess it was true. I couldn't help remembering the hot way the three of us had loved each other when we put on our little show for the rich Cantor Lord who looked like a fallen angel. I wanted to do this…I was just frightened. But maybe it was time to get over my fear.

I looked back and forth between them.

"You *swear* you'll be gentle?" I asked.

"So gentle you won't feel even a moment of discomfort," Lucian promised.

"And we'll stop if I say to?" I pressed.

"You'll be in complete control, baby," Drace promised. "If you say stop, we'll stop right away."

Lucian cupped my cheek in his hand. "Drace and I care about you, Rylee," he murmured. "We would never want to cause you pain."

"Well…"

Part of me couldn't believe we were doing this, but I couldn't deny my feelings for my guys any longer. *It's just once,* I told myself. *Just once and then we'll all go our separate ways. What harm is there is having a beautiful memory to cherish and remember when we're all separated?*

"All right," I said at last. "But let's get cleaned up first—I'm all sweaty."

"I think a dip in the cleansing pool would do us all a great deal of good," Lucian murmured.

"I agree." Drace gave me a wolfish grin. "Come on, baby—let's get relaxed and see where things go."

# Chapter Twenty-six
## Rylee

"Okay." I lifted my chin, trying to make my voice strong. "Let's do this."

I wasn't afraid of this, I told myself, wasn't afraid of being with both my guys at once. I could handle it.

I leaned down and started to take off my boots but Lucian was suddenly kneeling at my feet.

"Allow me, *ma 'frela*," he murmured.

"Yeah, baby—let us undress you." Drace was behind me, tugging at the hem of the red, long sleeved tunic I was wearing. I lifted my arms and let him pull it over my head, baring my breasts to both of them as Lucian slid the boots skillfully off my feet.

God, I couldn't believe I was doing this and yet it felt so right. The more I had their hands on me, the better and more natural it felt. It felt like the power inside me—the binding power of a *La-ti-zal* which everyone said I had—was reaching out towards both of them. As though I was *supposed* to be doing this somehow.

I didn't try to fight it. Before I knew it Drace was standing behind me, his arms around my waist, pressing his warm chest to my back while Lucian was pulling down the red leggings that went with the tunic.

I stepped out of them as Drace kissed my neck. I was embarrassed to note I was half naked now—down to the lacy red panties Drace had made for me.

"Mmm…I knew you'd look good in these when I simmed them for you," he murmured, running one big hand down my waist to cup my mound through the thin, silky fabric. I felt the warmth of his palm against my sex and bit my lip because it felt so good.

"You have become extremely good with the clothing simulator, bond-mate," Lucian complimented him. "You excel at making delicious undergarments for our female. Although not nearly as delicious as what is beneath them."

Still on his knees before me, he reached up, nuzzling the lacy edge of my panties, right where they met my inner thigh. Drace moved his hand obligingly and soon I felt Lucian's hot breath as he kissed me through the thin red fabric.

"Guys," I protested breathlessly, my heart pounding. "I thought...thought we were going to take a bath first."

"So we will," Drace growled. "Come on, bond-mate — let's get our female wet."

"With pleasure," Lucian purred.

Before I knew it, the two of them were lifting me up and setting me down, panties and all, into the steaming pool inlaid in the floor on the far side of the bed. The water felt wonderful lapping over my bare breasts and teasing my nipples but I didn't like being the only one in the pool.

"Hey!" I protested. "I thought it was going to be the three of us — I'm all alone in here."

"Not for long, baby," Drace promised. He and Lucian were rapidly removing their hiking clothes and boots. Before I knew it, I had company. The steaming water lapped lazily around all three of us, disturbed into ripples by the entrance of two huge muscular aliens into the pool.

"Mmm...feels good," Drace murmured, coming up to me. This time he was in front while Lucian was behind. They seemed always to keep me between them effortlessly — a silent dance they did where I was always in the center. It made me feel special and cherished and the center of their attention.

It made me feel hot.

"Are you talking about the water feeling good, bond-mate?" Lucian murmured, reaching around to cup under my naked breasts. "Or...something else?"

"I think you know what I'm taking about." Lucian let go of me for a moment and reached for one of the round homemade balls of soap. He rubbed it between his big hands, forming a spicy scented lather. "Tell me, *ma 'frela*," he murmured. "Do you still feel dirty? Do you wish for us to wash you?"

"I...I guess so." My voice came out high and breathless. I was very aware of the two, big male bodies bracketing my own in the steaming water. I could feel my nipples getting hard and my pussy was beginning to feel wet and swollen under the thin, soaked fabric of the red panties.

"You wash her breasts, I'll do her thighs," Drace murmured, reaching for another ball of soap.

"Agreed." Lucian cupped my breasts again in big, soapy hands, sliding smoothly over my naked flesh before capturing my nipples between thumbs and fingers to twist and tug lightly.

I moaned as sparks of pure pleasure ran down my body straight to the throbbing center between my legs.

"Uh-oh, bond-mate," Drace murmured, running his big, soapy hands up my thighs in long, caressing strokes. "I think you might have forgotten something—why are our female's underthings still on?"

"Her panties, you mean?" Lucian's breath was hot on the back of my neck. "I did that on purpose. I thought you might like to see the damp fabric clinging to her hot, wet pussy. If you look closely enough, you can even see the little bump of her clit. Would you like me to show you?"

"Please," Drace growled, his hands still busy rubbing up and down my thighs. God, I felt like I was going crazy but there didn't seem to be any stopping them—not that I really wanted to.

"Watch." There was a little lip just below the waterline on the edge of the pool. Lucian backed up to it and sat down, holding me in his lap. Then he lifted my lower body, supporting me, allowing my thighs and ass to float in the warm water. "Let yourself relax, Rylee, so that Drace can see how hot your sweet little sex looks with those wet panties on," he murmured in my ear.

I moaned softly and did as he said, leaning back against his broad chest and allowing my thighs to drift apart as Drace looked down at me.

"Mmm..." His hands were strong as he caressed and massaged my inner thighs. "I see what you mean, bond-mate. This wet fabric is clinging to her soft little pussy lips. Here…" He ran one teasing fingertip along the outer lips of my pussy. "And *here.*" The finger dipped inward, sliding along the cleft between my lips, dipping down to caress the throbbing button of my clit under the soaking wet fabric.

"Ahh!" I gasped, arching my back at the hot sensation. "Stop teasing me!"

"Of course we want to tease you, *ma 'frela,*" Lucian murmured in my ear, twisting my nipples gently but firmly. "We want you more than ready to take us."

"And you will be, baby," Drace promised hoarsely. "We'll make sure your hot little pussy is so wet and open you'll be able to take both our cocks with no problem."

I still wasn't sure about that but I was drowning in sensation, feeling too good to protest even though part of me was still afraid of what was coming.

*It's all right,* I told myself. *Drace and Lucian care about me – they're going to be careful and take care of me.* Just knowing that was true made me able to relax.

"I think she's wet right now—and I don't just mean with water," Lucian remarked softly. He tugged on my nipples. "Tell me, *ma 'frela,* can you spread yourself and allow Drace to see how wet you are? Can you allow him to slide his fingers under your panties and deep into your soft little sex to test your wetness?"

I gasped a little, sensations of fear and desire running through my body. Here I was, sandwiched between two huge, muscular alien men, wearing nothing but a pair of thin, wet panties, open, half-naked, and vulnerable. And now they wanted to do more than just wash and touch me…they wanted to touch inside me. Inside my pussy. Could I let them?

"Yes," I whispered, giving the approval they were asking for. "Yes, I…think that's okay."

"Good," Lucian purred in my ear. "Because I want to watch my bond-mate touch you, *ma 'frela.* Want to see his long fingers stroke into your sweet sex while you open for him."

"Spread your thighs, baby," Drace ordered, slipping the wet crotch of my panties to one side. I was ashamed to see that my pussy lips were hot and swollen — glistening with moisture that had nothing to do with the warm water we were bathing in. "Spread yourself wide and let me put my fingers all the way inside you."

"O-okay," I stuttered, opening myself as he had asked. My whole body felt heavy…languid with need and desire. I couldn't seem to say no to anything, couldn't seem to do anything but let them touch me — do what they wanted to me.

"Gods," Lucian murmured, watching from behind my shoulder. "Look at that hot little sex — look how she's opening for you, bond-mate. She needs to be filled, don't you think?"

"I do," Drace growled.

Both men watched avidly as he stroked over my glistening inner folds with two blunt fingertips, circling my clit to make me moan. The steaming water lapped at my slick flesh like a hot mouth, heightening every sensation.

"Look at that, bond-mate," Drace murmured to Lucian. "Our female's pussy is all swollen and wet with need. I think she needs our attention. Why don't you take over stroking her clit while I fingerfuck her?"

"With pleasure," Lucian purred and one of the hands that was stroking my breasts came down to hover over my pussy. Lightly, he began to trace around my swollen clit, never quite touching me exactly where I needed him — drawing out my pleasure by prolonging it until I moaned and squirmed.

Drace moved his own hand, sliding those two wet fingertips down to my entrance and swirling them teasingly just inside my pussy channel, barely touching.

I squirmed again, the hot water lapping all around me. All these light, almost-touches were turning me on so much I felt like I was melting from the waist down. It seemed like the two of them had made a silent pact to drive me insane.

"Please!" I gasped, my hips bucking. "You're making me *crazy!*"

"We just want you to be ready for us, *ma 'frela,*" Lucian murmured.

"Lucian's right. You're only feeling crazy because you need your pussy played with, baby. You need to be stroked and fingerfucked nice and slow, don't you?" Drace growled softly.

"Yes!" I admitted, past all shame now. "Please, yes!"

"Very well, *ma 'frela.*" Lucian looked up at his bond-mate. "Shall we give her what she needs?"

"I think so." Drace nodded. "I think she asked nicely enough."

"Indeed, she did," Lucian said softly. As he spoke, he finally let his fingertips dance over my aching clit, strumming lightly over and around my tight little bud, setting my whole body on fire with need and desire.

At the same time, Drace gripped my hip with one hand to hold me steady and then drove two long, thick fingers smoothly into my pussy. I gasped as I felt him hit the end and then draw back to press into me again.

"Oh," I gasped, suddenly right on the edge of orgasm. "Oh God, *yes!*"

"That's right, *ma 'frela,*" Lucian murmured in my ear, his talented fingertips still flying over my slippery clit. "That's right—beg for it. Beg for us to make you come."

"Please," I moaned obediently. "Please, I need to...need to come so badly! Please, Lucian...Please, Drace..."

"I'm sure you do." Abruptly Drace withdrew his fingers and Lucian stopped stroking me. "But not yet," he said when I moaned in frustration. "I think we'll save your first orgasm for when at least one of us is inside you. Or maybe even both."

"A good idea—her body will welcome us more easily if she comes on one of our cocks first," Lucian purred. "For now, I believe we are clean enough. Shall we adjourn to the bed?"

"Good fucking idea," Drace growled. "I can't wait to hold Rylee between us in bed again. I missed it last night."

"I did too," I whispered.

"And I," Lucian murmured.

Between them, they lifted me out of the water and began to dry me off with some of the spare furs, which surprisingly absorbent.

"But...but I've still got my panties on," I protested softly as they worked on me.

"We can take care of that, baby," Drace promised. He looked at Lucian, who was still behind me. "Maybe you'd like to pull down Rylee's panties, bond-mate?"

"I would love to," Lucian murmured. "I haven't explored our female's sweet sex nearly as much as I long to."

Before I knew it, big hands were tugging down the sopping panties and dropping them on the stone floor.

"To the bed," Drace ordered. "I think we need to spread out and relax so you can prepare our female's pussy properly, bond-mate. Don't you?"

I wanted to ask what they had been doing before if not preparing me but Lucian murmured assent and before I knew it, the three of us were on the fur covered mattress together. Drace was behind me, supporting me so that I leaned back against his broad chest and sat between his legs. Lucian was between my thighs, looking up at me.

"You want to taste her, don't you?" Drace asked, as he cupped my breasts and idly flicked the nipples with his thumbs. "I've tasted her twice—it isn't fair that you haven't even licked her sweet pussy once, Lucian."

"I'd like nothing more," Lucian murmured. "In fact, I was thinking..." He took a deep breath and looked at Drace full in the face. "Perhaps I should play the Beta during our...encounter. That way I can taste Rylee's pussy while you penetrate her to help get her ready to have both of us inside."

"Actually, I was going to offer to play Beta," Drace said in a low voice. "I've been thinking a lot of what Kess told us and I thought, well...maybe it won't be so bad."

"Why...why don't you both try being the Beta?" I couldn't believe the words that were coming out of my mouth. But I felt so turned on, so hot and shameless by now that I couldn't seem to help myself.

"How do you mean?" Lucian asked, frowning at me.

"Well...the Alpha, uh, slides his shaft inside while the Beta licks, is that right?" Just thinking of it made me feel almost lightheaded with lust. God, I couldn't believe we were doing this! But I didn't want to stop. I could feel my binding powers getting stronger, drawing the three of us together.

"True," Drace said. "Are you saying we should take turns doing the licking before we settle down to penetrating you together?"

"I think it might be easier for me to take if I was...was used to having you in me one at a time," I whispered, biting my lip.

"A good point," Lucian purred, stroking my thighs. "Very well, bond-mate," he said to Drace which one of us shall play the Beta first?"

"I will," Drace said decisively. "Rylee has already had you in her pussy once—it will be easier for her to take you again while I lick her sweet folds and tend to her clit. Then we can switch."

"As you wish. Then let me suggest a change of positions..."

We rearranged and before I knew it I, Drace was lying flat on his back while I straddled his broad shoulders with my pussy hovering above his mouth. Lucian was facing me, kneeling on the bed in front of Drace's head.

"Mmm, that's a fucking hot sight, baby," Drace murmured, looking up at me. "Love to see your hot folds all spread open—all sexy and wet right in front of me." Tilting his head up, he placed a hot, open-mouthed, sucking kiss full on my aching sex.

"Oh!" I gasped as he did it again, kissing my pussy the same way he would kiss my mouth. "Oh, *God,* you're good at that, Drace!"

"That's right, bond-mate," Lucian murmured encouragingly, his eyes filled with heat. "Spread our female's pussy with your tongue. Lap her hot clit and bring her pleasure. Make her wet so I can enter her properly."

As he spoke, he reached out and tugged at my nipples again, teasing me gently while Drace's hot tongue explored my open folds, sliding and slipping from my aching bud all the way down to the entrance of my pussy and back up again.

"Ah!" I moaned, grinding against Drace's mouth. "God, I'm close—so *close.*"

At which point Drace pulled away, much to my disappointment.

"Drace..." I begged, looking down at him. "Why did you stop?"

"He had to, *ma 'frela*," Lucian purred softly. "We need you to come on our cocks—remember? And speaking of that, are you ready for me to enter you?" He was facing me and now he scooted forward so he was kneeling, legs spread wide, with his long, thick shaft sticking out from between them.

"I...I think so," I said, a little uncertainly. "This is a little bit of an awkward position."

"Let me help," Drace offered. "It's the duty of the Beta to make sure the female is ready and to guide his Alpha's shaft into her pussy."

"You're certain?" Lucian looked down at him, a little frown on his face. "You don't mind?"

"I'm the Beta here," Drace growled. "So no, I don't mind doing what I'm supposed to. Remember, bond-mate—your pleasure is my pleasure."

"Very well." Lucian took his hands away from his erection and allowed Drace to reach up and take him in hand instead.

"Slowly," Drace commanded, bringing his bond-mate's shaft up to my pussy. He slid the broad head of Lucian's cock between my pussy lips, making sure to rub it against my aching clit in a slow, deliberate slide that made my back arch with pleasure.

I moaned and Lucian threw back his head and groaned as Drace continued to use his bond-mate's shaft to pleasure my pussy. And then, slowly, he guided Lucian to my entrance and slipped him inside.

"Thrust in, bond-mate," he ordered, looking up at Lucian who was looking down at the place we were joined. "Fill our female with your shaft and pump your precum deep in her pussy so that she can take us both."

"With pleasure," Lucian groaned. He slid forward and I felt him filling me—that long, hard shaft sliding deeper and deeper until he touched bottom within me.

I had expected him to move back and forth at that point but to my surprise he just held still, holding my hips so that we were joined tightly together.

Drace was still beneath us and I suddenly felt his tongue, lapping strongly around the place where Lucian and I were joined, sliding and licking around the tightly stretched opening where the thick shaft was invading me.

"God!" I groaned, my whole body clenching with need. "God this feels so good but why—"

"Why is he not moving?" Drace asked, looking up. "He's filling you with his precum, baby. A special kind of precum that helps you be open enough to take us both. If you concentrate you should feel it—some females say it's warm, almost hot—and there's a lot of it."

"All…all right," I whispered. Closing my eyes, I tried to do as he said and concentrate on what was happening between me and Lucian. Sure enough, as he thrust a little deeper, I felt him swelling inside me. Something hot and wet was spurting deep in my pussy, making me ready for him and Drace.

It was an amazing sensation and I swear I nearly came right there even though no one was moving. Just the feeling of Lucian pumping into me while Drace licked all around the place where his bond-mate's thick shaft was invading my pussy was almost too much.

At last, though, Lucian leaned forward and kissed me.

"I've filled her with as much precum as I can, bond-mate," he told Drace. "It's your turn now."

"Sounds good to me," Drace growled.

With a slow slide, Lucian pulled out of me. I looked down to see a clear, creamy liquid filling my pussy. It was amazing how much wetter and more open I felt now but I knew I could be even more open once my guys switched places and repeated the process.

We changed positions. This time I relaxed against Drace with my back to his broad chest. I straddled the long, thick pole of his cock as though I was about to ride him cowgirl style. But this time, it was Lucian's turn to help his bond-partner enter me.

"Are you ready, Drace?" he asked in that deep, smooth voice of his as he knelt beside us. "Ready to let me guide you into our female's pussy?"

"Do it." Drace didn't flinch when the other man grasped his thick shaft. As Drace had done, Lucian rubbed the broad, plum-shaped head of his bond-mate's cock against my inner folds, sliding across my swollen clit until I moaned and begged him to put Drace inside me.

"With pleasure, *ma 'frela*," he murmured and slid the head down until it lodged in the entrance of my pussy. "You can slide into her now, Drace," he told the other man. "But be careful—you're thicker than I am, I think. You need to be gentle while you fill our female's pussy."

"Of course," Drace murmured. "Stroke her clit with your tongue while I enter her, Lucian. Make her pussy tingle while I fill it."

"I'd love to." Leaning forward, Lucian grabbed my thighs and spread them wide, lapping and kissing my pussy eagerly while Drace filled me with his thick shaft.

I moaned as he entered me because Lucian was right—Drace was even thicker than he was. And yet, though I felt a stretching sensation as he filled me to the core, I didn't feel any pain. Though even if I had I'm not sure I would have noticed it—I was too busy enjoying the sensation of Lucian tasting me for the first time, lapping and sucking my clit as his bond-mate filled me completely.

"Gods, baby, you're so *tight*," Drace moaned in my ear as he finally bottomed out inside me.

"Tight and hot and extremely wet," Lucian agreed. "Fill her, bond-mate—pump her sweet pussy full of your precum and make her ready for me to enter her too."

"That's what I'm doing," Drace groaned and I felt that hot spurting sensation again as he filled me up the same way Lucian had. It felt *amazing*.

I lay back against his broad chest and just let it happen, enjoying the feeling of the thick cock spurting inside me while Lucian's hot tongue swirled around and around my clit, pushing me higher and higher with every moment.

"Ahh…" I moaned softly, burying one hand on Lucian's thick black hair and squeezing Drace's thigh with the other. "Guys… this is…I feel…"

"Are you going to come soon?" Drace growled in my ear, kissing the side of my neck. "Need you to come soon, baby — it'll be easier for Lucian to enter you if you're coming."

"I…I think I am," I admitted softly. "God, Lucian, that feels so *good.*"

"Lick her harder," Drace ordered, thrusting his cock even deeper into me. "Make her come, bond-mate. Come all over my cock so you can join me and we can breed our female together. Breed her and bond her to us."

"My pleasure," Lucian purred and then he sucked my throbbing clit into his mouth and lashed it with his tongue until I thought I couldn't stand it any more.

The duel sensations of being filled with such a large shaft and having the hot, wet tongue bathing my pussy was suddenly too much for me. With a low, broken moan I felt myself coming — coming so hard I could hardly breathe.

"Now!" I heard Drace say. "Enter her *now*, bond-mate. Join me in filling and pleasuring our female."

Lucian rose and repositioned himself between my thighs.

"Going to enter you now, *ma 'frela*," he told me in a low voice. "Going to fill you along with Drace so we can seal this bond. Are you ready?"

"I…I think so," I whispered, biting my lip as the pleasure went on and on. "God, I *hope* so."

"I think you are," Lucian assured me. To Drace he said, "Pull almost all the way out, bond-mate. Our shafts must be pressed together in order to enter our female at once."

"All right." With a long, slow slide, I felt Drace's thick shaft pull out until only the head was still inside me. Looking down, I watched as Lucian pressed his own shaft up alongside it and then, gently but firmly, he slid the head of his own cock into the entrance of my pussy so that it kissed the tip of Drace's.

"I feel you, bond-mate." Drace looked over his shoulder. "You ready? In position?"

"More than ready." Lucian cupped my cheek. "We're both going to enter you now, *ma 'frela*. Let us know if you have any pain or discomfort and I promise we'll stop at once."

"All...all right." The intense orgasm had died down some but I still felt pleasure running through me, like ripples in a pond that last long after you throw a stone into the still water.

"Now," Lucian said and with a long, slow thrust, both thick shafts entered me together and filled me to the core.

I don't know how long it lasted. The feel of both men inside me at once was so hot, so overwhelmingly intense, I could barely think of anything. All I could do was lie between them and let them take me—let them fuck me long and hard and deep, both of their thick cocks moving in unison with each other.

Though I had just come, I felt another orgasm rising inside me, threatening to drown me like a tidal wave. This one was going to be intense, I realized dimly, through the haze of pleasure that clouded my brain—*important*. It was going to tie the three of us together with an unbreakable bond that would be deeper and more meaningful than the tentative one we shared now.

*No, not unbreakable,* whispered a little voice in my head. *Because you're going to break it. That's the whole point of this – remember?*

But I didn't want to remember, didn't want to think of ever being parted from my guys. I just wanted to be with them forever—safe and loved and cherished, feeling them inside me. Inside not just my body, but my soul too.

"Gods, Rylee...love how tight you are around us," I heard Drace groan in my ear. "Feels so fucking good...so fucking *right* to share you like this."

"It does feel right," Lucian agreed, stroking my arms as they pushed inside me. "I can feel you binding us together with every thrust."

"Can't...can't help it," I moaned, dropping my head on his shoulder as he and Drace pulled out and thrust deeply into my pussy again and again. "It's...involuntary."

"It's all right," Drace assured me, stroking my shoulders. "All right, baby — we *want* to be together."

"Yes, we do." Lucian sounded a little surprised. "It feels good to be bound together. Feels so…Gods, *ma 'frela!*"

He groaned as he and Drace made an especially deep thrust inside me. My pleasure was building higher and higher and I knew I wouldn't last much longer.

"Guys," I panted. "I…I'm really close. Think I'm going to…going to come."

"Come on then, baby," Drace growled. "Come on our shafts while we pump you full of our seed. While we breed you."

His hot words and the feeling of both shafts filling me at once were finally too much. With a low cry, I threw back my head, my back arching and my toes curling as the incredibly intense orgasm ripped through me.

With a low groan from Lucian and a growl from Drace, I felt my guys tipping over the edge too — allowing my orgasm to trigger theirs as well. They spurted inside me, hot and wet…claiming me completely, making me theirs, breeding me and bonding me to them and encircling me with their love until I felt like I was overflowing with it.

When I felt their seed bathing the mouth of my womb, my orgasm jumped to a higher level. My whole body lit up and it felt like a freight train of pleasure had hit me square in the chest. For a moment, I could hardly breathe it felt so good. I saw stars dancing before my eyes and I thought,

*I love you! I love you both, so much!* in a burst of emotion I couldn't control or deny.

Then, to my surprise, I heard an answering voice — *two* answering voices in my head.

*Love you too, baby,* one growled — Drace.

*My heart is yours, ma 'frela,* Lucian's murmured.

Then the pleasure began to ebb and the intense connection was over, leaving me limp and panting, wilting like a flower between them.

But not *completely* over, I realized as I slumped back against Drace's broad chest and tried to catch my breath. I could still feel the new bond between us—a connection like a golden, fine-linked chain attached to all our hearts, tying us together.

We were bonded now and it was beautiful. Beautiful but also, incredibly exhausting.

"God," I groaned, closing my eyes. "That was…"

"Fucking incredible," Drace finished for me in a low, hoarse voice.

"Life changing," Lucian offered quietly. "Transcendent."

"What he said," Drace growled and I felt a sudden bubble of laughter rise in my throat. I giggled, unable to help myself. I just felt so *good* – so right and complete. It was like I'd been missing pieces of myself, pieces I'd been searching for without even knowing it for years. Drace and Lucian—they were the pieces, I realized. They made me whole—we made each other whole—and that was why I felt so good.

"What's so funny?" Drace asked, but he sounded like he might laugh himself.

"I don't know—you, Lucian, me…all of this." I giggled again and stretched between them, feeling sore but in a good way, like I'd just had the most amazing workout in history. Well, don't they say it's important to do your Kegal exercises every day? This would go down in history as the most intense Kegals ever. The thought made me laugh some more and I shook my head when Lucian looked at me quizzically and asked,

"Are you well, *ma 'frela?*"

"I'm beyond well," I told him. "I feel *amazing*. Like everything is perfectly right for me, both inside and out. I don't know when I've ever felt so good."

"I feel pretty fucking fantastic myself," Drace growled thoughtfully.

"And I am content and happy as I never have been before," Lucian agreed. "Do you think we can attribute all that to our bond?"

"Maybe. Or maybe it's just that our bond is special because Rylee's a Binder," Drace said.

"Maybe." Lucian nodded.

The feeling of warmth and contentment filled me too and now that my giggle fit was over, the safety and protection I felt radiating from my guys made me feel sleepy.

"Hey, I know it's the guy—or guys—who are supposed to fall asleep after sex…" I yawned and stretched. "But we've been tramping through the jungle all day followed by mind-bendingly intense three-way sex." I blushed a little as I said it but I didn't stop. "I'm tired," I told them. "Actually, *exhausted.* Can we…do you think we could just lay down for a little while and take a nap?"

"A good idea." Drace yawned too. "What do you say, bond-mate?"

"I'd like to rest—with Rylee between us," Lucian said. "Maybe we could finally rest peacefully instead of tossing and turning as we did last night without each other."

"Definitely." I sighed. "Come on, let's get, uh, untangled so we can get comfortable."

They slipped out of me and we all crawled under the furs, snuggling like sleepy children with Drace on my left and Lucian on my right. I let out a little moan of pure contentment as I felt the two big bodies on either side of me and then I closed my eyes and drifted off.

# Chapter Twenty-seven

## Lucian

"Lucian, wake up. Come on—wake up, bond-mate." A hand was shaking my shoulder and a familiar voice was murmuring in my ear.

"What? What is it?" I sat up, disentangling myself carefully from the sleeping Rylee. At first I didn't know where I was but then I looked at the fur covered bed and the dim, oval shaped stone room and the events of the last few hours came back to me. Bonded—I was bonded to another Alpha and our shared female and the bond was sealed.

*We'll be together for life,* whispered a stray thought in my head. A tingle of joy filled me at the thought. Finally, I was no longer alone. Finally I had a female I loved and a mate I cared for to share her with. It was beautiful...perfect...unspeakably *right.* I felt whole, complete for the first time in my life.

Then my bond-mate's next words ruined it.

"The Claw," he said. "It's free now. I mean—I can touch it. Look."

He was standing naked in the middle of the cave-chamber—none of us had bothered with any sleep clothes before our nap. Now he walked to the small pedestal which held the long, golden claw with its four, sharp-tipped points. Earlier it had been hovering in midair, clearly held there by some force beyond our understanding. But now it was lying on its side on the stone pedestal and the glow around it was gone. Drace picked it up carefully and showed me.

"See? No more force field, or whatever it was. It's ours now— we can have it."

"Oh. Of...course. That's good. So we can sever our bond whenever we want to." The words tasted sour in my mouth but I made myself say them anyway.

"Yeah. Of course." He looked down at the implement in his hand as though it might bite him. "How..." He cleared his throat. "How do we use it, I wonder?"

"I don't know." I shrugged. "I didn't see any directions on the wall."

"I don't either but...hey — look!" He came back to the bed and sat beside me, holding out the Claw. "See? Look on the shaft of it."

I bent to look at what he was talking about. Tiny black letters and symbols in the ancient tongue which decorated the walls were appearing up and down its golden sides.

"What does it say?" Drace asked me.

"It says..." I cleared my throat, reluctant somehow to read them, to speak the fatal words aloud. But that was foolish — we *wanted* to be parted. It was the point of our entire quest! I made myself go on. "It says:

"To sever a bond the Goddess has wrought

Is wrong and brings nothing but pain

But if you must, put the Claw to your heart

Draw blood and be lonely again."

Drace cleared his throat. "Um, okay. I guess that's pretty clear — we just scratch ourselves on the left side of our chest, right over our heart."

"I guess so," I said dully. It wasn't lost on me that the instructions on the claw mentioned the word "lonely." It was exactly how I had felt all of my life — and how I would soon feel again. "Do you want to go first or should I?" I asked.

"Uh..." Drace didn't look any more eager than I felt to break our newly formed bond. "Maybe...maybe we should wait," he said at last.

"For what?" I demanded. "I thought you wanted us to be free of each other? Why else wake me from a sound sleep to show me the instrument of our separation?"

"I just happened to wake up and see it lying there—I didn't go *looking* for the fucking thing," he growled defensively. "Okay then, you want *me* to go first?"

"If you like," I said coldly. So much for bonded bliss—we'd barely been together an hour or so (depending on how long we'd been napping) and we were already going to sever our newly sealed bond.

The prospect made my chest feel tight and I felt a deep unhappiness coming from Drace as well. Could it be, he didn't want to sever the bond any more than I did? But then why had he called my attention to the Goddess-damned Claw in the first place?

"Neither one of you is going first!"

Drace and I looked over and saw that Rylee was awake and sitting up. The furs were pooled around her waist, leaving her lush breasts bare and her hair was wild around her face. I couldn't help wanting her and I felt an answering surge of lust from my temporary bond-mate. Hmm—I hadn't thought of him as "temporary" for a while—the return of that word made me feel melancholy all over again.

"What did you say, baby?" Drace asked her, because Rylee was glaring at us both.

"I said neither one of you is going to break the bond—not yet!" she exclaimed. "What if we meet those damn horse-panthers again when we leave this place? What are we going to do if they decide to go for me because we're all unbonded and they can somehow smell it?"

I felt a rush of relief.

"Of course, Rylee is correct," I said. "We cannot break the bond until we bring her safely out of the jungle."

"You're right!" Drace also looked relieved. "Damn—can't believe we almost did that! Sorry, baby," he added to Rylee. "We weren't thinking straight."

"So you'll hold off—on severing the bond?" She looked at us anxiously. "Because I have to be honest—I feel much safer now that the three of us are linked. It's like…like we have a layer of protection we didn't before when we were only sort of half-way bonded."

"I agree," I said thoughtfully. "We're stronger together than we are apart."

"Absolutely." Drace nodded. "Fine—we'll just take the Claw with us and use it…when we decide to."

"A good plan," I agreed and then my stomach rumbled.

Rylee grinned. "Hey—sounds like somebody's hungry."

"Well, we *did* work up quite an appetite earlier," Drace said. "I mean, that was some hard fucking work."

"No pun intended?" Rylee asked dryly. "And are you actually saying that making love to me was *hard work?*"

"I was talking about the hike through the jungle and standing off those damn kr'awn," Drace protested. "Honestly, baby."

"All right—I forgive you." She laughed and slapped at his shoulder playfully. "Come on, let's get some food out of the packs. And please tell me you brought something besides hairy spaghetti and eyeball oatmeal."

"Actually, I simmed some of the Earth delicacies you call 'sandwiches,'" I said, answering her question. "Drace was making the clothes with the clothing sim, so I took charge of packing the food."

"Look at you two, working as a team! In more ways than one." She blushed, her cheeks going rosy under her creamy brown skin tones.

"Sharing you with Drace was incredible, *ma 'frela*," I murmured, reaching over to brush my knuckles over her hot cheek. "I hope you were able to accommodate us without pain."

"Not a bit of pain," she murmured, blushing again. "You guys, uh, prepared me really well. But how…" She cleared her throat. "How was it taking turns being the Beta? Did it bother you?"

"Not me." Drace sounded thoughtful. "I mean, it's not something that comes naturally to me, like it would a true Beta, but I didn't mind it. In fact…" He cleared his throat. "It was…"

"Surprisingly pleasurable," I finished for him, quietly.

"Yeah." He looked at me in surprise. "You thought so too?"

"Your pleasure is my pleasure, bond-mate," I said simply. "And Rylee's pleasure belongs to us both."

"True." He grinned at me. "We make a good team, don't we?"

It was on the tip of my tongue to say, *Why don't we stay that way? Why sever the bond at all?* But I wasn't sure how Drace or Rylee would react to such a radical suggestion. After all, we'd been all over Denaris on a quest that had almost killed us several times and all so we could be free of each other. Drace's family hated me and mine hated him—well, my mother did—and Rylee had her own life to lead back on Earth. There was no way the other two would want to stay together and try to somehow carve out a life for ourselves in such a hostile environment.

Or so I told myself.

"We do make a good team," I said instead, smiling back at my temporary bond-mate. "Come on—let's get some of those Earth delicacies and eat. I'm starving."

## Drace

We left the magical Chamber of Bonding the same way we had found it. Rylee insisted on straightening the furs on the bed and we made sure not to leave a speck of trash anywhere. In fact, the only change we made was the fact that I had the Claw tucked neatly into my pack when we stepped out of the egg-shaped room and back into the underground temple.

I didn't really like touching the damn thing—it felt wrong and somehow dangerous in my hands. But we'd come all this way for it so I felt obligated to pack it away, though I was careful to wrap it in several layers of clothing first.

We'd been a little afraid we wouldn't be able to get out the way we'd gotten in. But after climbing the steep and narrow staircase that seemed to go on forever, we finally found ourselves at the secret monolith door. Rylee had only to press the *Tanterine* Key to its surface once and it slid aside, letting us out into the jungle.

Though we'd been afraid the pack of supposedly extinct *kr'awn* might be waiting for us, the huge predators were nowhere in sight. Possibly because they could no longer smell Rylee after Lucian and I had sealed our bond with her between us.

Speaking of my bond-mate, I felt much more connected to him than I ever had before and it was a *good* kind of connection. Feeling his emotions no longer grated on me, even though the emotion I felt most from him was sadness.

Well, no—that's oversimplifying it. On the surface, he was happy—we all were. But underneath it was a deep sorrow, a feeling that this happiness was fleeting and would be over all too soon.

I understood Lucian's emotions because I was feeling the same way myself. But despite the unhappy choice to go our separate ways which was coming in the near future, for now we were all feeling pretty great and I believed it was because of our newly sealed bond.

I'd heard it said all my life how amazing it was to be bonded with a male you respected and a female you both loved—how wonderful it was to share her and take care of each other. But all the empty words I'd ever heard paled in comparison to the reality.

When I tripped over a vine in the forest, Lucian's hand was under my arm, catching me before I could fall. And when a poisonous *gareth* got too near his face and was about to strike, I severed its head with my brush cutter—what Rylee called a 'light-saber' for some reason—before it could spit the venom that would have blinded him. When Rylee took a false step and started sinking in a hidden pit of suck-sand, my bond-mate and I worked effortlessly as a team. Without even having to talk about it, we grabbed her under her arms and pulled her out before her first gasp of fear had even stopped echoing through the jungle. Together the three of us were like a well-oiled machine, anticipating each other's wants and needs without even having to think about it.

It was fucking beautiful.

The way we worked so well and so smoothly together made me think. And what I was thinking was, *Why are we in such a fucking hurry to sever our bond?* When we'd first been bonded, Lucian and I had been desperate to get it done—to be free of each other. But that was before Rylee and before we started to know and understand each other.

Of course, we came from radically different backgrounds and opposing clans and once that had seemed like a good enough reason to cut our bond. But now I understood that despite our differences, Lucian and I had something important in common, something that transcended anything else that might come between us—we both loved Rylee desperately and I was beginning to think I would rather die than let her go.

I wondered if Lucian felt the same—if he did, it was an emotion too deep for me to read or feel through our bond. I realized the only way to know would be to ask him—ask if he felt the way I did, that we should let our bond stand and just learn to live with the world's hostility towards our union.

But he had a lot more to lose than I did. I was just a lone artisan and if my family hated me for mating another Alpha, well, that was just too bad. Of course I didn't *want* to cause my parents pain but even if I did, it wasn't like it would affect my whole family on a more than emotional level.

For Lucian, things were different. His family was wealthy and influential. His fathers were the leaders of their clan. If it came out that Lucian was mated to another Alpha and an off-worlder girl, his parents' social standing would be ruined—their empire toppled. There was a lot more at stake for him…which was why I couldn't bring myself to ask if he'd stay with me.

Even if I had asked and he agreed, there was no guarantee that Rylee would stay too. And she was the glue holding us together. We both loved and cherished her—wanted to please and pleasure her—wanted to protect her from all harm. Without her to share between us, what did we have? Nothing.

So I kept my mouth shut and just kept cutting brush.

I didn't know what else to do.

# Chapter Twenty-eight

## Rylee

The trip back to civilization seemed to take a lot less time than the trip to the temple. By mutual consent, we didn't visit Drace's family again—Kess was wonderful and the kids were cute but nobody wanted to deal with Twyla and Porgy, especially now that the bond between the guys was completely sealed. Instead, we went straight from the jungle, back to the parking area.

Even though it was a long hike, it was totally worth it. Almost before we knew it, we were back in Lucian's ship, freshly showered, and relaxing in our jammies, feeding each other grapes and *nubu* – a Denarin fruit with a fuzzy green outside and a juicy red center. It had a flavor like watermelon and coconut and strawberries and cinnamon all mixed together – delicious.

"Mmm, this is so *nice*," I sighed, lounging on the sleeping platform between my guys. Tonight, Drace had simmed me a gorgeous, simple lace and silk nightgown in a warm cream tone that went really well with my skin. It was sinfully soft and practically see-through but I didn't mind, even though I could feel their eyes on my body all evening as we talked and relaxed. "I love spending time alone with just the three of us," I told them.

"I love it too," Lucian admitted.

"Me too," Drace said, his voice a soft growl. "Here, have some more *nubu*, baby." He pressed a slice of the juicy red fruit between my lips and a drop of juice ran down the side of my jaw. "Oops, let me get that for you." Leaning forward, he licked me, his tongue making a long, hot trail from the vulnerable side of my neck up to my chin.

"Mmm…" I moaned softly, my body lighting up at his touch. Despite the hot three-way sex we'd shared the night before, I still felt ready for more—still wanted my guys.

"Very nice," Lucian murmured. He had a hot, lazy look in his eyes, as though he enjoyed watching me and Drace together. "It's good of you to help our female clean up, bond-mate, but I fear you might have missed some. Just…here."

Leaning over me, he tugged down the top of my lace gown, baring my breasts. I gasped but didn't protest as he rubbed another ripe slice of the *nubu* fruit over first one nipple and then the other. The chilled fruit was cold against my tender nubs and I felt them get tight and achy immediately, begging for attention.

"Oh, I see what you mean," Drace growled, looking up at me. "What a mess—we'd better clean that up, baby."

"Yes," I said, my voice coming out in a breathless whisper. "You…I think you'd better do that."

Keeping his eyes trained on my face, Drace leaned over me. Starting at the bottom curve of my breast, he lapped upward, capturing the sticky juice on his tongue until he came to my tight left nipple which he sucked deeply into his hot mouth.

I expected Lucian to do that same to my right nipple but he was watching Drace with a thoughtful look on his face.

"I can't help noticing that you seem to have an excellent oral technique, bond-mate," he remarked in a low, aroused voice. "Every time you put your mouth on Rylee, you make her moan."

Drace let my left nipple slip from his lips and looked up with a wolfish smile. "It's in the way you swirl your tongue—watch." He positioned his mouth over my right nipple, still dripping with *nubu* juice, and demonstrated his tongue-work to Lucian.

"Oh!" I gasped, arching my back to press more of my breast into his hot mouth. God, I swear these two were driving me *crazy!*

"Hmm, very nice." Lucian nodded. "Tell me—do you use the same motions down below?"

"You mean when I taste our female's sweet pussy?" Drace stroked my thighs through the thin creamy lace gown, making me bite my lip to stifle another needful moan. "Sometimes…and sometimes I use a variation. Want me to show you?"

"I think that would be up to Rylee," Lucian murmured.

They both looked up at me and the naked lust in their eyes made something low in my belly clench with desire. But still, I wasn't sure…

"I…I want you to," I said. "To…to taste me, I mean. But, well…we're all going to be going our separate ways soon. Don't you think we should start laying off the kinky three-way sex?"

"We could," Drace said slowly. "Or we could take one more night to enjoy and appreciate each others' bodies. Give ourselves one last memory before we sever our bond tomorrow."

"Oh…" I bit my lip. "Are…are you guys going to do that tomorrow? I mean, you're going to use the Claw on yourselves? It's all decided?"

"I *thought* we were." Drace looked at Lucian. "Isn't that why you programmed a course for Y'brith? So we could give Mandrex back the Key after we, you know, severed our bond?"

"I suppose." Lucian looked deeply unhappy but then he seemed to make an effort to shake off the negative emotion. Looking at me, he gave me a slow, hot smile. "So if you want to have one more night to remember us by, maybe you should let Drace show me his excellent technique on your sweet little pussy, *ma 'frela.*"

I tried to let go of the sudden sadness that had overcome me at the thought that our time together was coming to a close. It wasn't just that I would miss them or be sad when I was back on Earth — it was that I felt like a piece of me — two pieces actually — would be missing when they left. It was like they were talking casually about cutting out chunks of my heart, as though it didn't matter.

*Stop it,* I told myself sternly. *You can't force them to stay together. Just try to forget about tomorrow and live in the moment — make a beautiful memory to keep with you for always.*

"All right," I whispered at last. "Drace can…can teach you his technique. I don't mind."

"Many thanks, *ma 'frela,*" Lucian purred, pushing up the lacy hem of my nightgown. "Now, if you would be so kind as to spread your thighs wide and give my bond-mate access to your pussy?"

Moaning, I did as he said, not protesting a bit when Drace got between my legs and began to tug off the lacy cream panties that went with the nightgown.

"Look at that, baby," he rumbled when he'd pulled them down. "Look how wet and ready your pussy already is. Gods, can't wait to taste your creamy little slit." He looked at Lucian who was on my other side, watching avidly. "Now look, the first thing to do is to spread her sweet pussy lips wide so you have clear access to her hot little clit…"

I don't know how long they worked on me—teasing and tasting, taking me right to the brink of orgasm but never quite letting me go over. Drace spent forever showing Lucian his favorite way to eat my pussy and then Lucian showed him his own favorite way to suck my clit and tease me with the tip of his tongue. By the time they finally let me come with Drace thrusting two thick fingers deep in my channel while Lucian lashed my aching little bud with his tongue, I nearly had an out of body experience.

"That's right, baby," Drace growled as I cried my pleasure while they touched and tasted me. "That's right—give it up for us. Love to watch you come, love to taste your sweet pussy while you lose control."

It was so good and the peak they'd brought me to was so high that the crash after orgasm was intense. *Never again,* I found myself thinking as I sank down, panting on the bed, my body and emotions wrung out by the incredible pleasure. *They'll never touch me like this again. My guys will be gone and I'll be all alone.*

It was all I could do to keep from crying.

But though I held back the tears, I couldn't keep the sadness back any longer—the sense of impending loss that made me feel hollow inside.

Drace and Lucian sensed my gloomy mood through our bond. Without asking, they slipped me between the covers and cuddled up on either side of me, lending me their heat, letting me feel their love. At last, worn out by the intense pleasure and safe in the cradle of four strong arms of the men who loved me, I fell asleep and dreamed…

*I was back home…back home in Tampa and I was all alone. A strange mist filled the streets and I was wandering through it, looking for something. No, looking for some**one**, but I didn't know who. He…no, **they,** were very special to me…or had been special to me once. But now I couldn't even remember their names. I only knew they were gone. They had left me alone. All alone.*

*Tears came to my eyes, hot and hard as bullets. They tore me up inside, pouring out like a salty flood of poison. It hurt so much to cry but I couldn't seem to stop, couldn't ease the loss that filled me and ate pieces of my soul.*

*"They're gone," I said, my words echoing in the mist that surrounded me. "Gone and they're never coming back."*

*I was alone and I would be alone forever…*

"Baby? What's wrong?"

"*Ma 'frela,* you are having a bad dream. Wake up!"

Two sets of hands were stroking me, two deep voices were talking in low, worried tones in my ear.

I finally managed to struggle out of sleep but when I did, I found my eyes were filled with tears. And even though I was awake, I couldn't stop crying.

"Baby, what is it?" Drace asked, cuddling me close to his broad chest.

"*Ma 'frela,* tell us—why are you crying?" Lucian pressed his warm chest to my back, stroking my hair.

"I…I'm sorry," I finally managed to gasp out as the tears ran down my cheeks and the sides of my face. "I just…I had such a horrible dream."

"Can you remember it?" Drace said softly.

"Some…I think," I whispered.

"Tell it then," Lucian urged. "In the Fang Clan we believe that dreams can be prophetic. Tell us what you dreamed, Rylee."

"I…" I closed my eyes, trying to remember. "I was back home but nothing was the same. I was…was wandering through a mist. I felt confused…disorientated. I was looking for someone—I think it was you guys. Only…" My voice started to waver again. "Only I couldn't even remember your *names*. I just knew...knew that..." A fresh sob broke from me and I had to work hard to stifle it. "I just knew I was alone and that...that I'd always *be* alone. I knew I would...would never see you two again."

I broke down again, then, sobbing as if my heart was breaking. And honestly, it was. This was the last night I was going to sleep between my guys — the last time I would even see them. After they left me back on Earth they were going to go their separate ways. Our beautiful three-way relationship — our Triumvirate — would be dissolved and none of us would ever see each other again.

"Rylee...baby..."

"*Ma 'frela...*"

Drace and Lucian tried to comfort me again but I was beyond comfort. All I could think was how I would never see them again and how I'd be lonely the rest of my life. Cold and alone without their love to keep me warm.

I sat up in bed and pulled my knees up to my chest, trying to stop the trembling that shook my whole body as I sobbed.

"Rylee..." The guys sat up on either side of me and rubbed my back but I was inconsolable, crying like I hadn't since I was a child. An all out sobbing that left me feeling breathless and choked and so miserable I wished I could just die.

From the corner of my eye, I saw them exchange a helpless glance and I could almost hear the nonverbal communication flying between them — *What are we going to do? I have no idea! She's really upset! I know but I don't know how to calm her down!*

For some reason their exchange — the way they fit so well together and were able to almost read each other's thoughts now — enraged me.

*It's not fair!* I thought, my pain turning abruptly to anger. *It's not fair — why do we have to be apart? They fit so well together and I'm their center. We're perfect together — why do we have to be separated? It's not fair!*

"*What* is not fair?" Lucian asked and I realized I must have said the last words aloud.

"Yeah, what's not fair, baby?" Drace echoed him.

"It's not fair that we have to be parted!" I burst out, finally giving vent to my sudden rage. "It's not fair that I'm going to lose you both and you're going to lose each other just because of what people say—because of what our families think!"

"Come now, Rylee," Lucian said dryly. "It is not *your* family who would not approve of our union. Drace and I are the ones who have to worry about that."

"You think my Aunt Celia would *approve* of us? Of *this?*" I made a motion with my hand, indicating the way I was naked in bed between two huge, muscular men. "You think she'd be okay with me shacking up with two guys at once? They have words on my planet for girls who do three-ways and none of them are very nice. And that's for girls who have three-ways with *human* guys. I have no idea what they'd call me if they knew I'd...I'd fallen in love with two aliens! If they—"

"Say that again." Drace was staring at me intently—they both were.

"Say what?" I demanded. "About how getting it on with two guys at once is frowned on down on Earth? Or how my Aunt Celia would most certainly *not* approve of our relationship?"

"Say the part where you admitted you love us," Lucian murmured. "The part where you said you had fallen in love with Drace and me."

"Oh, uh..." I came to a stumbling halt, feeling like my tongue was too big for my mouth. "I..."

"Is it true?" Drace demanded in a low, intense voice. "Really, baby? You love us?"

"You know I do," I said at last, unable to hold back any longer. "I told you—*thought* it at you—back when we were all, uh, bonding. You know."

"That was in the heat of the moment," Lucian pointed out. "Many promises are made and many things are said during such times."

"Well, it wasn't an empty promise to me," I said softly. I looked down at my hands, twisting in the covers, because I couldn't meet their eyes. "I love you, Lucian...and you, Drace. I love you both and the idea that I'm never going to see you again after you break your bond and take me back to Earth, well…it tears me up inside."

"It hurts me too." Drace's voice was low and choked. "Hurts so fucking much it feels like someone is ripping out a piece of my heart."

"I feel the same," Lucian admitted softly. "I see the necessity of being parted from you both but it is like looking on the necessity of death. I do not…do not know if I can bear it."

"They why bear it?" I asked, daring to look up at them. "I'm serious—why are we doing this? Why are we putting ourselves through all this agony to be apart when what we really want is to stay together?"

"That is a very good question," Lucian murmured. "One for which I do not have the answer."

"I do." Drace's voice was rough. "We're parting ways because it won't work for us to be together. I mean, it might work on a personal level but our families will hate it. And society—"

"Let society go fuck itself." Lucian's voice was low and angry.

Drace and I looked at him, extremely surprised. We didn't usually hear such language from him—dropping the F bomb was Drace's department.

"*What* did you say, bond-mate?" Drace asked him carefully.

"I said Rylee is right—why should we care what society thinks? Or our families either, for that matter?"

Lucian got out of bed and started pacing, a look of intense anger on his face.

"Do you know how *lonely* I have been all these years? And not because I couldn't find a Beta—I know that is a hardship too." He nodded at Drace, who nodded back. "But that wasn't my problem— I found several Betas that would happily have bonded with me. There was one in particular—Hylorn of the Scale-Clan. I met him in school and we were friends at once. I've never felt so close to anyone before—until the two of you, anyway," he said, motioning to Drace and me. "But I *knew*—knew at once that Hylorn and I ought to bind our lives together."

"What happened?" I asked. "Why didn't you?"

"I thought I would be allowed to," Lucian sighed and ran a hand through his tousled black hair. "The Scale-Clan are the Fang Clan's closest allies—many fine alliances have been made between Alphas and Betas of both clans. And yet, when I brought him to my home to spend the mid-winter holidays…"

"Your mom and dads vetoed the idea," Drace rumbled. "Is that right, bond-mate?"

"They treated Hylorn with a coldness that made me ashamed of them." Lucian spoke in a low, frustrated tone. "And later my mother dragged me aside and explained that we could never be together. Something about an old scandal in his family—a tragedy that happened years before. But as old as it was, she was afraid it would taint our family name if I was allowed to bond with him."

"So you weren't allowed," I finished for him in a low voice. "God, Lucian, I'm sorry."

"I let them do it to me once." He looked up, a savage expression of anger on his face. "I let my family ruin any chance I had of happiness in order to preserve their precious social status and reputation. Why should I let them do it again?"

"It hurt you badly, didn't it?" Drace asked softly. "I feel your pain through our link. I'm sorry, Lucian."

"I already thought of Hylorn as a bond-mate," Lucian said dully. "I'd allowed myself to feel for him—to get close—because I was so sure my family would approve. I didn't really believe, even then, that they would sacrifice my future and any chance I had of having a family of my own, just to keep up appearances. I didn't understand until it was too late that their pride was more important than my happiness." He looked up at us, eyes blazing. "Well fuck them!"

"Lucian!" I exclaimed.

"No, I mean it—*fuck them!*" he growled, sounding more like Drace than his own smooth, sophisticated self. "I'm not going to let them ruin my happiness a second time. I love you." He stabbed a finger and me and then Drace. "Love you *both*. And I want to stay with you. If…" He cleared his throat, some of the anger leaking from his eyes to be replaced by uncertainty. "If the two of you want to stay with me."

"I love you too, bond-mate," Drace admitted in a low voice. "But I didn't think…I didn't like to ask. You've got so much more to lose than I do," he said to Lucian. "Your family is rich and influential and — "

"Didn't I just finish telling you I don't give a damn what my family thinks or what happens to them? Let them watch out for themselves," Lucian growled. "I'm through letting them tell me who I can love…who I can be with. I choose you, Drace…and you, Rylee. If you'll have me." He looked at me. "Will you?"

"You have to ask?" I was half laughing, half crying as I put one arm around Drace's thick neck and reached my other arm out towards Lucian. "Come back to bed."

Lucian came willingly and before I knew it, we were entangled in the sweetest, three-way embrace imaginable. The kissing and caressing was beginning to turn into something more but suddenly Lucian sat up, looking serious. Reaching out, he put his right hand to my chest, just over my heart. And then he did the same to Drace, putting his left hand over the other man's heart.

"I pledge to you, bond-mates," he said in a low, serious voice. "I pledge my time, talents, and my treasure…my love and my loyalty. Even in death, may we never be parted."

I wasn't sure what was going on until I saw the awed, almost shaken look on Drace's face and felt a surge of emotion going through our bond.

"You're sure?" he whispered hoarsely, looking at Lucian. "You're giving us a heart-pledge? You want to go that far?"

"That far and farther." Lucian wore an intense look on his face. "I never want to be parted from you, my bond-mates. And I'll never let another come between us — this I swear."

Drace nodded and placed one hand over Lucian's heart and one over mine. "Then I pledge as well," he said, his deep voice rumbling with sincerity. "My time, talents, and my treasure…my love and my loyalty shall all be yours, my bond-mates. Even in death, may we never be parted."

Then both of them looked at me but before I could say anything, I had to wipe some tears from my eyes.

"I'm sorry," I whispered to both of them. "I...I don't mean to get all girly. This is just so...so beautiful."

"It is a heart-pledge," Lucian said simply. "It is about love and honor and sacrifice and loyalty—there is nothing more beautiful, no promise more enduring."

"That's what I want," I said. "Enduring—I want to be with you guys forever."

"Then make your pledge, baby," Drace said softly, "But remember, it's our most sacred vow—one that must never be broken."

"It won't be," I swore softly. Lifting my chin, I placed my hands over their broad, muscular chests and repeated the words." As they left my lips, I felt a surge of power flash out from me to encompass both of them.

*A Binder,* I thought deliriously. *I'm a Binder and I think this just tied us more tightly together than ever.*

It was an amazing feeling—a closeness I had never felt to another person and now I had it with *two* other people—my guys.

"I love you," I kept telling them both. "I love you so much—I never want us to be apart."

"We won't be—we'll never be parted," they promised. They took turns kissing me and then pretty soon, kissing turned to other things. Before I quite knew how it happened, the three of us were bonding all over again, the two of them holding me between them as they filled me with their thick shafts and spilled their seed inside my pussy for the second time.

It was even sweeter this time—a gentle, slow lovemaking that was still extremely passionate. We weren't just coming together out of necessity as we had been the night before. This time our three-way bonding was about affirming our love. It might have lasted hours—the rest of the night—I'm really not sure. Time seemed to blur into one long endless caress as Drace and Lucian held me tight and showed me how much they loved me, promising wordlessly that we would never be parted.

We came as one—all three of us—which pleased the guys. Apparently perfectly synced orgasms were the sign of an exceptionally strong Triumvirate. I didn't know about that and I didn't care. I just knew that when I finally drifted off to sleep a second time, held in the four strong arms of my loves, there was a smile on my lips and peace and contentment filling my heart.

*Together,* I thought sleepily as I nuzzled against them so that my cheek was pillowed on Drace's chest and my ass was snug against Lucian's groin. *We'll be together forever.*

If only I had known how wrong I was.

# Chapter Twenty-nine

## Lucian

"But Lucian, darling, it's only a little dinner party. Surely you don't mind."

"Yes, I *do* mind, Mother," I said through gritted teeth. "Especially since you're having it at *my* apartment without asking first. How did you even know I was coming here and when I'd get back?"

"Oh, I have my little ways." She smiled mysteriously until I glared at her. "Fine—I had a tracking device installed on your ship. Purely for your own safety, of course."

I made a mental note to have a good mechanic go over my ship with a fine tooth comb and to never again dock it in the same bay my family used.

"Mother," I said. "This really isn't a good time for a party." Not that any time would be.

"I thought it would be good for your fathers to meet your little…friends." She waved lightly at Drace and Rylee, who were standing behind me uncertainly. None of us had known what to think when we walked in my apartment and saw a catering team hard at work setting up expensive floral arrangements and hustling back and forth with platters of traditional Fang Clan delicacies. Of course, the moment my mother appeared, I knew she had to be up to something but I didn't know what.

"Drace and Rylee are my bond-mate and my female, Mother," I said firmly. "They're not just friends—I love and respect them both. I ask that you do the same—respect them, anyway." I knew there was no way in the Frozen Hells my mother would ever love them.

"But I thought that was all just *temporary.*" Mother's eyes widened. "You said so yourself—just a temporary arrangement that you were working to get fixed."

"It's become permanent," I said stolidly. "Drace and I have sealed our bond and the three of us have decided to stay together."

"Oh my..." My mother put a hand to her chest. "How...interesting. But I thought...thought you were going to go look for something to help you. You said...some kind of artifact, didn't you, darling?" She looked at me appealingly.

I wouldn't have answered but Drace spoke up.

"It's called the Claw—we found it in the Temple of Ganth in the K'drin Jungle," he said, frowning. "It has the ability to separate male bond-mates—even those whose bond has been sealed."

"And what did you *do* with it?" Mother asked, all wide-eyed curiosity. I wanted to tell Drace not to answer but he was already speaking.

"We brought it with us but we've decided not to use it."

"We're staying together." Rylee spoke up for the first time, lifting her chin high. "We love each other and that love is more important to us than any status or reputation."

"Well of *course* it is." My mother gave Rylee a simpering sweet look. "I hope you don't imagine I would ask you to give it up?"

"Well..." Rylee looked confused and Drace frowned. I was frowning myself—what was my mother up to?

"Just think of this as a little congratulatory dinner, darling" she said, smiling brightly. "A chance to introduce the rest of your Triumvirate to our family and friends."

"Friends?" I looked at her blankly. "You mean you invited other people? People *outside* our family?"

"Should I *not* have?" She put a hand to her chest again, a look of innocent uncertainty in her eyes. "I mean, you're not *ashamed* of your new bond-mates, are you?"

"Of course not!" I said quickly, watching Drace scowl from the corner of my eye. "I guess I just thought that you and my fathers would be...less than supportive of my choices. Like you have been in the past."

"Oh, the past…" My mother made a shooing gesture, as though the way she'd kept me from finding a bond-mate and true love for so many years was no more troubling than a fly.

"Yes, the past," I said stonily. "The past when you forbid me from bonding with anyone you deemed unacceptable. When you separated me from Hylorn—"

"My goodness, darling!" She cut me off with a light, breezy laugh. "Please don't speak so in front of your bond-mates. You'll give them the idea I'm an absolute *monster!*" She smiled at Drace and Rylee. "Now why don't you all just run along and get into the clothing I had simmed for you? My parties are *always* the talk of the city and you wouldn't want to be caught in anything less than your best if a news vid crew comes by."

"You invited a news vid crew?" I demanded. "You're really going public with this?"

"Well, no one *invites* those press people, darling." She patted my cheek. "They just tend to show up whenever someone prominent is hosting a soirée. So it's best to be prepared." She smiled at Rylee and Drace. "So nice to meet you both again. I know we're going to have a lovely time this evening. Now, if you'll excuse me—I see a catering disaster about to happen."

She ran off into the crowd of caterers and I saw her berating a male holding a platter full of *kiboth*-hump bites. Then several more caterers, carrying a heavy buffet table between them, passed in front of us, blocking our view.

I stood there for a long moment, speechless. What was going on? What was my mother planning? I honestly had no idea but it gave me an icy feeling in the pit of my stomach.

"Well…" Rylee shifted from foot to foot uncertainly. "Should we…go get dressed?"

"No," I said in a low voice. "We should go. I don't trust this. I don't trust *her.*"

"Really?" Rylee looked at me doubtfully. "But…she seemed so *nice.*"

"She can *seem* any way she wants to seem," I said. "It's one of her talents."

"Maybe you're judging her too harshly," Rylee said tentatively. "Maybe she's trying to make up for how she treated you in the past. I mean, she *did* say she was going to have reporters here. Why would she do that if she was ashamed of you and your choice to be with Drace and me?"

"The news vid thing makes me wonder too," Drace said, frowning. "Do you think maybe she's trying to get out in front of it—do damage control?"

"Maybe she's setting a trend," Rylee said brightly. "You *did* say she was the social queen of Y'brith. Maybe this is her way of making, uh, marrying outside the clan fashionable. Like, if she's doing it—or her son is, anyway—everyone else is going to pick it up and do it too."

"I highly doubt that," I murmured, thinking of the unspoken yet ironclad social laws that ruled Fang Clan society.

"Well, anyway—what harm can it do to just attend tonight?" Rylee asked. "I mean, she's your *mom*. You can't just blow off her party—especially when it's a party she's throwing for you. For *us*."

That was exactly what I wanted to do—just turn back around, walk through the front door, and spend the night on my ship with my bond-mates until I was certain the coast was clear and my mother and her army of caterers were out of my apartment. But the look on Rylee's face let me know that wasn't an option.

I knew from some of the pillow talk we'd had that Rylee had lost her mother at a young age and had been raised by a relative who cared for her but never really gave her much attention or affection. The bond of motherhood was important to her and if she thought there was any way she and Drace could make friends with—or at least get along with—my mother, she wouldn't waste the chance.

"Drace?" I asked, looking at my bond-mate. "What do you think?"

He sighed. "I don't like it and I feel like I'm going to be really fucking out of place at a fancy society party, especially a *Fang Clan* society party, but...well..." He ran a hand through his hair. "Family's important. And you guys put up with Twyla and Porgy for me—seems like this is the least I can do for you, bond-mate."

I sighed. It seemed my bond-mate and our female were in agreement—we would have to go through with the party.

"All right," I said grimly. "I still don't like it, but let's get dressed."

# Rylee

"So you've never tried *plonchik* stew before? I find that difficult to believe—it's a *classic* dish." The huge alien male, who had identified himself as a visiting T'varri, nodded at me and took a sip of the bright pink liquid which had been served to us chilled in tall metal cups. "Try it," he urged me. "Before it goes warm."

"Um…okay." I picked up the tall, fluted metal cup and raised it to my lips. The liquid inside looked like Pepto-Bismol and smelled a little like cherry-flavored vomit. Ugh—more high holiday food like the hairy noodles and eyeball oatmeal we'd been served at Lord Mandrex's house. I pretended to take a sip and put it back down.

"It's good, right?" the T'varri guy asked, looking at me intently. He was as tall as my guys—seven feet at least—with strange, vivid tattoos that crawled and shifted all over his skin in ever changing patterns.

"Yummy," I said, managing a weak smile. I really wasn't feeling very well but not because of the weird alien food or the too-tight, mint-green and pale pink striped dress which Lucian's mother had simmed for me and insisted that I wear. It was the fact that I was seated away from my guys—both of them.

Drace was at the foot of the long dining room table which held around twenty people. Seated to his left was a lovely Denarin girl with pale, pearly gray skin and a cloud of dark blue hair. She was laughing at everything he said and putting her hand on his arm in a flirtatious way that made me grind my teeth.

Lucian, on the other hand, was seated by a short—well, short by Denarin standards which meant he was only six feet tall instead of seven—male with pale purple skin and big green eyes. They were talking earnestly about something and I thought he must be someone Lucian knew.

I told myself it was foolish to be jealous or worried. After all, Lucian's mother's seating chart was probably just meant to let us meet new people and mingle. But though I tried to suppress my emotions, I couldn't stop the feeling that was growing within me — the feeling that something bad was going to happen and there was nothing I could do to stop it.

"So," the T'varri male said, giving me the eye. "Are you under contract to any other male?"

"Under contract?" I dragged my attention away from Drace and the girl sitting beside him who was now practically humping his leg as she fell all over herself to laugh at something he had said.

"Yes," he said patiently. "Are you contracted to another? You're very beautiful and unique. What planet are you from?"

"Earth," I said, craning my head to look at Lucian and the pale purple guy. I hadn't even known Denarins came in that color. I thought they were all green or red or blue.

"I'm asking if you're under contract because I want to play with you," he said and something about the way he said "play" made me snap my head up and look at him.

"Wait a minute—you're asking if I have a contract with someone else because you think I'm for sale? Like a prostitute?" I asked bluntly. "Because that's damn insulting."

"I never thought you were a pleasure girl." He held up his hands in a "don't shoot" gesture. "Among my people, we sign a contract before we become serious with a female. It avoids...misunderstandings."

"Well understand *this*, buddy," I snapped. "I'm with him." I stabbed my finger in the direction of Drace. "And *him*." I pointed at Lucian, who was so deeply engrossed in his conversation that he didn't even see me. "So no, I'm not available to 'play' as you put it."

He frowned. "Those are discourteous words considering I was only trying to pay you a compliment. If you were under contract to me, I'd have you out of that ridiculous dress and across my knee for some *serious* punishment to correct that attitude of yours."

"Back off, asshole," I snarled, glaring at him. "I don't know how you treat women in your culture but, on *my* home planet it's considered *rude* to threaten to spank your dinner companion!"

"Since you find my speech so offensive, I will refrain from speaking to you again," he said stiffly. "Enjoy your dinner."

He turned pointedly and began speaking to the person on his left—a man with smooth, green skin and wide violet eyes.

I balled my silver fabric napkin in my lap and gritted my teeth in irritation. I could have handled that better but I was so on edge, damn it! I just kept feeling like something bad was going to happen, only I didn't know what.

From the corner of my eye, I saw Lucian excuse himself from the table and caught a feeling of unease from him through our bond. He left the formal dining room (his apartment was really huge) and headed out into the hallway. After a moment the pale purple guy followed him.

*Now what the hell is that all about?* I wanted to get up and follow them, but I resisted the urge. What the hell was wrong with me, acting like a jealous wife who didn't trust her husband? Lucian probably just wanted to catch up with his old friend. I should just leave it alone and eat my dinner...or at least push it around on my plate so it looked like I had tried.

I sighed and went back to my food, trying to ignore the feeling of foreboding that hung over me like a dark cloud. Everything was going to be okay. We just had to get through this dinner party and then we could get away from Lucian's mother and her guests and reconnect with each other just like we had last night.

So I told myself, as I took a nibble of something that looked like gray cake and tasted like mashed liver and bananas. *Just take it easy, Rylee. Take it easy. Everything is going to be okay.*

I just wished I could make myself believe it.

# Drace

I watched my bond-mate at the other end of the table and felt the tremble of unease that came from him through our psy-bond. What was wrong with him? Was he still upset about the dinner party his mother had practically forced us to attend? It was a very fucking fancy affair—I would give her that—with multiple courses of high holiday foods, some of them so rare and rich I'd only ever heard about them. She'd gone to a hell of a lot of trouble with her seating chart too—placing Lucian and I on opposite ends of the long table with Rylee directly in the center.

Lucian's mother and her fathers were sitting all together not far from Lucian—his mother laughing and talking, presiding over the table like a queen and his fathers sitting silently on either side of her. I had noticed that so far the promised news vid crews had *not* arrived. Also, there were a lot more off-worlders here than Denarins. In fact, aside from myself and Lucian, his parents and a few other guests, everyone there was from another planet.

I was trying to keep an eye on both of my bond-mates—I didn't like the way the T'varri at Rylee's side was eyeing her—but the girl Lucian's mother had put beside me wouldn't let me pay attention to anyone but her.

"Come on now—tell me what Clan you're from," she cooed, stroking my bicep in an irritating manner. "Such a big, strapping Alpha like you. I bet you're Beak-Clan, aren't you? Or maybe Talon-Clan?"

"No," I said shortly. "Claw Clan."

I was hoping that would get her off my back since she was obviously Fang Clan herself. Instead, her eyes widened and she put a hand to her chest.

"How *exciting!* I've always *wanted* to meet a male from the Claw Clan. There's a reason you're our greatest rivals, you know," she went on, batting her fucking eyelashes at me. "It's because you're so big and strong the males of my clan fear you. Why, I bet you could beat any male at this table in a fight!"

"Maybe," I mumbled, trying to ignore her babble. At the other end of the table, Lucian was engaged in an intense conversation with a Beta of the Scale-Clan. I knew he was Scale-Clan because they're the only Clan on Denaris where the males have purple skin coloration. Some people say it's a mutation of the usual blue, which may be true—I don't fucking know. All I knew was that the unusual coloration made them highly prized as bond-mates.

And I also knew that the Beta Lucian had mentioned wanting to take as a bond-mate had been Scale-Clan. Hylorn—hadn't that been his name? Was this him—the male who Lucian was talking so intently to?

*So what if it is?* I asked myself uneasily. *He's a grown male – he can talk to who he wants. Plus we're bonded and Lucian is too honorable to cheat. Everything is going to be fine.*

*Isn't it?*

And then Lucian got up and left the table. After a moment, the little Beta followed him, trotting eagerly after my bond-mate into the dark, shadowy hallway.

*It's fine,* I told myself, though I felt another tremor of unease flow through our bond. *They're probably just talking – catching up. There's nothing wrong with that.*

But I couldn't shake the feeling that somewhere, something was getting seriously fucked up. I just couldn't put my finger on what it was.

"So does your Clan hold the feats of strength each year?" the girl beside me asked. "I'm sure you must win *all* the prizes."

"Sure," I muttered, still watching the hallway that Lucian and the Beta had disappeared into. "All the fucking prizes."

"Ooo!' She squealed. "Make a muscle for me, please? I'm dying to –"

I got up, leaving the Fang Clan girl in mid-flirt, and went looking for my bond-partner.

## Lucian

"Thank you for agreeing to speak to me alone." Hylorn turned his big, green eyes up to me earnestly. "It's been so many years – I never thought I'd see you again."

"Nor I, you," I said, leaning stiffly against the food-prep counter.

Hylorn had asked me to find us an empty area to speak in but for some reason I didn't think that was such a good idea. Most of the caterers my mother had hired were gone now that the dining area was set up and the food had been served, but two or three of them still lingered in the food-prep area. This gave us only limited privacy, which was fine with me. It seemed…safer somehow.

"What did you want to say to me that couldn't be said in the dining area?" I asked him.

He looked at me, his eyes wide. "That I still care for you, Lucian. I have never bonded myself to another because I always hoped you would come back into my life."

"Hylorn—" I began, uncertain what to say, how to tell him.

Suddenly, Hylorn was in my arms. "I've missed you so much, Lucian," he murmured, nuzzling against me. "I've thought of you every night for years. And now we can finally be together."

"No," I said, "we can't." I wanted to push him away but he was clinging to me too tightly. And I felt bad for him—bad for what I had to tell him. We had meant everything to each other once—a ghost of that affection still lingered in my own heart. "Hylorn," I told him as gently as I could. "I'm already bonded—I have a bond-mate and a female that we both love."

"I heard that was only temporary." He looked up at me, his heart in his big, green eyes. "Heard it was an accidental bond to another *Alpha* of all things!"

"Drace *is* an Alpha," I said shortly. "But—"

"Really? I thought it was a joke!" Hylorn looked at me wide-eyed. "Lucian, be real—you can't possibly be bonded to another *Alpha*. What you need is a sweet, submissive Beta—someone who's going to take care of you."

"Hylorn—" I began, still trying to find a way to push him away without hurting him.

"He can't please you like I can," he whispered. And then he placed his hand over my heart. "Bond-mate," he said, looking me earnestly in the eyes. "I heart-pledge to you—my time, my talent, and my treasures, such as they are. My love and loyalty, always and only for you. May we never be parted."

"Hylorn…" I put my own hand on his chest to push him away from me.

And that was when I saw Drace—standing in the doorway of the food-prep area with his arms crossed over his broad chest and a scowl on his face. I had no idea how long he'd been watching or what he had seen and heard.

"Drace!" I exclaimed, trying to extricate myself from the unwanted embrace. But by the time I finally disentangled myself from Hylorn, my bond-mate was gone. Though I searched my entire apartment, calling his name, I couldn't find him anywhere.

## Drace

"Well, well, I *thought* I might find you here."

I looked up from my pacing, startled. I'd been walking up and down the long main corridor of Lucian's ship for the past hour, trying to make sense of what I'd seen.

Lucian, in the arms of a Beta—of the same Beta he'd told Rylee and me about—the one he'd been so desperate to tie his life to and bond with. The two of them heart-pledging to each other—then the look of horror on Lucian's face when he saw me. And after that, the terrible surge of guilt that had come through our bond as loud as any confession.

*Fucking cheating bastard!*

He'd called out to me but I hadn't stopped—not even to talk to Rylee, who had watched in confusion as I left the apartment. I needed to be alone, I told myself—needed to think without anyone else around to cloud the issue. But an hour of solitude hadn't done me a fucking bit of good—I was still madder than hell and as hurt as if Lucian had taken a konji blade and stabbed me right in the heart. Not only had he broken the pledge he had made to Rylee and me—he had pledged himself to another! It was the worst kind of treachery and I didn't know how to deal with it.

And now, to top it off, I had company.

"What are *you* doing here?" I asked, frowning as Lucian's mother stepped into the ship and closed the pnemo-seal behind her.

"Looking for you, of course, dear. I heard what happened from poor Hylorn." She shook her head sadly and made a *tsking* sound. "Such a shame."

"Yeah, a real fucking shame," I muttered. "How did you even get in here?"

"Oh, I make it my business to have access to my son at all times." She smiled smugly.

"You really like to keep him under your thumb, don't you?" I gave her a look of deep disgust. "I know what you did to him—

keeping him from bonding with a Beta just because he couldn't find one you approved of. Making him stay alone—lonely—all his life."

"I don't think he's lonely anymore, do you?" She raised an eyebrow at me archly. "Not now that *Hylorn* is back in the picture."

"You set that up," I accused. "You invited that fucking Beta just to lure Lucian away from Rylee and me."

"All I did was invite Hylorn to the party. I didn't *make* Lucian heart-pledge to him. He did that all on his own." She shrugged easily, the high collar of her fancy silver dress rustling.

"You—" I began.

"It's actually a good thing you bore witness to their tender moment—even if it *was* a little awkward," she went on, ignoring me. "At least now you know who Lucian's heart *really* belongs to. It's good to get it out in the open—before things between you and my son and that *off-worlder* girl got too serious."

"He heart-pledged to me and Rylee too," I snarled. "And we sealed our bond. That seems pretty fucking serious to me."

"Yes, but you can break that bond with the nifty little artifact you found," she pointed out, her eyes glittering. "And if you love Lucian—if you have any feelings for him at all—that's exactly what you're going to do."

"Why in the Frozen Hells would I do that?" I demanded. "Why should I give you the satisfaction of letting your son go just so you can keep your social status?"

"It's not just about social status—although that *is* part of it," she said, all wide-eyed sincerity now. "Lucian is the sole heir to the Chiefdom of the Fang Clan. But there's simply no way his fathers can pass the mantle of leadership on to him if he's psy-bonded to a mortal enemy of our clan, not to mention another *Alpha*. I'm sure you can see how impossible that would be."

I felt my stomach turn but I kept my face blank.

"Lucian doesn't want any of that. He told Rylee and me he'd rather be with us."

"I'm sure he did—he's been very lonely, as you said, for many years." She made a sad little face. "Now, I'll admit that part of that was my fault. I've been…very *picky* about who Lucian associates with."

"I know you have." I gave her a fierce, unhappy grin. "You must have just about shit a brick when you found out he was mated to a nobody of the Claw Clan and an off-worlder female."

She sniffed. "I will admit that when Lucian finally chose to rebel he certainly went about it whole-heartedly." She lifted her chin. "But that's all right—we can fix it."

"You know, he's a grown male with a life and a business of his own. Did it ever occur to you that it's time to butt out of his life?"

"No," she said blandly. "But I *am* hoping that very notion will occur to *you*. Think about it, Drace—he's happy now. He finally has the bond-mate he's wanted all his life."

"The one you denied him, you mean," I growled. "Hylorn wasn't good enough for him before but suddenly, the minute Rylee and I come into the picture, he's just perfect."

"I wouldn't say 'perfect' exactly, but he's certainly a much better choice than *you*." she cocked her head to one side. "I had you checked out you know, Drace. You have no status in your own clan—you're a nobody. A *loner*. Even your own family thinks you're strange. You're—"

"All right," I snarled, cutting her off. "You've made your fucking point."

"I believe I did." She nodded, unperturbed by my anger. "Lucian has a bright future ahead of him, Drace. He and Hylorn can be psy-bonded and then find just the right female to complete their Triumvirate."

"And I just bet you've got 'just the right female' all picked out, don't you?" I growled.

"And if I do?" She shrugged, as if it didn't matter, her dress rustling again. "The point is, you and Lucian *don't work*. It might be a salvageable situation if you weren't another Alpha but as things stand, you'll only be an impediment to my son. You'll drag him down with your poor Clan status, your abysmal manners, the fact that you're not the proper Beta he deserves…"

"He told me he didn't *want* a Beta," I snapped.

"Well...I think we both know *that* isn't true, now don't we?" Lucian's mother gave me a small, cold smile. "Or he wouldn't have heart-pledged to Hylorn."

"You—" I started but she talked right over me.

"Lucian will never inherit the leadership of his Clan or rise to the heights he should with you and your little off-worlder female dragging him down." She put a hand on my arm and looked up at me earnestly. "*Think* about it, Drace. If you love him, you need to let him go."

I would have told her to fuck off, that her interference wasn't needed or wanted. I would have said that Lucian and Rylee and I were happy together—that none of us wanted or needed anyone else.

I would have said all those things if I didn't remember Lucian telling us that Hylorn was practically the love of his fucking life before his mother separated them. And if I hadn't seen his hand over the other male's heart.

"Fine," I said, looking down at the metal floor of the ship. "I'll let him go."

It felt like tearing a piece of my heart out to speak those words, but I knew it was for the best. She was right—I would only drag Lucian down. Being mated to another Alpha and an off-worlder like Rylee would ruin his perfect, golden life. I thought dully that maybe Rylee and I could stick together and find a Beta somewhere. But the idea of sharing her with anyone but Lucian just seemed *wrong* somehow. No, it was probably better that we all go our separate ways, even if it meant parting from the two people I loved most in the universe.

"Fine," I said again.

"Oh, *good.*" Lucian's mother looked vastly relieved. "I'm so glad you've come to your senses. Now if you'd just—"

"Look, I admitted I'm garbage that would just drag your son down," I growled at her. "And I promised to let him go. Now I have nothing else to say to you so would you please just get the fuck out of here and leave me alone?"

"Very well." She nodded stiffly. "I'll go tell my son he and Hylorn can start planning their bond-mate ceremony. Oh, Lucian will be *so* happy."

"I'm sure he will," I muttered. "After all, he's finally getting the mate he always wanted—the one you denied him for so many years, you *bitch*."

"There's no need to be nasty," she snapped, frowning. "I did you a favor, Drace—*believe* me. How long do you think a relationship with two Alphas would last, after all? The only reason the two of you were able to be together at all was because that little off-worlder you found is a Binder."

"How did you know about—?"

"Rylee? Lucian told me about her—imagine how surprised I was when his claims about her actually checked out!" She smiled triumphantly. "I told you, I'm very picky about the people Lucian associates with. You and that off-worlder *La-ti-zal* aren't right for him at all. And if it hadn't been for *her*, the two of you would never have even gotten it into your heads to stay together."

I wondered if she was right. If Rylee was the only reason Lucian and I had thought we could make a go of it. Probably so—we both loved Rylee to distraction. Picturing her sweet face and big eyes when I broke the news that Lucian and I would be using the Claw after all, I nearly wavered.

But then I remembered Lucian's hand over Hylorn's heart. The way I'd heard Hylorn pledge his undying love and loyalty. And I knew I had to let Lucian go—even if it was like ripping my heart out, I had to do it.

There was no other way.

# Chapter Thirty

## Rylee

"Here you are! Lucian and I have been looking all over for you!"

I was so relieved to see Drace standing there in Lucian's ship that I ran to throw my arms around him—but he didn't hug me back. He stood as rigid as a statue, not returning my embrace. When I looked up at him, I saw him glaring daggers at Lucian over my head.

Lucian glared back but there was something besides anger in his face. I sensed shame as well—a low level guilt that flowed like poison through our bond.

"What?" I said, looking back and forth between them. "What's going on with you two? What's wrong?"

"I want to use the Claw," Drace said abruptly. "We need to be separated. Our bond needs to be severed."

*"What?"* I looked at him in disbelief. "Drace, you can't be serious? What's all this about?"

"It's about something he saw," Lucian said stiffly. "But it was a mistake—a misunderstanding."

"I don't think there was any mistaking that fucking pledge I saw you in with Hylorn," Drace growled. "You were all over each other."

"No!" Lucian protested. *"He* was all over *me.* I—"

"Save your fucking excuses," Drace snapped. "It never would have worked between us anyway. I'm doing you a favor, Lucian— letting you run back to the one you really want."

"I don't want anyone but you and Rylee," Lucian protested. "I swear it, bond-mate!"

"Don't call me that. Not anymore." Drace took a deep breath and looked the other man straight in the eye. "I disavow you, Lucian," he said in a slow, even voice. "I want nothing more to do with you."

Lucian made a low sound in his throat, something like a cross between a gasp and a groan, and staggered back, as though Drace had punched him in the gut.

I got a sick feeling in my stomach. A feeling that something bad had just happened. No—not just bad—*horrible*. Something that couldn't be taken back.

"What happened? What does that mean?" I demanded. "Will the two of you please *talk* to me?"

"Drace has expressed his need to be free of me in the strongest terms possible," Lucian said stiffly, finally regaining his composure. "To disavow a bond-mate is to ask for a complete and permanent separation."

"*What?*" I looked back and forth between them wildly. "What is going on? What caused this?"

"Drace walked in on Hylorn heart-pledging to me." Lucian looked down at his hands. "He...I didn't know how to get free of him. I cared for him for so long and—"

"And now you can finally fucking *have* him!" Drace snapped.

"Wait a minute—I'm sure this was all just a big misunderstanding," I said urgently, looking from Drace's stony face to Lucian's guilty one. "I'm sure we can talk this out. We shouldn't make any rash decisions before we sleep on it, at least."

"No, I don't want to wait another second," Drace snarled. "Tonight—we must be severed *tonight!*"

He lifted his hand and I saw that he'd been holding the long-handled, golden Claw down by the side of his leg where it hadn't been visible before. The ship's overhead lights caught on its four sharp talons and they glittered wickedly.

"Very well," Lucian said coldly. "If that is the way you want it."

"It is," Drace assured him.

It was my turn to gasp. Seeing the Claw in Drace's hand seemed to bring everything home to me—this wasn't just a quarrel between the two of them. Drace was actually asking for a divorce—or what passed for divorce here on Denaris. And Lucian was willing to give it to him.

"Wait a minute!" I shouted, glaring at both of them. "Don't *I* get any say in this matter? I'm part of this relationship too!"

Drace's face softened for a moment, the granite melting.

"Baby, you're the *heart* of our relationship," he said, sounding sad. "And I'm so, *so* fucking sorry to do this to you. But it's time you and I let Lucian go."

"Let him go? Just because you caught him hugging someone else for half a minute?" I shouted.

"It wasn't a simple embrace," Drace growled. "They were heart-pledging."

"I never—" Lucian began but Drace cut him off.

"Save it. I know how you feel about Hylorn—well you can fucking well have him!"

"Are you crazy, Drace?" I demanded You *love* Lucian! We *both* do!"

"Not anymore." Drace's face went hard and dark again. "Now I only want to be free of him."

"Fine," Lucian said tightly. He opened the fancy jacket his mother had made him wear to the dinner party and started unfastening his shirt. "I wish to be free of you as well. Do you wish to use the Claw first or should I?"

"I will." Drace was opening his shirt and jacket as well.

I felt sick. They were *really* going to do this. Right in front of me they were going to sever their bond and pull us all apart. How could this be happening? And how could it happen so *fast*?

"I don't believe this," I said blankly. "Just last night we were promising to love each other and stay together forever. I was willing to leave Earth—to leave my home planet and never go back again—all because I loved you both so much and I *thought* you loved me."

"We *do* love you, *ma 'frela.*" Lucian spoke softly. "I am sorry beyond measure that you are hurt by the conflict between us. I cannot—"

He stopped talking, his eyes wide. Drace had taken the golden Claw and placed it on his chest, right over his heart.

"Drace, n—" I started to say, but before I could get the words out, he was dragging the four sharp points down his muscular left pec, leaving four bloody parallel lines in his dusky blue skin.

"Ahh!" As the blood began to flow, crimson over blue skin, I felt part of our bond crumble to dust. It hurt so much it was like someone carving off a piece of my heart. I put a hand to my own chest as Drace passed Lucian the Claw without comment. "Please!" I gasped out in a choked voice.

It was no use. Lucian was already dragging the awful instrument of separation, its wicked points still bloody from Drace's wound, down his own left chest.

I felt a second stab in my heart as another part of our bond collapsed. This one was so strong I stumbled to my knees.

"Baby—are you okay?" Drace knelt by me at once.

"*Ma 'frela,* are you well?" Lucian was on my other side.

Both of them looked terribly concerned—maybe even remorseful. But I realized that though I could see the emotions on their faces, I could no longer *feel* them inside me. The place where they had been connected to me felt numb—like an amputated limb. It simply wasn't there anymore.

*It's done—it's really done. We're separated and we'll never be together again.*

The realization was too much. I shrugged off both their hands and curled into a ball. I could feel the tears threatening, stinging and hot, just behind my eyes. But I couldn't let them come out. If I started crying now I would never stop—I'd just be a basket case who cried the rest of her life.

*Home,* I thought miserably. *I just want to go home and forget any of this ever happened.*

Which gave me an idea…a way to cope. Maybe the only way that would keep me from going crazy with grief…

# Chapter Thirty-one
## Rylee

"You're sure this is what you want?" Lucian asked me for maybe the tenth time. He and Drace were standing on either side of me, just as they always had. But this time I felt no love or protection coming from them—our bond was gone...gone forever.

*No, don't think like that! You'll go crazy if you think like that. Just keep it together, Rylee – keep it together for a little while longer.*

"I'm sure," I said, lifting my chin. "If you think the two of you can work together just one more time?"

"For you, baby – anything," Drace said hoarsely.

"No," I said, looking at him sadly. "Not quite *anything.*"

He flushed and looked away. "I'm sorry—it was for the best," he muttered.

"Tell that to my heart," I said and looked up at Lucian. "You're sure you can take all of it away? Every last memory from right before I got sucked up in the mirror until now?"

"If that is what you really desire, *ma 'frela.* If you really want to forget us completely."

"I do," I said steadily. "I'm barely holding it together here. If I let myself start crying I'll go *crazy.* I need to forget you two—forget everything we did together...everything we meant to each other. The...the love we shared." I choked on the words and almost couldn't go on. "It's...it's the only way to keep my sanity," I finished in a wavering voice.

"Are you nearly finished with your farewell rituals?" called the squeaky voice of the head Commercian—or the head Blue Centipede Guy, as I called him in my head.

"Almost," I said. "You have that thing tuned to my apartment?"

"We'll be depositing you right back in front of the mirror you were first transported through," the Commercian—Char'noth I think his name was—said.

"Good, that's good." I took a deep breath and looked up at my guys for the last time. "All right," I said. "Wipe me. I don't want to remember *any* of this. *Ever.*"

"We will do a very thorough job—just as we did on your former paramour," Lucian promised. He looked up at Drace. "Are you ready bond-m—" He broke off abruptly.

"Yeah, I'm ready." Drace acted like he didn't notice the slip but I was pretty sure he had. They positioned themselves on either side of me, each with a hand on the side of my head, just as they had done when they erased Phillip's memory what seemed like a million years ago.

"I'm sorry," Drace said to me one last time. I had the feeling he was regretting using the Claw to sever himself from Lucian so quickly, without really thinking about it first. But of course, it was too late now. "I love you, baby," he added in a low voice. "I always will. I'll never forget you."

"Nor I. I love you as well, *ma 'frela,*" Lucian said.

"And I love both of you," I said, feeling the tears prick behind my eyes. "But our love wasn't enough, was it?" They started to answer but I shook my head. "No please—put me out of my misery. Help me forget. *Now.*"

"As you wish," Lucian said and then I felt a thick, gray mist blanketing my mind. A numbing mist, that made the pain go away—that banished the sharp ache which was all that was left in the place where we had once had a beautiful three-part bond. I wanted the mist to cover me completely, to erase everything, to leave nothing behind.

I closed my eyes and let myself fall into it. Closed my eyes and forgot.

* * * * *

I woke up with a splitting headache and the feeling that there was something important I had to remember. But what? I sat up in my bed and ran a hand over my tangled hair. What was wrong with me? I felt so *strange*.

I'd had a dream—I vaguely recollected. A really strange dream about someone tucking me into bed and kissing me goodnight. No...*two* someones. Huge men...one green and one blue? But that didn't make any sense.

The moment the image began to form in my head, it was obscured. A thick gray mist seemed to cover it, hiding any details of my dream that I might have remembered.

Well, dreams were fleeting. I shrugged and swung my legs over the side of the bed, groaning as the sudden motion jostled my head. It felt like my skull was stuffed with glass shards and cotton and I had the *worst* headache. Seriously, an up-all-night-drinking-morning-after hangover kind of headache. What had I been doing last night?

I frowned as I tried to remember but all I could come up with was a vague idea that I might have seen my gay clients—the ones who were fighting over their pet French Bulldog-labradootle mix. That didn't seem quite right, but it was the best I could come up with. I couldn't recall anything else except the idea that there had been a divorce—a nasty one that hurt everyone involved. But was it my clients' divorce I was thinking of...or someone else? I didn't know and trying to remember made my head hurt even worse.

*It'll be okay,* I told myself uneasily as I clutched the side of my head and shuffled to the bathroom to take some ibuprofen. *I just had a bad night. I'll feel better after a shower.*

Only I didn't. The headache persisted, a throbbing, debilitating ache which made me want to crawl back into bed. The eight hundred milligrams of ibuprofen I took didn't even touch it.

*This is awful! It's like a migraine,* I thought, wrapping a towel around me and hobbling back to the bed like an old woman. *What's wrong with me? I never get migraines.*

Only it seemed like I had one now and it was in no hurry to go away. Groaning and clutching my head, I sat back down on the side of the bed. God, it hurt *so much* – what was I going to do?

*I'll go back to bed,* I told myself. *At least I don't have to call in sick – I work for myself now. I can take a sick day without worrying someone might fire me for it. I'll just go back to sleep but first I'll call and cancel my appointments.*

This involved a lot more effort than I wanted to expend at the moment. First I had to find my phone—which was missing from its usual spot by the night table. The phone turned up lying on the floor on the living room which was just damn weird. How had it gotten there? Had I gotten up in the middle of the night and dropped it by accident? But why hadn't I picked it up? It made no sense.

After finally locating the phone, I found that it was dead—completely dead. Which was so unlike me—I always keep my phone charged in case of emergencies.

I plugged it up to the charger and resurrected it only to find that I had something like fifty voicemails and tons of unanswered texts from friends, family and clients. Most of them were variations of, "Where are you? I can't reach you and I'm getting worried." My Aunt Celia had called me ten times at least, each call more concerned than the last.

There was also a message from an old friend who knew my ex, Phillip. She wanted to know if I had been watching the news—somehow Phillip had turned up naked and disoriented in a town in Australia and now he was apparently trying to get back home. The story had been picked up by a prominent Internet blog and had gone viral.

I frowned. Well, *that* was bizarre and even stranger was the way it messed with my head. I had some kind of idea about Phillip—a feeling that I might know something about his bizarre disappearance and reappearance, naked down-under. But the moment I tried to access my memory, the fog came rolling back and my headache got worse.

I gave up and went back to my other messages and texts.

"What in the world?" I muttered, scrolling through the contents of my phone. "What happened? How did I get all this mess in one night?"

Then I looked at the date on my phone. It hadn't been just one night. Somehow I'd been gone for days and days. But how? And why?

A memory tried to surface again—me between two huge men. One of them with blue skin and one with olive green. They—

But the moment the memory started to come back, the fog rolled over my brain again. I couldn't remember—I had lost over a week of my life and I couldn't remember where I had been or what I had been doing or who I had been doing it with. I only knew my head ached so badly I couldn't stand it.

Lying on my side on the bed, I put one hand to my throbbing temple and closed my eyes. Something had happened to me…something bad. But I couldn't remember what it was. All I knew was that I *hurt* and I couldn't seem to stop hurting…

# Chapter Thirty-two

## Lucian

"Rylee's in pain." Drace's face over the viewscreen was grim. "I can feel it. I shouldn't be able to—especially not at this distance and after we severed our bond—but I do. She's *hurting*."

It was the first time my former bond-mate had contacted me since I'd dropped him off near his home by the K'drin jungle over a solar week ago. The call was a surprise—I'd never expected him to speak to me again.

He had been silent and taciturn on our trip back from Earth to Denaris, saying barely three words to me. I'd thought about trying to explain myself again—about how everything he'd seen was a big mistake. But what was the point? Our bond was broken and I was fairly certain there was no way to restore it, even if we had wanted to—which Drace most definitely did not. So, really, there was nothing to say except goodbye.

I came back home and spent the next week feeling completely shredded, refusing to see or speak to anyone. Hylorn and my mother both came to try and cheer me up but I sent them away without even opening the door of my domicile. I couldn't help it—I wasn't fit to be seen. The loss of my bond-mate and the female we both loved was a pain so great I was nearly incoherent with grief. For the first time, I understood how people felt when a loved one died. Because, for all intents and purposes, both Rylee and Drace were dead to me now.

But now, here was my former bond-mate, back from the dead, confronting me with this startling claim.

"Can you feel it?" he asked me abruptly. "Can you feel her pain too or is it only me?"

"I don't feel any pain," I said slowly. "But...I *do* have dreams. I keep seeing her curled up on the sleeping platform, clutching her head. I keep telling myself they're only dreams but..." I trailed off uncertainly.

"Goddess above," Drace muttered angrily. "Are there any side effects to that damn memory-wipe we did on her? Anything that can go wrong?"

"Not if it's done properly," I said bristling. "By a bonded pair of males."

"But we *weren't bonded* when we did it," he pointed out.

"No...but it *did* work," I said, frowning.

"*Did* it?" he demanded. "How do you know we didn't abandon the female we both love—*loved* anyway, in your case—to a lifetime of debilitating fucking pain? Can you promise me we didn't?"

I pursed my lips, ignoring his insult. "I've never heard of such an outcome before. But Rylee is human, a Pure One and a *La-ti-zal*. It's possible that her body reacted differently to the wipe than anyone else from the Twelve Peoples would have."

"We have to get to her. We have to check and make sure she's all right," Drace growled. "*I'm* going anyway. I don't care if you come or not."

"Of course I'm going," I said coldly. "You said it yourself—she's the woman we both love. Just because we don't...don't care for each other anymore is no reason I would stop caring for her."

"That's not what I hear," he snarled. "But fine, you go in your ship, I'll go in mine."

"That will take too long," I objected, ignoring his dig. "What if there really *is* a problem and I need you to help me help Rylee?"

"And how do you think *I* can help you if the problem has to do with the mind-wipe?" he demanded. "Our bond is severed."

"Yes it is—you saw to that yourself," I said sharply. "As to how you can help—I don't have any *fucking* idea. But we started this together, it seems logical it will take both of us to remedy whatever is wrong with Rylee."

As always, when I swore, Drace seemed taken aback.

"Fine," he said at last. "Pick me up where you dropped me off. We'll go together."

"On my way," I said and cut the connection. It was time to pay a visit to the AMI and have the Commercians zero in on Rylee so we could find out what, if anything, was going on.

* * * * *

# Drace

Lucian picked me up and I swear we didn't share five fucking words between us on the trip back to Earth. There was nothing to say, I told myself. What was I going to do—ask him how his new bond-mate was working out?

I knew that my former bond-mate had already psy-bonded himself to Hylorn because Lucian's mother had called to tell me—with poorly concealed glee—that they were already an item. She went on and fucking *on* about how the two of them were attending society balls every night with the female she had picked out for them. Apparently the three of them were the toast of the town. The cream of Fang Clan society and the envy of everyone everywhere.

*Fucking asshole.*

And all the while I sat at home in my bachelor's lair and kept to myself, as lonely and miserable as I had been before. No, actually *more* lonely and miserable because now I knew what I was missing. Hearing about how Lucian had moved on only made me hate and resent him even more.

*That bastard,* I thought while his mother was prattling on and on about how well he was doing and how happy he was. *He never cared about Rylee or me in the first place. If he had, there's no way he could move on so quickly.* At last, I wound up hanging up on her—I couldn't stand to hear anymore of his golden boy exploits. They made me sick. Sick with longing for Lucian and Rylee both, even while I hated him and missed her. Sick because I couldn't stand to let them go—at least, not in my mind.

I told myself to get over it. That the pain I felt was due to the psychic trauma of severing our bond so abruptly, that I would move on eventually, just as Lucian already had. But would I really?

It sure as hell didn't feel like it.

When we got to the AMI and docked with the Commercian's station, which was camouflaged among the space junk in low Earth orbit, we got a surprise. There was another ship also docked with them.

"What's this?" I muttered to Lucian. "I thought they only saw one client at a time?"

He shrugged. "You know the Commercians—always eager to make more profit."

We went through the airlock and found the Commercians already busy with two customers—an Earth female with long, silky brown hair and a huge Braxian male with blue skin and curving black horns. He had the black-on-black eyes of his kind and they didn't look friendly when he turned to us.

"Are these the ones?" he asked Char'noth, the head Commercian as he pointed to us.

"Yes, my Lord Grav, these are the males who purchased the *La-ti-zal* female called Ry-lee," Char'noth piped up, pointing several arms at us.

"Who the *fuck* are you and what do you want with Rylee?" I growled, taking a step towards him. Braxians were some of the most feared of the Twelve Peoples—they could unleash a berserker rage that was seriously insane in its intensity. But if this bastard wanted to mess with Rylee, he'd find out I could get more than a little berserk myself.

Beside me, Lucian also stepped up, fangs bared, which surprised me a little, since he was already practically life-bonded to Hylorn and the female his mother had picked for them. I told myself he was probably just feeling responsible for Rylee because of the way he *used* to care for her.

"Who the fuck am I?" The Braxian growled, his black-on-black eyes narrowing to slits. "I'm Gravex N'gol, here by order of the new Goddess-Empress, Sundalla the 1000th to find out what's going on with the Commercians' little business. And what I want with Rylee Hale is to find out what you two fuck-ups did to her that left her lookin' like *that.*"

He stabbed a finger at the AMI lightscreen. I stepped forward and saw that it was showing Rylee—but not the happy, laughing, vibrant Rylee Lucian and I had known. She was curled on her side, her hands pressed to the sides of her head with tears leaking from the corners of her eyes.

She was in terrible pain. I felt just a tingle of it, the kind of feeling you might get in a limb that's had extensive nerve damage and isn't expected to recover full function.

"Gods," Lucian whispered in a stricken voice. "This is what I dreamed! I can't believe it's *true*."

"Believe it, asshole," Grav snarled. "The poor little thing is suffering and you two fucks have something to do with it! She's a friend of my mate, Leah." He nodded at the brown haired Earth female who had a worried look on her face. "And she's pretty damn upset by this. I want to know what you did to her and I want to know *right fuckin' now!*"

"We wiped her memory of us after we severed our bond with her," Lucian said, answering for both of us. "It's a talent the males of my Clan have, to erase bad or painful memories. But I've never seen anyone have these kinds of effects from it before."

"Wait a minute—you *severed* your bond?" The Earth girl frowned at us. "I've never heard of that before. I mean, I don't know much about your people but don't you guys bond for life?"

"A bond between Denarin males is...complicated," I said in a low voice. "Normally you can't break it. But we found a way."

"Oh you *did*, did you?" Grav's eyes narrowed even more. "And what way was that? Did you sacrifice this little female's health so the two of you could get free of each other?"

"Of course not!" Lucian exclaimed. "We would never hurt Rylee—we *love* her!"

"You mean *I* love her," I snapped. "*You're* already bonded to another male and having the time of your life with the female your mother picked out for you!"

"*What?*" He shook his head, looking genuinely confused. "What are you talking about? I'm not bonded to anyone!"

"You deny it?" I crossed my arms over my chest and glared at him. "You're telling me you're *not* already psy-bonded to Hylorn and looking to get life-bonded to a female you both care for?"

"Of course I deny it!" he snarled. "I haven't seen Hylorn or anyone else in the past week. I've been holed up alone in my apartment feeling like shit because *you* severed our bond!"

"Stop *lying!*" I shouted. My hands balled into fists and I longed to punch him in his stupid, lying face. "Your own *mother* called to tell me all about how fucking *happy* you are now that Rylee and I are out of your life!"

"My...my mother?" His voice faltered and he put a hand to his head. "She said all that?"

"Guess she just couldn't resist rubbing it in," I said bitterly. "She went on and fucking *on* about how happy you are now."

"She lied." His voice was cold and flat. "She lied to you."

"Oh, so being with Hylorn and having the 'perfect female' *isn't* making you happy?" I demanded sarcastically. "I'm so *sorry* for you, Lucian. What a fucking disappointment."

"No, I mean she lied about *everything*." Lucian sounded stunned, as though he was discovering some great treachery he still couldn't quite believe. "She lied about Hylorn and the female and about me being mated to them. And she lied back at my apartment when she said she wanted to throw a party for me to introduce you and Rylee as my bond-mates. It was a set-up all along—an excuse to bring Hylorn back into my life and let you see us together."

"Well that part of it worked, anyway," I said sharply. "Seeing the two of you heart-pledging—"

"*He* pledged to *me!*" Lucian snapped. "And I did *not* return his pledge. Because it wouldn't be right—not when I was already pledged to you and Rylee." His voice dropped to a whisper. "Nothing is right anymore without the two of you."

I stared at him, wanting to believe but not sure if I could.

"So that scene with Hylorn in the food prep area was—?

"A trap planned by my mother," he said dully. "And you and I both fell directly into it."

"But she came to me afterwards," I protested. "She said you truly cared for Hylorn. And told me—"

"That if you cared about me you'd let me go because you'd only drag me down and ruin my life, right?" he finished for me.

"How—?" I began.

"How do I know what she said? Because it's the same exact thing she said to Hylorn when she separated the two of us so many years ago." His voice was little more than a whisper. "How could I not see this? How could I let her ruin my chances for happiness and drive away the people I loved *again?*"

I didn't know what to say. The pain on his face was real—as real as the pain in my heart now that I understood what had happened.

"It's not your fault," I said in a low voice. "I should have listened to your explanation about you and Hylorn instead of losing my temper. I should have given myself time to cool down before using the Claw to sever our bond and demanding you do the same."

"The Claw?" Grav, the big Braxian demanded. He and his mate Leah had been standing back, watching quietly as Lucian and I argued and shouted and finally came to the truth. But now he stepped forward, a frown on his face. "What the fuck is this 'Claw' you two are talking about?"

"It is an instrument we found in a sacred place on our own planet," Lucian explained icily. "We were led there by a prophesy of one of the Wave-Dwellers."

"Wave-Dwellers?" Leah shook her head. "Who are they?"

"One of the Twelve Peoples," Grav told her. "They live in the seas of Denaris and have the lower half of a sea creature when they're in the water. But when they come up on land, they're able to change their appearance and look completely, uh, normal. Or at least, like the rest of us—with legs and everything."

Her face brightened. "Mermaids? You're saying there are real, actual *mermaids* on Denaris?"

"Dunno what mermaids are but sure," her mate growled. "But listen, I'm more interested in the 'Claw' these two used to sever their bond." He nodded at Lucian and me. "If it's what I think it is…" He shook his head. "It could be bad fuckin' news."

"I have it with me," I said.

"You brought it *with* you?" Lucian gave me an incredulous look.

"Thought we might need it. I don't know." I shrugged defensively.

"Get it," Grav demanded. "I need to see it."

I went back to Lucian's ship and rummaged in my pack. The golden Claw was wrapped in a shirt and I unrolled it carefully, not wanting to be stuck by it again. It's four, wickedly sharp tips were stained maroon from my blood and Lucian's and I was struck again by how *evil* the thing felt in my hand.

Carrying it away from my body, I brought it back to the AMI.

"Here." I held it out to Grav.

"What *is* that? It looks like some kind of weird golden backscratcher!" Leah put out a hand but Grav quickly pushed it away.

"Don't touch, baby — that thing is fuckin' dangerous," he growled. He glared at me. "Do you know what you have there? It's a Goddess-damned Braxian soul-devourer."

"The Claw is Braxian?" I frowned at the dried blood on its tips. "You're sure?"

"Sure I'm fuckin' sure," he growled. "They've been outlawed on my home planet for over a thousand years but you still see them pop up from time to time — usually after they fucked some poor bastard to the Frozen Hells and back."

"What…" Lucian cleared his throat. "What are the side effects of a 'soul-devourer then? We only used it to sever our bond."

"Yeah, it'll sever a bond all right — by taking a bite out of your fuckin' soul," Grav said, frowning. "And leaving you in crippling pain afterwards."

"I haven't experienced any pain," Lucian protested.

"Me either," I said.

"It looks like Rylee is, though." Leah's voice was soft and worried.

I looked over her head at the AMI lightscreen where Rylee was still curled in a ball and bit back a curse. Could it be that the pain which should rightfully have come to Lucian and me after severing our bond had landed on her instead? A wave of guilt and horror so deep it threatened to drown me washed over me. What had we done to the female we both loved?

One look at Lucian's face let me know he was feeling the same.

"But...how could this happen?" he demanded. "We followed the instructions—Drace and I both marked ourselves, over our hearts."

"Yeah? And what about Rylee—did you use the soul-devourer on her too?" Grav demanded.

"Well...no," I said. "We didn't think it was necessary. It was just Lucian and I wanting to sever our bond. So Rylee—"

"Is the one who wound up getting the pain all *three* of you should have shared," Grav finished. "Goddess-damn it! Do you realize what you've done? Rylee still has a part of her bond to both of you because she wasn't marked by the soul-devourer. And because *she's* the one who still has a little bit of the bond, she's *also* the one who got the pain!"

"Fuck!" I threw the evil Claw on the metal flooring of the Commercians' station. It clattered and landed points up, giving me a bloody grin with its stained talons.

"What can we do?" Lucian asked in a low, urgent voice. "Both of us love Rylee to distraction and this has all been a horrible mistake! We should never have severed our bond. How can we ease her pain and get back our bond?"

"You can't,' Grave growled. "Can't get your bond back, I mean. Once a bond is broken—eaten, really—by a soul-destroyer, there's no restoring it. But since Rylee still has her part of the bond, it *might* be possible to at least ease her pain."

"How?" Lucian asked. "How can we do it? If our bond is lost, at least we can take away her suffering."

"Skin-to-skin contact—as much as possible," Grave said. "It helps dissipate the pain."

"But don't you see—we *can't* hold Rylee between us and touch her! Not now!" Lucian exclaimed. "We did a memory-wipe on her—she doesn't even *know* us anymore!"

"Damn it!" I snapped. "We can't just leave her in pain, Lucian!"

"Again, she *doesn't know us*," he spat. "We'll scare her to death if we bring her up here and demand the three of us get naked together."

"Then don't bring her up to the AMI." Leah spoke up, looking thoughtful. "You guys go down to her instead."

"Wonderful plan," Lucian said acidly. "So two huge, naked aliens she doesn't know suddenly show up in her sleeping chamber? *That* won't be frightening at all."

Leah pursed her lips in a frown. "You're right—that *would* be terrifying. Tell you what—let me go first and talk to her."

"You're sure?" Grav frowned at his mate. "I thought you didn't like traveling through the AMI system."

"It's not very comfortable," Leah admitted. "But it's my fault Rylee's in this mess in the first place. I gave her the, uh, *La-ti-zal* virus or whatever you call it, so I should be the one to help her. And I *am* a Healer—that's my *La-ti-zal* power," she explained to us. "So maybe I can help."

"I wish you could, baby, but I kinda doubt it," Grav growled softly, stroking her long brown hair. "Usually this kind of psychic pain can only be helped by whoever caused it in the first place."

She got a stubborn look on her face. "Well, at least I'm going to *try.*"

"All right, try then. I know better than to argue with you." Grav turned to Char'noth, the head Commercian who had been standing by, waiting for orders. "You guys get your transporter or whatever the hell it is ready to go. My female is going down first and then you're going to bring her back up and send these two down." He nodded at me and Lucian.

"At once, my lord Grav." Char'noth bowed obsequiously, his blue, worm-like body writhing with the gesture. "Only…who will pay the costs of all these transferences? Travel between our station and the Earth takes immense amounts of energy, you know and energy is not cheap."

"I'll fuckin' pay," Grav growled. "I've got an unlimited expense account from the Empress to keep tabs on you little bastards. So get going!"

Char'noth scurried away, his multiple legs clacking on the metal floor.

"All right." Leah took a deep breath. "I'll try my best to help her remember you. Or if that won't work, at least to let her know you guys just want to help ease her pain."

"We do," Lucian said fervently. "I'll never forgive myself for letting her be hurt like this."

"I won't forgive myself either," I growled. "To think she's been in pain all this time—we're fucking idiots, bond-m—" I stopped myself just in time but Lucian shook his head, looking sad.

"Bond-mate," he finished for me quietly. "My fondest wish is that you could call me that again, Drace—and I could call you the same. When we were joined with Rylee between us, I never felt such a sense of peace and rightness."

"And I've never felt more alone or fucked-up since we parted," I said in a low voice.

"You can't get the bond back," Grav growled. "Right now you need to concentrate on easing that little female's pain." He nodded to Rylee's image on the lightscreen again.

"Before I go, tell me a little about how you and Rylee met and the things you did together," Leah said urgently. "Any little details that might jog her memory would help."

"Okay," I said. "Well it started because Lucian and I were looking to break our bond…"

We talked quickly, trying to give her the important points and details—the highlights of our adventures together—while the Commercians prepared their transport. Leah nodded rapidly and I hoped she could keep all the strange things the three of us had been through together straight.

"My lord Gravex—we are ready." Char'noth's high, piping voice informed us. "Please have your female disrobe if she does not wish to lose her clothing in the transfer."

"That's for my eyes only." The Braxian's face darkened. "You two go back to your ship. I'll let you know when it's time for you to transport."

"Go back to the ship?" I protested. "What the fuck are we supposed to do there?"

"Pray," Grav growled. "Now get the fuck out of here."

Lucian and I looked at each other. What else could we do? We left and went to wait in his ship, hoping against hope that Leah could convince Rylee to let two alien males she no longer remembered come into her room and comfort and touch her.

*"Please Goddess,"* I prayed as we stepped back through the airlock. *"Please let Rylee be okay. Let us be able to ease her suffering and take away her pain. Even if we're never able to be together again, let us at least do that much."*

I didn't hear any answers or feel any warm glow but I did get the sense that someone was watching. Watching and waiting to see what Lucian and I did and how we cared for the female we both loved.

# Chapter Thirty-three

## Rylee

A week later, the headache still hadn't gone away. In fact, if anything, it had gotten worse. I'd gotten in contact with my Aunt Celia who had come to take me to the ER. Nobody said the words out loud but I think we were both worried about some kind of brain tumor or aneurism. But first a Cat Scan, then an MRI showed nothing. I was having headaches for no reason and no medication the doctors could give me would make them stop.

I was in constant pain—feeling so bad I couldn't bear to even get out of bed. My Aunt or one of my cousins came once a day to check on me, make me some soup, and get me in and out of the shower, which was really sweet of them. I hadn't realized what a close knit family I had until I was feeling so bad. When I mentioned how grateful I was to my Aunt, she stroked my hair out of my eyes and gave me a worried smile.

"Of course I'll take care of you, child! You're like one of my own. Just wish we could find out what's going wrong with you. Are you sure you won't let me take you to the hospital again?"

"So they can hook me up to all kinds of tubes and wires and run more tests that don't show a damn thing?" I said. "No, Auntie—I'm better off in my own place."

Brave words and I'd meant them when I said them. But now, a few days later and feeling much, *much* worse than I would have dreamed possible, I was beginning to reconsider. I hurt so much I was beginning to feel like I was going crazy…which was probably why I wasn't that surprised when I turned over in bed and saw Leah, the friend of Zoe's I'd helped with her divorce papers, walking out of my bathroom.

"Hi, Rylee." She gave me a little wave. "I hope you don't mind me showing up unexpectedly like this."

"Uh...no." I struggled to make my brain and mouth work together. "But...what are you doing here? If you're looking to get any legal paperwork done, I'm sorry but I'm really not up to it right now. I have a *massive* headache that won't go away."

"I know you do." She came over to my bed and sat on the side of it, a concerned look on her pretty face. "And I'm not here for any paperwork."

"Uh...okay." I closed my eyes again, the pain overwhelming me. "Sorry. I just...just feel so bad."

"I know, honey." There was compassion in her voice and I felt her cool hand stroking over my forehead. To my surprise, the headache eased up, just the tiniest bit. It still throbbed dully just behind my eyes but at least I didn't feel like I was going to pass out from the pain.

"Hey, how did you do that?" I muttered. Looking up at her, I noticed something else. "And why are you wearing my bathrobe?"

"It was the only thing I could find in your bathroom when I got here. It was either this or a towel or go naked." She nodded down at the pink, terrycloth robe which had been a present from one of my cousins the Christmas before. "I didn't think you'd mind."

"It's fine," I said, frowning. "But...did you just come over here to borrow my bathrobe?" Even with my head singing *The Hallelujah Chorus* that seemed like a strange idea. "And how did you get in, anyway?" I asked. "Did my aunt leave the door unlocked the last time she left?"

"No..." Leah took a deep breath. "Look, the way I got here, and your headache, and even the reason I'm wearing your bathrobe are all kind of...interconnected."

"What?" I shook my head and winced as the sudden motion set off new flares of pain behind my eyes. Okay, should *not* have done that. "I don't understand," I groaned, putting a hand to my throbbing temples.

"Do you remember two big guys named Drace and Lucian?" she asked me softly. "One of them had kind of olive green skin and the other was dark blue?"

"Blue and green skin? What?" I squinted at her, feeling my head throb even harder. "I don't know any —"

Suddenly an image flashed before my mind's eye—there and gone so quickly I wasn't even sure I'd seen it. Me, sandwiched between two huge, muscular, male bodies, both of them touching me…both of them…what? What were they doing?

The moment I asked myself the question, I felt the familiar gray fog begin to roll over my mind. I tried to fight it but that only made my head throb. At last, I had to give up.

"Do you remember?" Leah asked, looking at me anxiously.

"I tried," I said, pushing my hair out of my face weakly. "I *almost* can but it hurts my head to try. Who are they, anyway? And what do they have to do with me?"

"Well…" She hesitated. "How good are you at believing impossible things?"

"I don't know," I said. "Try me."

"All right. Leah took a deep breath. "Here goes…

* * * * *

"So…I got sucked up into an alien spacecraft and went on a bunch of adventures with two alien guys who wanted me to help break their psychic bond?" I said, when she was finally finished. "And instead I ended up bonding with them…only the bond got broken anyway and that's why I can't get rid of this horrible headache?" I narrowed my eyes at her Are you for *real*, Leah or am I having another weird dream?"

"I'm telling you the truth," she said earnestly. "And the reason I'm telling you is, well…we think the only way to ease the pain you're in is to let your guys come see you again."

"What like…bring them through the mirror the way you came?" I still couldn't believe I was saying all this. And yet, her words to me *did* seem to stir something inside me. Some strange memory that kept getting hidden by the fog every time I tried to grab hold of it.

"Exactly." Leah looked at me earnestly. "Will you let them try? They feel *horrible* for what happened to you. And…Rylee, I think they both still love you."

"Love me?" I shook my head, making it throb again. "I don't know, Leah—this is too weird."

"Please just give it a shot," she begged. "I want you to be okay, Rylee. Because part of this is my fault too. I'm the reason you're a *La-ti-zal* in the first place, which makes you stand out on the AMI database."

"Okay, I still am not understanding half of what you're saying," I groaned. "But at this point I'll try anything to get rid of this pain. It's *awful.*"

"So I can send them down?" she asked cautiously. "And you promise you won't freak out?"

"I'll *try* not to," I said. "As long as they don't try anything, uh, funny."

"They just want to hold you," she assured me anxiously. "They just want to take away your pain."

"Well..." I sighed. "What have I got to lose? Okay, sure I guess. Bring 'em down."

"I'll send them in a minute," she promised. Leaning down, she kissed me on the check. "Get better, Rylee. Zoe is dying to see you again and my other friend, Charlotte wants to meet you too. She said to tell you she's got a spot all picked out for you in her court if you want it."

"A spot in her court?" I looked at her uncertainly. "What does that mean?"

"Well, Charlotte used to be a medical intern but now she's the new Goddess-Empress of the galaxy," Leah explained. "She—well look, it's another *really* long story. The main thing is, everything is going to be okay."

"Okay, sure." I shrugged. "Thanks, Leah."

"I'll see you in a little while," she promised, rising from the bed. "I'll go send Drace and Lucian down first."

Then she disappeared into my bathroom where she'd come from and the door clicked shut behind her.

I stared at the door for a long moment, trying to decide if I'd imagined the whole thing or not. *I must be dreaming,* I told myself.

*Aliens and bonding and spaceships and psychic pain and the Empress of the galaxy...that can't be real, right?*

I had just about decided I was in so much pain that I was having hallucinations and I had better call my Aunt Celia to take me to the hospital after all, when the bathroom door opened again.

This time two huge, muscular men, both around seven feet tall, shuffled into my room. They wore remorseful expressions on their faces and tiny white towels — *my* towels I realized — tied around their waists.

"Oh shit," I whispered as I stared at them. It *wasn't* a dream!"

# Chapter Thirty-four

## Rylee

"No, *ma 'frela,* it was no dream," the one with olive green skin murmured. He had thick black hair and a deep, smooth voice that seemed to go right through me.

"Are you okay, baby?" the other one, who had blue skin rumbled. "We're so fucking sorry you're sick."

"We want to help you feel better," the other one said.

"Wait..." I half sat up, despite the throbbing in my head, and pointed at them. "You're...Drace and...you're Lucian. Right?"

"She remembers!" Drace looked at Lucian with a grin. "I can't believe — she remembers!"

"No, I don't remember you two," I said sharply, cutting him off. "It's just that my friend Leah was here and she told me your names. She — *ahhh!*"

My last words ended in a groan because the pain in my head, which had receded just a little while Leah had been with me, had abruptly come back with a vengeance. I felt like someone was stabbing rusty iron spikes in both eyes and scraping the back of my skull just for fun.

"*Ma 'frela!*" Lucian was suddenly on the bed beside me, on my right.

"Baby, are you okay?" Drace demanded, insinuating himself between me and the wall on my left side. My little bed — which was only a full sized one — was suddenly crammed full of big, muscular, alien bodies and I didn't know what to think.

"Hey, wait a minute — I don't even *know* you guys," I said — or wanted to say. What came out was just another groan — I was literally too weak and in too much pain to do anything to stop them.

Even though I was only wearing a thin oversized t-shirt and a tiny pair of white panties and I knew this level of intimacy with strangers was totally indecent, I couldn't do a damn thing about it.

Big hands stroked over my forehead, my throat and shoulder and arms...sliding down my back in long, soothing strokes, touching my thighs. And all the while they were whispering to me, telling me how sorry they were, how much they loved and adored me, how they wanted to make me feel better...to feel good.

"Hey," I protested weakly. "You can't...I'm only wearing a nightshirt. I mean..." But I stopped in mid protest. As strange and frightening as it was to suddenly have two guys who seemed to be complete strangers in my bed, I realized that when they touched me, the awful, throbbing pain in my head faded. Or started to fade, anyway.

"*Ma 'frela*," Lucian murmured, kissing my forehead gently. "How we have missed you! Missed holding you between us and caressing you like this."

"Did you?" I whispered, wide-eyed in the semi-gloom of my dim bedroom. "Did you guys really, uh, have me between you a lot?" As the pain faded, a different sensation was taking its place. A kind of need...a hunger that I didn't quite understand was growing in me.

"All the time, baby," Drace rasped in my ear. "Wish you could remember. Lucian and I loved holding you between us."

"But..." I cleared my throat. "I'm guessing that, uh, *holding* wasn't the only thing going on, was it?"

"No," Lucian murmured, looking into my eyes. "How do you feel about that?"

"I...I'm not sure," I whispered. "I mean, I don't even *know* you two."

But though my mind didn't know them, my body was no stranger to theirs. As they held me between them, the pain faded farther and farther into the distance and a warm tingling took its place. I felt surrounded by them, enveloped completely by their big bodies. And there was something else that was familiar—their scents. They filled my senses—a cool, crisp ocean aroma from Lucian and a dark, spicy musk from Drace. Both were equally delicious but when they mixed together, they made the hunger inside me grow.

"You *do* know us," Drace murmured from behind me. "You just don't remember. Gods, I wish we could find a way to bring your memory back."

"Unfortunately there is no way to reverse a mind-wipe." Lucian sounded regretful. "Unless…no, never mind."

"What?" I asked, looking at him. "What were you going to say? *Say* it."

"Well…" He shifted uncomfortably. "I was thinking that maybe if Drace and I were to…to touch you in the way that we have done in the past it might…bring back primal memories. But…" He shook his head. "That is far too familiar now, especially when you do not even remember Drace or myself."

"I don't *remember* you," I said slowly. "But…you're both very familiar. And when you touch me it…"

"Takes the pain away?" Drace asked hopefully.

"Yes," I said. "But something else too. It…" I blushed but made myself go on. "It makes me want…more somehow."

"More of what?" Lucian cupped my face in his big hands. "More of this, *ma 'frela?*" he murmured and pulled me in for a gentle, delicious kiss.

"Yes," I whispered breathlessly when he finally released me. "More of that."

"What about this, then?" Drace asked and one big hand crept around to cup my breast from behind. He was touching me over my nightshirt and he held me tentatively at first. But when I moaned and pressed my breast forward to nestle more fully in his hand, he growled softly and pinched my nipple, sending sparks of pleasure through my body.

"Yes," I whispered, pressing my ass backwards and feeling something hot and hard brush my inner thighs. Part of me felt like I shouldn't be doing this—I didn't even know these guys, after all. But my *body* seemed to know them—to know them and their gentle, demanding touch intimately. And it felt so good not to be in pain anymore I didn't want to stop.

"You have such beautiful breasts, Rylee," Lucian murmured, watching with apparent pleasure as Drace stroked and pinched my nipple through the thin cotton t-shirt. "Would you allow us to bare them and pleasure you with our mouths?"

"Did…is that something you guys did…used to do to me a…a lot?" I somehow managed to get out.

"Oh yeah, baby—Lucian and I love sucking your sweet, ripe nipples," Drace growled softly. "It always makes your little pussy so *wet.*"

"Well…" I bit my lip, trying to rationalize it. "Maybe…maybe Lucian is right and it would…would help if we did things we used to do before…before I lost my memory. Maybe it would help me remember and…and feel better."

"It is certainly worth a try," Lucian murmured. "So may we take off this little night-garment you are wearing?"

"Okay," I whispered. "But… leave my panties on."

"As you wish, *ma 'frela.*" And then four big hands were lifting my thin white t-shirt over my head, leaving me mostly naked and incredibly hot.

"Gods, I love your body," Drace growled, when I was lying between them again with nothing but my lacy white panties on. "Look how *tight* your nipples are."

"That's because you were…were pinching them," I reminded him in a soft, breathless voice.

"Aww, did I hurt you baby?" There was a hot light in his eyes and his voice was a deep, hungry growl.

"If you did then it is our duty to sooth the ache you made in our female's sweet nipples," Lucian purred. "Don't you agree, Drace?"

"Absolutely," Drace murmured. And then two hot mouths were on me, sucking my aching buds—hard and deep for Drace and with light, ticklish teasing sweeps of his tongue for Lucian.

I moaned as the two different but equally pleasurably sensations filled me. Moaned and arched my back as I buried my hands in their thick hair, wanting more. So much more…

*They used to do this,* whispered a little voice — maybe the voice of memory in my head. *They loved to suck my nipples and it always felt so good even though they have such differing styles.*

Could it be I was finally beginning to remember something? I grabbed onto the memory and tried to follow it, tried to remember more but I couldn't. I needed something else to help bring it into focus. But what?

"Uh...guys?" I whispered, still pressing my breasts up to their mouths.

"Mmm?" Lucian looked up, allowing my right nipple to slip slowly from between his lips. Drace kept sucking a while longer, nursing long and hard at my tender peak before finally raising his eyes to mine.

"I...I *think* I'm beginning to remember something," I told them hesitantly. "But it comes and goes. I...I feel like I might be able to remember more if..."

"If we would show you other things the three of us used to do together?" Lucian purred.

"Yes." I nodded, my heart galloping in my chest. God, was I really going to do this? Was I really asking them to go farther, to touch me more intimately? It seemed that I was and I couldn't even bring myself to feel guilty about it.

"Sure, we can show you, baby. But you'll have to let us take these off..." Drace's big hand drifted down to stroke lightly over my lacy white panties.

I bit my lip as his light touch started a fire inside me.

"Drace is correct," Lucian murmured in my ear. "We used to take turns touching and tasting you, *ma 'frela.* I remember one notable occasion when Drace showed me his special technique for making you come on his tongue."

"You guys did that? You...took turns with me?"

"Took turns *pleasuring* you," Lucian corrected me gently.

"Your pleasure always comes first with us. We just want to make you feel good, baby," Drace growled softly.

"All...all right," I whispered, lifting my hips. "You can take them off. As long...as long as you're gentle."

"Always gentle with you, *ma 'frela,*" Lucian promised as he slipped the lacy white panties down my thighs and tossed them over the side of the bed.

"Gods, look at her sweet pussy—she's so fucking *wet.*" Drace's harsh, growling voice was thick with lust. "Do you want to lick her first or should I?" he asked Lucian.

"You lick her," Lucian murmured. "I enjoy watching how hot riding your tongue makes our little female. I will take my turn after."

I bit my lip and moaned as Drace slid down to get between my thighs, splitting them wide with his broad shoulders. God, I couldn't believe I was doing this! The sight of him dipping his dark head to my open pussy made me close my eyes with lust and shame.

"No," Lucian's voice murmured in my ear and I felt his arm come around me, encircling my shoulders so he could cup my breasts in his hands. "No, *ma 'frela,* watch as Drace tastes your pussy and laps up your sweet juices. How else can you remember all that we have done together...how much we mean to each other?"

Well, he had a point—I had to admit. Though I still felt embarrassed and uncertain, I opened my eyes and watched as Drace spread my pussy lips wide with his thumbs. Then, looking up at me to read the expression in my eyes, he began a slow, hot lapping, starting at the very bottom of my slit and dragging his tongue upwards over my slick inner folds. I moaned again, breathlessly, when he reached my clit, dragging his hot tongue relentlessly over my tender, sensitive bud.

"Does it feel good, Rylee?" Lucian murmured in my ear as he twisted and rolled my nipples between his fingers. "Does it feel good to let Drace spread you wide and lick your hot little pussy?"

"God," I whispered. "It...it does. You know it does."

"And does it bring back any memories?" he asked earnestly. "Think, *ma 'frela*—it's important. If you could remember us maybe...maybe we could somehow be together again."

"I...I think I'd like that," I whispered. Though I still couldn't remember them completely, the feel of their two big bodies surrounding mine felt right in a way I could neither explain or deny. I tried to remember if this had happened before…tried to recall the times they had spoken of.

For just an instant the gray fog that wanted to cloud my mind slipped aside and I had a clear memory…Drace and Lucian taking turns between my legs, each one showing the other his technique for lapping and sucking my pussy, each one eager to make me come…

"I remember," I whispered eagerly as Lucian pinched my nipples again. "At least…a little. "I remember the two of you taking…taking turns. And you —" I broke off, blushing.

"What? What else do you remember, baby?" Drace asked eagerly, looking up from between my thighs. His full lips were wet with my juices and I felt my heart pounding like a drum when I saw the hope in his eyes and heard a similar hope in Lucian's voice when he urged me to tell them what, if anything, was coming back to me.

"I…I remember this wasn't…wasn't the only way the two of you, uh, took turns with me," I whispered at last, feeling both mortified and hot at the same time.

"You're right, *ma 'frela*," Lucian murmured. "But Drace and I didn't know…we weren't certain how you might feel about letting us…"

"Make love to you," Drace finished for him.

"I'm not sure either," I admitted. "I think…think maybe we should take it slow. Let me see you — both of you — first."

They seemed to understand what I meant because both of them shed the white terrycloth towels they'd had wrapped around their waists and came to sit on either side of me again.

"Holy crap!" I muttered, looking at them. They were *huge!* Lucian's shaft was a little longer and Drace's was a little thicker but both of them were way bigger than anything I'd ever had in me before.

*Anything you **remember** you mean,* whispered a little voice in my head.

Without thinking about it, I reached out to take on thick shaft in each of my hands. As I touched their hot, silky skin and felt the guys shift restlessly under my touch, I had another memory.

"Someone was telling the three of us what to do," I whispered. "He looked like a fallen angel with huge black-feathered wings. He made us touch each other…taste each other…"

"Fuck each other," Drace finished with a growl.

"That was Lord Mandrex," Lucian murmured. "He loaned us the Tanterine Key which we used to get into the hidden Temple of Ganth." He frowned. "Which we still have not returned to him."

"Later for that—she's beginning to remember us." Drace thrust eagerly into my loosely fisted fingers. "Does it help to touch us, baby? Does it help you remember?"

"I remember…" I bit my lip, trying to roll back the fog. "I *think* I remember you, uh, being inside me." I looked shyly at Lucian. "Only I don't see how that's possible. You're so *big* – both of you."

"You don't remember but Dracian males produce a special kind of precum which allows our females to stretch to accommodate us," Lucian told me. He nodded down at his own shaft, still gripped loosely in my fist. "I am beginning to make some now—my body is responding to yours as is Drace's."

"Really?" My eyes widened as I looked down at the pearly, opalescent droplets welling at the tips of their broad heads. "You could…I mean just, uh, rubbing against me you could help me, um, open up."

"That is what we have done in the past," Lucian assured me.

"You did? And you were…able to fit inside that way?"

"Not just one of us," Drace assured me. "Both. At the same time."

I had no memory of this, though his words *did* seem to stir something inside me.

I bit my lip. "You mean…one in the front and…and one in the back?"

"Actually, neither of us has claimed your sweet ass yet, *ma 'frela*," Lucian murmured. "What Drace means is that both of us were able to put our shafts inside your pussy at once. That is how we bonded you to us in the first place." He looked sad. "Before the bond was severed, anyway."

The longing I heard in his voice and saw in Drace's eyes made me wish with all my heart I could remember what they were talking about. But I just didn't know about having two of them inside me at once. I still wasn't sure about taking just one of those big shafts inside me. But if it was the only way to remember...

"All right," I said, making up my mind. "You can...can show me what you mean. About the, uh, precum helping me to open up, I mean."

"Which of us should it be?" Drace asked, frowning.

"I think it should be you, bond-mate," Lucian said softly. "You are thicker than I am—if you can slide your shaft deep into our lady's pussy with no difficulty it will prove to her beyond question that it is possible for her to accommodate us."

"You sure?" Drace rumbled. "You didn't even get a chance to lick her pussy yet."

"But I will," Lucian promised. "When you are inside her."

Drace's eyes widened. "You'll play the Beta?"

"With pleasure." Lucian nodded and raised an eyebrow. "Unless you do not wish me to?"

"No—of course, I don't mind." Drace looked at me. "How do you want to do this, baby?"

"I think it would be easier if you lay on your back." I pushed at his broad chest, feeling both hot and nervous at the same time. "Lay back and let me, uh, ride you."

"With pleasure." Drace's voice was a low, lustful growl as he lay back in the center of my bed.

I positioned myself over him, straddling his lean hips. His thick cock jutted up from between his muscular thighs and I bit my lip. Had I really taken all that inside me? And could I do it now?

"Gently, *ma 'frela.*"

To my surprise, Lucian was suddenly on my right side, murmuring in my ear. He rubbed one big hand over my back and with the other, he grasped Drace's thick shaft.

I expected the other man to protest but instead, he held still, his eyes half-lidded with lust as Lucian used the head of Drace's cock to part my pussy lips and rub all over my slick folds.

"Allow the precum to work on you, *ma 'frela,*" he murmured as he slid the other man's shaft against my open pussy. "Especially your sweet little clit—the more pleasure you have, the easier it is for you to open."

I moaned softly as I watched him insert the head of Drace's cock into the entrance of my pussy. God, it felt so good and it was *working*. I kept catching flashes of the three of us doing these kinds of things before. I felt like I was close, very close to breaking through the gray fog and regaining my memories of them completely. And I wanted that—God, how I wanted it!

"Now, lean back," Lucian murmured. "Keep the head of Drace's cock inside you but sit back a little and spread your legs. I need to lick your sweet pussy to help him slide inside you.

I did as he said, fisting my hands in the covers on either side of me as Lucian bent between me and Drace. I felt his tongue, hot and ticklish, sliding over my swollen clit and the place where Drace and I were just barely joined. Another little piece of memory slipped into place just as Drace slipped another inch of his thickness into me.

*We did this—one of them entering me while the other one licked me. I remember—I remember now!*

As Drace's shaft leaked the special precum inside me and Lucian's tongue continued to work its magic, I felt myself opening to both of them. Suddenly the impossibly thick shaft slid into me all the way.

I gasped as I felt Drace bottom out inside me. God, he was in me—all the way in—and it didn't hurt a bit, just like they had promised. There was a stretching sensation, but it was a *good* feeling, being so open and exposed and vulnerable.

"God," I whispered, working my hips to feel the thick shaft move inside me. "This is…amazing. And…and I think it's helping me remember."

It was certainly helping with my pain. My headache was completely gone by this time, although I had a feeling it might come back if we stopped. That was all right though—I didn't want to stop.

"That's good, Rylee...so good." Lucian had stopped licking me and moved around behind me so he could whisper encouragement in my ear. "Just open your pussy, to Drace," he purred softly. "Let yourself be open enough so he can fuck you."

"What...what about you?" I whispered breathlessly. I could feel his broad chest pressing against my back and the brush of his hot, hard shaft against my ass. "Do...do you want to be in me too?"

I couldn't believe I was asking him this—practically inviting him. But it seemed wrong, somehow, to have one without the other.

*I need both of them,* a little voice whispered in my head. *Both of them inside me at once.*

"I would love nothing more than to enter you at the same time Drace is inside you," Lucian murmured. "But not in your pussy...we cannot re-bond, as much as we might want to. I would, however, very much like to use your sweet little ass."

"My...my ass?" I whispered, feeling uncertain all over again. I've never been much into that kind of thing and the idea of having one thick shaft filling my pussy and another filling my ass at the same time made me feel nervous. Nervous but also hot and excited.

"I'll be gentle." Lucian was already rubbing my tightly puckered rosebud with the head of his broad shaft. "My precum will help your ass open, just as Drace's helped your pussy open."

"Well..."

I tried to think past the lust that was clouding my brain. Should I do this? Should I let them go this far? It seemed wrong but...what if it was the only way to finally remember them...to remember the love they said we'd shared between the three of us. I wanted that, wanted it desperately even if it couldn't be like it had been before.

"All right," I said at last. "But gently. And *slowly.*"

"I'll be so gentle you'll barely feel me," Lucian murmured.

I doubted that but leaned over obediently, my pussy still impaled on Drace's thick cock, to give Lucian better access to my rosebud.

"God, your pussy is so tight, baby," Drace growled as my breasts brushed over his face. "Can't imagine how much tighter it's going to feel once Lucian has his shaft buried in your tight little ass."

I couldn't imagine either but then, I didn't have to. Already Lucian was breaching the back entrance to my body, pressing the broad, plum-shaped head of his cock inside me and inching slowly inward.

"Ahhh!" I moaned as he filled me. God, it felt good but it was a *tight* fit.

"Gently, *ma 'frela*," Lucian murmured, cupping my breasts from behind so he could roll my nipples, sending sparks of pleasure through my whole body. "Drace, tease her pussy," he ordered, looking over my shoulder at the other man beneath me. "Stroke her ripe little clit and give her pleasure so that she can open more easily."

"Gladly." With a low growl of lust, Drace slid one big hand between my thighs and began to explore me. His blunt fingertips found my swollen clit quickly and he began a maddening, slow circling of the sensitive little bud, making me cry and grind my hips against him even as Lucian slid deeper into my rosebud.

At last I felt Lucian's hips flush against the rounded curves of my ass and knew he was all the way inside me—filling me up just as Drace was doing in front.

All three of us moaned with the incredible sensation. I couldn't believe what I was doing—kneeling naked on my bed with my legs spread, sandwiched between two huge, muscular alien males, both my ass and my pussy filled with their thick shafts. And yet, it felt *right* somehow—as though this was meant to be between us.

I was close, so *close* to remembering them completely. I only needed a little more to banish the thick, gray fog forever and bring me back to my guys. Up until now, they'd both been holding still inside me, waiting for my word. But now I needed more.

"Lucian...Drace?" I murmured. "I...I need more. I think...I think I need both of you to move. To...to fuck me."

"Gods, baby," Drace groaned. "Thought you'd never ask!"

"It will be our pleasure, *ma 'frela*," Lucian murmured. And to Drace he said, "Slowly and gently, bond-mate. Our lovely little female is a lady and we must treat her as such."

"Of course, bond-mate." Drace nodded. I wondered if the two of them realized they were calling each other "bond-mate" when their bond was supposedly severed. But before I could say anything about it, they started to move.

I don't know how long it lasted—the deep thrust of both shafts inside me at once. They were moving in unison—in perfect harmony, that much I remember—both of them pulling out and thrusting back in at the exact same moment. And all the while they were filling me, Lucian's hands were on my breasts, touching and teasing my nipples while Drace's thick fingers continued to stroke between my legs.

It seemed like forever…it seemed like no time at all when I felt my pleasure beginning to peak, felt my body begin to clench around their hard, deep shafts thrusting into me so deeply.

"Ahhh!" I gasped, throwing back my head to rest it on Lucian's broad shoulder. "Oh God! I…I'm coming! You're making me come *so hard!*"

"Come for us then, baby," Drace growled, his fingers still sliding over my aching clit. "Come all over our cocks while we fill you up—fill you with our seed."

"Yes!" I moaned breathlessly. This was what I needed, I suddenly realized. Feeling them both in me at once, coming in me at once—this was what would lift the veil and blow the fog away forever.

I felt Drace's thick shaft swell even thicker inside me and then he was spurting, even as Lucian's cock began to throb in my ass. I gasped as my own orgasm continued to grow, breaking over me like a warm, all-encompassing wave. And then I was floating, flying free at last as both my men claimed me all over again.

The intense, exquisite pleasure blew away the last of the fog and banished my pain completely as well. I suddenly knew the men who were loving me so intimately—knew them completely. And more than that, I could actually *feel* them too. Not just inside my body, although that was certainly unmistakable, but also inside somehow. I could feel their emotions—their regret that our bond had ever been broken, the love they still had for each other and for me, and their desperate wish that we could be restored to our former relationship.

*"Love you"*, I thought at them as hard as I could. *"I love you forever, Drace...Lucian. I heart-pledge myself to both of you from now until forever."*

*"We love you too, ma 'frela,"* Lucian's deep, smooth voice filled my head.

*"Love you forever,"* Drace's rough voice added. And then I saw his eyes widen and he gasped out loud, "The bond!"

"It's back." Lucian's voice was full of wonderment and disbelief. "But how? We weren't even performing bonding sex."

"Maybe we didn't have to. Rylee *is* a Binder," Drace pointed out. "And maybe since she still had a little piece of our bond it allowed her to grow it back."

"I don't care how it happened," I said, and suddenly tears of joy were pouring out of my eyes. "I'm just glad we're back together. Oh guys, I missed you both *so much!*"

"We missed you too, baby," Drace growled.

They both slipped out of me and the three of us lay on our backs in the bed with me between them, cuddling and loving each other, reveling in the feel of being together again.

"I love you," I told them, out loud this time. "Love both of you so much. Let's never be apart again."

"Agreed," Lucian said firmly. "I am going to renounce my clan and my family so that we can find a place to live together."

"I will too," Drace said. "And I think we should move off-planet. Denaris is never going to be a good place for us."

"I agree." Lucian frowned. "It's a shame we wouldn't fit in on Earth. But since it's a closed planet, none of them even know there *is* extraterrestrial life outside their little world, I don't think it would work."

"No, Earth is definitely out, although I *do* want to introduce the two of you to my Aunt Celia before we go. But..." I snuggled between them. "We *might* already have a place. My friend Leah said that her friend Charlotte is the new Empress and she has a place for me in her court—whatever that means. I'm sure there would be room for you guys too. We could at least go check it out."

"Go live on Femme One?" Lucian sounded thoughtful. "Well, why not? The Ma*jor*ans are en eminently civilized people."

"If the three of us are accepted there for what we are, I'm for it," Drace growled. "Let's give it a shot."

"All right then." Lucian kissed me on the forehead. "It's settled—we'll take the Empress up on her offer and take positions in her court. But first we must return the Key of Tanterine to Lord Mandrex—we cannot fail to fulfill our promise to him."

"Sounds good to me." I yawned and cuddled against them, my face pressed to Lucian's broad chest and my ass rubbing against Drace's muscular hips. "But first I want to take a little nap—taking on the two of you at once is enough to wear a girl out!"

"Rest, *ma 'frela*," Lucian murmured. "And know that we will guard your dreams."

"Love you," I whispered sleepily. "Love both of you, so much."

"We love you too, baby," Drace growled softly. Lucian said something too, but I didn't catch it.

I had already drifted off, safe in the arms of my men and knowing I would never leave them again.

**End**

# Epilogue

## Rylee

"So you found what you were seeking, I trust?" Lord Mandrex arched one black eyebrow at us and cocked his head curiously to one side.

"We did," I said firmly, handing him back the fist-sized triangular stone. "But it wasn't what was in the Temple of Ganth. What we found was each other."

His eyes widened in surprise and he looked at Drace and Lucian.

"So you decided *not* to sever the bond between you after all?"

"We did sever it—for a while," Drace growled. "Turned out to be the worst fucking mistake of all our lives."

"Thank the Goddess of Mercy we were able to reconnect with each other," Lucian said soberly. "I do not think it would have been possible if Rylee wasn't a *La-ti-zal* with the power of binding."

"Is that right?" Mandrex sat forward, his tall black wings rustling with interest. "And it was by your power that the three of you were *made whole* again?"

The way he said 'made whole' made me frown a little. There was an intense interest burning in those swirling, Angel's eyes of his.

"Well…I guess so," I said.

"And are there more with powers like yours on your home world?" Mandrex demanded.

"I *think* so. I don't really know." I shrugged.

"There *must* be. But you probably wonder why I am so interested." He stood up from the throne-like chair which was cut to comfortably accommodate the huge, rustling wings at his back and began pacing. "You probably also wonder why I am not welcome on my home world of Cantor."

"Of course not—it would be rude to ask such questions," Lucian said smoothly.

"You don't have to tell us anything," Drace added.

"*I'd* like to know," I said softly, taking a step forward. Mandrex's receiving hall was gorgeous and the soft little slippers Drace had simmed me made no sound on the thick, richly woven carpet in front of his chair.

"This is the reason—one of them, anyway."

With a rustle like a hundred birds of prey taking flight at once, Mandrex spread those gorgeous, black-feathered wings of his. I gasped at the sight—he had a wing span that was over fifteen feet long on each side when his wings were fully extended...or he would have, if both of them had been able to extend.

His left wing appeared to be crippled somehow. It wouldn't completely unfold and there was a jagged, featherless scar running down the inside of it, just at the fold of the joint.

"Oh..." I reached forward to touch it but my fingers had barely brushed over the glossy feathers before Mandrex took a step back and abruptly closed his wings tight. "I'm sorry," I said, biting my lip. "Should I not...have done that?"

"Only a Cantor's mate may touch his wings," Lucian murmured to me. "It is a very...intimate part of their body."

Oops, apparently I'd just felt up our host by accident.

"Sorry," I mumbled. "I didn't mean to, uh...they just look so soft."

"Soft and broken." Mandrex looked down at the floor. "That is one reason I am not welcome on my home world of Cantor. There are...other, more complicated reasons as well, but nothing can be done about them. I did think, however, that perhaps something could be done about my wing." A wistful look came into his swirling, predatory eyes. "I would like to fly again," he whispered harshly. "To feel the wind against my face, bearing me aloft. I would love that above all things."

"If you wish to seek a bride from the Alien Mate Index, you should go soon," Lucian advised him. "The new Empress is in the middle of evaluating it and putting up stricter guidelines about which females may be taken."

"I don't need a bride," Mandrex growled. "No female would have me as I am now—that much I know. But if one would be willing to try and heal me, well...that would be worth trying."

"Go try then," Drace advised him. "Just don't be surprised if things don't work out quite the way you planned." He grinned at me and Lucian and we smiled back. "You never can tell what's going to happen when you get a female from the Alien Mate Index. Anything is possible."

*Author's Note:   Hi guys, for the half of you that voted for Kindred 18 Uncharted, it will be coming soon.*

\* \* \*

*Author's Note--if you have enjoyed Severed, please take a moment to leave a short review. Good reviews are worth their weight in gold--they help readers decide to take a chance on a new book. Also, they give me the warm fuzzies. : )*

*Thanks for being such an awesome reader! : ) Evangeline*

## Want more Alien Mate Index?

Of course you do! And don't worry, the next book is coming. (And yes, I'm going to write more Kindred too.)

Hugs to you all, Evangeline

.

# Also by Evangeline Anderson

You can find links to all of the following books at my website:
www.EvangelineAnderson.com

**Brides of the Kindred series**

Claimed  (Also available in Audio and Print format)

Hunted  (Also available in Audio and Print format)

Sought  (Also Available in Audio and Print format)

Found  (Also Available in Audio and Print format)

Revealed  (Also available in Print)

Pursued  (Also available in Print)

Exiled  (Also available in Print)

Shadowed  (Also available in Print)

Chained

Divided

Devoured  (Also available in Print)

Enhanced

Cursed

Enslaved

Targeted

Forgotten

Switched  (Also available in Print)

Brides of the Kindred #18: Coming Fall of 2016

Mastering the Mistress  (Brides of the Kindred Novella)

**Born to Darkness series**

Crimson Debt (Also available in Audio)

Scarlet Heat  (Also available in Audio)

Ruby Shadows (Also available in Audio)

Cardinal Sins (Coming Soon)

**Alien Mate Index series**

Abducted (Also available in Print)

Protected (Also available in Print)

Descended (Also available in Print)

Severed (Also available in Print)

**The Institute series**

The Institute: Daddy Issues

The Institute: Mishka's Spanking

**Compendiums**

Brides of the Kindred Volume One

  Contains Claimed, Hunted, Sought and Found

Born to Darkness Box Set

  Contains Crimson Debt, Scarlet Heat, and Ruby Shadows

**Stand Alone Novels**

Purity (Also available in Audio)

Stress Relief

The Last Man on Earth

Anyone U Want

Shadow Dreams

Mastering the Mistress

**YA Novels**

The Academy

# About the Author

Evangeline Anderson is the New York Times and USA Today Best Selling Author of the Brides of the Kindred, Alien Mate Index, and Born to Darkness series. She is thirty-something and lives in Florida with a husband, a son, and two cats. She had been writing erotic fiction for her own gratification for a number of years before it occurred to her to try and get paid for it. To her delight, she found that it was actually possible to get money for having a dirty mind and she has been writing paranormal and Sci-fi erotica steadily ever since.

Find her online at her website: www.EvangelineAnderson.com

Come visit for some free reads. Or, to be the first to find out about new books, join her newsletter.

**Newsletter** – www.EvangelineAnderson.com

**Website** – www.EvangelineAnderson.com

**FaceBook** – facebook.com/pages/Evangeline-Anderson-Appreciation-Page/170314539700701

**Twitter** – twitter.com/EvangelineA

**Pinterest** – pinterest.com/vangiekitty/

**Goodreads** – goodreads.com/user/show/2227318-evangeline-anderson

**Instagram** – instagram.com/evangeline_anderson_author/

**Audio book newsletter** – www.EvangelineAnderson.com

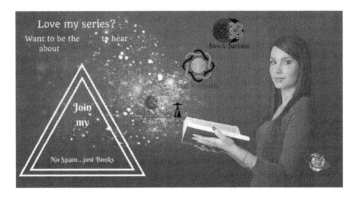

*Join my newsletter at www.EvangelineAnderson.com*

*Or if you love audiobooks, I have quite a few of those too...*

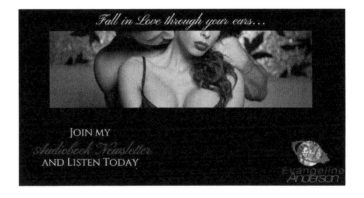

*Join my audiobook newsletter at www.EvangelineAnderson.com*

98940

Made in the USA
Middletown, DE
19 October 2016